LIGHT ME UP

KARLA SORENSEN

Cover Designer: Najla Qamber, Najla Qamber Designs

Interior Designer: Indie Girl Promotions

This is a work of fiction. Names, characters, businesses, places, brands, media, events and incidents are either the products of the author's imagination or used in a fictitious manner. The author acknowledges the trademark status and trademark owners of various products referenced in this work of fiction, which have been used without permission. The publication/use of these trademarks is not authorized, associated with, or sponsored by the trademark owners.

To my boys.

Our house is always a disaster now, I can cry at the drop of a hat, am lucky if I shower twice a week, and my meals typically consist of the cold, soggy food you don't want.

But you two showed me what true love is, and I got to channel just a little bit of that love into this story.

Please, please never feel the need to read my books.

1

—————

RACHEL HENNESSY WAS about thirty seconds away from committing murder.

"Raaaaaaaachel! Did you even bother to check these flowers? This bunch of hydrangeas isn't even close to being fluffy enough for this centerpiece. The mayor will be at this table; anything less than absolute perfection isn't acceptable."

Scratch that. Two seconds away from murder.

Pre-meditated, calculated and completely justifiable homicide. Emily's nasally, imperious, I-am-the-unofficial-queen-of-the-world voice caused every hair in her ear drums to shiver in rebellion. Rachel briefly closed her eyes and jammed the tip of her pinky finger in her ear, hoping to drown the sound out. That one request by its lonesome would be acceptable, because hey, nobody likes a droopy hydrangea.

But add it to the eight hundred and forty other minuscule issues that Emily had found with every aspect of the decor that Rachel had put together for the cancer research benefit, well, it meant that any ol' event planner would be ready to snap too. The edges on the napkins weren't crisp enough. Couldn't Rachel just quick press them? The cushions on the chairs? Not thick enough.

The draped linens across the ceiling? Well, she just didn't remember agreeing to that shocking of a white. What Rachel wanted to do was scream. The intricately folded napkins looked amazing, the cushions had been approved by everyone, including Emily, and the thin white linens swooping down from the center point of the ballroom ceiling looked incredible. The large, austere space looked more intimate, almost heavenly with the whites, creams and golds around the room.

But, Rachel was a friggin professional, so she slicked her tongue across her teeth a tad bit harder than necessary and turned with a smile. "I'll be right over to swap that out, Emily. I asked the florist for extra buckets of all the flowers just in case."

What she failed to mention was that she'd asked for the extras because she knew Triple E would find some inevitable flaw in even the most pristine centerpiece.

For the last year, Emily Elizabeth Eaton had been the proverbial thorn in Rachel's ass. When Platinum Occasions was hired to do the cancer research benefit put on by one of the local hospitals, it had been a huge deal at the office. Platinum was a small, high-end firm in West Michigan with a stellar reputation. And while it wasn't the biggest event they'd ever been in charge of, it was the biggest one where Rachel had been project lead. The decor concept was hers, she'd crafted every detail down to the panko crusted crab cake bites smothered in a roasted pepper and chive aoili. And of course, Triple E was chairperson of the benefit. Her daddy's wallet, and the way that it endlessly opened for the hospital, meant that Emily was free to reign supreme over, well, everything. Including Rachel.

So for almost three hundred and sixty five days, she had smiled and nodded and taken every single criticism that Emily had thrown her way. And by sunrise tomorrow, she'd hopefully never have to deal with her again. All she needed to do was get through this final run through of the venue, go home to shower and slip into her favorite black dress for these kind of events, then come back later that night to make sure that everything went perfectly.

After she'd canned the offensive off-white hydrangea for a vastly fluffier one, she did a final sweep of the tables. Wait staff, already decked out in their crisp black and white uniforms, straightened salad forks and turned coffee mug handles to a perfect angle. Rachel pulled in a deep breath, and with it, caught the whiff of her boss Deidre's perfume. J'Adore by Dior, the same floral scent she'd worn as long as Rachel had known her, was a perfect match for Deidre. Her boss was dainty, overtly feminine. The kind of woman who had every conceivable color of the classic Chanel suit, held her pinky finger out when she noiselessly sipped her tea, and said 'Oh, bless her heart' when someone was on the verge of a complete mental collapse. So yeah, Rachel and Deidre were pretty fricken different, considering that Rachel had just been contemplating all the ways she could possibly hide Emily's body.

"Looks fantastic, Rachel," Deidre said from just behind her, her southern accent slipping back into her voice. "You should be very proud of yourself."

Her lips curved in a smile, wishing that Triple E was within earshot, because it did look pretty damn good, and hearing her boss say it was just the validation she needed after the day from h-e-double-hockey-sticks. She pulled her eyes away from where a shaggy haired waiter almost knocked over a set of champagne flutes and looked back towards Deidre. Her boss's sable colored hair was pulled back in its standard chignon, never a single strand of hair daring to fall out of place. Cripes, her hairspray must be straight-up shellac. Best not light a match around her.

"Thanks, Deidre. That means a lot coming from you. I really appreciate you giving me the chance to be lead on this."

A small smile tugged on one side of Deidre's perfectly lipsticked lips. And after seven years working with her, Rachel knew that little tilted smile didn't happen often. "You were past due for your chance. And Marie Steadman was very insistent that we should work primarily with you on this event."

Oh, *bless her heart* indeed. Marie Steadman, her best friend Casey's mom, had been in Rachel's life for more than fifteen years, and had always been a surrogate mother to her, miles and leagues and oceans and universes away from the emotional Mt. Vesuvius that was Rachel's own mother. And if Marie had put the bug in Deidre's ear, then Rachel would be sure to thank her.

Rachel was not exactly easily intimidated. In fact, she should probably be a bit more intimidate-able. But Deidre? That pastel wool clad, J'Adore-wearing, peach-lipstick-sportin' southern belle made every inch of Rachel's hourglass figure quake in absolute fear. Rachel was no taller than her, both of them only a few inches above five feet. But damn, chick was scary.

Deidre ran her pink-tipped nails along the back of one of the gold chairs, and swept her shrewd gaze over to Triple E, who was quite inconspicuously straightening every single fork and spoon and knife that the wait staff had already perfected.

"She's important to this fundraiser, Rachel."

Well no shit, Sherlock.

"I know," Rachel said, figuring a more diplomatic answer would suffice. "And by tomorrow morning, I'm sure that Emily will be quite happy to not have to deal with me again either. She'll probably want to plan a whole other party just to celebrate."

"You joke, Rachel, and I'm aware that that's your way to deal with stress, but a referral from someone like Emily Eaton would be very beneficial to Platinum Occasions. Keep in mind that she is our customer. And we aren't happy with customer satisfaction. Customer *loyalty* is ..."

"... is the unyielding foundation of Platinum Occasions," Rachel finished by rote. Deidre had all but tattooed it on all of their foreheads. And wowza, would she ever be surprised if Triple E was feeling at all *loyal* after this. And Deidre would not be happy with Rachel if they received anything but a gleaming gold star on their report card at the end of the night.

"That's right. Keep that in mind until the last plate is cleaned tonight, Ms. Hennessy."

Oh well then, it was Ms. Hennessy now. Awesome. Fricken great.

When Deidre did a precise turn and headed towards the exit, Rachel expelled a heavy breath. Thumbing through the last minute checklist she kept for all her events on her phone, she felt comfortable heading home to get ready.

"Rachel?"

Le sigh.

She turned from where she had been leaning against one of the serving stations to see Emily, one French-manicured hand perched on a curve-less hip. "You're not done, are you?"

"Is there something you needed me to wrap up, Emily? Because I think the staff here has everything else under control, and I need to go home to get ready."

Emily narrowed her beady little blue eyes (in reality, they were not at all beady, but annoyingly large and bright and *ugh*), clearly filtering through a myriad of reasons why she could harp on Rachel. The silence stretched for a moment past comfortable, and Rachel knew there was absolutely nothing she could bring up. This place was perfect. Pristine. Immaculate. Impeccable. Faultless. Beyond compare.

Yeah, yeah, she'd spent some time with a thesaurus.

"Hmmm," Emily hummed, running a finger across her lips, eyeing Rachel from head to toe. "I suppose you can go. It's probably a monumental task to make yourself look even remotely presentable."

Oh no, she di-in't. Rachel opened her mouth, probably to say something that had absolutely nothing to do with unyielding foundations of customer loyalty, but stopped when she felt a small, shockingly strong hand close around her shoulder.

"Emily, we're so looking forward to this evening. With your kind indulgence, could I interrupt to speak with Rachel about some final things to make sure tonight is perfect for you?"

And wasn't Deidre just so good? Emily practically melted, sucking up the simpering tone like a dried-up sponge that got tossed in Lake Michigan. Rachel held the eye roll that was threatening at the backs of her eyelids, curved her lips in a tight smile, and followed Deidre to the hallway outside of the ballroom.

The mint green of her boss's suit looked sickening against the deep jewel tones laced through the carpet and hallways of the hotel. She whipped around and froze Rachel with a tight-eyed look.

"I *get* that she's an entitled bitch who has raked you over the coals for the last year, but if I ever see you even remotely close to snapping at her again, you *will* lose your job. Do I make myself clear?"

Rachel clenched her jaw and nodded, fighting against every burn of every non-existent tear that pushed at her throat. No crying. Absolutely never, ever any crying.

"Deidre ..." she swallowed roughly and then tried again, straightening her spine when she pushed all that completely unnecessary emotion down. "Deidre, I'm so sorry. You know I've never had this problem with a client before."

"I know, and that's the only reason I'm even being this lenient. You're excellent at details, Rachel, and most clients love your, *ahem*, brash personality. But a successful businesswoman must recognize the time and place to keep it at bay. And if you're missing my point, *now* would be the time to keep it at bay."

With the 'blessing' of Deidre, she drove home on auto-pilot. Home, meaning the place where she was currently shoved into her childhood bedroom because she was forced out of her *former* house because her *former* boyfriend Marc was caught cheating on her with an anorexic-looking brunette. She knew that her parents and younger sister Kate weren't home, thank the Lord in heaven above, because all she wanted to do right now was stand under a frigid cold blast of water to snap herself back into professional mode before the event tonight. No way was Triple E worth losing her job.

When she pulled her black 1970 Camaro into the driveway, she pulled the key out, letting it fall into her lap with a clunk. Giving herself one dramatic sigh, she heaved herself out of the car and trudged in the house. In the kitchen, she sat on the black granite counter top and stared into the refrigerator door, willing it to make some Diet Coke magically appear.

When that didn't happen, she took the necessary freezing cold shower and went about the 'monumental task' of making herself look acceptable. Rachel twisted her red hair into a low bun on the nape of her neck, letting a few strands fall around her face. By the time she'd finished her makeup and slipped into her black wrap dress, she felt like she finally had a handle on the Triple E situation. And by that, it meant she'd scrolled through motivational quotes on Pinterest until she felt sufficiently inspired and totally under control.

Life is 10% of what happens to you and 90% of how you react to it.

In one minute, you can change your attitude and in that minute you can change your entire day.

Change your thoughts and you'll change your world.

Negative people need drama like it's oxygen. Stay positive and take their breath away.

Don't keep calm, slap that bitch, hard.

Okay, so the last one had done nothing for her composure other than to make her laugh. Tonight was just another night at work. It would be crazy and chaotic, and that she could handle. Marie Steadman would probably show up an hour after she got back to the hotel ballroom, and outside of her two closest friends, Casey and Liz, no one would be able to keep her steady better than Marie.

She sat down on her bed, the metal frame squeaking the

same way that it did her entire childhood, whenever all the weight was centered on the right corner. She slipped on her nude heels, thankful for the three-inch boost that it would give her for the rest of the evening. The ding of her phone sounded across the room, and she smiled when she picked it up and saw it was from Marie. Her smile all but collapsed as she read the text.

Marie: Mr. Steadman is sick and being a horrible baby about it, so I'll be bringing Tate as my plus one. I hope that's okay!

Rachel sank back onto her bed, the squeak not quite as loud as it was covered up by the horrified groan crawling up her throat. She reread the text, hoping that it might change. Maybe Marie was bringing her youngest son, Dylan. Or one of the other boys. Or, yes, maybe she'd bring Casey.

Nope. Still that same pesky T name.

The third of Casey's four older brothers. The lawyer. The recently single, insanely hot, not even remotely fun, ridiculously inconvenient star of all her very inappropriate dreams as of late.

And now he'd be there tonight, when her sanity was already hanging by a thread, wearing a tuxedo and being all Tate-like.

Awesome. Fricken great.

2

"Mom, I ... I just can't."

Silence. The oppressive silence that only a mother can achieve practically vibrated through the phone. Tate slumped back in his brown leather desk chair, wondering if he could wait this out. Five seconds ticked by.

She won. Of course.

He rubbed his forehead. "Why can't Dad go again?"

"He's sick. He has a really bad cold, and I don't need him hacking over everyone sitting at our table."

"Hmm. And I'm the only one who can go with you?" *Please say no.*

"You are, my favorite third born. We paid for the plate, so it makes no sense to waste it. How come you don't want to go?"

Because there was absolutely no way he could answer that question honestly, he did what any good lawyer would do. He lied, straight through his teeth.

"No particular reason, just a really busy day. And even though I've still got four months left on my lease with Jake, I want to start looking at houses."

Tate had rented a newly-renovated duplex from Jake Miller,

his sister Casey's landlord/boyfriend. When Tate had broken off his engagement with Natalie, he'd been at a little bit of a loss. Asking Jake for a short term lease seemed like the best temporary option. It was nice to have a place to stay, and being close to Casey was a bonus, though maybe not for her. He'd only caught her sneaking back into her place once when he was on his way out of the door for work early one weekday. She'd given him a narrow-eyed look when he wagged his finger at her through his car window, but the bright red blotches on her cheeks made him chuckle, because she knew she was caught.

Most nights after work, he still felt like he didn't know what to do with himself. What did Tate Steadman do with his free time? Five years of his life in a relationship that had been comfortable at best, manipulative and confining at worst. Natalie had taken up all of his time outside of work, and she'd done it so quietly and masterfully that Tate had barely even noticed. Every night he distinctly felt the novelty of being able to sit and read a new James Patterson book or watch the entire Jason Bourne trilogy, or basically do whatever the hell he felt like.

Just being able to say 'hell' if he wanted to. It might be childish, but there was still a pulse of rebellion in him left over from his years with Natalie that made him want to sit on the couch all night, wearing only his boxers, drinking beer out of a can, and watching Sports Center for four straight hours, not caring in the slightest that he'd see the same headlines over and over and over.

"You always were the one who planned ahead the farthest, but Tate? The houses will be there tomorrow night, just waiting for you to discover them."

He snapped out of his Sports Center fantasy, and let his head fall back against the chair.

"I know they will."

"So? What's the issue?" The silence became weighted again, and Tate fixed his stare across the cream colored walls of his office to the framed family picture from last summer. He was thankful now that his mom had a 'spouse only' rule when it came to family photos. He'd hated it if he'd had to remove that picture because Natalie had been sitting with the rest of them on the beach of Lake Michigan. His mom was actually the first to cave during this stretch. She spoke softly, consolingly. "Tate, I'd really appreciate it if you'd come with me. Please."

He smiled, grudgingly, but he felt the tug of his lips. His mom could have written the book on delivering the *please* in a way that no one was immune to.

"Fine."

She squealed. His mother, graceful and composed, actually squealed. "Wonderful! Wear that charcoal suit with the blue shirt and blue and silver tie that Casey got you for your birthday last year. Pick me up at six."

And with that, there was a click and more silence. He exhaled a laugh as he set his cell phone down on the cluttered surface of his desk. He checked the time, and since he only had an hour to go home and change, he shot off an email to the client that he was working with on drawing up some stock purchase agreements and then told his assistant to take off when he passed her desk. Maggie looked surprised he was taking off at four-thirty on a Friday, but she quickly recovered, and her football helmet shaped brown hair never moved when she nodded and grinned in response.

Traffic was light on his drive home, and the two identical duplexes on either side of the one he currently called home were quiet when he pulled in. The way that the three buildings sat back from the road ensured that it was usually a peaceful place. There were enough large spruce and fir trees bordering the property that neighboring houses were never seen. He knew why Casey had fallen in love with the place, and for the short time he'd lived there, he'd already shifted the amount of land he was going to look for in his new house.

It didn't take him long to swap one suit for another, and he grudgingly pulled out the tie his mom had requested. He stood in front of his bathroom mirror, scrubbing a hand across his jaw and trying to decide if shaving off the five o'clock shadow went hand in hand with a formal event. Since he didn't have the dark hair of his mom, Casey and Dylan, he decided to forgo. Because in no way, shape or form was he trying to impress anyone that night. Nobody would care whether his jaw was a bit scruffier than normal. Because nobody would be paying much attention to him. Nobody would care whether it was prickly. And nobody, repeat nobody would be getting close enough to feel it.

He snagged a granola bar out of the pantry for the short ride over to pick up his mom, and had just finished locking up when he heard the slam of a car door from the garage that Jake and Casey shared.

"Well, well, don't you look handsome, big brother." He smiled when Casey reached up to straighten the knot on his tie after giving him a brief hug. She grinned back and shoved his shoulder a bit. "Nice tie. You must know someone with impeccable fashion sense."

"That I do. But as talented as she is in picking out clothes, she has horrible taste in men."

He laughed when she rolled her eyes, because everyone in their family loved Jake. "Ha, ha. Very cute."

"You don't look terribly surprised to see me dressed like this on a Friday night."

She shook her head, her long dark ponytail coming to rest over her shoulder. "Talked to mom already. She told me she practically had to do Chinese water torture to get you to agree. I figured, if nothing else, you would relish the chance to see Rachel in action."

And there it was. Tate swallowed and looked down at his watch, hoping Casey didn't notice the way his jaw clenched involuntarily at the mention of Rachel's name. He pulled in a deep breath, schooling his facial features and smiled at her.

"Are you kidding me? If anything, I'll be the one who walks away damaged. I'm not sure my delicate constitution can handle anymore of her clever little nicknames for me."

"Good point. Though I don't know why she keeps thinking up new ones. 'Assassin of all things fun' is by far my favorite. Though 'prophet of doom' was a close second."

Tate sighed, going for nonchalant, though he would be gigantic liar if he didn't admit that Rachel's nicknames for him didn't cut a little. There was something about those names, said in jest, that chaffed. Like dragging his hand against the scruff on his chin. "Once. I drive you three home from a bar once, and I'm the prophet of doom."

Casey laughed, shaking her head, like that was the only conceivable reaction to Rachel. Tate pointed to his watch.

"I need to go get Mom; she'll hang me if I'm late. See you around, Case."

She waved and headed to the door of her own place. Casey called back to him just when he'd started walking away. He shaded his eyes from the early evening sun when he turned back to face her.

"Be nice to Rachel, okay? This is a stressful event for her."

Tate swallowed again, and somehow managed to nod in agreement.

Be nice to Rachel. *Be nice to Rachel.* If Casey had absolutely any idea what kind of *nice* he wanted to be to one of her best friends, she definitely wouldn't say that. He made the drive to his parents' house on auto-pilot. He somehow managed to compliment his Mom on how she looked in her ice blue cocktail dress, and when he turned his car over to the black suited valet at the hotel, he had an impending sense of doom that almost made him laugh out loud. Prophet of doom it was tonight.

If it hadn't been so maddeningly ironic, he really would have laughed. But as it was, he walked with his mom down the wide hallways, softly lit with wall sconces, her heels clicking loudly along the ivory marble; he felt like her hand tucked into his elbow was the only thing keeping him from tucking tail and flat out sprinting back to his car.

And the moment they passed through into the ballroom, dreamy and elegant in its lightly colored decor, he knew exactly why he would have felt no shame in running.

Because Rachel Hennessy looked like perfection.

Not the kind he had been used to with Natalie. Natalie was beautiful, but subtle. She was an Audrey Hepburn kind of perfection. Rachel was not subtle. Even draped in that ridiculously boring black wrap dress, which did nothing to detract from curves that could probably make a eunuch hard as nails, Rachel was the kind of sexy that made her seem untouchable.

Her red hair, flaming and bright and swept up to show the length of her neck, was like a siren pulling him in to his destruction if he wasn't careful. She was gesturing to one of the wait staff, and the way that she turned in order to show the kid something, he actually groaned at the way it highlighted the steep curve of her waist. His mom looked up at him in concern.

"Are you okay?"

Spectacular show of restraint, Steadman.

"Yeah, just smelled those appetizers and realized how hungry I was."

At that she smiled, and he almost wept in relief that she'd actually bought his lame explanation. "Just wait until you try them. Rachel worked with the executive chef here to make a fantastic menu."

Tate followed his mom as she meandered through the room, making small talk with the people she introduced him to, and did everything in his power to actually pay attention to what they were saying. When the wife of the mayor was asking him questions about the type of law he practiced, he managed a somewhat articulate answer when he felt *her* staring at him. Raising his head, he saw Rachel standing next to a table about twenty feet away. The hum of conversation around them made it impossible to do anything but smile at her. She didn't smile back, but even with dozens of people milling around both of them, he didn't miss the way her bright hazel eyes tripped down his frame. He raised one eyebrow, knowing she'd hate it. She smirked, not looking even the least bit repentant that she'd been caught blatantly checking him out. And that made every inch of his skin tighten up.

He turned back to the mayor's wife and made his excuses, but when he stepped around the table, Rachel was gone.

3

RACHEL GRIPPED the back of the chair in front of her, where it was safely tucked in the alcove leading to the restrooms, the cold lacquer of the curved back a welcome relief to her overheated ... everything. She sucked in a few deep breaths like she'd just done a marathon. The short walk out of the ballroom seemed like it actually *had* been twenty six miles, because when one flees in abject terror, apparently distance is multiplied. Multiplied by like a hundred.

And as she gathered her breath and calmed her heart, she could admit the total cowardice behind her exit. It wasn't even how ridiculous Tate looked in that damn tie she'd helped Casey pick out a month ago, it wasn't the sexy fricken little quirk of his eyebrow, because she'd seen him do that about million times more than was necessary when he got all judgey, it was the look in his dark eyes when he did it.

She had never, ever seen Tate look at her like that. Lordy, if it wasn't completely embarrassing to admit, she might even go so far as to say that her traitorous knees had been preparing for a mutiny when she'd seen that flicker of interest in his freakishly chiseled face. And wouldn't that be perfect?

She could just imagine Triple E staring down at her with disdain stamped over her features, causing Rachel to crumple to the floor. Then the mayor would probably have had a heart attack triggered by a droopy hydrangea and then Natalie would have chosen that exact moment to glide, yes *glide*, into the room and lay one on Tate's mouth.

She straightened up and smoothed a hand down her dress, snapping out of the nightmare that would never come to fruition.

No droopy hydrangeas could be found on the entire premises of the hotel.

Natalie wasn't here and wouldn't be getting close to Tate's lips.

And she, Rachel Nora Hennessy, had no weak knees.

She pivoted to head back into the ballroom, knowing that she needed to double check that the vegetarian meals were going to the right seats, and almost ran smack into Emily.

It went down like nails covered in glass and then coated in tar to admit, but Triple E looked flawless. The gold sequined column dress covered her lithe frame in a way that was sexy and still classy.

Bitch.

"Why are you hiding back here? Trying to escape the train wreck of this event you put together?"

Aaaaaaand there went her heart rate again. Rachel clenched her jaw and pulled air in through her nose.

"I'm not hiding," she replied, her tone staying miraculously even. "I just needed to use the restroom."

"Already? You've been here for like two minutes."

"I've put in ten hours just today, Emily. I think you're well aware of that. Now, if you'll excuse me, I have to check a few things in the kitchen, and then make sure the silent auction items are set up correctly."

Emily crossed her slim arms across her chest and narrowed her eyes, and Rachel stepped to walk past her. She was about clear the alcove when Emily spoke from behind her.

"You're insane if you think I'll recommend you or this company to anyone after this."

Don't do it. Don't do it. Customer loyalty is ... the ... the ... something something ...

Job. Paycheck. Can't be stuck at parents forever. Don't. Do. It.

Rachel whirled around, not really giving two shits about the pep talk Deidre had given her earlier. "What exactly is your problem? I don't know what I ever did to you, but I am not going to let you treat me like the shit that your Louboutins stumbled into. If you feel insecure because of how little you scare me, then I truly am sorry." She stepped towards Emily and got a ridiculous charge from the way her skinny little shoulders jerked at the sudden movement.

She scoffed. "You're delusional if you think I feel insecure around you."

"Then please," Rachel said, spreading her arms wide. "Explain it to me. Because it looks incredible in there. I have been nothing but professional with you, and I have put up with every possible snide and degrading comment that you could come up with over the past year. I organized a damn good event that will bring in a lot of money, so why else do you hate me so much?"

Emily tilted her head, and oh, did Rachel want to smack it back into place. "I don't hate you. I couldn't possibly bring myself to feel that strongly about you."

"Okaaaaay, fine. Then what is it?"

"You're exactly the kind of woman that makes my skin crawl, Rachel."

Scriiiiiiiiitch. That sound when the needle crawls across a vinyl record? Rachel heard it echo through her head.

And then she laughed. "What?" she gasped out when she finally collected herself. "I'm what kind of woman?"

Emily narrowed her eyes. "The kind who laughs at a moment like this. I literally hold your job in my hands, and you can't find even a modicum of respect. You think that being the sarcastic, brazen redhead makes you something special. You're worse than a cliche. You're a clown, a caricature."

Rachel's chest heaved, and she struggled to pull her tongue from where it stuck to the roof of her suddenly dry mouth. She could have bit down on her tongue until it drew blood and it wouldn't have made a lick of difference.

"Well, color me impressed. That's a lot of alliteration for a blonde."

"A derisive comeback, how original. I'd almost pity you, if I wasn't so excited to watch you get fired."

"Oh, take your pity and shove it up your scrawny ass, if you can pull your head out of it long enough."

"Rachel!" Deidre's voice was like a crowbar smacking against concrete. Rachel dropped her chin to her chest, not willing to look at Emily's face. She felt the soft brush of air against her arms as Emily swept past her without a word. The hum of conversation in the ballroom across the hall was an incongruous backdrop to the absolute silence in the alcove.

Even the breath sawing through her lungs felt freakishly loud while she waited for Deidre to talk. The subtly patterned wallpaper on the wall closest to her suddenly looked very interesting. It shouldn't have gone with the deep, rich colors of the carpet and the chairs, but it did. Casey would've loved it. She was unnaturally concerned with wallpaper. And still, this mental rambling was so not helping.

"Rachel," Deidre repeated, and while the volume may have been softer, the tone was still just as hard. An elderly woman walked past them, smiled politely and then pushed open the door of the restroom, completely unaware that she was witness to the imploding of a career. Rachel turned to the side, and met her boss's unflinching eyes. "I warned you, and I expect my employees to be able to follow simple instructions."

Rachel nodded, figuring it was in her best interest to keep her mouth firmly shut this time. She felt so much bubbling up inside her, that she wouldn't be surprised if it was coming through her skin. Chief among the emotions battling for dominance was mortification. She had made it until the night of the event, and she let Emily claw her way under her defenses. She was so, so stupid.

And ooooh, this was all Tate's fault. She knew, just *knew*, that him being there was going to send her off into orbit one way or another. Little did she know that it was going to send her straight into the unemployment line. Unemployment. Any visions she had of escaping from under her parents' roof vanished in an annoying little poof. One more mood swing from her mom, and Rachel was guaranteed to go postal, and the irony of *that* was not lost on her. She'd worked so hard during her teen years and through college to not become her mother, completely ruled by her emotions. And nights like this? Oh boy, did they put all that hard fought control to the test.

"As much as I know that you wouldn't have said something so completely unacceptable without being provoked, you know that I don't have much of a choice here. I warned you what would happen, Rachel."

"I'm sorry, Deidre. You have to know that."

Deidre's face smoothed out, losing the pinched look that gathered on her forehead whenever she was stressed. She looked Rachel head to toe, and shook her head once, like she couldn't believe what was happening. Yeah. Join the club, lady.

"You're terminated effective immediately, but I'll give you Monday to clean out your office. I'd prefer if you come after five, I'll be there until six thirty."

Rachel bit the inside of her cheek, effectively tamping down one of the tidal waves knocking at the back of her eyes. She'd been relegated to a post-work footnote, to ensure that no one else felt uncomfortable. After Deidre left to return to the ballroom, Rachel sank into the chair that had been her support a mere fifteen minutes earlier. And look at that, Rachel had managed to go from mildly and inconveniently turned on to raging bitch monster without a job ... all in *fifteen minutes.*

The woman from before walked back out through the bathroom door, pausing when she saw Rachel slumped in the chair.

"Are you all right, dear?"

Rachel looked up, and tried valiantly for a smile. "Peachy."

After the lady had left, she stood to go get her purse and almost ran over Marie Steadman. Sympathy was stamped all over her features and it made something twist up inside of Rachel.

"Good news travels pretty fast here, huh?" And miracle of miracles, her voice stayed relatively even.

"I overheard Deidre tell the chef, I'm so sorry, honey." Marie reached out, but before she could touch her, Rachel took a tiny step back.

If Marie touched her, she'd probably hug her, and heaven help her, if she was hugged right now, she'd lose it. She held up a hand in apology. "I ... I have to go. I'm sorry, Marie."

She grabbed her purse and jacket from the coat check, threw a tip at the counter and fled the hotel, knowing that the exact kind of place she needed right now was just down the block.

TATE COULDN'T REMEMBER the last time he'd had to pay a cover to get into a bar, but he figured if there was ever a time that it was warranted, it was now. The stone-faced bouncer made a cursory glance at his ID, even though he was thirteen years over the legal drinking age. His mom had told him under no uncertain terms that he would be disinherited if he didn't follow Rachel and make sure she was okay. The Cliff's Notes version was that she had been fired, but he didn't get a whole lot more information than that.

The valet outside the hotel had seen her turn a corner into a bar/nightclub that was attached to the hotel and the heavy bass throbbing through the walls gave him an uneasy feeling. The club scene was so far removed from his personality it wasn't even close to funny. And what made the whole situation even more humorous, was that he was coming to check up on a woman that would probably be more likely to knee him in the balls than talk to him about what had happened. He strode down a dimly lit hallway, not seeing a single person until he turned the corner to the main bar area.

The place must have just opened, staff was prepping for what would probably be a busy Friday night, and only a few tables and booths that lined the open dance floor were occupied. Everything had an industrial look to it; concrete floors and bar top, black metal tables, and booths with clean lines and dark colors, the same as all of the staff. Steel beams hovered across the large space, bracketing the open brick walls on either side. The wait-resses all wore tight black halters with dark pants. Besides the bouncer, there was only one other male working, and he was behind the bar pouring out two shots for the beautiful, incredibly pissed-off looking woman in front of him. The grin that the bartender aimed at Rachel told Tate that he probably had women eating out of his hands at the end of every night.

Tate's hands curled into fists at his side, and the action was so unconscious that he actually looked down in confusion. He relaxed his hands and couldn't help but smile. If there was ever a woman in the history of the world that did not need a man getting overly-protective, it was undoubtedly Rachel. She had an incredible, and somewhat terrifying, ability to hold her own. In fact, if a man ever tried to rescue her, she'd probably take out the white horse he rode in on.

Right as she was about to tip back the first of two shots that the bartender had poured for her, Tate slid into the stool next to her and motioned to Rachel.

"I'll have the same, please."

Her shoulders stiffened as soon as he spoke, and the bartender simply nodded and walked away to mix a couple more of whatever Rachel had just smoothly tossed back. She tipped her head back until her chin pointed at the ceiling and the long line of her throat stretched more gracefully than it should have considering she had just pounded straight liquor. They sat in silence while the bartender finished up the two shots. He set a receipt down in front of Tate, along with glasses filled with a medium dark liquid. Tate brought one closer to his face and sniffed it.

"Oh, for shit's sake, my grandma can take shots better than you."

Tate sent her a long look, not willing to concede his relief at the fact that she finally cracked first and spoke. With Rachel, that was a major tactical victory. Without responding, he tipped back one shot, then the next, somehow managing not to cough when the hot liquor slid down his throat. Everything warmed inside of him, starting in his stomach and weaving outward until he felt it on the surface of his skin. He slid the empty glasses towards her.

"Best get caught up, little girl. That shot isn't going to drink itself."

She turned towards him and arched one brow. "Little girl?"

"You're what? Six years younger than me and about a foot shorter. I'd say that's accurate."

Rachel crossed her legs, and the way that they had lights mounted underneath the bar top only served to highlight her smooth skin capped by dangerous looking heels. She picked up her second shot glass, clicked it against one of his empty ones, and tossed it back. She blew out a breath and he caught a whiff of the Southern Comfort.

"I get what you're trying to do, Tate. Be a peach and go work your mind tricks somewhere that's not by me."

"No tricks, I promise."

She scoffed.

"So, what kind of shot was that?" he asked when she didn't respond.

"It's called a Short Southern Screw. Seemed appropriate tonight." His confusion must have read on his face, because she rolled her eyes. "My boss ... well, former boss, Deidre, is quite the southern belle. And considering my impending unemployment, I most definitely got screwed. But I'd wager a guess that you already knew that, judging by your presence at this fine establishment that you would probably normally never step foot in."

Tate was surprised that she brought up her firing so easily. Letting her statement pass for the moment, he flagged down the bartender again, who'd moved down the length of the bar to try his luck with a pair of coeds that had parked themselves on some stools a ways down.

"And you accuse me of being judgmental. You don't think this is my kind of place?"

She turned towards him finally, her cheeks holding a slight flush from the back to back shots. He had to shift his eyes away from her face because of how good it looked on her. *Your sister's best friend. Your sister's best friend.* He chanted it over and over in his head, to absolutely no avail.

"This is so not your kind of place. Because people only come here for two reasons: to get wasted and try to sweat out everything they've imbibed on that dance floor or make conversation where the most substantial thing that gets said is 'Your place or mine?'"

Tate laughed, because she was absolutely right, and then handed the bartender his credit card, motioning for him to start a tab. He pushed a glass towards her, and picked up one of his own.

"Fair enough, I wouldn't normally come to a place like this. I like it though, it was a good choice." He looked around, and then landed back on where she watched him with a speculative look on her face. "What are we toasting to?"

She blinked a few times, her hazel eyes burning in the dark atmosphere. "To being pleasantly surprised."

They clicked glasses, and the only time she moved her eyes

from his was to flick down to his mouth when he lowered his empty shot glass. And he felt that look like she'd dragged a lit match down his spine.

"Okay, Steadman," she said, her voice a little huskier than it had been before. He told himself it was strictly the effects of the drink. "I assume you didn't come here just to get blitzed with me. But before you try to pry my feelings out of me, you have to answer a question."

He smiled. "Of course I do. Shoot."

"Fabulous, because I've been wondering this for a while. Could you, in terms that even a peon without a law degree can understand, please explain why the ever-loving hell you were with Natalie for so long?"

Tate stared at her for a few charged seconds, wishing she had asked just about any other question, then turned and motioned to the bartender again.

"We're definitely going to need a couple more of those."

4

WATCHING Tate try to answer her question was like watching one of those screens at a train station, everything flipping and changing and never staying in one place too long, the destinations and times filtering through until it hurt your eyes to keep staring. She figured it was a long shot for him to answer her in the first place, but shit, she had always wanted to know why someone like him stayed with someone like her for so fah-riggin' long.

Rachel had run into Natalie Firestone more than a dozen times over the years that Tate was with her. She wasn't outwardly bitchy like Triple E was, but she always managed to stare down her long, thin nose in that 'I'm so much better than you' way that seemed to be ingrained into rich girls since they day they left the womb. She didn't talk much at the Steadman gatherings that she hadn't been able to avoid, just throwing small smiles like she was giving extra tithe to the poor. Rachel wasn't even convinced that Natalie had teeth, as she'd never actually spread her lips wide enough to show the inside of her mouth.

She had always been perfectly put together, hair always shiny and smooth, the blunt brunette edges swinging just past her bony shoulders, and her big brown eyes made her look a little bit like Bambi. She was the kind of woman who knew how to arrange cut flowers and could pull off pearls with every outfit and somehow not look matronly. Natalie looked like a perfect little wife for a lawyer.

Unfortunately, she had also turned out to be a raging, manipulative bitch whore. Whore might be a tad strong, but Rachel would stand by it even if someone shoved a gun in her mouth. Tate had stayed with her through every single attempt to rein him in over the years, separating him from his family at every chance, constantly making up reasons why he had to stay home. And obviously, Rachel had no real personal interest in Natalie, but hearing all of Casey's stories over the years made it impossible to want them to stay together. Tate was just simply too *good* to be stuck with someone like that. Because he was so honorable, he would be one of those married forever types, just like his parents were.

"Have you ever worn a veil?" Tate finally said. He was staring down at his shot glass, turning it in small circles on the concrete bar top.

"Sure. Why? The more important question is have *you*?"

"I can imagine what it would be like. You can see through it, even though it's covering your face. There's just enough transparency so you don't always remember that you're not seeing everything clearly. That's sort of how I felt with Natalie. She was a veil. Beautiful and fragile. You couldn't move it a single inch and still have it work the same way. I could see, I could breathe, I could keep going on with life and somehow manage not to realize just how stifling everything had become. And the second you move it off your face, you realize just exactly how solid it was, because you can finally pull in a deep breath." He looked sideways at her, taking in her expression, which Rachel figured must look pretty serious, because he grinned a little, then looked back down. "Sorry."

"What are you apologizing for?"

"You came here to be distracted, and I'm pretty sure I just gave the most depressing answer possible to your question. Did you expect something different?"

She thought about that for a few seconds before answering. "Truthfully Tate, I didn't know what you'd say. I know you're too much of a gentleman to give some idiotic answer like you stayed with her because she was killer in the sack."

He laughed. And she could do nothing but sit back on her stool a bit to take in the glory that was Tate Steadman mid-laugh. When that man smiled, Lordy, it was like everything sparkled around her just a bit while she watched. He didn't have dimples, because those might somehow detract from the wide, bright smile that made his brown eyes squint a bit. No, instead of dimples, he had deep, bracketing laugh lines that weren't even slightly noticeable until he grinned. She wanted to cup his face and rest her thumbs right inside those curved lines, so maybe her fingers would know what it felt like to frame that perfect smile.

And that particular desire was monumentally more disturbing to her than the one where she wanted to rip his clothes off and then secure him to the bed with his own tie. Because the last, absolute last thing she could possibly need right now in her newly-jobless, living-at-her-parent's life was to have mushy, gooey, want to stroke his handsome face, feelings for Tate.

So she elbowed him in the side and relished the way he flinched in surprise, cutting him off mid-laugh. "Don't laugh at me, Tate. You know that men have a tendency to overlook a few personality quirks for a good roll in the hay. I'm just glad you're not one of them."

He rubbed his side, giving her what he thought was an effective glare. He'd never met Deidre, so he didn't realize just how unscary his version was.

But something did actually bother her about his answer. So,

after looking around the bar that was starting to fill with bodies as the hands moved around the clock, she turned back to him.

"You *really* didn't realize how bad she was? I find that hard to believe."

"How so?"

"You aren't exactly a moron, Tate."

He pretended to fall backwards, hands gripping his chest. "Be still my beating heart, Rachel. I do believe that's the nicest thing you've ever said to me."

She tried not to smile, she really, really did. But she couldn't, so she turned her head away from him. When she had her traitorous lips under control, she looked back to where he was smiling that cursed smile again. So annoying, and so, so hot. Her pleasantly numb tongue ran along the edge of her front teeth, and she decided to just ask, while they were being all drunk and honest and shit.

"So, when you overheard that phone call, that was seriously the first time you thought about breaking up with her?"

Tate closed his eyes briefly, and when he opened them again, she saw the pain there. Just like she had the night he was at Casey's and they found out what happened to make him leave Natalie. Casey had been recovering from an attack from a freakazoid customer, and thank God, he had been stopped before actually raping her, but it had been terrifying for all of them to see the always smiling, unflagging optimism of Casey even a little bit beaten down. And as the cherry on top of the shit sundae of that week, they'd pried it out of Tate that the reason he'd broken up with Natalie was that he'd heard her tell someone on the phone that Casey's attack had been her own fault, that she'd deserved it.

Rachel gripped her shot glass a little tighter, bright red rage coursing through her veins just thinking about it, the hot rush of anger feeling out of place among the liquor cloud around her head. That night, oh that night, she'd felt murderous seeing the look of defeat shadowing Casey's eyes after hearing what Natalie had said. And still, months later, Rachel wouldn't exactly be sad if she were walking through a dark alley, wearing some brass knuckles, and happened to run into Natalie. Fun, *so* much fun, could be had in that situation. Thankfully, he spoke again, breaking her out of her 'let's dream about roughing up Natalie' daze.

"It may sound insane, but yes, it was. Hearing her say that about my sister." He pressed a fist above his heart and his face hardened and Rachel figured he was hearing it all over again. "It was the first moment in almost six years that the light bulb really went off for me. There was no way I could ever marry someone who could say that about *anyone*, let alone Casey. Of course over the years, I had moments where I wondered if I justified her behavior too much. Wondered if she was clingy because she just loved me that much, or if it was more controlling in nature. But honestly, Natalie and I had a peaceful relationship. In all those years, we never fought once."

"Shut up. Not once?" Rachel asked, highly skeptical. Who never fought? How was that humanly possible? She and Marc hadn't fought a lot, but they'd had a few yelling matches over the years.

He shook his head. "Never. It was rare when it happened, but Natalie was very passive aggressive when she disagreed with me. I know her mother is the same way, because she always said she wanted a marriage that was like her parents. Which should have raised yet another red flag, because while her parents tolerate each other, they certainly aren't happy."

She gave a small laugh, shaking her head.

"What?"

"Nothing." No way was she going into her parents' relationship with him. After that many years with Natalie, he'd never understand the love/hate, back and forth tempestuousness she'd lived with her entire life. Her parents loved each other, no doubt about that, but she'd seen them screaming at each other as often as she'd caught them making out in the hallway. Or the bathroom. Or their room. Or in the backyard. She remembered one morning before school, she'd found her mom a sobbing wreck at the kitchen table, after heaving a coffee cup at her dad's head for some ridiculous reason. Ten minutes later, they had been in their room to 'take a nap'.

At seven-thirty in the morning.

Her parents had mellowed a bit after being married for thirty years, but they were still jealous and territorial, her mom's latest issue being that yoga instructor on their anniversary cruise had apparently been hitting on her dad. So her mom had decided that she'd demonstrate in front of the entire class just how talented Mr. and Mrs. Hennessy were at doing a joint downward facing dog. Ew, ew and *ew*.

As an adult, she appreciated the fact that her parents still loved each other that much, but it was not what she wanted for the long haul. No siree. Because it was possible to have love and happiness without all of that insanity, right? Dear God in heaven, she hoped so. And really, she knew it was, after seeing the Steadmans for so many years. Not that Tate needed to hear about all of that just now though. She smiled over at him, hoping he couldn't read that whole inner monologue on her face.

"Geez, you must have had the most boring almost six years ever. All that makeup sex you missed out on."

It was a risk. Saying something like that to Tate. She doubted that he got teased too much outside of his family.

He didn't laugh like she expected him to. He stared at her for a few long seconds, and she felt it straight down to her lady bits. That look warmed her faster than any of the shots she'd taken so far. And while she was on the topic of shots, she raised her hand to wave down cutie-patootie bartender boy. The evening had taken a serious turn she wasn't positive she was prepared for.

"You sure you need another one?" Tate's voice was a little

rough when he said it, and she had to force herself not to look at him when she nodded. "Then I'll take another one too."

They took the drinks in silence this time, neither of them flinching any more at the burn of the alcohol.

She swallowed roughly, and felt herself move along to the beat of the song that had just started, just a slight shifting of her shoulders where she sat in her seat. Oh, she wanted to dance. The music was getting louder and louder as more people filed in, the bar itself seeming to pulse along with the thumping, rumbling bass. She excused herself to the ladies room, and took a few extra moments in the dark room to splash some cold water on her flushed cheeks and along her chest. She stared in the mirror and could see the effects of the four, or maybe it was five, or hang on ... six shots. Removing herself from that barstool next to Tate and his stupid smile, even for a minute, made it so that every percentage point of that alcohol rushed through her blood-stream in one delicious, running swoop. She laughed at how pathetically relieved she was to feel it.

Yup, being buzzed was good. It made everything dull around the edges just enough so she didn't feel the quelling disappoint-ment of getting fired from her dream job, or the stifling embar-rassment that her boyfriend's infidelity had hit her waaaaaaay out of left field. Because really, who doesn't realize that their boyfriend of over three years has been cheating with the same woman for a year of that time?

Her, apparently. She'd loved Marc, truly she had. Maybe not the *in love* that caused heart shaped tattoos or anything, but it was still love. He'd understood her need for independence and never pushed her on it, he had sympathized with her fear of becoming her mother, who was ruled by a never ending flux of rampant emotions, which caused Rachel to shut down whenever she felt anything threatening to take her over.

But it was absolutely staggering how quickly she'd been able to flip that switch and erase Marc completely from her heart. It almost scared her. Because if she could do that to someone she loved, then what hope did she have of forming anything else permanent?

Before those types of *ifs* could overtake her completely, she pushed her hands into her hair, pushing it out of the careful twist so that she had no choice but to pull the pins out and go with the slightly wild, very 'I just got felt up in the coat check' look. She laughed, thinking about Tate's face if she were to suggest just that, and she sounded slightly hysterical in the empty restroom.

Maybe she should just drink water for a while. Thinking about Tate dragging her into a dark room made her lean forward and grip the edge of the counter with one hand. The mental image literally took her breath away. She dragged a finger down the edge of the neckline of her dress, still feeling some of the cool water clinging to her finger, loving the way it felt against her skin.

He had followed her, left the event he'd been at with his mom, and made sure she was okay. He was sitting with her, in a bar that catered to the kind of people that were so completely different than him, for her. Not just because she was Casey's friend either, if that was the case, he would have made sure she got home and that was it. No, this was something different. And that knowledge made her so hyper-sensitive. She felt it everywhere, and Rachel couldn't decide whether she hated or loved it. But all she knew was that this was the kind of realization that could change everything.

She moved out the restroom and down the hallway, the air around her feeling sluggish, thick. People moved past her like they were in slow-motion, like she could predict exactly what direction they were going to go. She shifted around them, surprised at how full the dance floor had become in the few minutes she had been away from the bar. As she moved through the crowd, she felt herself move along with the music without making a decision to do it. And even as the space cleared out so she could have made a straight shot back to her seat, she felt herself slow.

There were people all around her, some moving together, some moving on their own, but Rachel stopped where she was and let her hands drift above her head, surrendering to the sounds that literally made her spine shake inside her body. She could feel Tate watching her, and she closed her eyes, her entire being swaying to the music. She couldn't place the song through her alcohol-fogged brain, but it was sultry and sexy. A woman with a throaty voice, Lorde maybe, that made her want to dry hump (cough, cough, Tate) something. She tipped her head back, not particularly caring who was singing and making her feel so weightless.

Because back at the bar was this man who tempted her beyond reason, and waiting with him was the reality of her entire situation. So instead of taking the few steps back to it, and to him, she gave herself up.

TATE CURLED his hands into fists. Not because he was mad, because he had never felt this way before. Sitting there, watching her dance, was the most acute kind of torture that he could have conjured for himself. She was so fluid, so perfect in how she moved. Everything about him felt heavy. His brain certainly, because he couldn't remember the last time he'd drank this much. But his limbs were heavy too, and unfortunately, they weren't weighted in a way that made him want to stay on his stool. He actually wanted to go to her.

It had to be the shots. Because he did not dance.

Ever.

Maybe a slow dance at a wedding, the kind of buttoned up, tuxedo affairs he'd gone to with Natalie over the years, but not *this* kind of dancing. There were bodies all around her, women who were wearing tiny scraps of dresses, men who were staring at all the exposed places, but no one was pressing in against Rachel. It was like she had her own private space that no one even noticed. And he was thankful for that, because he had nothing obscuring his vision of her. He knew that if he moved from his seat and went to stand behind her, she probably wouldn't push him away.

He pulled at his tie, feeling like it was choking him tighter and tighter the longer he watched. His throat felt thick, and he couldn't pull in more oxygen. Bad, this was so, so bad. What the hell had he been thinking? Coming here and drinking with Rachel. If he wanted to set himself up in the worst possible situation with her, he'd done an incredibly spectacular job. Because as much as he should stay level-headed around this woman, he was definitely the opposite while he sat there watching her.

Another song started, and she tipped her head back, her red, tousled hair brushing down below her shoulder blades draped in the black fabric. He turned in his stool, even though every fiber in him wanted to keep his eyes on her. He sank his head into his hands and blew out a breath. Flexing his fingers against his skull, he relished the quick bite of pain.

"Need another one, dude?" The bartender's voice was flat and disinterested, but when Tate raised his head to look at him, he had an amused look on his face.

Tate forced a smile. "That obvious?"

He set the shot glass down in front of Tate before shifting his eyes out to the dance floor. "This one is on the house, man. Looks like you're gonna have your hands full tonight."

Tate tossed back the liquid, no longer feeling the burn down his throat. That alone should have worried him for the rest of the night. But right then he decided that he just did not care. He never did stuff like this. For six years, and even before then when he was still finishing college and law school, he didn't do stuff like this. Drink more than he should, flirt with a beautiful, albeit completely inappropriate woman, and close down a bar. And if a man hadn't done things like that at the age of thirty-four, when could he?

Yes. That entire line of thinking made perfect sense through the lens of a Short Southern Screw. That was what cab companies were for. And coffee and Advil for the inevitable hangover. Which reminded him of *another* thing he'd never done: experienced a hangover.

It was so pathetic, all he could do was laugh. He collected himself when the bartender gave him a strange look. Tate was about to turn back around and see how little miss dancer was doing, when he felt her brush up against his arm to take her seat again. His skin tightened when he felt how warm she was. Rachel waved a hand in front of her, fanning her face.

"Could I get a water, please?" She was slightly out of breath, and he actually started feeling a little disgusted at how he couldn't keep his thoughts even remotely clean. No matter how often he might remind himself that she was too young, too wild, too much his sister's friend, too ... too Rachel, it wouldn't be enough tonight. Any control he may have had at the beginning of this evening started deteriorating at a surprisingly rapid pace when he watched her lift her hair off her neck and try to tie it up again.

"What are you doing?"

She looked over at him in surprise. Rachel moved her hazel eyes over his face, and after a few moments she seemed satisfied with whatever she found. She didn't answer, just drained half the glass of ice water that had been set in front of her by a new bartender. The young woman had given Tate a very un-ladylike undressing with her heavily made up eyes when she had taken her place behind the bar, and she was currently settling that gaze over Rachel. The new girl shook her head and shrugged one shoulder, and for some reason, that rankled. Like she didn't get it, them being together. So he turned on his stool, his legs settling on either side of where Rachel stood next to her own seat.

Rachel set down her glass and quirked an eyebrow. "What are *you* doing?"

"You didn't answer me, why should I answer you?"

Her lips curled up in a little smile. He'd never really paid close attention to her lips before. And just then, he couldn't imagine why. Her lower lip was fuller than her top lip, and both were glossy from the condensation on her glass. Her smile spread and he snapped his eyes up, knowing he'd just been completely caught ogling. All of a sudden, he really didn't care that he had. It cleanly snapped the filter between his brain and mouth.

"You shouldn't have stopped dancing."

"What?" Her smile dropped in an instant and she barely whispered it, but he heard it perfectly despite the pounding sounds around them.

"You looked incredible. I could've watched you like that all night."

"What are you *doing*?" She sounded suspicious as she repeated the question, much more serious this time, but her eyes- they gave her away. The fire inside of her was burning as brightly as it was in him. Those hazel irises seared through him, and they were so full of desire that it knocked the breath out of him for a second.

"For the first time in a really long time, Rachel, I have no clue."

He felt something relax inside of him when she grinned, like she understood how important it was for him to say that. She took another long sip of her water, and then looked over her shoulder back at the dance floor that had somehow added another crush of bodies.

"So, will you dance with me then? Or do I need to find a different partner?" Her smile was wicked, curving sin. He just shook his head.

"I couldn't keep up with you, even if I tried." And there was so much truth behind that, it almost pulled down his buzz. But then she laughed and leaned forward, resting one hand on his shoulder to steady herself.

"I'd slow down for you, don't worry." Her lips brushed his ear when she said it, and her throaty voice reached down inside him, pulled his hands up and settled them on her hips before he even realized that they were moving. Her fingers curled into his dress shirt when his tightened around her soft curves, and he forced himself to keep his gaze steady. The sweet, static warmth of the alcohol sliding through his blood didn't feel even a fraction as good as she did. Marc was the biggest dumb ass ever born to let this woman go, to think that anyone could have even a fraction of the appeal that Rachel did.

Someone shoved into Tate from the side, and it snapped the moment. The guy slapped Tate on the shoulder and yelled an apology, but Rachel had already stepped back, and he could have kicked himself in the balls. The problem was that he wasn't exactly sure why. For putting his hands on her in the first place, because that's what he *should* think, or for not pulling her in the way he actually wanted to. He went to check the time on his phone and noticed a text.

Mom: Are you still with Rachel? Is she okay?

Looking sideways at her, he saw she was trying to flag down one of the bartenders. He tapped out a reply while her attention was diverted.

Tate: Yes, I am. I'll make sure she gets home safely. I think she'll be fine.
Mom: There was a reason your dad got sick and I brought you with me, and I think this is it. Be safe.

Rachel slid another shot glass towards him after he tucked his phone back in his pocket. He quirked an eyebrow. *I should not do this, I should not do this, and holy crap, she looks so beautiful staring at me like that.*

"How many more of these are we going to take?" There was no way she'd be able to hear the defeat that colored his voice, but it was definitely there.

"I'm not sufficiently numb yet. A couple more and I should hit my optimum level."

He laughed, because she looked completely serious. "Optimum for what?"

"Think about what I should do next, without all the other crap getting in the way. Alcohol kills all that other crap, haven't you figured that out yet?" She was enunciating carefully, like she had to think a little bit harder about what she wanted to say. And now, finally, almost two hours into the evening, they'd swung back around to the whole reason they were there.

"Is there another event planning firm you want to apply to? I'm sure they're not the only one like that in West Michigan."

She shrugged a shoulder, but wouldn't look at him. Her tongue darted out to wet her lips and Tate didn't think he could look away if his life depended on it. Then she wrung her hands together, and his shot-soaked brain finally caught up.

"C'mon Rachel, spill it. What's going on in that head of yours?"

SHE COULDN'T DO IT. She'd never really talked about it. And of course, it would be Tate that could drag it out of her. Well, Tate and a lot of ill-advised shots. Rachel peeked over at him, and couldn't help the small grin at the slight pink that touched his cheeks. His dress shirt was a little wrinkled, and he'd loosened his tie at some point in the evening. She'd never seen Tate even slightly rumpled and it made her want to lick him from head to toe. And spend a few extra minutes (hours, days, whatever) in the space in between.

"I'm thinking about starting my own event planning business." She blurted it before she could rein in her misbehaving little tongue. His eyebrows shot up, but his mouth spread in an immediate smile. And everything in her relaxed at the look on his face. It wasn't helping the licking fantasy in the slightest. Bad, bad tongue.

"Rachel." He shook his head. "I think that's a phenomenal idea."

"Really?"

"Of course," Tate said resolutely. "One of my favorite parts of my job is helping people incorporate their own business. And I know, without the shadow of a doubt, that you would do an incredible job. If you decide to do it, and I absolutely think you should, let me know and I'll help you through all the legalities."

She bit down on the inside of her cheek, cursing the shots and her horrible, awful evening on the blazing burn of emotion crawling up her throat. Of course he would say the absolute perfect thing. Once, she'd almost told Marc that she had dreams of starting her own business. RH Events, Inc. She already had the logo designed. And when she'd started to bring it up to him, what she might do if she didn't work for Deidre, he'd flicked his stupid, lying, cheating bright blue eyes over to her and said, "I guess it's good you have a job at a place like that, it'd suck for you if you didn't." And not one to be a glutton for punishment, she'd never brought it up again.

Until now.

And Tate looked so inexplicably excited at the prospect of her doing this that she didn't think twice about leaning forward and throwing her arms around his neck. He froze for a second, and she had the brief thought that if she'd been even slightly sober, she would have pulled back. Instead, she tightened her arms and pushed her nose into the warm skin underneath his ear.

Oh, ohhhhhh holy things that were ever possibly holy, he smelled really good. Spicy and manly and exactly like she imagined Tate would. And then he wrapped his arms around her and tightened right back. She knew he was in shape, she'd seen him in swim trunks a couple times over the years. Man did not let sitting behind a desk be a reason to slack off. But feeling the bands of muscle in his biceps close around her made Rachel feel a wee bit lightheaded.

Shit yeah. Being buzzed (okay, drunk) with your friend's insanely hot brother, the one whom you'd had inappropriate thoughts about for well over a couple years was freaking awesome. Somewhere in the back of her foggy mind, Rachel registered the thought that this might be a monumentally horrible idea. But instead, she pulled back to see his face and relished the look of absolutely unconcealed lust that she saw looking back at her. She slid off of her seat and settled herself in between his legs, wanting to smile in complete and utter triumph when he moved into her.

She placed both of her hands on either side of his face, leaned forward and dragged her teeth along his lower lip. He groaned, and with that low, rough sound, she lost her flipping mind. Her fingers, acting on their own accord at this point, moved around the back of his head and dug through the thick locks. Her head, not caring in the slightest about what might come after tonight, tilted to meet his mouth at a better angle. Her lips, absolutely mindless at this point, fit themselves perfectly in between his. And her tongue, that selfish little ho, snaked through and touched his. His tongue pushed back, and she couldn't help the whimper that escaped when they met over and over and over.

Everything about the moment was warm and soft and hard and hot, and still managed to make perfect sense to her. Not timid in the slightest at this point, she pressed along Tate so that every inch of her from the belly button up could feel him. His hands pushed up, and she moaned into his mouth. Absently, she wondered if she should care that hundreds of people could see them just then. And nope, she sure did not.

He pulled back, breathing hard, with one hand still settled on her lower back, and hello, the other gripping her thigh just under the hem of her dress.

"Tate." She met his eyes and practically dared him to look elsewhere. "I want you. And just in case you need a little time to get used to that, I'll order us one more shot so you can decide what you want to do about it."

He smiled slowly, never looking away.

And that was the last thing she remembered until the next morning, when she woke up in his bed.

5

AN ENTIRE PARADE of freight trains had taken up residence at the base of her skull. Everything from the top of her head to her exceedingly sore feet pounded in perfect tandem with the train engines. Rachel groaned and flopped onto her back. Thick cottony dryness coated her mouth and throat. Oh, this was shooting straight to the number one spot of her top ten hangover list. In fact, it may take spots two, three and four as well.

Then something moved next to her, and she almost shrieked when she felt the warm brush of skin against her leg. Rachel froze, thinking that it may not be the best idea to make a ruckus if a serial killer was parked next to her in her bed. Then her grainy, dry eyes noticed the khaki and white striped sheets of a much higher thread count than her own. And the sheets covering the bed at her parents were most definitely a light purple. Which meant one horrifying thing.

Not her sheets.

Not her bed.

Tate and shots and a tongue-tangling kiss throbbed through her slow-moving brain. Then more shots, and she was pretty dang sure that at some point after that she'd given him an incredibly ill-advised lap dance, her facing away from him while she swiveled her hips along with the music. His nose had been lodged at the base of her skull, where he'd kept kissing her damp skin, and his strong hands gripping her around her waist, his fingers digging into her dress just past the point of comfort. And that, oh yeah, that she vividly remembered loving.

Ohhhhhhhhhhhhh shit.

She slowly turned her head to the side and pried her eyes open. And there he was.

Hair mussed, muscled chest bare, the sheet draped somewhere around the area of his defined abs. She had slept with Tate. Oh no. No, no, no, no. She couldn't have. Could she? Rachel pulled up one corner of the material covering her and dared a look down.

Shit, shit and triple shit. Naked. She slapped a hand over her mouth, and seriously, honest to goodness, she felt the sudden movement all the way down to her vajajay. She was sore, which effectively ended any denial that had been shuffling through her mind. *Deliciously sore*, to quote every romance novel she'd ever read. She so got that now. And completely unstoppable in that moment was the tiny smile that pulled at her lips. Tate Steadman made her sore. And she couldn't freaking remember any of it.

Ladies and gentleman, winner of the biggest slut and worst friend to Casey Steadman award? Rachel 'I'm a hussy' Hennessy. She edged herself to the side of the bed and held her breath when Tate shifted to the side, only an inch or so closer to her but enough that it made her freeze. She frantically tried to filter through foggy memories to piece the rest of their night together. Everything stayed just out of reach, and it was enough to make her scream. She didn't though, because if she could get out of here without waking him, she'd be the happiest camper on the block. And the cherry on top of that would be somehow escaping without Casey seeing her doing the walk of shame out of Tate's place. She groaned before she could stop the sound coming up her throat. She clamped it down and froze all over again when one of Tate's arms slithered around her waist to pin her in place.

Multiple curse words in multiple languages screamed through her brain at the hot, heavy weight of his arm across her. She couldn't, not even for a fraction of a second, think about how good it felt. Rachel felt prickly all over at just how badly she wanted to turn and burrow into him. It was choking and terrifying and it almost made her feel as panicky as when she'd been fired.

In the harsh light filtering through the shades of his bedroom window that they hadn't closed, it was so screamingly obvious that he was only in the position because of her. He never would have come to that bar, never would have gotten drunk, never would have needed to take a taxi home. That's it! The taxi ride back to his place.

She vaguely remembered that now: swinging one leg over his lap to settle herself on top of him, the driver yelling at her that there was no sex in his cab. Her burying her head in his shoulder, laughing and his hands shifting up her back while he laughed too. Then she'd dragged her tongue up the hot skin of his neck, and when she'd nipped at his earlobe he had cursed under his breath and pulled her face back up to his to give her slow, drugging kisses.

But there is no way he would have done that under normal circumstances. She'd quite effectively gotten Tate Steadman drunk and then slept with him when he couldn't think clearly. So awesome. And so pathetic.

She looked over at him, and grinned when he emitted a small snoring sound from his perfectly straight nose. He was so handsome it almost hurt to look at him. Or maybe it was the hangover stabbing at the back of her eyeballs that made it painful, but either way, she spent a few minutes soaking in the sight of him draped across her. Because this was never gonna happen again. It couldn't. If she woke him up now, oh he'd probably apologize profusely and spend a few harried minutes making sure that he hadn't taken advantage of her. It was laughable, because of how completely opposite of the truth it was.

If anyone had been compromised, it was him. A teeny, tiny crush over the years had come to an alcohol-fueled head. And that would be that. She could walk away, and have these small pockets of memories of her wild night with Tate. She had to walk away. Awake for five minutes with him, and she already felt bipolar. This was the kind of shit that terrified her. Next thing she knew, she'd be locking him out of the house because he looked at a woman in the grocery store a little bit too long. And yes, her mom had done that once too. The next day, her parents had renewed their vows. Again.

So this one little moment, this was something she could give herself. Carefully lifting one hand, she traced the bottom curve of his lip, barely touching the skin as she took her thumb from one corner of his mouth to the other.

Rachel took a deep breath, and then let it out slowly, gaining incremental control over the riots going on inside her. She lightly clasped Tate's wrist and lifted his arm just enough that she could shift to the side in tiny, barely detectable increments. She got to the edge, and having cleared his arm, she kept a hold of him and in a very impressive move, slipped off the bed and gently laid his arm back down without him so much as flickering an eyelid. She silently fist pumped into the air, and then mentally groaned when the quick movement shot arrows of pain through her throbbing skull. And then she looked down.

Still naked.

And that wouldn't do, to have Tate wake up after all her hard work to escape his muscley clutches and catch her naked fist pumping. She bent down and found her underwear peeking from underneath the dust ruffle on his bed. She snorted, thinking he was probably the only man in the world who lived by himself and had a dust ruffle on his bed. It was the same masculine, solid brown micro suede as his comforter, but still.

Tate shifted, and she wanted to face plant on the floor just in case he opened his eyes, but when she peeked over the edge of the bed, he had simply moved onto his back. She quickly found her bra, one shoe, and, thank you Lord, her dress. Figuring that the loss of one shoe was an acceptable sacrifice at this point, Rachel tiptoed out of the room. She was careful to avoid the pile of Tate's clothes that had landed on the floor next to the bed, and tried to ignore the bright flash of memory that came with it, her pulling the ends of his shirt of out his pants, running her hands up his hard stomach and curling her fingers into the skin above his heart where it felt dangerously close to thrashing out of his hot skin.

And crimeny, it made her want to crawl right back into that very comfortable bed to do a reenactment. After she left his room and eased the door shut, she smacked a palm onto her forehead, not completely positive if she was doing it to shove the memory out, or to jar some more loose. And hey, there was her other shoe just outside the bedroom door. Scooping it up as she crept towards the bathroom, she carefully closed the door behind her.

"Stupid, stupid, stupid!" she whispered to her rumpled reflection in the bathroom mirror as she quickly dressed. And seriously, Rachel almost felt weak where she stood just thinking about how differently last night could have gone. She had been reckless and, well, stupid. Even if Tate hadn't shown up, she probably would have had just as many shots. And she wasn't this person, not really. She liked to have some drinks with her friends, and yes, that one time she had too many at the bar and Tate had to ride in on his fricken horse and save them, but if a cheating a-hole boyfriend isn't reason to drink a lot, then what is?

Still. She had to be just a little grateful that Tate was smart enough to call them a cab and that neither of them had been insane enough to attempt to drive. Her cell phone had about eight percent battery left, since plugging it into a charger was incredibly low on her priority list last night. She quickly looked up a cab company and dialed the number.

"Great Lakes Cab." His voice was gruff and loud and for some reason she was afraid Tate could hear it down the hall.

She cleared her throat. "Hi, I need a cab as soon as possible please."

"Address?"

Well shit. "Uhh, hang on." The man sighed on the other end of the phone, and she had to fight not to feel judged. C'mon, he worked for a cab company, like they weren't used to stuff like this. She didn't find anything on his ridiculously clean kitchen counters, and knowing that he had the second bedroom set up as an office, she treaded carefully down the hall. Hallelujah, a pile of mail sat on the corner. She picked up one envelope and quietly read off the address to the guy on the other end of the phone.

She heard a few clicks of a keyboard while she hurried back down the hallway.

"Okay, he'll be there as soon as he can."

"Wait, how long is soon?"

Another sigh. "Well, my closest guy is dropping someone off at the airport right now, should be there in about fifteen minutes."

"Fifteen minutes?" she whispered as angrily as she could, then cringed at how loud even that sounded in the empty room. "You don't have anyone closer than that?"

"Sorry, sweetheart. That's the best I can do right now."

Rachel chomped down on her tongue to keep from responding to the condescending nickname. "Fine, I'll be waiting."

She relayed her credit card information to him since she didn't have cash. The guy clicked off the phone and she slumped against the counter, pushing one hand against her throbbing temple.

Even though she'd shut the bedroom door, she walked

around the kitchen as quietly as possible and searched through his fridge until she found a full pitcher of water. She poured herself a large glass, and was lucky enough to find a bottle of ibuprofen in the first cupboard she opened. Tossing back three pills with the water, she decided that since they'd slept together, she would be forgiven for eating one of his bananas. Feeling a little bit better after draining two more glasses of water, Rachel couldn't help but think that it was a little cold to leave without even a note. But what was she supposed to say?

Thanks for the great time. I think. I don't really remember. I'm sure you were great though. Obviously you were since my hoohah feels like I was in a rodeo yesterday. Please don't tell your sister. Or I'll kill you.

She laughed, but really, it wasn't even slightly funny. She had never kept a secret like this from Casey or Liz. And she rubbed at her sternum thinking about doing it now. They'd been friends for so long, and been through so much together, that it killed her to do this. But the fact was that Liz would have her and Tate as good as married if she heard about it, and Casey would probably excommunicate her for the sheer fact that she'd seen Tate naked. On purpose. And kinda sorta would love to do it again, but sober.

She sank into his couch to wait for her ride to show up. The large window in his family room faced the front of Jake's property, so Rachel had a clear view of the long, curved driveway. Large oak trees provided a barrier from most of the road, and watching the branches full of bright green leaves put her in a bit of a trance. And she let it. She couldn't keep thinking about Tate and what they'd done and how he made her feel.

Crazy. She felt freaking crazy. She wanted to scream at him, and then kiss him, and then figure out if he remembered last night, and then run away. Far, far away. But first make sure to tell him he wasn't allowed to touch any other woman the way he'd touched her last night. Because she seriously felt like she might go all Lorena Bobbit on his ass if he did.

Oh no. No, freaking no way. Rachel speared her suddenly

shaking hands into her hair. She was totally becoming her mother. She was so focused on watching for a vehicle to turn off the street, and having a mild identity crisis, that when someone pounded on the front door, she emitted a little shriek and about fell off her perch on the couch.

"Hallooooo, Tate. Do you have a minute?"

Rachel let out a weighted sigh of relief that it wasn't Casey on the other side of the door. The British accent definitely belonged to Tori, the fifty-ish year old woman who shared the other half of Tate's duplex. Rachel had met her a couple times when visiting Casey. Tori was an ex-pat who was definitely more than a little bit lonely.

She was always sitting outside of her front door, perched in a bright red Adirondack chair with a giant glass of wine clutched in one hand. She seemed nice enough, so Rachel figured that opening the door to talk to her was less of a risk than letting her pound away at the door and possibly wake Tate. She glanced down the hallway and was happy to see the bedroom door still firmly shut.

Rachel couldn't help but smile at the big-eyed look of shock that was planted on Tori's face when she opened the door and not Tate.

"Well, uhh, Rachel, isn't it?" Tori stammered after she pulled her mouth closed. Rachel nodded, and angled herself in the opening so Tori didn't think she could come inside, and while she seemed to understand that clear gesture, she did crane her neck to look inside. "Is Tate around? I need some legal advice."

"Oh, umm. He's here, but ..."

Tori must have sensed her hesitation, and an annoying, sly smile crossed her thin lips. "Not awake yet, however. I see, I see. You're Casey's friend, aren't you?"

"Mmmhmm," Rachel ground out between gritted teeth.

"And you and Tate are ..."

"Nothing. Tate and I are just friends." And maybe if Rachel

didn't have a bright red hickey stamped on the side of her throat, her sentence would have sounded a bit more believable. But Tori's blue eyes narrowed right in on it, and she let out a low laugh.

"Bloody hell, I need to find the kind of friends that you have."

Rachel slumped against the doorframe. "Please Tori, please don't say anything to Casey. I'll tell her."

Tori raised an eyebrow.

"Eventually. I'll tell her eventually. I promise."

"Well then, what's this little secret worth to you?"

"You're blackmailing me?" she asked incredulously. "I thought you Brits were supposed to be all nice and shit."

Tori hooted out a laugh. "Let's just say I'm enterprising when it suits. So now, what's in it for me?"

"Fine." Rachel crossed her arms across her chest and pursed her lips while she thought. "Two bottles of that Leelanau Cellars Great Lakes Red that you like so much."

"Pffft, two bottles will only see me through a Tuesday night. Four bottles and my mouth stays zipped indefinitely."

"Deal. But you never saw me, do you understand?"

"Never saw you where, exactly?" a low, rough, probably very hungover voice asked from behind her. Rachel pinched her eyes shut and tried to ignore the way that Tori was hunched over in laughter.

"Oh, this just keeps getting better and better, now doesn't it?"

Rachel looked over her shoulder and tried her darnedest not to gape at Tate, who was wearing only black gym shorts, hanging low on his hips. His hair was a complete mess, probably from Rachel shoving her greedy little hands in it at every opportunity over the previous six hours. Tate reached over her head and pulled the door open wider.

"Tori," he said in greeting, squinting a bit at the obnoxiously bright sun. "Is it okay if I talk to you later?"

Like *any* woman would say no to anything he said looking

like that. A little roughed up, and ridiculously hot, even obviously hungover. Tori said she'd call him at his office on Monday, and as Tate was about to usher Rachel back inside, her taxi driver chose that moment to pull up the driveway and circle around to pull in front of Tate's garage door. Tate's face was stamped with bewilderment when he looked down at her.

"You were just going to leave?"

And yup, instantly defensive. She wrapped her arms around her waist. "What? Did you expect breakfast in bed or something?"

Tate shot her look that showed her how much he appreciated her attempt at humor, a dry squint of the eyes that kinda made her want to shrink behind the couch. He swiped his wallet from the table by the door, and walked outside and up to the driver's side window. They spoke a few words, Tate tapped the roof of the car, and then he headed back towards her. He was so focused on her, his eyes so dark and intense that she backed up a few steps. He quietly shut the door behind him and sagged against the dark wood. It was almost eerily quiet, just the sounds of his deep breaths acting as heavy punctuation marks in the thick, weighted silence.

She wanted to run out that door so freaking bad it made her feel itchy.

"Why the hell do people drink?" he groaned. He opened one eye and saw her smiling at his obvious misery. "No, really, I think you need to explain this to me. I feel like I might actually be dead right now."

She shifted, not exactly comfortable with this informal, 'let's sit here and chit chat after we had inappropriate bed time activities' thing he was doing.

"Yeah," she hedged. "Hangovers are straight from the fiery pits. Umm, I really should get back home; I'm sure that cab driver has the meter running."

His brows lowered. "I already gave him some money to wait."

"And you're just assuming that I'd want to stay around any

longer?" Oh, is this what blind panic felt like? She thought losing her job was bad? Well, apparently it's got nothing on being forced to stick around for the morning after conversation.

"Don't do that."

"What?"

He pushed off the door, and she immediately backed up. "Don't act like this was some meaningless thing, some mistake that you have to run from."

She laughed, and kinda hated the way that the harsh sound made his face look pained. "Wasn't it though?"

"No." And oh holy crap, he sounded so sincere that she felt the blank look cover her face. "No," he said more firmly. "This was *not* a mistake. At least not to me."

"I'm Casey's best friend and we had drunk sex last night. How is this anything *but* a mistake?"

He held up his hands, obviously trying to be non-threatening to the unstable hungover girl. "Rachel, I'd like very much to back up and start this morning over again. Maybe actually wake up next to you and just take a second to see how you looked in my bed. Maybe tell you that I'd like to take you out to dinner tonight. Because I think I should."

Should. He *should* take her out to dinner. Not *want*. Apparently white knight syndrome wasn't taken down by a massive hangover. And it made her want to smack him. She wasn't anyone's pity dinner date. And damn if it didn't make her pulse with anger.

"Are you insane?" she shouted. And then hated herself, because the sound pounded through her skull.

He dropped his head into his hands and groaned again. "Please don't yell. My head feels like it might explode."

"Drink some water; you'll get over it."

Tate straightened again, and raised an eyebrow. "Why don't you tell me what's going on in your head right now, Rachel? Talk to me about what you want to see happen here."

She narrowed her eyes. "Don't lawyer me, Tate."

"I'm not lawyering you."

"Ha. You can't even help it."

He walked past her into the kitchen and poured himself the same size glass that she had started with. And then the same amount of ibuprofen. He braced his hands on the counter, his head hanging down between his shoulders. And she tried, really, truly tried not to notice how that stance made a muscle pop out in his bicep. She sighed, loudly enough that he turned to watch her.

"I just want to know what you're thinking, Rachel. I'm not...I'm not used to this either."

Her shoulders drooped from their defensive posture. She spoke quietly once she'd thought about what she could say right now that didn't make her sound like the raging bitch that she'd already been this morning. "I don't know what I'm thinking, Tate."

Which was a bright red, bald-faced lie. She was thinking he was making her certifiably insane.

"I don't think I can apologize for what happened," he said slowly, shaking his head. "Because I'd be lying if I did."

And just like that, her traitorous heart started thrumming. And if she could have pinned it down to make it stop, she would have, because she had no place in her completely pathetic life right now to get excited over anything hungover Tate had to say to her.

"No apology is necessary," she conceded, and knew she'd at least done the right thing by saying that, judging by the look of relief that covered his features. "I think we're both equally to blame for what happened."

"Don't say blame, it sounds too negative." His eyes searched her face, which she tried to keep as blank as possible. "I'd still like to take you out to dinner though, and we can kill two birds with one stone, talk about incorporating your new business while we're there. I'd be honored to help you."

She swallowed a giant boulder down her throat. He remembered. She lifted her eyebrows and laughed a little. "If I actually start my own business, that is."

"You will, and you'll be great," he said simply.

"I might take you up on it then. But I don't think dinner is a good idea."

"Why not?"

"You seriously want a list? Because I could give you one. The first item on it starts with a C and has the same last name as you. And it doesn't stop there."

"So you're going to ignore the list of reasons why we should?" he shot back at her. "Because I could give you one too."

She shook her head and turned to pick up her purse. He didn't mean it. He couldn't. He just felt bad. Her breath started coming faster, and she couldn't get to the door fast enough. She'd cave. If she kept staring at him and his eyes and his muscles and his fricken sincerity ... she'd cave.

"Tate, I have to go."

"Rachel, please, don't make it like this."

She stopped at the open door and took one more look over her shoulder, allowing herself to stare for a few long seconds. "I'm sorry, Tate. But it *has* to be like this."

And then she left.

6

RACHEL SANK her head against the headrest of her car, thinking that the distance from her comfortable seat to Casey's door seemed inordinately long. Did they push her house back? Add a half a mile of driveway since the last time she was there? Liz was already there for their bi-weekly Ladies Night, and Casey had sent them both a text saying she would leave the door unlocked as she might not get there before them. And that was odd; Casey was normally always cooking up a feast of Pinterest Queen level proportions for their drinks and movie nights.

She'd seen Casey since her night with Tate, but she still felt like she was wearing a giant 'I'm a big fat liar' sign on her forehead. And it really freaking sucked. So having a few more minutes of reprieve before she had to slip on her game face was very welcome. Rachel figured this feeling would fade eventually. It had to fade eventually. It had to get to the point where if she heard his name brought up in conversation she wouldn't immediately flash to a rotating collage of the memories that she did have. Oh, she really wanted to get to that point.

Shoving anything remotely close to that night out of her head, she figured that she wouldn't be missing anything. Just close her eyes and take a little nap until Casey got there. Napping was infinitely better than remembering.

And she would have, until Liz decided to rap her knuckles on the driver's side window. Rachel jumped about a mile.

"Geez, Blondie, can't you see I was sleeping?" she grumbled when she pushed the door open. Liz smiled at her, as usual, completely un-intimidated by the grumpiness that seemed to have invaded Rachel for the last month.

One month. Four weeks. Thirty days since the loss of her job and the infamous, no matter how she tried but still could not forget it, one-night-stand with Tate. Thirty days of still living in her parents' house, trying to keep her younger sister Kate from stealing her shoes. Thirty days of working her completely exhausted ass off trying to start her own business.

She'd spent the first week doing an excellent sloth impression. Sleeping in past ten every morning, watching the horror that was daytime television, and generally eating everything her mom put on the table. One excellent thing about being home: meals from scratch that were made by hands other than hers. At the beginning of the second week, she'd taken a long, hot shower and let her mind whirl feverishly.

She could do this. She was going to do this.

After putting together her business plan, Rachel decided to wait on applying for a business loan and take advantage of her rent-free living situation. She developed her advertising, started her website and Facebook page, and ordered some friggin fantastic business cards with the same gray and white chevron design she'd be using for all her branding. Her dad had really wanted her to rent a small suite in one of the office buildings he owned. And while the 'daughter discount' kicked major ass, she decided that it would be prudent to actually get a few clients first before doing that.

"Hello, earth to Rachel. Are you coming in?"

"Oh, yeah. Hang on, I have to gather my strength to pick up my purse."

Liz peered in at her. "Are you okay? You're not sick are you?"

"No," Rachel shook her head, but still didn't move. "Just really, really, really tired. If Casey picks the wrong movie to watch tonight, I think I may be out in about ten minutes."

"You fell asleep two weeks ago at my house too."

"Well yeah, you pick the most boring movies in the world. It's amazing I don't fall asleep every time it's at your place."

Rachel heaved herself up out of the car with an exaggerated groan, and then hefted her purse over to Liz, who swung it easily onto one slim shoulder.

"*Emma* is not boring, it's witty. You're just so shockingly uncultured. It's not my fault you don't appreciate a classic."

Rachel stepped back while Liz held the door open for her. "You could have least picked *Clueless*. Now that's a version of *Emma* I can get behind."

They helped themselves to the chips and dip that Casey had left ready for them, along with a hot pink post-it note explaining that she'd hunt them down if they didn't save some margaritas for her. Rachel picked up the note and stared at it, snorting a laugh at how Casey drew pictures of little margarita glasses around the edge.

"Where is she anyway? It's super weird that she's not here."

"I think she's meeting someone who's buying some of her shoes off of Craigslist."

Rachel dropped her chip full of dip back onto the table. "I'm sorry, what? Casey is selling her shoes? Casey Marie Steadman? Our best friend since seventh grade?"

Liz shrugged her shoulders. "I guess so. I didn't ask her about it because she sent me the text about it while I was at work. I couldn't reply because I was trying to finalize some stuff for the class I'm going to start in a few weeks."

"Her. Shoes. She's selling them?"

"Rachel," she said on a sigh. "I'm sure you can grill her when she gets here. Do you want a margarita while we wait?"

Rachel scrunched up her nose when she caught a whiff of the pitcher that Liz pulled from the fridge. "Ugh. No thanks. Doesn't really sound good to me tonight."

Liz quirked an eyebrow and poured herself the smallest glass of margarita in the history of the world. "Doesn't sound good? And you're sure you're not sick?"

"Eh, maybe I am coming down with something."

"Well, if you don't feel better in a few days, promise me you'll go see a doctor." Liz's blue eyes were serious, and it made Rachel smile a little.

"I promise, Mom."

"Bite me. Now, show me those business cards you ordered. I want to put one up on the library community board."

They chatted for a few minutes before they heard Casey's Honda whip up the driveway, then the click clack of her heels across concrete. She walked in the door, face completely blank when she walked straight past Rachel and Liz. Rachel lifted her eyebrows at Liz, who shrugged. Casey plopped onto her couch and stared at the dark television screen.

"Are you high, Casey?" Rachel finally asked and Casey snapped to attention.

"Have you ever found yourself in a situation where the only thing you can think is 'holy balls, I cannot believe this is happening to me right now?'"

A memory, hot and striking, whipped through Rachel, of Tate's large hand gripping into her hair and his teeth sinking into the curve of her shoulder. The shift of his muscular shoulders as he held himself above her.

"Uh-uh, nope. Definitely not," Rachel said emphatically. Maybe a bit too emphatically, because Liz pushed her eyebrows together and stared at her.

"Because I just did," Casey continued. "I was selling some of my shoes to someone who saw my Craigslist post."

"Yeah, Blondie told me. What's up with that?"

"Not the point right now, just gimme a second."

"Okaaaaaay."

Casey shifted so she was sitting sideways on the couch. "So, a couple days ago, I got an email from a lady named Loren, saying she wanted to buy all the shoes I had posted, and I put like eight pairs of shoes up. And I'm talking nice shoes, you know, those yellow patent ones that I adored but they hurt like crap and the bright red suede ones that I got from Nordstrom's that I never found anything to wear with, and the black leather ones with the silver spike heel ..."

"Casey-" Rachel interrupted. "Focus."

"Sorry," she said, still obviously flustered. "So, I'm waiting to meet Loren in the parking lot of that Target by my work, you know, crowded parking lot just in case they're a psycho or something? Well, the white Trailblazer pulls up next to my car, and I get out to put the shoeboxes on the trunk so she can look at them. And umm, it wasn't a she."

Liz tilted her head. "What do you mean?"

"I mean, it was a dude. A middle aged, overweight, bald dude wearing a wrinkled polo and horrid khaki shorts."

Rachel choked on her chip. "Shut up."

"Well, maybe he was picking them up for his wife," Liz said hopefully.

Casey just shook her head. "Nope. Because he told me that they looked like they'd fit him perfectly."

Rachel lost it. By the time she could finally speak again, she almost cracked all over again when she saw the misery all over Casey's face. "What's the issue? I mean, he paid you, right?"

"Well, yes, but ..."

"But, what?"

Casey pulled her shoulders up and held them for a second,

her expression covered in pure torture. "But what if all those beautiful shoes just sit there? In his closet. Never to be worn in public. Because he likes to stare at them or something."

Even Liz snorted out a laugh at that. "And that's a bad thing?"

"Yes!" Casey shouted, slapping her hands down on her thighs. "It was hard for me to part with those. I promised myself I would sell the stuff that I didn't really need, since I'm all financially responsible now, and I figured I'd sell them to some down on her luck girl, who would cherish them forever."

"Ohhh," Rachel drawled. "I think they'll be cherished."

Finally, Casey laughed. She dropped her head back onto the couch and stared up at the ceiling. "I cannot wait to tell Jake this."

They made their way into the kitchen, demolishing the chips and dip, then got comfortable on the couch.

"Alright Casey, oh great benefactor of cross dressers, what movie do you got for tonight?" An orange throw pillow came sailing across the room and whacked Rachel right across the face with an oomph. She laughed, and tossed it back. "Hey, don't shoot the messenger, you know I speak the truth."

She snuggled back down into her seat while Casey cued up *Where the Heart Is*. Typical. Casey, always the romantic, never failed to go for a rom-com, or some sappy-ass movie that had a completely unrealistic happily ever after. And it looked like the Walmart baby was it for tonight. She sighed, expecting that she'd succumb to her exhaustion within minutes.

So, suffice it to say, she was more than a little surprised to find herself biting the inside of her cheek so that she wasn't bawling like a freaking baby when Ashley Judd's character was recovering from an abusive relationship and talking about what her kids had endured as a result.

Lord have mercy. She was losing her ever-loving mind. She cleared her throat and abruptly stood off the couch when her eyes started burning. Liz sniffed noisily and looked up at where Rachel was standing, looking out Casey's living room window.

"You okay, Red?"

"Uh huh, sure. Just need to pee."

And she fled the room, sinking against the door when it closed. What was the matter with her? Exhaustion. That's what the problem was. And duplicity, apparently. Not telling one of your best friends that you slept with her brother sure took it out of a girl. But while she was in there, her bladder was awfully full. She sat and went like, two tablespoons.

Huh. Weird.

Her anti-crying shield firmly back in place, she settled in for the rest of the movie.

When the credits started rolling, Casey turned to face her. "Have you talked to Tate recently?"

"What? No. Why?" Rachel felt the heat rushing into her face, and Liz gave her another confused look. She took a deep breath. "Did he say he talked to me?"

"No, my mom must have talked to him though. He said he was waiting for you to call him at work or something. What's up with that?"

Relief swept through her and she couldn't help but smile. "Oh, he mentioned that he'd help me incorporate my business if I wanted. I don't know though. I haven't decided if I want to do it yet."

Which was a lie. She just hadn't decided if she could actually sit across a desk from him without wanting to throw herself on top of it and pull him down with her.

Casey nodded. "Well, I think you should still talk to him. He's a smarty-pants. If he thinks it's a good idea, it probably is."

Yeah. Because Tate never, *ever* had bad ideas. Rachel could think of at least one very specific example to the contrary.

"I will, I'll probably call his office tomorrow."

"You could walk over to his place now, he's probably home."

Rachel snorted before she could think better of it. Then coughed to try and cover it. "Yeah, maybe I will."

Or maybe she wouldn't. Maybe she'd put on a gasoline soaked dress and walk over some open flames instead.

Liz came into the kitchen, still wiping mascara from under her eyes from the movie. Rachel rolled her eyes. "Geez, they ended up together. Why are you crying?"

With a soft laugh, she leaned against the counter next to Rachel, then bumped their shoulders. "You say that like you weren't getting all teary eyed at one point too."

"What?!" Casey shrieked. "Is the sky falling? Is the apocalypse upon us?"

"Ha, ha," Rachel said dryly, but turned to grab her keys and purse. "I'm out. Pray I can stay awake long enough to drive home."

After giving quick hugs to Casey and Liz, Rachel walked through the door, and then about tripped over her feet when she saw Tate's car pulling into his opened garage door. She froze, thinking maybe she'd get lucky and blend in with the siding and still be able to escape unscathed. Unfortunately for her, she was wearing a kelly green coat that was not even remotely close to the slate blue siding. He eased his black BMW into the garage, and she practically sprinted to her fully restored Camaro, the greatest car in the world, and probably would have made a clean exit but Tate called out to her just before she could open her door.

"Shit," she whispered when she knew she was good and stuck. She pasted on a smile and turned towards the sound of his footsteps. He looked so yummy. He wasn't wearing a coat over his solid black suit, so the jacket opened over a bright blue oxford that made him look almost criminally handsome. His eyebrows pinched over tired-looking eyes, and he approached her almost warily. And she couldn't blame him one little bit.

"Rachel," he said in greeting, and gave her a cautious smile. "I'm really glad I caught you."

She crossed her arms in front of her, the only armor she had, and it felt horrifically flimsy. "Hey, Tate."

"Didn't you get the voicemail I left you a couple weeks ago?"

His face was blank when he said it, but his dark brown eyes actually looked a little wounded.

She had. In truth, she hadn't been by her phone when his call came through, but it had still taken her two days before she worked up the courage to listen to his message. She'd waited until she had crawled under the covers one night, and even though it was completely dark with the comforter pulled over her head, she'd unnecessarily pinched her eyes shut and listened to his low voice scrape across her. And in just a few moments of weakness in the days that followed, she'd played it again. And again. And again. And then after the fourth time, she'd hit delete before she could talk herself out of it. Not that deleting it would make her forget what was on it.

"Rachel, it's Tate. I saw Casey yesterday, and she told me that you're really doing it. Starting your business. I was serious, you know, I want to help you. If you'll let me." He'd paused for a few long seconds, and she thought he was going to hang up. But he let out an audible breath. *"Damn it, Rachel. It's been over a week since I saw you. Twelve days, actually. I hate this. I get it, why you didn't want Casey to know what happened. But I wish you'd just ... I don't know ... talk to me. I hate that this feels like you're going to do your best to never talk to me again. And that, that I'm not okay with. I'll stick to work stuff if that would make you more comfortable. Just ... call me back. Bye."*

And looking at him now, she felt like it was practically screaming from her that she was too gutless to return his call. And that was so not her. She wouldn't let this make her some weak-kneed, shrinking violet.

She straightened where she stood against the side of her car. "Yeah, I got your message. I'm sorry I didn't return your call yet."

"Yet? So you were going to?" His tone was disbelieving, and she couldn't blame him.

"Eventually," she admitted, not meeting his unwavering gaze for more than a second. "I'm still not sure it's worth all of your time and my money to incorporate my business. It's not like I'll even have any employees."

His shoulders relaxed, probably feeling like her- on more solid footing with a business conversation.

"That's exactly when you should do it. You can use your own social security number to file your taxes. Beyond the tax benefits, it'll protect you more as the business owner." He looked so intent, so bright talking about it, that a grin tugged at her lips before she could stop it. "Ah, there it is. I was thinking I'd never get to see that smile ever again."

So she flattened it, and squinted down the driveway, shivering a bit in the brisk October wind. He noticed.

"Do you want to come inside? I don't want you to stand out in the cold if you want to talk about this more."

"No," she said firmly. Inside with him would be bad, bad, bad. "I think that's a ... bad idea."

He nodded and looked like he was fighting a smile. "You trust yourself around me so little?"

She shifted her squint into a glare and aimed it right at his handsome face. "Arrogant much? No. Once was enough of a mistake. I'm just exhausted and want to go home."

"Twice."

"What?"

"You said once was enough of mistake, but it was twice."

Her jaw fell open. "Shut up. We did it twice with the amount of alcohol we drank?"

Well, that was all sorts of sexy and impressive and hot. And sexy. Not like she'd tell him that.

"You don't remember?" He looked incredulous and more than a little hurt.

She shifted uncomfortably, shoving her cold hands in her coat pockets. "I remember bits and pieces. Just flashes. Like someone spliced out big chunks of the night."

"Sounds like some fairly important chunks are missing."

"Is this funny to you?" she nearly screeched, then looked back to Casey's door that Liz had yet to exit.

Tate reached a hand up and ran it through his hair, leaving it there before it dropped back to his side. "No, Rachel, it's not funny to me. I remember all of that night, and I'm sorry that you don't, because-"

"You're still here, Red?" Liz's voice preceded the slam of Casey's door. "Hi, Tate."

Rachel turned her head, and attempted a smile, even though she wanted to scream at the top of her friggin' lungs from wanting to know what Tate was going to say next. "Yeah, just talking to my lawyer here. He's going to make sure I don't screw this up." She quirked an eyebrow back at Tate. "Right?"

"Right," he said quietly, seriously. And he meant it. It radiated off of him, and that knowledge made her feel pleasantly warm. "Call my office tomorrow and my assistant will get you on my calendar. She'll let you know what you need to have done before meeting with me. Goodnight ladies."

She pulled in a few breaths, the cold air feeling good in her lungs. And after saying goodbye to Liz, she took her time driving home, successfully avoided seeing her parents, and flopped into bed. Laying in the dark, the only light visible coming from the window. Staring over at the light purple curtains that she'd obsessed over as a sixteen year old, she couldn't sweep Tate's interrupted sentence from her mind. *I remember all of that night, and I'm sorry that you don't, because ...*

Because why?

Beeeeeecause she was clearly a glutton for punishment, she rolled over, snatching her phone from the black nightstand. Rachel swiped her thumb over the home screen and pulled up her messaging app. Her thumbs started moving, punching in Tate's name, then moving down into the body of the message. It ached, everywhere, from how badly she wanted him to finish that sentence.

I think you should finish telling me why you're sorry I don't remember all of our night. Because if it's more of what I already do remember ...

Rachel stared at the words, not sure what she would say next, how she would finish that thought. And knowing that going down this path would only serve to ignite the black edged, glowing orange embers that wouldn't quite go away since she'd kissed him, she started deleting the text, one letter at a time. Plugging her phone back in and carefully setting it back where she found it, she rolled back towards the window, knowing that sleep would be a long time coming.

7

ONE PLACE that Rachel certainly never thought she'd find herself, two weeks after seeing Tate that last time in the cold driveway he shared with Casey, was sitting in the corner of her shower, fully dressed, arms hugged around her knees, counting to one hundred and twenty. She'd shut the glass door, somehow feeling like that would bar her from leaving this little safe place before her time was up. Because that might somehow change what was waiting for her on the bathroom counter.

Her seventh pregnancy test.

The first six? Well, she was banking on a fluke. The first three had a reeeeeeeeeally faint lines, like she could only see the second line if she turned it at just the right angle. She'd taken those last night. Because even though the instructions *clearly* said that the best results came from the first pee of the morning, well, ha, the person who wrote these *clearly* had never been in her situation.

The next package of tests gave her mother-effing smiley faces as a result. SMILEY FACES. Which made her think that buying the tests from a dollar store might not have been the best idea. And that left her in her current state: waiting for the expensive test to decide her fate. No messing around this time; she got the good kind, the 'pregnant' or 'not pregnant' kind.

One hundred and eighteen, one hundred and nineteen, shit, shit, shit, holy shit, I can't do this, one hundred and twenty.

She pushed herself up to standing, and let the shower door open slowly, only a slight squeaking of the hinge breaking the silence in the bathroom. With a shaking hand, she picked up the small piece of white plastic from the cream granite counter. Rachel had no clue why this one felt so different, so real. No numbness this time, no denial, and before she flipped it over, she took a really deep breath.

Pregnant.

There it was, in a dark, unassuming font. As if those eight letters didn't spell out the most life-changing thing a woman could go through. A freaking baby. She was pregnant with Tate Steadman's baby.

"Oh. Holy. Crap," she said to her reflection, barely recognizing the clammy-faced, wide-eyed, crazy-haired person staring back at her. "What am I gonna do?"

She didn't know how long she stood there, but when a fist pounded on the bathroom door, she didn't even flinch.

"Rach! Move your ass! You're supposed to drop me off at campus, remember?" Her younger sister Kate's voice was muffled through the door, and on autopilot, Rachel reached over and twisted the brushed nickel doorknob to let Kate inside. In a flurry of long brown hair, Kate whipped past her and pulled a brush out of one of the drawers. "What's your deal? We need to leave in like thirty seconds and you're still in your ugly PMS pants."

"Sorry," Rachel said, and belatedly realized that 'the test' was still sitting next to her on the counter. She darted her eyes over to where Kate was hurriedly putting mascara on and thankfully not paying much attention. Rachel slowly moved her hand and tried to pick it up when something zapped her like a fricken lightning bolt. Kate was going to be an aunt.

Her twenty-year-old sister was going to have a little niece or nephew. Which meant her parents, oh Lord help her innocent little offspring, were going to be grandparents. Because she was going to be a mom. Some little person's mother. She didn't have her own home. She had just started her own business. And she was going to have baby. Rachel dropped her head into her hands and tried to hold in the sob threatening to crawl up her throat.

"Uhhh, Rachel?" She felt Kate move closer to her, and then a hand settled on Rachel's heaving shoulder. "Is ... is that ... a pregnancy test?"

Rachel lifted her head and met her sister's gaping look in the mirror.

Then she gulped and nodded. "Yeah."

"Are you ...?"

And then Rachel started shaking, her legs sinking away beneath her. Kate wrapped an arm around her waist and walked her out of the bathroom, down the hallway and into Rachel's room. They both sank onto the bed, and Kate turned so that she was facing Rachel. She chewed on her bottom lip, so Rachel knew she was probably about coming out of her skin waiting to say something. Holy balls, she was going to have to say it. Out loud.

"I'm pregnant."

"No shit, Sherlock. Whose is it? Is it Marc's? Did you have breakup sex or something?"

"No!" Rachel said, and slugged Kate's arm. "I broke up with him like six months ago. Do I look six months pregnant?"

"Your boobs do."

"You're just jealous, A-cup."

They both smiled, and Rachel had to admit, she was glad her sister was here. Because there were eight years in between them, and Rachel had Casey and Liz, she and Kate hadn't always been close. Whenever she'd thought about being married and having kids someday, all those fuzzy hypothetical situations that seemed so far off, Rachel had never imagined herself confiding in Kate first.

Oh shiiiiiiiiiiiiiit, she'd have to tell Casey. After she told Tate. And right then, she seriously didn't know which one sounded worse. Rachel flopped back on her bed, rolling until her face was buried in her pillow, wanting to scream, but keeping it in.

"C'mon hooch, quit holding out on me. Who's your baby daddy?"

Rachel shifted to her side, facing Kate. "Tate Steadman."

Kate's dark eyebrows shot up her forehead, and her mouth dropped in the opposite direction. "Wait. Casey's hottie-patottie older brother? The lawyer?" Rachel nodded and her sister threw her head back and laughed loudly. Then she wiped a finger under her eye. "Wow, I gotta say, I did not peg you going for him."

"I didn't *go* for him, Kate. We just had a one night ... thing. It wasn't planned. And why wouldn't I?"

Kate shrugged. "He's got that sexy professor vibe. You know, all business in those hot ass suits, but underneath? Probably a fricken animal."

Rachel breathed out a laugh and dug a hand into her hair. "You're such a perv."

"Animal though, right? C'mon."

"I admit nothing." But yes. Yes, he was. And just thinking about it made every single inch of skin feel like it was completely combustible. Oh geez, this had to be hormones. She kept her eyes fastened up on the ceiling, and she could feel Kate's stare, but was thankful that she stayed quiet. "Mom and dad are going to freak out."

Her sister hummed in agreement, then added her next question quietly. "What are you gonna do?"

Die of embarrassment. Hide under a rock. Move into a convent. No, scratch that. She'd lose her mind in a convent. She closed her eyes and just breathed for a few seconds.

"I have to tell Tate," she whispered. "I have an appointment with him tomorrow anyway, he was going to help me incorporate my business. I don't ... I don't want anyone else to know before he does. It doesn't feel fair."

"Good plan. Don't be one of those stupid biatches who think they can get away with not saying anything, thinking they're making the best decision for him, only to have him find out in like, the worst way possible, and then he never trusts you again."

Rachel quirked an eyebrow. "You read too many angsty books, Kater."

"Maybe," she sighed, then bit down on her lip again. "So ... you're going to keep the baby?"

"Yes," Rachel said firmly. And truthfully, nothing else had occurred to her. She wanted to be a mother, always had, but the timing had never been precisely right. And apparently this was as good a time as any. But the rest? The rest was up to Tate, and she had a horrible, creeping feeling that she knew what he was going to have to say about this little development. And it involved something waaaaaay more permanent and legal than she was ready for.

She let her sister wrap her in a hug. They stayed that way for a few minutes before Kate pulled back and looked towards Rachel's closet.

"So, what the frick do you wear to go tell your one night stand he's gonna be a daddy?"

Rachel smiled, but it felt awfully forced. "I have a feeling it really isn't gonna matter."

LESS THAN TWENTY four hours later, she stood outside the heavy mahogany door to his office, thinking that she had probably made a good choice after all. The canary yellow sweater dress was one of her favorites. The gray pumps were probably ill-advised considering that her legs felt like jello. Shit, that outfit usually made her feel like fricken Heidi Klum when she wore it.

If Heidi Klum was short. With red hair and big boobs.

But today, she didn't think anything would help her feel stronger. During the walk from her car to the entrance of the small law firm he worked at, all she could think about was that the whole 'I'm expecting a teeny tiny human' thing wasn't actually going to feel real until she got the words out to Tate. The receptionist directed her back to another desk, where an unassuming middle-aged woman with unfortunate hair sat pecking away at a computer.

She greeted Rachel with a beaming smile and told her to head on back, that he was expecting her. With shaking hands, Rachel undid the belt on her coat, pulled it from her shoulders and folded it over the arm carrying her files she was required to bring. She'd practiced this. A hundred times in the last few hours. She'd just say it. Tell him. They'd discuss it for a few minutes, then move on to business. Yeah. That would work.

Rachel stopped with her hand on the cool metal handle and kept her forehead from dropping on the door. That would *never* work. Tate was going to freak out. She quickly stepped back, wondering if it was too late to cancel her appointment and just tell him at his place. What the *heck* was she thinking? Telling him at work?

There was no fah-reaking way she could sit in a room with him for any extended amount of time without him noticing that she was losing it. She had to cancel. Like now. She spun in place and was about to take a step when the door opened behind her.

"Rachel?"

She turned back to face him, swallowing loudly at the absolute perfection of Tate in his lawyerly element. He must have taken off his suit jacket, and had just a white dress shirt underneath a freaking vest. A VEST. It hugged his chest in a way that was kinda ridiculous, because all she wanted to do was rip the damn thing open and see what was underneath it. Well, she knew what was *actually* underneath it, but another little peek wouldn't hurt.

"Can I get you some water or coffee before we start?"

His face was polite mask, but his eyes practically singed her everywhere they touched over her face and body. Guess Tate enjoyed the yellow dress too.

Good to know.

"Water would be great, thanks," she said as she walked through the door he held open for her. She took a seat in one of the armchairs that he had sitting across from his desk, and she tried, she really tried to stay in her seat and not snoop a bit. Unfortunately, Tate must have been walking three miles to get the water, so she had too much time unattended. Rachel walked around the large desk, trailing her finger across the glossy surface.

He didn't have any personal photos on his desk, no extra clutter. A large photo of the entire Steadman family on the sand dunes framing Lake Michigan was directly across from where he sat every day, and that made her smile.

They were just all too good-looking. Tan and smiley and happy. If she didn't love Casey's family so much, she'd probably totally hate them. Staring at all those faces that she'd known and loved for so many years, she felt a tightening in her chest thinking about how amazing they'd be as family to her child.

All she had to do was get through this meeting with Tate, maybe pretend like she forgot something and ask if she could drop it off to him later. Okay, yes, that would work. Tell him somewhere that he could process it easier. Rachel walked past the picture, trying to blank her mind of all things pregnancy-related, reading through the spines of the books filling the large book shelf on the opposite wall when she heard him come back through the door.

"Sorry," she said. "I'm peeking where I probably shouldn't be."

He shook his head and gave her a sheepish smile. "Nothing too exciting to find in here, I'm afraid." He handed her a cold bottle of water and gestured for her to sit again. "Well, this should be a pretty easy process if you filled out the articles of incorporation that my assistant sent you. But let's review them to make sure everything is ready to go to the Secretary of State."

All Rachel could do was stare while he spoke. Would their son or daughter have his dark brown eyes or her hazel ones? Her red hair or his dark blond hair? And just like that, her heart started pounding, absolutely *pounding* against her ribcage, and her lungs felt like a Hummer had parked on top of them for as much as they moved when she tried to make them expand.

Thankfully, he was shuffling through some papers and didn't notice when she finally pulled in a full breath. Her movements stiff, she handed him what he'd asked for. Tate tapped his green Cross pen against the paper, and if she hadn't been thirty seconds away from having a complete mental breakdown, she probably would have made fun of him for using such an expensive pen.

He must have asked her a question while she stared at him, so when he said her name, she flicked her eyes up to his where he looked at her expectantly.

"I'm sorry, what did you say?" She ran her hands along the tops of her thighs, momentarily grounded by the feeling of the soft material of her dress. When she crossed her legs, she so did not miss the way Tate's eyes tracked the movement. Nope. Not helping, buddy. Rachel cleared her throat and absolutely loved the way his cheekbones showed a little pink when he focused back at her face. He gave her a self-deprecating grin, and she returned it. Yeah, he wasn't even going to deny it.

And this is exactly what got them in trouble in the first place. Tate and his wandering eyes and hot dress shirts and her complete inability to deny him. And his innate goodness and decency. All of it, him, made her so friggin weak.

"Tate," she spoke softly, but he heard her. He lifted his eyes from the papers and lifted an eyebrow. "I'm so sorry."

He tilted his head. "For what?"

"I didn't want to do this here," she said, her breath catching in her throat. *Oh God, give me strength.* "Tate, I'm pregnant."

And before his expression could even change, the jarring beep of the phone on his desk screamed through the room.

"Tate, I'm so sorry to interrupt," his assistant's voice sounded tinny through the speaker. "But Natalie is calling back. Again. She insists, again, that it's urgent. Do you want me to put her into your voicemail one more time?"

He'd sunk back into his chair, one hand speared into his hair, his eyes fixed right into Rachel's. If she thought her heart was pounding before, ha. She felt it everywhere, louder and louder until the sound was galloping through her eardrums. Tate blinked rapidly, then picked up the phone receiver.

Oh. Hell. No.

Just the thought of Natalie having any single second of this moment was enough to push her to her shaking feet. Rage coursed through her, hot and thick. She vaguely heard Tate shout her name when she pulled open his office door so hard that it bounced back against the wall. For a brief moment, her conscience bellowed at her to stop, to just give him one second, but she smacked that nosy bitch back into place with the picture of Tate pulling his eyes from Rachel to pick up the phone.

The sound of his voice faded as she practically sprinted through the door into the parking lot. And then she just drove.

8

TATE YELLED a curse word into the phone that he typically tried not to use when Rachel didn't stop.

"Excuse me?" his poor assistant said on the other end of the line.

"Sorry, that wasn't aimed at you."

"Mmhmm, I'm guessing it's aimed at the redhead that just did her best Olympic sprinter impression into the parking lot."

"Yeah," he said, still staring at where his office door moved from the force with which Rachel pulled it open.

Pregnant.

Rachel was pregnant. With his child.

The bright burst of excitement he got was quickly tempered by all the logistics that went with her statement. He'd known, and known immediately, that something was off with her when she had walked into his office. And it was no wonder. She was probably freaking out.

"One thing at a time," he said on an exhale, which Maggie wisely didn't respond to, just waited patiently. "Okay, put Natalie into my voicemail, that way it's on me when I don't return her call. Then if you could get my realtor on the line, I'd appreciate it, I have another quick phone call to make before I talk to him."

"Sure thing. I'll put him on line three once I have him."

Tate placed the phone back on the cradle and sank into his chair, then scrubbed a hand down his face. And the hand was shaking a little bit when he set it back on his desk. He'd always wanted kids. Never a single doubt that once he and Natalie were married that he wanted to start trying right away. It was actually one thing they'd agreed upon after he proposed. Neither of them were getting any younger, and Tate didn't want to be a father that was in his sixties when his child graduated high school.

And despite the way it happened, and the millions of unanswered questions he had right now, and the fact that Rachel was probably insanely pissed at him, a slow smile spread across his face.

He was going to be a father.

His hand came up to rest over his suddenly racing heart. And as badly as he wanted to tell his parents, and soak up any single bit of advice they would give him, he needed to find Rachel.

Tate called her first, though he wasn't surprised in the slightest when he was sent to voicemail after two rings.

He pulled up Casey's contact information and hit the call button. Given that his ass hadn't been chewed out by her yet, she probably didn't know about Rachel's little bombshell. So he'd play dumb unless Casey hinted otherwise. She picked up after one ring, and he didn't even let her finish saying hi.

"Where would Rachel go if she was really ticked off?"

"What did you do, Tate?" The tone of her voice told him two things. One, she was narrowing her eyes, and two, she had one hand on her hip. Apparently, he was two for two today when it came to offending important women in his life.

He rubbed at his forehead. Nope, she definitely didn't know. "I'll tell you, I promise. But I need to talk to her first. Would she go home?"

"I doubt it. Did you try calling her?"

"She sent me to voicemail."

"Yikes. You do realize that it takes a special kind of stupid to piss her off, right? Any cliché you've heard about the redheaded temper is like, nothing compared to Rachel."

Oh yeah, that was helping him feel better. "Trust me, I'm well aware."

Tate heard a muffled voice in the background, Casey must have covered the speaker on her phone while talking to herself. Finally, she let out a long huff of air. "Fine, she's probably at the airport."

"The airport?"

"Yeah. She doesn't go very often anymore. But I know she said her dad used to take her and Kate to watch the planes take off and land, and that it was a good distraction if everything else in her life was going crazy. There's a small observation area on the north side of the airport where you can park your car to watch, right in between those train tracks and the fence that runs around the property."

He nodded. "Yeah, I know where you're talking about. And you're sure she'd go there?"

"It'd be my best guess. She went a few times after she found Marc cheating with miss slutty pants."

The light blinked on his phone telling him that Maggie had gotten through to his realtor.

"Thanks Case, I have another call I have to take really quick. But I'll start at the airport as soon as I can leave."

"Will you let me know if you found her?"

"Sure thing. And don't screw it up any more than you already have."

He was smiling when he clicked the line over to Robert.

"Thanks for holding, Robert."

"Not a problem, young man," his voice boomed through the line. Robert was a friend of his parents, and the first person he thought of calling when he needed to find a house. Tate had been fairly specific in his search parameters so far, not willing to make an offer on just anything. The market had been picking up in the last year in West Michigan, making it so that if he found a house he loved, he'd need to make an offer quickly. He trusted Robert to keep an eye on anything that fit what he was looking for. Tate had seen half a dozen houses so far, none exactly what he wanted though. "What can I do for you?"

"I need to make a change in what I'm looking for in a house."

"Oh?"

"Yeah. Hey, do you mind if I call you back on my cell phone real quick? I need to leave the office."

Robert agreed, and Tate quickly pulled up his contact information on his cell.

Tate shut down his laptop, grabbed his keys and suit coat, wedging the phone in his shoulder so he could lock up his office. He waved to Maggie as he walked past her deck, studiously ignoring the blatant curiosity on her face.

Once he'd cleared the door into the parking lot, he took a deep breath. "Okay. I want something with one more bathroom and at least one more bedroom than I originally told you, minimally an acre of land, but I want most of that to be in the backyard, in a good school district, and definitely no pool."

He was met with silence. "You have something to tell me?"

Tate smiled, not at all surprised that he would come right out and ask. But since Robert had known him since he was about two years old, he wasn't offended in the slightest.

"Just decided I need some more space," he answered as evenly as he could, thinking of all the ways that extra space would be filled.

"You know I wouldn't say a word to your parents unless you said it was okay."

"I know that, Robert. But I appreciate you saying it anyway."

"Well, I guess you gave me some homework then. I'll poke around and email you the links of what I find."

"Thanks. I appreciate it." He disconnected the call by the time he folded into the driver's seat of his car. While he let it warm up, he finally let his mind swarm with everything that had been pressing in on him the last six weeks since his night with Rachel.

Despite the ridiculous amount of alcohol he'd consumed that night, nothing this side of heaven would be able to erase what he'd felt. He gripped the cold steering wheel thinking about Rachel rising over him after they'd caught their breath from the first hard, feverish, frantic joining. The way she'd dragged her fingernails down his chest and stomach and made every hair on his scalp tighten up. The way she'd moved on top of him. The way she had leaned down to drag her tongue up his jaw, pressing small kisses along the way.

How her skin was so insanely soft and warm. How she curled into him after they'd finally found their way firmly into exhaustion. He'd dragged his hand over her hair for a few minutes after she fell asleep, barely recognizing the fire that was still coursing through him. Even after having her twice, he wasn't nearly satisfied.

No woman would ever be as breathtaking to him as she was that night.

Then she'd completely shut him out. And he had felt like she'd literally ripped his intestines through his skin. That's how much her silence hurt him. Tate had been with Natalie for so long that he had absolutely no clue how to do this. To dance around feelings like this.

And *feeling* seemed to be his fate with Rachel. Feeling but never quite reaching what was just beyond those emotions.

He wanted, but he certainly couldn't have.

And, for lack of a better term, it sucked. A lot.

But the things he had felt during her six weeks of silence were crickets compared to what swamped him when she'd said she was pregnant. The rush of emotion was unlike anything, *anything* he'd experienced in his entire thirty-four years combined. Nothing could even come close to touching it.

At least until he was able to meet and see and hold his son or daughter.

Just the *thought* of that moment made his chest tighten and then swell with hope and fear and then terror, and then back to overwhelming excitement.

And he would do anything in his power to be certain that his child would have the absolute best life possible. As he turned his car onto the packed dirt road next to the inconspicuous chain link fence following the boundaries of the airport, he knew exactly what the first step would be to making sure that happened.

Maybe he could have Rachel too.

Maybe the attraction that was practically a physical presence between them wasn't exactly the way he'd imagine building a life-long relationship, but looking deeper past that gave him more than enough to start from.

Beyond being beautiful, Rachel was smart and funny and driven. She was loyal. The way she morphed from concerned friend to a tigress, ready to maul Natalie on behalf of his sister, was almost overwhelmingly appealing to him. She felt so deeply and strongly that her reactions couldn't be masked. Even the way she'd stormed out of his office earlier, he knew why she did it. She'd been mistaken, but he could actually understand why.

And the way that she was so visible, so vibrant, made it easy to want to show her the same honesty. He owed her that now. And every fiber of his being was practically vibrating with the knowledge of how they could, how they *should* do this.

He swung his car next to hers, but it was empty inside. When he stepped out into the brisk, biting air, he spotted her fiery hair. She was sitting on a dark bench just on the other side of her car, and since no planes were coming or going at the moment, she was staring at her phone. When he carefully shut his car door, he saw her head turn slightly, followed by a straightening of her shoulders. She knew.

Tate walked slowly, trying to sift through everything he wanted to say. Other than intermittent sounds of cars on the nearest street, and the rumble of plane engines taxiing down the runway on the opposite side of the airport from where they were parked, it was eerie. He could see exactly why she came there. When he stood next to the bench, she still hadn't turned towards him.

And as much as he'd love to stand there in silence with her, just watching her, he knew one thing that couldn't wait. "I wasn't picking up to talk to Natalie. I'm sorry that it appeared that way. I was just telling Maggie to send her to voicemail. I have no intention of returning her call."

"Well," she sniffed and shrugged one shoulder. "It's *possible* that I shouldn't have run out. I was a little ... overwhelmed. Not that that's an excuse."

"I know the feeling," he agreed easily. She tipped her chin up and watched him for a few seconds before turning back to her phone. The silence was heavy, but he let it stay that way for a few seconds longer, hoping she'd speak next. Then he smiled a little, thinking there was no way she was going to make this easy on him. "Have you been feeling okay?"

"Other than being completely exhausted, I'm fine. I never thought it was possible to be ready to go to bed before seven, but apparently it is."

He nodded, relaxing a little at her sharing just that tiny piece of information. He blew out a short breath of air and shoved his hands into his pockets. And it was utterly ridiculous how much he wanted to be around to help her get into bed that early. Make her breakfast in the morning if she didn't feel like getting up yet. They could do this, they could get through this mind-blowing life change together. He could feel it in his bones. It was inconceivable that she didn't feel it too.

"So, you're about six weeks pregnant then?"

"Yeah," she said, flicking her eyes up to him quickly before lowering them again. Because the grass was practically dead after too much frost and the trees had lost almost all their leaves in the last couple weeks, the hazel color of her irises looked brighter than normal. He wished he could see them again. "I called my doctor this morning, I won't have my first appointment for another three to four weeks."

"Well, just let me know when it is and I'll come with you."

"No," she said quickly, her voice hard but quiet. "I mean, I know how busy you are. You don't have to do that. I'll let you know what happens, I promise."

"It's not an inconvenience, trust me. I would really like to be at your appointments with you."

Rachel turned finally, her body angling towards him, her face finally showing some vulnerability and it practically cracked him right down the middle. "You're not just saying what you think I want to hear?"

He smiled. She probably didn't realize that she just as good as admitted she wanted him to come with her. He shook his head, not answering until he knew he could speak evenly. "No, I'm not."

She turned back to the tarmac, where a plane was going to take off, and exhaled heavily, probably hoping he wouldn't notice how full of relief it was, and he grinned widely. Tate rocked forward onto the balls of his feet, watching while a 747 made its way down the runway, the engine a low, loud noise that he could feel in his chest. The wheels tucked into the belly of the plane, and it rose quickly into the gray sky then banked towards the east.

He felt like he was at the sharp edge of a gaping precipice, and this one was so different than any others he'd experienced before. And the quiet conversation they'd just had helped ease him. Just enough that he felt like he could walk right off the edge of the cliff in front of him. Because he knew she'd be next to him.

So he shifted so he could face her, taking in her profile. Too still to not be paying attention, Tate knew she was watching him in her peripheral. "Besides," he said, not turning away despite her still facing forward. "I'd never expect you to go by yourself once we get married."

Tate didn't precisely know what he expected in reaction. He'd just figured she'd feel more comfortable showing her relief if he didn't make a huge production. But the way that her features didn't move, how they hardened in place, made him shift in place.

"Rachel?"

Her eyes flicked down to the phone still gripped in her hand, but her lips thinned into a tight line. He could see the screen shift with different colors and screens with the quick jabs of her thumb.

"Rachel?" he said a little louder. Nothing. Well, shit. "Come on. You can't keep ignoring me."

"When I'm working I can." Her voice sliced through him. He took a step closer, trying to see what she was doing, and she turned the phone so all he could see was the lime green cover. He snatched it out of her hand, ignoring the creative combination of swear words she managed to string together. Tate raised an eyebrow at her after looking at the screen. "Pinterest?"

"It's called research, asshole," she snapped, color rising in her cheeks. "My first bride wants a blue and yellow theme and I need to make sure it doesn't look like a Michigan pep rally puked all over the reception."

"So that's your answer?"

"Oh, I'm so sorry, did you ask a question that I missed? Because, if I'm not mistaken, all you just did was announce an edict."

Tate pinched the bridge of his nose. "Fine, I could have done that a little better."

"Gee, ya think?"

"This is new to me, Rachel, cut me some slack, okay?"

"Really?" she bit out as she stood to face him. Her eyes were blazing again, her chin thrust towards him at a stubborn angle, and Lord help him, he felt so inconveniently turned on in that moment. "Because I was under the impression you'd already asked someone to marry you. But maybe Natalie warranted a polite request since you didn't happen to knock her up."

And that shoved all the air out of his lungs for just a second. He almost felt like he should swipe a hand across his chest to make sure she hadn't plunged a knife into it. And the hell of it was, she was so right. If it hadn't been for the briefest flash of regret in her eyes, he might not have backed down.

He let out a self-deprecating laugh, staring at the ground. What was wrong with him? He shook his head, trying to figure out just what the hell he had been thinking. "Wow. I'm not sure I could have done that any worse if I tried. I'm so sorry. There's something about you, Rachel, I just lose my mind when you're around."

Tate looked up, at least expecting a small smile, but her face was completely blank. He'd meant it as a compliment, but clearly, it wasn't taken as one. She stared for a moment, giving absolutely nothing away.

"Well," she said flatly. "We can't have that. I'm afraid I'll have to turn down your proposal, Tate, given that it's not 1953 and I'm perfectly capable of managing this without a husband."

"I wasn't saying you weren't capable--"

"Not directly, no, you weren't," she interrupted. "I can't do this right now. I need to get home and get back to work."

He stared helplessly at the top of her head when she bent down to pick up her purse off the bench and then swung the handle over her shoulder. A smart man knew when to shut his mouth, and this was definitely one of those times. A little reprieve would probably benefit them both, so he stepped aside, clenching his fists to keep himself from reaching for her. He caught a faint whiff of a perfume that was slightly spicy and he greedily pulled a deep breath of it into his lungs.

"Rachel," he called out when she'd reached her car. "You'll let me know when your appointment is, right?"

She nodded quickly and ducked into her car. Tate moved to sit on the bench that she'd vacated, staring numbly at plane after plane taking off, until he was too cold to stay any longer.

9

BABIES. There were big-eyed, smiling babies everywhere she looked. On the walls. On brochures. On magazines. Perched in car seats, drooling up at their exhausted-looking mommies. And despite the fact that lately, all she was capable of thinking about was the microscopic little person inside of her, sitting in this office made everything so freaking real. Tate shifted in the chair next to hers, and she tried to move away so she wouldn't keep feeling the heat of his shoulder brush up against hers. From across the crowded waiting room, a wail of epic proportions came from the mouth of a child that looked about fourteen years too young to make that kind of sound. She sank down in her chair, digging her fingernails into her palms.

"Are you okay over there?" Tate asked calmly, quietly. Of course he wasn't freaking out. He'd been annoyingly steady since his faux proposal that she was doing an excellent job of pretending had never happened.

Because yeah, if she thought too much about a pity marriage proposal from Tate because he was trying to do 'the right thing' she would go postal. She was so glad she hadn't been looking at him when he'd said that so casually. She would have smacked the shit out of him. Kinda like she felt like doing now.

"Oh yeah, I'm awesome. I just had to piss in a tiny plastic cup and then somehow write my name on it without spilling pee all over my hands."

He was silent for a second, tilting his head towards her. Good. That ought to shut him up.

"You can always write your name on the cup beforehand."

Rachel rolled her lips inward, focusing on the sharp pain of her teeth on the sensitive skin inside her mouth instead of responding to Tate's annoyingly rational response. Everything he'd done in the last four weeks had been rational. Supported her when she'd asked him to wait until after her doctor's appointment to tell his family.

He'd sat with her when she'd told her parents last week. Smiled calmly when her mom had started weeping copiously and begging that her first grandchild be named after her. Shook her father's hand when he'd made the entirely inappropriate remark about having 'excellent swimmers'. Held her hair back when she threw up in the trash can in his office during their last attempt at finishing her incorporation paperwork. Didn't flinch when she cursed him in between dry heaves. But hey, it *was* his effin' fault.

All those little things felt like someone was trailing her, scratching rusty nails down a chalkboard. It was almost uncomfortable in how steady and supportive he was being. Because she damn well knew that he wasn't forcing it. This was just him. And he'd offered to do this for her, forever.

"Rachel?" The smiling blond nurse in pink scrubs called her name from the doorway leading back to the exam rooms. She and Tate rose from their chairs, and he graciously looked away when the nurse asked her to step on the scale before entering a room. She took Rachel's blood pressure, asked a few basic questions, and then patted Rachel's knee before she left the room. "My name is May. We'll be seeing a lot of each other for the next nine months, so don't be afraid to call if you have any questions in between appointments."

They sat in silence, but it wasn't awkward. Rachel fidgeted with the white paper she sat on, the crinkling noise filling the room. Tate looked up from the magazine he was flipping through. Of course he was reading a parenting magazine. The headline "How much caffeine is safe for pregnancy?" flowed across the top in purple script. She narrowed her eyes at him when he smiled back into the article.

It was almost eerie, this back and forth they'd developed in the month since she'd told him. They exchanged text messages almost every day, often instigated by Tate, asking how she was feeling, if she needed him to do anything for her. And without discussing it, both of them seemed content to wait to have a talk about how this whole parenting thing would actually go once the baby got here.

Truthfully, she wasn't positive it was smart to let it go, but if Tate was feeling anything like she was at the moment, she was still having to take baby steps towards this new reality sinking in. Pun intended. She'd asked him once how he felt about it so far, right before she went to bed a couple weeks ago. They'd just finished texting about her preference to wait until her doctor's appointment to tell friends and family, the only reason she'd been forced to tell her parents was the tiny fact that they'd both caught her puking in the kitchen sink when she couldn't make it into the bathroom.

Rachel: So, you're okay with all of this?

Tate: Of course, I understand why you want to wait to announce it until closer to the end of the first trimester.

Rachel: Thanks for that, but that's not what I meant. The whole baby thing ... you're okay with it? I'm kind of a bitch for not asking before.

SHE HAD PACED to the bathroom, taking her time brushing her teeth, not able to sit and stare at her phone and wait for his answer. While she was rinsing her mouth, she heard the chime on her phone, the one she'd assigned to Tate.

Tate: Please don't talk bad about the mother of my child.

She had blushed. And then grinned like a fool. And then felt her heart squeeze when his next text came in.

Tate: You may not believe me, but there is very little that could make me happier right now.

And ever since that night, despite the multitude of unanswered questions they still had facing them, she'd felt at least one weight lift off her shoulders. A soft knock on the door had Tate setting down the magazine.

Her doctor, with her fuzzy brown ponytail and bright purple plaid Danskos, looked more like an intern fresh off the set of *Grey's Anatomy*, but Rachel loved her. She made introductions to Tate, and then started going over a few basic questions about how she was feeling. When Tate asked about the best brand of prenatal vitamins, Rachel only rolled her eyes when Doctor Madison beamed in response.

"Well, my dear, if you don't have questions or concerns for me, we'll see you in four weeks."

"Wait," Tate said. "Aren't you going to listen to the heartbeat?"

"I usually wait until after twelve weeks, because it can be hard to find before then, and I never want the parents to freak out if we can't find it. But I'm happy to try if you'd really like me to."

Tate looked over at Rachel with one brow raised in question. Even if she wanted to wait, which she didn't, she would never have been able to turn him down right then.

She smiled and nodded to Dr. Madison. "Let's do it. As long as you don't tell me you can hear like six heartbeats."

Her doctor laughed and pulled out a tube of gel and a hand-held wand thingy from one of the drawers. Rachel laid back on the table and edged her pants down so far that she was kinda glad she'd done a little shave job earlier that morning in the shower. She inhaled at the feel of the cool gel on her skin and stared at the ceiling tiles when the doctor reminded them that it wasn't uncommon to not hear the heartbeat yet. Suddenly, she was nervous. She really didn't think she would be, so it surprised her that her own heart started galloping. When she started fidgeting with the edge of the paper again, Tate's warm fingers closed around hers.

She turned her head to meet his dark eyes while the doctor pressed the rounded end of the wand at various spots on her stomach. He smiled a little when she started to pull her hand away, but before she could, a fast *wop-wop-wop-wop* sound filled the room. She tightened her fingers where they were woven through his. Tate's small smile spread into an almost blinding grin, and she felt an unexpected wave of relief swamp through her.

In that moment, everything was perfect. So perfect, it pricked at the back of her eyelids.

"There we are," the doctor said with the same broad smile on her face that matched Tate's. "Sounds great. And I think there's only one."

"Thank you," Rachel said sincerely. Doctor Madison left the room, and while Rachel closed up her pants, Tate just shook his head.

"That was ... that was the most amazing sound I've ever heard." And he smiled at her again, wide and open, making her heart constrict in a whole different way than she had ever felt. The pressure on her chest wasn't bad. It was warm and solid. And supremely annoying.

While they walked out into the parking lot, he stayed with her until they reached her car where it was parked in one of those awfully convenient expectant mother spots.

"Thanks for letting me come with you."

"You're welcome," she said, jingling her car keys in one hand. As much as she wanted to thank *him* for being there, for her not having to do it alone, she just smiled. "So, now that we've heard the heartbeat, are you going to tell your parents tonight?"

"As long as you feel comfortable with it."

She nodded. "Thanks for waiting. A lot of guys wouldn't have."

"Rachel." He looked at her so seriously, searching her face. "I hope I never respond the way *most guys* do. We're in this together, okay?"

Swallowing proved difficult, but pushing the boulder down her throat helped take away the pinprick of yearning that was hovering beneath her skin. She had a sudden wave of gratitude, that this man would be the father of her child. No other way around it, her kid had won the lottery.

Which meant that she'd won the lottery too.

"I know telling my parents with me wasn't the most fun thing, so if you want me to repay the favor when you tell yours, I'll come with you." She straightened her shoulders, even though the thought of facing Marie and Elliot Steadman to inform them of this little bombshell made her knees practically shake. She'd only ever been 'Casey's friend', and now she'd be providing them with another grandchild. He just smiled and shook his head.

"That's okay. Besides, don't you have your ladies night tonight? I'm guessing you'll do some announcing on your own."

"Oh, son of a bitch, I forgot." She smacked a palm on her fore-head. "Your sister is gonna flay me alive."

He laughed. "Nah. I don't think she will. This will be a great distraction for her anyway, since Jake's leave just ended, she's probably pretty down." Rachel blew out a deep breath, and Tate reached a hand up and rubbed her upper arm. "It'll be fine, Rachel. I promise."

Rachel turned to open her car door, his hand dropping off of her, and she had to grit her teeth to not feel like a big gooey mess from that small supportive touch. Looking back in her rear view mirror as she pulled out of the parking lot, Rachel took a sliver of comfort that he was still standing there, watching her pull away.

Her mom's car was in the driveway when she got back home, and that in and of itself was weird during the work day, but when she saw two large bags sticking up above the passenger side window, she groaned. Two purple bags with 'Babies R Us' written on them.

She cautiously opened the door, and her jaw dropped when she walked into the kitchen.

"Mom," she breathed. "What the hell did you do?"

"Oh Rach, I couldn't help myself. I stopped to just look at a few things, and I thought, you know, this is the only first grand-child I'm ever gonna get. And Lord willing, your sister won't be getting impregnated for another ten years, so this my only chance to spoil for a while."

Her mom sat on the dining room floor, literally swamped between bags and boxes. There were blue clothes. And pink clothes. Stuffed animals. Hooded towels. Three boxes of diapers. And if she wasn't mistaken, a diaper genie. But it was the borderline dreamy expression on her mom's face while she held up a tiny lavender sundress with white ruffles on the butt that kept Rachel's mouth shut. This was a different kind of happy than she'd ever seen on her mom's face. And because they looked so similar, same hair and eyes, Rachel had to wonder if that's what she looked like earlier, laying on the exam table.

"Oh! How was your appointment?"

Rachel walked over and sank into a chair next to the kitchen table, running a finger over the silky ear of a big white teddy bear wearing a black bow tie. She could do this. Have a normal, well-adjusted conversation with her mom. At least they weren't talking about Rachel's dad. "Good. We heard the heartbeat."

And then her mom burst into tears. Rachel dropped her head onto the table, banging it on the hard wood a few times. Breaking the news to Casey and Liz suddenly looked very appealing.

Except, four hours later, after Pinterest-ing her little heart out looking for ideas for the bride she got a signed contract from yesterday, she retracted the idea that telling her friends looked even remotely good. Her hands were actually shaking when she opened Liz's front door. Liz was the only one of the three of them who owned her own home, and normally Rachel loved going there. It was cozy, cluttered with books, almost fairy tale-like. But the small stoop that held large terra cotta pots full of brightly colored mums felt downright claustrophobic at the moment. Casey's car was already parked in the small, cracked driveway, so she knew there wasn't much room for a reprieve.

When she walked through the entryway, she heard Casey's soft weeping, so she hurried around the corner into the kitchen.

"What did you do to her, Blondie?"

Liz gave her an unamused look from where she sat with an arm wrapped around Casey's shaking shoulders. "She's just sad about Jake leaving. Just because you're allergic to emotion doesn't mean the rest of us don't get to show it."

Even though the quietly spoken statement wasn't meant as a barb, it stung a little. Rachel pursed her lips and snatched a still warm chocolate chip cookie off of the kitchen counter. Casey wiped a streak of black mascara from her damp cheek and gave Rachel a watery smile.

"Don't listen to her. She's had to put up with me for last half an hour. I know he's done deployments before, I just ..." She sniffled and shrugged her shoulders. "I'm worried. And I'm gonna miss him so, so much."

"How long until he's back for good?" Rachel asked, praying that it didn't unleash the waterworks again.

"Probably five to six months."

Rachel nodded, mind swimming over the fact that by the time Jake returned home, she'd be in her third trimester. "He'll be fine, Casey. Jake's way too much of a bad ass to have anything happen to him."

"Rachel's right-"

"Don't say that like you're surprised, Liz," Rachel huffed.

Liz only smiled when Casey let out a shaky laugh. Then Casey blew out a breath and slumped back in her chair, pushing her dark hair out of her face. "Okay, we need to change the subject. I've been a weepy mess since he left yesterday. Please tell me that one of you has something better to talk about."

And there was the door, opened way the hell up. All Rachel had to do was walk through it. She cleared her throat, and the small sound held such a nervous tinge that both Casey and Liz looked over to her. Rachel slid her hands forward on the hard surface of Liz's white-washed table, knitting her fingers together.

"I have something to tell you guys," she said slowly, looking directly at her hands. "And I'm really fricken nervous, if I'm being totally honest, so I just need you to wait until I finish before you say anything."

Out of the corner of her eye, she saw them look at each other. She swallowed and then pulled in a fortifying breath. "The night Deidre fired me, I went to that club right down the street from where the benefit was, and your Mom sent Tate after me to make sure I was okay." She saw Casey nod a little, and it was a small relief that at least that part wasn't a surprise. "Well, we sat there all night, talking and drinking. A lot of drinking, unfortunately. And, umm, I went home with Tate." She heard a quick gasp of air, but didn't dare look up to see who it was. "And I swear, Casey, I swear I didn't intend for that to happen, and I wasn't going to let it go past that one night. But, a few weeks ago, I found ... I uh, I found out that I was, I am, um, pregnant."

"Holy shit," Liz whispered at the same time that Casey's jaw fell open.

Rachel covered her face with her hands and fought, for what felt like the hundredth time this week, the urge to cry. She was the worst friend in the world.

"I'm so sorry, Casey," she started when the silence became oppressive.

"You're sorry?" Casey said, voice incredulous. She slowly stood from her chair and walked around the table, then sank down in front of Rachel's chair. Her bright aqua eyes were full of tears again, but they didn't spill over. She shook her head, reached to pull one of Rachel's hands down off the table, and squeezed it in between her own. "Rachel ... you're pregnant. You, one of my favorite people in this entire world, are pregnant with my niece or nephew. What on *earth* do you have to be sorry for?"

How she ended up with a friend who'd react this way was truly humbling to her in that moment. In no way did she feel like she deserved it. And one, just one tear pushed out from the burning mass behind Rachel's eyes and dashed down her cheek. She swiped at it with her one free hand.

"You're seriously not mad at me for sleeping with Tate?"

Casey lifted one shoulder. "I'm not blind, Rach; you guys kinda spark whenever you're in the same room. Is it an ideal way for you to start a family? Of course not. But, you couldn't ask for anyone better to go through it with than Tate."

"I can't believe you're pregnant," Liz said in between sniffles, not making the effort to wipe her face the way Rachel had. "How far along are you?"

And here was part two of the bombshell. She pinched her eyes shut. "Ten weeks."

"What?!" Casey screeched and shot up onto her feet. "And you waited until now to tell us? Wait, do my parents know? I can't believe you let us miss almost your entire first trimester!"

"See, I knew this whole understanding thing would only stretch so far."

"Rachel," Liz interjected. "You can't blame us for feeling a little blindsided. You being pregnant is one thing, but you're pregnant with a man I've never heard you admit to having feelings for. You just started your own business, you're living with your parents, and oh, by the way, this pregnancy is almost a third of the way done."

"Wow, tell me how you really feel," Rachel snapped, knowing full well that Liz's statement was fair.

"Fine," Liz crossed her arms and her face set into hard lines, something that didn't often happen with her. "I'm happy you're pregnant, I can't wait to love your child, but I am worried for you, Rachel. Where are you going to live? What about insurance? Are you and Tate going to have joint custody?"

And when Rachel's hackles were good and raised, Casey laughed. "Oh, knowing Tate, he'll be herding Rachel to the altar as soon as he can manage it."

Rachel's facial expression must have betrayed her, because Casey groaned. "He already proposed, didn't he?"

"He did?" Liz's face finally lit up, die-hard romantic that she was, this was the kind of crap she lived for.

"Good Lord, Liz, is that really what would make you feel better about all this? If I entered into a marriage of convenience?"

Undeterred, Liz met her gaze. "You obviously have feelings for each other. I think you two would be wonderful together."

"Sure, because a drunken sex fest is a fantastic foundation for a marriage."

Casey clapped her hands over her ears. "La, la, la, la, I didn't hear that."

Rachel winced, knowing that if anything would shove her into hussy-who-seduced-Tate category, it would be little reminders like that. "Sorry. But, c'mon, he doesn't love me."

"Not yet," Liz replied.

"Okay, ladies, back to your corners. Geez. Liz, I'm not used to taking over your peacemaker role; it's kinda awful." Casey flipped her eyes back and forth between Rachel and Liz, then crossed her arms across her chest. "I'm sure Rachel and Tate will figure out what's best for them."

"Thank you, Casey. It's not that I don't expect questions from you, Liz, but trust me when I say you're not bringing up anything I haven't thought about."

"I know, I'm sorry." Liz shook her head, then speared her hands through her white blond hair. "You're going to be a mom, Rachel. This is ... insane. How do you feel? Wait, do you need water? Are you staying hydrated?"

"I swear, this pregnancy has the uncanny ability to make everyone lose their flippin' minds. Yes, I'm staying hydrated. And I've been a little pukey in the mornings and thoroughly exhausted, but other than that okay."

Motioning for them to move into her family room, the three of them took their usual spots on her white furniture. When Rachel sank back into the plush love seat, she reveled in the feeling of relief that settled in her. That hadn't been terribly awful, and considering the worst-case scenarios that had been filtering through her head, a little snipping with Liz wasn't too shabby. By unspoken agreement, it seemed that no movie would be watched tonight.

"So," Casey started after she kicked off her heels and settled a light blue pillow on her lap. "I've got to know. How did he propose?"

Rachel snorted. "Believe me when I say this is not a story you're gonna like."

"Wait. Did this happen the day he called me and I told him about you possibly being at the airport?"

"Oh yeah." Rachel dragged a finger along the white stitching on the armrest. She told them everything that had happened at his office. Liz slapped a hand over her mouth and Casey muttered something under her breath when she got to the part about him picking up the phone. She paraphrased their conversation at the airport, considering she'd cursed like a sailor a few times in there, but when she got to the part where Tate laid out his little plan, Casey slapped a hand on her thigh.

"You're shitting me. That's how he did it?"

"What an idiot," Liz whispered. Rachel tipped her head back and laughed, long and hard, and it felt so good after the past few weeks of uncertainty.

"Yeah, he can be. I don't think he meant to be hurtful. He apologized right away."

"But it did hurt." Casey said it, not as a question, as a statement of fact.

Rachel nodded, knowing it would be completely pointless to lie to them about it. "Yeah. No woman wants to feel like an obligation, and Tate ... he just ..."

"He wants to save everyone," Casey finished. All three sat in silence for a few long moments. It wasn't uncomfortable, but it was pensive, heavy.

Liz spoke first, having been relatively quiet up until that point. "So, besides his less than romantic proposal, what do you feel for Tate? And pretend that it's not Casey's brother, just some guy."

Rachel closed her eyes and just let the question breathe through her. She kept them closed while she answered, because she wouldn't be able to look at Casey and stay honest.

"He's so far under my skin that he absolutely terrifies me. And it would kill me to trap him somewhere he didn't really want to be." When Rachel forced her eyes open, she caught the tear falling down Casey's face. "It's almost annoying how pretty you look when you cry. I don't know if I can be friends with someone who doesn't look ugly when they cry."

The smile on Liz's face was nothing but satisfied, and Rachel knew she'd played right into her scheming little romantic heart with her answer. For some reason, admitting it out loud to them, even though it was depressing as shit to be in this situation for the man she was going to have a baby with, she felt stronger, on more solid footing.

"You know it'll probably be a boy, right?" Casey said, her eyes dry now and sparked with humor. "I was a complete fluke in this family."

Rachel groaned, even as the thought of a little boy that looked like Tate flashed through her mind and made her heart beat faster. "Great. Just what the world needs. Another Steadman male."

"Speaking of Steadman men," Casey said. "Liz, you don't have any unrequited feelings for Dylan, do you? Because he's the only single brother I have left. Please, please say no. I need to have at least one friend that I can talk to about their sex life."

They all laughed at that, and to Rachel, the sound was the second most perfect thing she'd heard that day.

10

TELLING his parents had gone about as Tate expected. Shocked faces and a few long silences, but overall, they were being supportive. His mom, of course, had immediately asked how Rachel was and how he planned on taking care of her. He'd been honest about their conversation at the airport, and the sharp smack on the back of his head from her made it more than clear how she felt about his proposal technique.

"You don't think I should marry her?" he had asked, rubbing the back of his head and feeling like a chastened teenager.

"Tate," she'd said, disapproval clear in her voice. "I love Rachel. And I love that your father and I raised a man who's willing to step up to his responsibilities. But, if *you* don't love Rachel and she doesn't love you, then you're walking into a disaster. If you ask her for the right reasons, then your father and I will be your biggest supporters."

And that was the thing. He knew he could easily love Rachel, even if he wasn't there yet. She did *something* to him, as vague as that sounded. There was no other way to put it. He loved watching her pretend like she wasn't nervous at the doctor, and he loved pushing her buttons even more when she was like that.

The way the color rose in her cheeks, the way her hazel eyes practically shot electricity at him. He'd never been an antagonistic person in his life.

With Rachel though? Riling her up like that was pretty much the best kind of foreplay possible without actually putting his hands on her. It made his skin practically hum when she looked like that. And what was more, he loved that she was bringing out that side of him. But with one stupidly delivered sentence, he'd effectively signed his own death sentence when it came to pursuing a relationship with her. Because that's what he hadn't actually done. Pursue a relationship.

Starting from scratch with her, trying to rebuild any semblance of trust in his feelings given the situation they were in, wasn't going to be easy. But it wasn't impossible. They communicated every day. He wanted to call her, but decided that starting small was best. He hadn't sent her a text yet today, so he pulled his phone out from his pants pocket and tapped out a message quickly.

Tate: I keep hearing the sound of that heartbeat over and over in my ead.

Rachel: Me too. How did it go telling your parents? Did they have to explain to you how birth control worked all over again?

Tate: Funny. Went well, you'll be happy to know my mom smacked the shit out of my head for what I said to you about getting married. As she should have.

Rachel: I'm jealous.

Tate: ?

Rachel: I wish I could have been the one to smack you. But

**since I have to be a good example for our unborn child now, I
should probably avoid a violent first reaction.**

Tate laughed, having seen Rachel actually punch a guy for
placing his hands on her in too personal a manner. Even then,
and that instance was easily five years earlier, he was so in awe of
her strength, her backbone. And now, in these daily snippets that
they shared, he could still feel it.

**Tate: Don't change a thing. I can only pray that our child will
inherit your strength.**

She'd read his text. He knew it. And he knew because of her
silence. He smiled, because it was so easy to be able to say things
like that to her. Telling Rachel the truth about how he saw her
felt effortless. He just had to make sure she *knew* they were the
truth for him.

"Tate? Your one o'clock is here. Shall I send them in?"

He looked over to his calendar, where it was up on his
screen. Maggie had entered this one in, putting very little information as to what the appointment was about, which was very
unlike her.

"Yeah, I'm ready."

He tidied the few piles of papers on his desk and stood to
open the door, but before he could clear the side of his desk, the
sight of his two oldest brothers, Michael and Caleb, walking
through the door made him stop.

"What are you guys doing here?"

"Can't we come and have lunch with our little brother?"
Michael asked, dropping a large brown bag on the coffee table,
the smell of Chinese food filling his office. Caleb clapped him on
the back before he took the other open seat. The oldest in the
family, Michael and Caleb were identical twins who were only
two years older than Tate; he was more than used to them step-

ping in when they thought a younger sibling needed unsolicited advice.

"You talk to Mom this morning?" It was phrased like a question, but all three of them knew it was more like a statement. Leaning up against the edge of his desk, he watched with amusement when Michael and Caleb looked at each other briefly, obviously trying to decide who would speak first. "C'mon, someone has to spit it out, preferably before the food gets cold."

"Yeah, she called me this morning before I got to the job site," Caleb started, focusing very intently on pulling white and red takeout containers from the bag. He handed Tate one without asking what he wanted, along with a set of unopened chopsticks. "Thought you might want someone to talk to."

"Ah, I guess I'm not surprised she called one of you before sunrise. She was practically salivating to talk to Casey last night. How was she when you talked to her? She still ticked at me?"

Lifting his chin, Michael grinned. "Maybe not ticked. But she did mention that if you're able to give her a granddaughter she may not kick your ass so bad."

The twins let out the same low chuckle, and Tate scoffed. "Yeah, not sure I can do anything about that at this point."

Oh hell. A little girl. A little girl with red hair like her mom's. It twisted him up imagining that, like someone was yanking his heart down into somewhere around his kidney. He'd tried not to think too much about what the gender was. Truthfully, he didn't care one way or the other what they had, and he and Rachel had mutually agreed to wait to find out. It had been a surprise when she'd brought it up in a text one day, but a good one. They'd decided that in keeping with the theme of this whole situation, letting this be another surprise would be appropriate.

His brothers dug into the food in front of them, and Tate settled himself more fully on the desk so he could eat from the fragrant container of kung pao shrimp that he'd been given. "Not that I don't appreciate free Chinese and time with my big brothers, but my phone does work. You guys make it feel like this is an intervention."

Michael lifted a hand in concession. "Well, maybe we shouldn't have gone through Maggie. We just wanted to make sure you had time for us. You know that I understand a little of how you're feeling. Didn't want you to think that we weren't going to support you where we can."

"That was different though," Tate pointed at him with his chopsticks. "You and Jen were already engaged when you found out she was pregnant."

Still, Tate remembered vividly when Michael and Jen had told the family they were bumping up the date of their wedding by six months. Something about the wedding dress not fitting. The kind of stuff that Tate, as a new law student living away from his family, hadn't paid too much attention to. He just showed up, wore the tux they told him to, stood at the front of the church where the scary wedding coordinator had taped a little x for him, and watched a glowing Jen walk down the aisle.

"Of course it was different, it just sped up the inevitable with me and Jen. Hell, I was just happy she had to marry me even sooner." He grinned, looking so much like their Dad. But he sobered, setting down his food and leaning forward in his chair. "But what I remember is that 'oh shit' feeling when you're dealing with a terrified woman who isn't expecting to go through it. Not knowing what you can do to help."

Yeah. That was a feeling that Tate still had soaking through his bones.

"I reckon Rachel isn't the terrified type though," Caleb added, mouth full of rice.

Tate blew out a short laugh. "If she is, she's not telling me about it."

"I guarantee you that she is," Michael said seriously. "Knowing you're going to be a parent for the first time, before you meet that child, is the most awesomely terrifying thing you will ever experience. And believe me, we only feel a tiny fraction of what the woman does. She feels that baby move inside her, feels it make her body ache in ways she never thought possible, both good and bad, and thinks about that child every second of those forty weeks. Trust me, she's scared shitless."

He set the food down next to him, letting Michael's words settle through him. Tate shrugged. "So, what am I supposed to do? I was ready to marry her to help, not that I went about it in the best way, but if she doesn't want me there as her husband, what more can I offer her?"

"Lord have mercy," Caleb said, wiping a napkin across his face. "For such a smart guy, you're a friggin idiot, Tate."

"Thanks," he drawled.

"Listen," Caleb continued, "she may *never* want a romantic relationship with you. Are you prepared for that? I mean really and truly prepared for that? That she'll just be someone you share custody of a child with and that you send a check for child support to every month?"

Tate stared at a spot on the wall until his eyes dried out with the need to blink. It made him ache, thinking about that. Not in the jealous way, of her possibly being with someone else, just at the thought of *him* never being with her. With her and their child.

"I guess if that's what she really wants," he swallowed roughly, fairly choking on the words, "then yeah."

"Good," Caleb said. "Because you are the only person who's really going through this with her, no matter how many people she has that love her and support her. You are the person who can do the most to make this okay for her. So, the wooing and the shitty proposals come second right now, okay?"

Tate hung his head into his chest and laughed. "Okay."

"We love you, little brother, and we just want to help," Michael said as they finished cleaning up the food. "Thanks for not kicking our asses for barging in."

"That's not my style; I'm not Dylan." They all laughed,

because their youngest brother probably would have. Tate walked them out, hugging them both, receiving bone-crushing thumps on his back from them.

Maggie waved a hand in front of her face when he walked past her desk. "Lordy, you do have good lookin' brothers."

He raised an eyebrow. "Looking to rob the cradle, Maggie?"

She swatted at him with a manila folder. "You know I'm happily married. No harm in looking. Your realtor called while you were walking them out. I sent him to your voicemail."

He thanked her and shut the door to his office behind him. The message just told him to check his email, that there were some great options. Both had just been put on the market that morning. Tate pulled up the links and couldn't stop the grin from spreading when he started looking through the first one. He couldn't flip through the pictures fast enough. Then he looked at them again.

Barely taking his eyes off his computer screen, he called Robert.

"Hey, it's Tate. The one on Constellation Court, I want to see it as soon as possible."

"Wonderful, I had a feeling you would."

"Oh yeah. This is it, Robert. It's perfect."

"Sometimes you just know. I'll call the listing agent right now. If it's not occupied, how soon can you meet me there?"

A quick look at his calendar didn't show anything that couldn't be rescheduled. "Whatever works for them. I'm flexible."

"Excellent, I'll send you a text with the time."

Folding his arms behind his head, Tate leaned back in his chair, feeling a lightness that hadn't been around for a while. It was a different feeling than what thinking about the baby gave him. Like Michael said, that was a terrifying sort of awe, at loving someone he'd never met. This was the most concrete, tangible thing he could do for the future of this little family that was now his. Unable to help himself, he looked through the pictures again.

This was it. He could feel it so fiercely that he couldn't wipe the smile off of his face if he wanted to. And man, he didn't.

A plan started threading through his brain as the pictures crossed his computer screen. And as he looked at them a third time, it cemented.

His phone chimed.

Robert: If 5pm works for you, I'll meet you there.

With a quick response to Robert, he hit the button on his desk phone to call Maggie.

"Yeah, can you call Mike and see if he can come at three-thirty instead of four? I've got to go buy a house."

11

I<small>T WAS</small> the perfect scenario for a serial killer. Defenseless pregnant chick driving down a long driveway, huge trees arcing over the quiet street, the first dusting of snow making everything stark and eerie. She was unsure of her destination, so if a masked guy carrying a chainsaw jumped out from all the groupings of trees, she probably would have asked him for directions.

Tate, adding a new twist to their daily text messaging, had sent her an address and asked her to meet him there a few hours later.

Rachel: Why?

Tate: Can't you just trust me?

Rachel: This from the man who impregnated me out of wedlock. Sure thing, Tate. I'll get right on that.

Rachel: Fine. I'll see you there. But this better be good, it's cold and it's the only reason I have to leave the house today.

Tate: Don't worry, it'll be good.

That, Lordy, she had taken in such a dirty way it was almost ridiculous. Pregnancy hormones? No flippin' joke, that was for sure. Because she knew, and knew with utmost certainty, that Tate could deliver on the promise of 'good'. She snickered as she drove, thinking that Tate would probably looooove knowing that one innocently sent text had pretty much forced her to take an, ahem, extra-long shower before she met him. In rebellion of him making her leave the house, she'd stayed in yoga pants and her sweatshirt from her alma mater, Grand Valley State University. If he thought she was getting all cute just to meet him at some random place? Ha. The next six months should clear that up for him pretty damn quick.

She saw the mailbox with the number he'd sent her, so she took the turn onto the street. Looked like a private drive. Huh. In her rear view mirror, she noticed a bright green and white sign that she hadn't noticed when she drove past. A real estate sign. Her eyes narrowed when she saw Tate's car by itself in front of, well, pretty much the most perfect house she'd ever seen.

The driveway did a large curve before looping around to meet back up to where Rachel had pulled in. The three stall garage sat perpendicular to the front of the home, which had thick white pillars propping up a gorgeous wide front porch. The dark gray siding and black shutters looked rich against the snow on the ground. Layers of river rock sat along the bottom of the house, and large windows all along the front showed that there were already warm lights blazing inside. She stared for a few seconds, not willing to look over at where Tate stood on the front porch, hands braced on the white railing.

What the *hell* had he done?

She blew out a breath before she exited, making sure that her face stayed blank. What she wanted to do was run inside and look, having a really fricken strong gut feeling about what was happening here. The slam of her car door echoed around the property. It was completely silent while Tate looked at her, and she looked right back. His face was serious, and it made her heart beat faster.

"Whose house is this?"

"Why don't we go inside? It's cold."

She held up a hand. "Tate whatever-your-middle-name-is Steadman, if you're trying to buy me off with a big ass gorgeous house, it is *not* going to work."

"You know my middle name is Elliot."

Not moving from her spot, she continued to stare up at him.

He grinned. "Have I ever told you how much I appreciate your ability to get to the point?" Rachel screwed her lips together and glared. He sighed. "Will you please just come and look at it?"

A bitter wind came through the trees, and she stomped up the dark treads of the stairs. The porch was beautiful and wide, with hooks that probably held a swing in warmer weather. Tate gestured for her to open the heavy door, painted a bright cheerful red.

And inside? Well, the inside kicked the outside's ass, if that said anything. Dark, glossy wood floors stretched into a large family room with a soaring cathedral ceiling. And at the peak of the ceiling was where the stone fireplace started, and spread down the entire length of the wall. It was empty of furnishings, but the way the room flowed into a huge dining area and kitchen, it didn't matter one bit. The cherry cabinets above seemingly endless lengths of dark granite counters surrounded a giant island in the center of it all.

She finally found her voice when she'd wandered around the kitchen. Tate stood silent by the massive windows looking out into a, oh yeah, of course, giant ass backyard.

"Tate," she waited until he turned and faced her, "whose house is this?"

"You sure you don't want to look around more before we talk?

The master bedroom is down that hallway, second bedroom is across from it. And there are three more downstairs."

She barked out a laugh. "Five bedrooms? I'm not going any further until you tell me what the hell is going on."

He crossed the room and stopped on the other side of the island from her, his large hands looking stark against the dark counter. They were more calloused than she'd expected when she had finally felt them on her skin. She felt a warm flush and averted her eyes.

"We'll compromise. You look at the rest of this level and then I'll explain."

"Fine. Let's get this over with."

Compromise, she wanted to spit the word back out at him. Man didn't know the meaning of the word. Rachel, marry me. Rachel, hold my hand while I force the doctor to find our child's adorable little heartbeat. Rachel, come look at this amazing as hell house that I can afford to buy because I'm a snooty ass lawyer.

Then she stopped when her anger-fueled steps took her into the master bedroom. There were lots of windows and a huge amount of space, but the double doors that were set open to the most perfect of all perfect closets stood open, welcoming her like a long-lost friend. She stood in the opening, mouth hanging open at all the custom shelving and hanging space. Carrie Bradshaw deserved a closet like this. And if Carrie did, then damn it, so did Rachel.

"Never mind, maybe you can buy me off after all." He laughed softly behind her, and he must have been standing close, because she could swear she felt her hair move. She pinched her eyes shut and stepped into the closet, dragging a hand along a shelf. "Okay, I looked. Now spill."

He took a deep breath. "Let's go back into the kitchen, then you can sit down."

"Wait, I might as well see the bathroom while I'm here." But she shouldn't have. Because it was awesome. Sunken tub with the mother-load of jets, double sinks and a fully tiled, double show-erhead, glass-enclosed shower, everything in warm tones. It looked like a spa.

Shit.

With a peek in the second large bedroom across the hall from the master, she followed Tate back into the kitchen. When she slid onto a stool perched at the island, thankfully he decided to sit on the counter next to the fridge so that he wasn't right next to her. She didn't want to look at him. For some reason, it was worse today, knowing what she'd admitted to Casey and Liz about how she really felt about him. So, like she did when she was at Liz's, she stared at her hands.

"So, you want to know whose house this is?" he finally asked.

"No, I just asked four times to be polite." One of his eyebrows slowly rose up, and she rolled her eyes. It was his favorite facial expression apparently. "Sorry."

"Barring complications, and there shouldn't be any, this house will be mine in two weeks. They accepted my offer last week."

And even though she knew it, she freaking knew it, hearing him say it out loud knocked the breath out of her lungs. "Wow. It's really ..." Amazing. Perfect. My dream house. "Big. Congratula-tions." He smiled, just one side of his lips, while he watched her. Ass probably knew exactly what she was thinking. "So, why am I here?"

"I have a proposition for you. But I wanted you to see the house first."

"A proposition, huh? Is this anything like your last 'proposition'?"

"No," he shook his head, and ran his hands down his thighs a couple times. Wait. Nervous gesture and Tate didn't usually go together. "Rachel, have you thought about what you're going to do after the baby is born? Like where you're going to live?"

Her teeth clenched together, and one finger traced along the design of the counter so that she didn't snap unnecessarily. Valid question, that one was. But sitting in the most amazing kitchen she'd ever seen, it burrowed right into her defenses. "My parents have made it very clear that I'm welcome to stay with them, at least for a while."

Tate nodded, staring at her intently. "Like you said, this is a big house. I did that on purpose."

"Okaaaaaaay."

"Well, in the lower level, there's three more bedrooms, a family room, and a small kitchenette. And you haven't even seen the rest of this floor."

"Sounds like you're getting your money's worth."

He continued like she hadn't even spoken. Jerk. "I'd like for you to move in here. You and the baby."

She pushed her stool backwards and gaped at him. "Is this a joke?"

"Absolutely not. I've given this a lot of thought, and it makes sense."

"Makes sense," she repeated slowly, trying to let her racing mind catch up with what he was saying.

Leaving his seat on the counter, Tate walked around the island and stopped next to where she was glued to the stool. He moved his hands like he was going to touch her, but she gave him a warning look that he wisely heeded.

"Yes, Rachel, it makes sense. The master bedroom would be yours, the nursery can be in the room across the hall from you. I'll stay downstairs. I'll have my own space, but still be able to be here for you and the baby. No trading weekends or dropping off one night a week. I'm sure you'll have a lot of night and weekend hours once you start getting busier with weddings, and I'll be able to be here, as much as you need me. We can do this. Together."

Her elbows dug sharply into her legs and she speared her shaking hands into her hair, not particularly caring how much it was ruining her ponytail. Crap, she did not want to admit that every single deeply-spoken word he had just said made sense, so much fricken sense. She *would* have a lot of night and weekend hours as she drew closer to the wedding dates of her brides. Right now, their seven wedding dates were perfectly spaced out, one every month starting in February. Two on the opposite ends of May, clearing up her schedule just a couple weeks before her June due date.

But, after the baby came? She'd need brides in order to have steady income, and that meant odd hours in her line of work. The beauty of being able to do most of it from home would be wonderful, but Tate was right, she'd need help.

But moving in with him? A vivid memory of him walking through his own place wearing only his gym shorts plagued her, because if that was the kind of shit she'd have to see all the time? She'd jump him before the first month was up.

And beyond jumping him, which felt like an almost tangible problem at the moment, she was desperately and mind-numbingly afraid that living under the same roof as him, parenting with him twenty four hours a day, would catapult her head first into falling completely in love with him. The kind of soul-altering, permanently-etched-onto-her-heart love that she'd been terrified of her entire adult life. And to be that close, all the time, without being able to do anything about it just might kill her.

She'd lose her mind, slowly and steadily, until the inevitable day when he would find someone else, and it would snap her cleanly into a million fragments. Dragging her eyes from where she stared down at her lap, Rachel looked at Tate's face. He still looked nervous. But more than that, she could see in his eyes just how badly he wanted her to say yes to this.

She swallowed down her immediate refusal. "Can I see the rest of the house?"

"Yes, of course," he said, eyes widening in surprise. And the rest of it was as amazing as the part that she'd already seen. She wanted to cry a little when he showed her the office that was tucked around the corner from the dining room. One entire wall of white shelving and a custom built in desk along the back. The same dark floors that ran through the entryway, kitchen and dining room. It would be hers, he said firmly, as if it would help her make her decision.

Tate let her wander at her own pace, trailing her as she went back through the family room to where the stairs going into the lower level were framed by two white squared-off columns and a gorgeous wrought iron railing that enclosed them from the rest of the room. The steps going down ended in a huge family room and kitchenette. No stove in the lower level, but a full size sink and refrigerator and stools tucked in underneath the high counters. Down the hall were three decent sized bedrooms, and two full bathrooms.

Once she made her way back into the family room, she stood in front of the slider that opened to the gigantic backyard. No way was this place much less than two acres. She noticed a play set tucked in the corner that she hadn't been able to see when they were upstairs, but Tate didn't say anything when he caught her staring at it. Smart man.

When she followed him back up the stairs to the main floor, she could feel everything bubbling under the surface of her skin. It was so overwhelming, this place and this offer he was handing her on the proverbial silver platter, but she was determined to give his idea the consideration it deserved. So she struggled to keep her tone even despite the roiling, raging feelings coursing through her.

"When did you first see the house? I'm assuming Casey doesn't know since she didn't call me panting with the big news."

He leaned back against the wall, hands jammed in the pockets of his black dress pants. His eyes searched hers for a few moments before he answered. "No, she doesn't know. Only Maggie and Robert, my real estate agent, know I was looking at it. But, I saw it last week Tuesday evening. Put an offer in on

Wednesday after talking to my bank. They accepted it Thursday morning."

"Busy week."

"An expensive week," he conceded with a grin. "But, I knew the house was perfect. So it's worth every penny."

She nodded, trying not to feel like she was being pushed back into a very difficult corner to escape from. One where she'd feel like the biggest bitch in the world if she told him no. The man had just bought a house. A big, expensive, beautiful home in order to house their impromptu little family.

"And," she said, quietly clearing her throat, "what if I say no? Is it still worth every penny?"

He stayed leaning against the wall, but she didn't miss the way his entire frame stiffened. "Are you going to say no?"

"I'm just asking a question. I think I'm allowed to have a few considering the situation."

His features had immediately brightened when she'd said that, and if she had been at all able to look away from him, she would have. "What can I do to make you say yes?"

The way his lips curled around the words made her feel flushed, and she thought about the last time she'd said 'yes' around him. Pretty sure she'd shouted it, actually. A firm mental bitch slap knocked her back to a less hormonally ruled frame of mind. *Lord have mercy, pull yourself together, woman.*

"I just need to think about it. It's a really big deal to move in together, Tate. It's not something I'd do lightly, no matter how amazing that closet is. I mean, do I pay you rent? Do we eat our meals together? Do we have certain nights we're expected to be home? What happens when one of us starts dating? Or gets married? Are Tate Junior and I out on the streets if someone else enters the picture for you? Or if I find someone?"

And the optimism faded from his face as she shot the questions at him, unable to stop them rolling out of her mouth. She wasn't even paying attention to what she was saying, let alone how he might react.

"Are you thinking of dating?" He all but growled it.

"Oh yeah," she pointed a surprisingly shaky finger in his direction. "Go ahead, start acting like an alpha male asshat and you'll just keep racking up points in the 'reasons I will never move in with you' category. That shit may fly in romance novels, but it does *not* with me. You don't get to be territorial."

"I'm not *acting* like anything, Rachel," he snapped back, volume rising while he pushed off the wall and stepped towards her. "But do you want to look me in the eye right now and tell me that it wouldn't bother you if I started dating someone?"

She huffed a laugh and stripped off her sweatshirt, thanks to a pregnancy-induced heat wave combined with rampant anger that he seemed insanely skilled at provoking in her. His brown eyes heated when he looked down at the plain blue t-shirt she had on, the deep V showing the cleavage that she had in abundance even before pregnancy.

She shoved at his hard chest, satisfied when he actually fell back a step. "Don't check me out right now. What is the matter with you?"

"Do you think I want to?" He flung his arms out to the side and stepped right back to where he was before she pushed at him. "I can't *help it*."

"Well, try!" she snapped, yanking the ponytail holder from her hair since half of her hair was falling from it anyway.

"You have no clue, do you?"

"Any clue of what?" she yelled back him, thinking that maybe she should be smart right now, try to diffuse the electricity that was snapping and popping around them. He stepped forward again, and she backed up the same amount of space, feeling the column that framed the stairs against her back.

Be smart, be smart, be smart. She chanted it in her head along with the way her chest heaved with the need for oxygen.

"Any clue how insanely sexy you look when you get mad." He said it low and hard, biting at the consonants, and the only thing she thought when he took the last step to press against her, pushing her into the equally unyielding surface behind her, was that being smart was highly overrated.

12

BEFORE RACHEL COULD TAKE in a full breath, Tate gripped the sides of her head, stamping his mouth over hers. She felt branded. His fingers curled around the back of her head, tangling in her hair, and when he tightened his grip even more the sharp bite of pain at her scalp made her whimper. His tongue, when it . pushed into her mouth, was an unequivocal command, a daunting challenge. And holy hell, she'd never backed down from a challenge a day in her life.

She curled her tongue around his and sucked it back into her mouth, drawing a deep, tortured groan from him. Practically mindless from what that sound did to her, she rocked her hips into him, and the hardness that she encountered, his chest, his stomach, his back, his, well ... yeah, made her want to sink into a puddle at his feet. He moved his hand from her head and gripped her cotton shirt and the back strap of her bra, pulling them both away from her body with his tight grasp, but she wanted to feel skin. Yanking the bottom of his shirt from where it was tucked into his pants, she pushed her hands up along the hot skin of his back.

Everything about him felt so good, so right, that she felt no shyness in meeting his every movement with a matching one of her own. When he pushed one large hand down past the edge of her pants, palming her completely, she twined a hand into his hair, tugging to the point that he let out a ragged moan. It was like the best kind of battle for dominance, where even the loser was a winner. But when he pressed into her, trapping her against the hard surface behind her, she gladly ceded control.

When he nipped at her bottom lip with his teeth and pulled at it just a little bit, she had the distinct feeling that someone was lighting firecrackers under her skin. Everything inside of her tingled and throbbed and felt on the verge of some sort of unholy detonation. When he followed the line of her jaw with tiny bites, ending by sinking his teeth into the soft flesh of her earlobe, she actually cried out at how unearthly good it felt.

This was so, so different than anything that had happened their first and only night together. That was jumbled memories and flashes of heat, all blanketed in a slight haze of alcohol. This was so vivid, so sharp in the way that she felt it all over her body, in her head and definitely, most definitely in her aching heart. Every push, nip, and sinking of his lips against hers zapped her straight down to her curled up toes. She pushed up on the balls of her feet, and their lips and tongues collided again, over and over and over, until she had to pull away just to breathe.

"Tate," she groaned. "What are we doing?"

He pulled back to look at her, dragging his thumb across her lower lip and her eyelids fluttered shut at just that light touch. Without the stimulus of his handsome face clouding her vision, she dropped her head back on the column behind her and listened to his heavy breathing, felt where it hit her overly sensitive neck, and breathed in the clean, masculine scent of his body wash. She felt so raw, still pressed up against him, that if she opened her eyes right now and saw the way he was probably looking at her, she'd never be able to walk away from him, never be able to think clearly.

"We're not doing anything that I haven't wanted to do for the last few months." And after he said it, he pressed his lips on the side of her neck. She shivered and pinched her eyes shut harder. He didn't move, just left his mouth resting above her skin. He groaned again after pulling in a deep breath. "You smell so damn good."

And because she didn't immediately push him away, his arms wrapped around her waist, tightening even though there wasn't any spare room between them in the first place. Against her better judgment, which was screaming bloody murder in her head right now, she tightened her arms right back. He was so much taller than her, so she pressed her forehead against the steady, rapid thrumming of his heart and tried to gain control of the turbulence inside herself. One of his fingertips dragged along the skin right above the edge of her pants, and it seemed like he couldn't decide whether he wanted to feel her overheated skin above or below the ridge of soft cotton.

"Tate, this--"

"Please don't say this was a mistake."

Rachel lifted her head and stared up at him. "That's not what I was going to say."

"Good," he said, smiling a little.

She carefully extracted herself from his all too comforting embrace and moved until she was a few feet away, where she felt like she could breathe without wanting to suck on his tongue again. "I was going to say that *this*, whatever this was, or is, doesn't help me think it's a good idea to move in with you."

He'd shoved both hands into his hair, a flush still tingeing his cheeks. But after staring at her for a few seconds, he nodded slowly. "I just shot myself in the foot again, didn't I?"

The shaky breath that came out sounded awfully pitiful. "Obviously I was an active participant, but yes, it confuses the issue for me. If we're going to be parents slash roomies, then hot make-out sessions probably aren't the wisest idea. Right?"

She felt almost panicked at how much she needed him to agree right now. There was no way that they could keep doing this. She'd go ass-over-elbows nuts in no time flat if they stayed in this weird limbo.

The silence through the house felt weighted, significant, while she waited for him to answer. Currently, he was staring at his black leather shoes like they held the secrets of the universe. And as much as she didn't want to, she couldn't stop staring at how his hair was standing up at all sorts of crazy angles as a result of his hands. Rumpled Tate was almost hotter than Angry Tate. Shit. No. No, no, no. No versions of Tate should be hot right now.

"Right."

Her head snapped up, having almost forgotten that she'd asked him a question. Right. He'd agreed with her. And there was no way she could think too deeply on why she suddenly felt like something shriveled up and died inside of her.

No. Freaking. Way.

After picking up her sweatshirt, she quickly slipped it back over her head. Apparently the power of her pregnancy cleavage was not something to take lightly. Best keep those puppies covered up. Which was for the best anyway, since she kinda felt like she'd slit someone's throat if they breathed on them in the wrong way-they were so overly sensitive.

Tate walked with her to the front door, and she couldn't help one look back at the family room and kitchen. It could be hers. At least for a while, if she wanted it. The biting cold air pushing through the open door was a stark contrast to the heat they'd generated just a few minutes earlier. She pulled her eyes back up to Tate's face, willing herself not to pull back at their close proximity. He'd tasted like cinnamon, and it was hard to forget that when she could smell it on his breath.

"Just give me a few days to think about it, okay?"

"Of course. I appreciate you actually taking the time to think it over."

She raised an eyebrow. "Are you insinuating I'm a hothead who can't be rational about making a decision?"

"I would never dream of it," he said, full of mock seriousness. "Be careful on your drive home, you've got some precious cargo."

One hand drifted to her barely-rounded stomach, and she smiled. One of his fingers tipped her chin up so that she looked at him.

"Both of you are."

He didn't look anywhere but her eyes when he said it, and somehow, that made it so much sexier. She had to force herself to walk slowly to her car after she descended the stairs, instead of fleeing at a dead run like she kinda wanted to. There was something oddly disconcerting about Tate calling her precious.

Precious. C'mon, who did that? Hot. She'd heard hot. She'd heard sexy. It came with the territory when she'd ended up with the definition of va-va-voom, Jessica Rabbit curves at the age of fourteen. But no one had ever called her precious. It made something slowly blossom inside of her, and she couldn't wipe the stupid ass grin off her face the entire drive back to her parents, even though the darkness that arrived so early in the winter in Michigan was pressing in on her, casting odd shadows on the quiet, wooded streets.

She knew from earlier in the day that her mom would be the only one home tonight; Kate had a night class and her dad had some chamber of commerce meeting. The thought of a quiet house was nice after the roller coaster of an afternoon, but she had a sinking feeling that her mom was waiting to ambush her with all the really big things that Rachel had avoided talking about with her family. Things like where she was going to live and how she was going to support her child. It wasn't that she thought she wouldn't have their help - she knew she would.

Despite all the crazy her parents subjected her and Kate to, they always gave absolute trust and support.

"I'm in the dining room, sweetheart," her mom called out as soon as Rachel walked through the garage door. With a fortifying sigh, she toed off her shoes and hung her purse on a hook in the coat closet. Snagging a banana on her way through the kitchen, she shook her head at the picture her mom made at the dining table.

Rachel prayed she aged like her mother. Madelyn Hennessy was a knockout. Her mom wore her hair longer than Rachel did, only a little bit of gray threading through the red hair that hung well past her shoulders. They shared the same hazel eyes, the same cheekbones and mouth, and though Rachel had always been a bit envious of the more slender frame that her sister and mom shared, one reassurance she had looking at her mom's perfectly unlined sixty-year-old skin, was that Rachel's ivory skin was the exact same.

At the moment though? The knockout effect was in short supply. Her hair was up in a sloppy bun and she wasn't wearing a stitch of makeup, which showed off some fairly impressive dark circles under her mom's eyes. It gave Rachel a little pang to think that she might be the reason her mom wasn't sleeping. But, considering the spread of pregnancy books and magazines in front of her mom, chances were good that it wasn't caused by anything else.

"What's all this for?" Rachel said, flicking a finger along the edge of a stack of books at the edge of the mahogany dining room table.

"Just pulled out all the pregnancy books people gave me when I was pregnant with your sister, brushing up on all the stuff I should know to help you." She flopped her head down on folded arms and let out a gusty sigh. "But, damn it, all of this is outdated; how the hell am I supposed to know what size fruit the baby is right now? Son of a bitch, I need all new books."

And people wondered why Rachel felt comfortable with all sorts of four letter words at the age of fourteen. She sank into a chair across the table and pulled a large hardcover book in a horrifying shade of purple into her lap, flipping open to a page towards the back. Her jaw dropped when she saw a black and white picture of a gross, goopy head coming right out of some poor woman's hoohah. After slamming the book shut and dropping it on the floor next to her, she watched her mom gnaw on the corner of her thumbnail.

"A peach."

"What?" her mom mumbled, a finger still jammed in between her teeth.

"The baby. It's about the size of a peach."

"See?" She threw her hands up in the air, then slammed them back down on the table, causing a mini-avalanche of magazines. "How the hell am I supposed to know that? These books are useless. *I'm* useless!"

Rachel had two options. She was well aware that they were the *only* two options when one was faced with a meltdown of these proportions. One was to coo and coddle. The other was to use heavy, unconcealed sarcasm. And that? Well, given her current state of affairs, that was a no-brainer.

"You know, it's too bad there's no such thing as some virtual source of information that you could, I don't know, access from your computer and find everything you could need to know about pregnancy with just a few clicks of a mouse. Someone should invent that."

The soft laugh that her mom exhaled made Rachel smile. "I know. I'm just kinda freaking out a bit. A baby? I can barely sleep thinking about it. I go from terrified - at how you'll be able to do all of this - to so damn excited I can hardly breathe. You and your sister are the only other times I felt so much love for someone I'd never met. But this is different, you know? My daughter is having a baby. Oh God, my *baby* is having baby."

It was never-ending roller coaster. Rachel couldn't even be shocked at how many different ways her mom could swing in a few sentences. And it wasn't like she didn't get it, obviously she did. But coming from that house with Tate, and his quiet, rock steady reassurances to *this*? Well, it was like walking from a library straight into a rave.

"So, did you have a meeting with a bride?" her mom asked when Rachel didn't respond to her last statement.

"No, just had an errand to run." Lie. Blatant, bold-faced lie. And Rachel was so incredibly okay with that. Her mom would probably freak if she knew Rachel was actually considering moving in with Tate when they had no romantic relationship. Er. Or kind of didn't have one.

"Are you all ready for your style shoot tomorrow? I saw those centerpieces you put together. The next time your dad and I renew our vows, I'll have to use those. The lemons and limes in the vase were so pretty."

"Thanks. I'm excited to have it done. The photographer owes me a favor from the last referral I gave her."

"Oh!" her mom exclaimed before the sentence was barely out of Rachel's mouth. "Do you want to come see what I figured out? I can move my desk and bookshelf from that upstairs nook into the living room, and we can fit a crib and changing table in there. It'll be tight, but babies don't need a ton of space, right? Your dad, pfft, well he says we should just add an extra room off the back of the house, make a little baby suite, kinda like Steve Martin did in *Father of the Bride Part Two*, but then I said he was just trying to one up me and be the favorite grandparent. Ha. He doesn't understand that you'll need that precious little bundle right by you for those first few months when they're getting up at all hours."

"Mom," Rachel interrupted, pressing two fingers up against her suddenly throbbing temples. "Please don't argue with dad about something like that. And he's insane if he thinks I'm going to let him put a big ass addition onto your house."

"Thank you. I knew you'd see sense."

"Let's just ... not worry about stuff like that yet. We've got plenty of time, okay?"

And the more you ramble, the more Tate racks up points in the 'living with him is the best idea ever' column.

"Okay, sweetheart. Hey, did I tell you that I watched some of your *Sex and The City* DVDs? Miranda got in this same position, you know. It worked out fine for her."

Sinking her face into her hands to muffle the outburst of laughter was instantaneous. While Rachel generally felt that *Sex and the City* was the greatest thing to ever hit television, thinking of her mom watching any of them was more than mortifying.

She pushed some air through pursed lips after her laughter had faded, the events of the whole day piling onto her until she practically felt her shoulders sag with the weight of it all. "Yeah, I suppose it did. But, I was always Team Steve."

"I don't know why you've never made me watch those before. Samantha played some games with Smith that were *pretty* interesting. I might need to remember some of those."

The sound of Rachel's forehead thunking against the dining room table couldn't hide the laughter from her mom.

"Seriously, Mom? I just, I don't want to hear that."

Her mom stood from her chair, still smiling, and came around to Rachel, smoothing a hand over her hair, probably still a bit wild from Tate's hands digging in like he owned every strand. "Why don't you go get in bed, sweetheart. I'll bring you some of those lemon cookies that you said helped settle your stomach. I baked two dozen more."

Fresh, homemade baked goods. Delivered to her in bed. Two points in the Mom column.

"Besides, I need to tell you all about how I want to get your father's name tattooed over my heart. I've got the font all picked out, but I'm not sure if that's trampy at my age, to get one there."

And over the next three days, with that horrifying visual in her head, she kept a running tally, texting Tate when she had questions.

Rachel: So, would I pay you rent? And don't tell me I'll earn my keep by cooking and cleaning up after you, because that shit won't fly with me.

Tate: If you'd feel more comfortable paying me, I'll put it in an account for future college money, but I certainly don't expect you to.

Two points for Tate. One for letting her make the decision. Two for thinking about college money already.

One point for her mom because she insisted on doing Rachel's laundry. And actually ironing stuff.

Rachel: I don't really have much furniture to contribute to that monstrosity. Is that a problem for you?

Tate: I have furniture in storage that I could use downstairs, but I would be buying stuff for the upstairs anyway. Casey was going to help me pick stuff out if that makes you feel better.

Rachel: Well, I assumed there wouldn't be posters of naked women on cars all over the walls, but thanks.

Tate: That you know of. You think you'll be allowed in my bedroom?

The man was funny. It was still a bit surprising to her, after so many years of teasing him about being boring. It was definitely a two-pointer in his column. The beautiful house that she probably would have only admired on Pinterest was another two points. After hearing her mom weep for two hours after watching the home video of her sister being born, her way of preparing for the impending birth, yet another two points for Tate. But, her mom had done things like swaddle babies, change dirty diapers and give baths to those slippery little suckers. Having her around probably wouldn't be so terrible.

Rachel: What if I want my mom to come stay over for a few days to help me after the baby is born?

Tate: Two Hennessy women under my roof? I can't think of anything better.

Rachel: Kiss-ass

It was highly unlikely she'd want that anyway, but geez, couldn't he at least pretend to give a wrong answer?

The light purple paint of her childhood bedroom made her feel sixteen again, wishing that Jason Michaelson would pass her a note in English. Like she'd stopped aging after she'd decorated the room that way. The grime of the glow-in-the-dark stars still clung to the ceiling, where she'd placed them in random patterns. A fresh palette, more points for Tate.

Rachel: What if I want to paint my bedroom? Can I do that?

Tate: In your delicate condition, no, you cannot paint your room. But, I have a sister who works at a home improvement store and can outfit me with everything I might need in order to paint it for you.

Rachel: What if I want to paint it hot pink?

Tate: Then I would kindly ask you to keep the door closed at all times.

"Damn it," she muttered and chucked her phone onto the bed, where it bounced harmlessly. Across the room, sitting on her dresser, sat the eight ball that she'd bought with babysitting money during seventh grade. While she crossed the room, she absently rubbed her belly, which now required a rubber band to keep her jeans closed. Palming the black plastic, Rachel gave it a small shake.

"Should I move in with Tate?"

Concentrate and ask again.

"Yeah? Screw you, eight ball."

13

"HEY PREGGO, what are you doing here?" Casey beamed from where she held open her door to let Rachel in out of the cold. Jake's German Shepherd Remy pushed past Casey's leg to shove his nose against Rachel's stomach, sniffing furiously. She scratched behind his ear as she walked in.

"Oh you know, just felt like driving in this beautiful weather. It was the freezing rain that really cemented my decision."

Casey snorted and motioned to a pan of something she had boiling on her stove. "Want me to make you a cup of hot chocolate? This milk is almost ready."

Peering into the stainless steel pot, and then back up to Casey, Rachel kicked one eyebrow up. "You do know you can just microwave water and dump one of those little pouches into it, right?"

"Blasphemy. Sit on the couch and I'll bring it to you, then I'll sit and listen while you rave about how freaking awesome my hot chocolate is."

She let out a short laugh and did as Casey said, dumping her coat onto a dining room chair on her way to the couch.

"Not that I'm complaining at the surprise visit, but seriously, why are you here?" Casey said from around the corner in the kitchen, where Rachel could hear her the clink of a spoon against the side of a ceramic mug. Arching her back to try and alleviate a dull ache that was just slowly taking up residence there, Rachel groaned before she answered. Remy plopped down on the floor next to her and let out a short snuff of air.

"Well, I wanted your advice on something, and I thought face to face might be better."

Casey poked her head around the corner. "What, you're having triplets and Tate isn't the father - Dylan is?"

Rachel scoffed. "Bitch. No."

"Sorry, I couldn't resist," Casey giggled. "I should have at least six more months of giving you crap about this." She had two large rust colored mugs in her hands, and she carefully handed Rachel one of them before she took a seat on the opposite side of the couch from Rachel. Casey blew into her mug before taking a small, noisy sip. "Ohhhh yeah. That's the bomb. You just wait."

"The bomb? What, are we back in 2002?" But Rachel leaned to take a sip as well, and couldn't help the tiny moan that escaped when she got the rich, creamy, chocolaty, minty amazingness flooding her mouth. "Holy shit, Casey ... what did you put in this? Hot chocolate crack?"

But her friend just gave a tiny smile and took another drink. "My little secret. I can send some of the mix home with you if you want."

"Um, yes. I want. And I'm pregnant, so you have to do what I say."

After she'd swallowed, Casey watched her for a second. "So, let's drop the cryptic. What's up?"

Wrapping her hands tightly around the hot mug, Rachel soaked in the warmth for a moment before answering. "Well, Tate bought that house, right?"

"Right. Asshole pretty much bought my dream house."

Yeah. Get in line. "You've seen it?"

"No," she said, sounding bummed. "He sent me the link to the listing. Man, the things I could do with wallpaper in that house. That master bedroom? It is *screaming* for this new handcrafted paper from York that just came in. I about orgasmed when I saw it. Seriously, it's this silver paper with a really thick, textured cream pattern." And she shivered. Actually shivered.

"It is mind boggling. You look normal, but really? Just. Not at all," Rachel said, shaking her head.

"Say what you want. You'd love it."

And, oh man, she had to work to swallow, because it actually sounded kind of amazing. And she could do it. She could put that orgasm-inducing wallpaper in her room. If she had the lady balls to say yes to him. And maybe that's why she was here, why she'd driven out in absolutely craptastic weather. For Casey to tell her she wasn't insane for doing it.

"So," Casey dragged out the word so that it sounded like it had four syllables. "Why do you want to know about Tate's house? Does it make you feel weird?"

Rachel snapped her eyes up to Casey's. "Weird? Why?"

Casey shifted her shoulders, almost looking uncomfortable. "Well, he's moving into this amazing house, by himself, and you'll be staying at your parents after that baby is born, right?"

"Right," Rachel said quietly. "Well, no. That's kind of why I'm here. I ... umm ... I don't know that I want to stay at my parents."

"Really?" Casey perked up, a broad smile covering her face. "Do you know where you'd live?"

"Well ... that's kind of why I'm here-"

"Because I have a great idea," Casey finished on a rush.

Rachel almost tipped over her mug when Casey shifted forward on the couch in her excitement. She sucked the few drops of hot chocolate that had spilled over the edge onto her fingers. "You do?"

Casey nodded, practically vibrating. "Move into Jake's. We

decided not to rent it out while he's deployed, so it's just sitting empty. And you'd be right next door to me. I could help you! And even though Tate will be moving soon, he'll be only like fifteen minutes away. What do you think?"

What did she think? She was thinking that this came way the hell out of left field. Option C, rolled out right in front of her. Carefully she leaned forward and set her mug on the coffee table so as not to spill anything on the ivory couch underneath her. "Wow. I wasn't expecting you to say that. Wait, what about when Jake gets home?"

Casey waved a hand. "Eh. He can move in with me. C'mon, we were practically living together for two months before he left anyway." She reached a hand out to where Remy had sat up when Casey had started doing her little excited dance and scratched underneath his jaw. She smiled when the dog let out a contented groan. "And this beast doesn't care either way where he lives."

And all of a sudden, all the points she'd been mentally tabulating for the past few days wavered just a bit, like a Jenga tower that wasn't quite ready to fall. It was a viable option. A support system close by, she knew that Casey would never offer something that she wouldn't follow through with. She'd be over wiping dirty butts in a heartbeat if Rachel needed her. Hell, Casey had five nephews already, she was a baby pro.

Best friend next door. Two points.

Rent. Ugh. Actual rent that wouldn't be going into some cushy little college fund. Negative two points.

And that? That was a really, really big negative two points. While Rachel had been happy to sign all her brides quickly, and even better, all but two of them had wanted the biggest (and most expensive) of her three wedding planning packages, she'd feel a lot more comfortable taking on a large monthly cost of rent and utilities if she had a few more signed up.

"Well, before you keep telling me what an amazing idea this

is, and it's really incredible for you to offer, I should probably finish telling you why I came to talk to you."

"Oh! Crapola, sorry. Bad friend, right here," Casey said, pointing a finger back at herself.

Rachel shifted again, yanking the rubber band from around the button of her jeans, then took a deep breath at how much fricken better that felt.

"Give it up, Rach," Casey said, with an unrepentant grin. "You need maternity jeans."

"Blah, blah, blah. I was hoping I'd be one of those women who'd get hateful stares because they just have this tiny basketball stuck under their shirt and can still wear their normal pants." Once she could actually breathe comfortably again, she took another sip of the crack hot chocolate. Oh yeah, baby liked that. She set the mug down again and turned towards Casey, putting on her shit's-about-to-get-serious face. "So, I did see Tate's house, a few days ago."

"You. Bitch. I'm so jealous. How big is that master closet? Wait, why did he show it to you? I mean, I get it, baby momma and all, but yeah, never mind, I don't really get it."

"He sent me a text asking me to meet him there, I didn't even know where I was going." Rachel paused when Remy leaned back against her legs and plopped his head down in her lap. "Why is your dog looking at my stomach? That's weird."

"Apparently he's weirdly intuitive when women are knocked up, Jake told me that," Casey said impatiently, then gave Rachel a hard look. "Now, keep talkin'."

She heaved a sigh. "Your brother asked me to move in with him there."

"What?" Casey shrieked, and Remy's ears twitched comically. "Wait, like living in sin move in with him, or co-parent roommate living with him?"

Rachel burst out laughing. "Living in sin? Good grief, Casey. I don't care how weird you are about wallpaper, I'm gonna keep you around for sheer comedic value. But, the second one, co-parent roommates. He's pretty much offering me the upstairs and he'll be in one of the lower level bedrooms."

Casey's aqua eyes took up half of her face, they were opened so wide, like freaky wide. "Holy crap balls, that's quite an offer."

"Ya think?" Rachel scoffed. "Why do you think I wanted to come and talk to you?"

Rising from her seat on the couch, Casey paced the length of her living room a few times, biting down on her bottom lip like it was made from Dove chocolate or something.

"Comments? Questions? General feedback? C'mon Case, gimme something. Anything."

She stopped her pacing and fisted her hands on her hips. "What about rent?"

"He said if I really feel like paying it, that he would just put it into a future college fund for little nugget."

Casey's jaw dropped. "Seriously?"

Rachel nodded.

"And you didn't say yes on the spot? Have you lost your mind?"

Wait, what? Rachel blinked a few times, making sure this Casey wasn't a subconsciously fueled mirage. "Soooooo, you really think it's a good idea?"

Holding her hands out and raising her eyebrows up in a very clear *duh* gesture, Casey shook her head and then sat back onto the couch. "Look, I'll be the first to admit that his marriage proposal was lacking-"

"Statement," Rachel clarified with a raised finger. "It was a marriage statement, not a proposal."

"Right. Whatever. But, my point is this, he didn't really think that through, he didn't have the time to. Rachel, this is big. He would not offer to do this unless he really, truly thought it was the best possible idea for all of you. Rent-free, in an amazing house, with the father of your child, who is willing to help you whenever you need him to? I mean, c'mon, as much as I'd love to have you and my newest little nephew to live next door to me, that's kind of a no-brainer."

"We don't know it's a boy yet, Case, I could be carrying your niece."

"Pfft, please. This isn't my first rodeo. And I have four brothers and five nephews to prove it. Let's just say I'd bet my entire wardrobe that you're carrying another Steadman male in that cute little belly of yours."

Rachel smiled and looked down at where Remy still had his nose pointed straight at the belly in question. "So, you think I should do it? That wouldn't be weird for you?"

Casey shrugged. "Weirder than you being pregnant with my brother's child? No. I think I hit my weird quota already this year. And trust me, I wouldn't tell just anyone to take up this kind of offer, but because it's you and Tate, I actually think it would work. You're both strong personalities, but in totally different ways. You'd be good about setting boundaries with each other, and not taking advantage of the other person."

Having a smart friend was the shit. It was an angle of this situation that Rachel hadn't really thought about before. Could everyone do what Tate was offering? Probably not. But there was no way Rachel would walk all over him, and she knew that Tate wouldn't push her beyond her comfort zone either. Good Lord in heaven. This meant she was doing it, didn't it? From a money standpoint, it made as much sense as living with her parents. But from an emotional standpoint? Tate won by a landslide. And it felt good. Really, really good. And really, really terrifying.

"And judging by the look on your face, you've obviously decided to take him up on it?"

"But," Rachel said, feeling a twinge of nerves. "What if I want to kill him?"

"Well, if you didn't, then he'd be the perfect man. And honey, we both know there's no such animal. I love Jake with all my heart, but when he makes fun of my shoes, I want to smother him in his sleep." They laughed, but Casey laid a hand over Rachel's knee. "As long as I don't have to play referee between you two, you know I'll support any decision you make."

Watching her friend, Rachel felt a smile tug her lips. "You're kinda awesome, you know that, right?"

"Obviously. How could I not?"

"And so humble too."

Casey slapped her hands down on either side of her. "Hang on. So, you're really doing it, right? You're not going to change your mind?"

"No, I'm not going to change my mind," Rachel said suspiciously. "Why?"

A smug smile lifted Casey's mouth, and she leaned back against the couch cushions. "You love me, right Rachel?"

"Why do I feel like this is a trick question?"

The grin spread on Casey's face, and she wiggled her eyebrows.

"Oh shit. The wallpaper. That's what this is about, isn't it?"

"If you give me free reign to surprise you with the master bedroom, I'll make you meals to have ready in your freezer for the first month you live there."

"So, let me get this straight, you're going to decorate my room and make me food?"

"If you're giving me free reign, then yes." Casey said, and the calculated gleam in her eye made Rachel start rethinking.

She pointed a finger. "No purple."

"Deal," Casey said, and held out a hand for Rachel to shake. Then she started laughing.

Rachel eyed her. "What's so funny?"

Wiping a finger under one eye when she finally calmed down, Casey smiled. "Oh nothing, I just wish I could be there when you tell your mom you're leaving the baby central she's created in their house to go live with Tate. Bring some tissues, that's all I'm sayin'."

"Oh zip it and go get me some more hot chocolate."

14

"So, you don't completely hate it?"

Casey walked around her dining room table to get a good view of the centerpiece Rachel had put together that morning, so Rachel stood back to let her make a complete circle, pressing a balled up fist into the small of her back to try and alleviate the non-stop ache that seemed to live there.

"No, Rach, I really like it. Since you're not a florist, you don't want the centerpiece to be too much of a show stealer, the short vases across the whole length of the table like that is perfect. It looks classy, elegant. I mean, I wouldn't say no to this as the reception decor at my wedding."

Rachel lifted an eyebrow. "You trying to tell me something?"

Casey laughed and straightened one of the white napkins laying against a silver charger plate. "Nope. Besides, if Jake proposed to me via Skype, I'd fly to Afghanistan myself to kick his ass. You know, the only thing I would add is maybe some crystal pieces in the flowers. Against the white roses, it would look nice. Let me go look if I have something that would work."

Rachel nodded, loving the idea and tipped backwards into the couch behind her, immediately propping up her feet. "See, this is why I have you around. You actually keep stuff like that in your spare room."

The sound of Casey's laughter came down the hallway. Rachel smiled, glad she'd decided to get a second opinion. She'd decided to have booth space at the West Michigan Bridal Expo, and while she knew it probably wouldn't garner her a lot of actual brides, the networking would be good, and give her an opportunity to put her face in front of some of the vendors that she'd worked with at Platinum, but hadn't seen since she went out on her own. But when she'd paid for the space, she hadn't been pregnant. And last month, when she'd started thinking about what she was going to do to fill her eight-by-eight space, she was more than dreading two solid days on her feet. But, oh, that had been before she'd connected with one of her profs from college.

And now, thanks to dear Professor Elizabeth Marin, she had two brand spankin' new senior interns from the Hospitality and Tourism Management program at GVSU. They had a certain number of hours in unpaid internship hours that were required in order to graduate. Unpaid. Shittier than shitty when she'd been a college student putting in hours every week, but as a brand new business owner? Halle-freaking-lujah.

Now she had a Peyton and a MacKenzie that were the most eager little sorority sisters she'd ever encountered. It was amaze-balls. They'd gladly accepted some of the hours at the bridal expo, leaving Rachel free to do the setup and work the first shift on her own. Get a feel for what they'd need to do the second day.

But she'd been unsure of how to set up her space. Enter Casey Marie Steadman to the rescue. She was an interior designer without the degree to make it official - not that any of her customers gave a shit - and had flawless taste that Rachel had sought out more than once. Casey came down the hallway, her quick steps preceding the triumphant grin across her face.

"Ha! I knew I would need this someday." She handed a small

box over to Rachel, and she was right, they were perfect. A single crystal perched on the end of a bendable sturdy wire, the crystal no larger than one inch in diameter. Enough to add some sparkle, but not look cheesy.

"You're handy, Steadman, I'll give you that. Now, stick a few in there; I'm too lazy to move."

Casey smirked and took the box back, carefully placing a few crystals in each bouquet. She clapped her hands at the finished effect, and Rachel shook her head at the little dance Casey did. There was a knock at the door at the same time that someone opened it.

"Is it safe for me to come in?" Tate's voice called out, and it made Rachel pull in a deep breath. She hadn't seen him yet since she'd sent him a text telling him she was going to take him up on his offer for her to move in. She'd sent it as soon as she left Casey's that night.

Rachel: Well, since you said yes to me painting my room whatever color I want, I'm in, if the offer is still on the table.

Tate: Changed my mind about the hot pink. That's banned. You, on the other hand, will always be welcome.

Rachel: I've given your sister free reign to decorate my bedroom. I'm guessing hot pink is *not* one of the options.

Tate: I've thought of it as your bedroom from the first day, it suits you. So, when do you think you'll move in?

Rachel: Considering I'm not due for five more months, not for a while.

HER PHONE HAD REMAINED CONSPICUOUSLY silent after that, like, *screaming at her* silent. Only Tate could manage to communicate complete disappointment and disapproval through an unsent text message. It had made her twitchy. She'd paced her room. Stared at her phone, before she set it down. Then, picking it up and making sure she hadn't lost a signal and his response wasn't coming in due to that. She'd been damn near ready to crack and send a shouty caps text saying "FINE! I'LL MOVE IN NOW!" but she'd been saved by the chime.

Tate: Obviously you can move in whenever you feel is best, but I meant it. You are always welcome. You could move in tomorrow and it would be fine with me.

Oh, *screw him*. She didn't mean it, of course. But, screw him because she'd actually thought about it. Because c'mon, she'd told her parents that morning of her decision, and the odd silence from her mom had made her feel like she'd been shoved into someone else's skin. Uncomfortable. Didn't fit. Like she wanted to stretch out her arms to make it snap into the right places.

She'd expected tears. Wailing and gnashing of teeth. Instead, she got silence.

But really, Rachel knew why. Her mom, believer in soul mates and one true loves, was probably wary of this type of arrangement. Separate bedrooms, but under the same roof, parenting together. Rachel didn't need to hear the explanation. She'd seen it in the way that her mom's slightly over-plucked brows had drawn together, in the way that her eyes had looked a little sad. Not sad because Rachel would be moving out. It was a worried sad.

And for whatever reason, the worry from her mom freaked her out even more than any emotional fireworks would have.

She'd pushed that aside though, focusing on work, which was a pleasant, albeit busy, distraction, full of centerpieces and place settings and rehearsal dinner themes and brides who had questions about everything under the sun. And by doing that, she'd been able to sort of, kind of, not really push aside thoughts of Tate too. Until hearing his stupid deep voice coming from Casey's kitchen. She snapped up from where she laid on the couch, and felt a sharp, burning tug on the lower part of her belly.

"Owwwwwww," she groaned, pushing down on the area. Oh Lord, she really hoped this wasn't what a contraction felt like. What with being only in her fourth month. Tate was suddenly crouched in front of her on the floor, one hand gripping her knee, the other pushing her hair out of her face. His eyes were dark, his face pinched with concerned lines.

"What's wrong? Are you okay?"

"I don't know," she answered honestly, looking between him and Casey, who was hovering by Rachel's side. "I tried to sit up too quickly, and I felt this sharp jerk of pain underneath my belly."

"Does it still hurt?" Tate asked, pulling his phone out from the back pocket of his dark pants.

Rachel shook her head. "Maybe I should try to stand?"

"No," Casey and Tate said at the same time.

"I'm going to call your doctor," Tate continued, "see if I can bring you in. I'd rather not take a chance, okay?"

Rachel swallowed against the rising panic. Even though there was no pain, the way he was staring at her, like he could fix whatever was going on just by looking at her, it made her feel an equal amount of relief and apprehension. Because that was a feeling she could get used to, Tate being around to take care of her. She looked up in surprise when Tate rattled off her birthday to the person on the phone, even Casey's eyes widened. Okay, apparently he was paying attention.

Tate pulled the phone away from his ear. "Do you feel it on your belly anywhere? Like a tightening feeling?"

She shook her head. "It was just that sharp tug, down below."

He relayed that to whoever he was talking to, and then he asked her to try and stand, the apprehension clear in his voice. She gripped one of Tate's outstretched hands, using her other to push up from the couch, and as soon as she put weight onto her right leg, the pain flashed through again, in the exact same spot. She groaned without opening her mouth, trying not to alarm them, but really wanting to curse like a freaking sailor. Tate moved beside her and wrapped an arm around her, practically lifting her off the floor - he was taking so much of her weight. He agreed with the person he was talking to and slipped the phone into his pocket after he'd finished the call.

"That was May, Dr. Madison's nurse. She's pretty sure you just pulled a muscle, but she wants you to come in to make sure. Casey, if you could help her into her coat, I'll go warm up my car and move it closer to your door."

Rachel tried to pull away from where his hand was tucked into the curve of her waist, pushing against his chest. "If it's a pulled muscle, I'll just go get checked, and then I'll be fine. There's no need for you to freak out."

She could practically hear the crackle of the thunderclouds gathering above Tate's head, practically see the steam begin to pour from his ears. It made her try to shove down a nervous gulp that inched up her throat.

"No need to freak out? No need to *freak out*?" he said slowly, like he didn't understand the words as they came out of his mouth.

"Aaaaaand this is part where I go hide in my room. Rach, I'll pack up all this stuff for you. Text me when you're done at the doctor." And with that, Casey pretty much sprinted down the hallway to her room and, geez Louise, Rachel wanted to follow. She stared at the white buttons on Tate's charcoal gray dress shirt, not daring to meet his eyes.

"If you could just help me to my car, I'm perfectly capable of getting myself there." She said it quietly, but kept her voice firm. And it was met with a stony silence that practically lifted goose bumps on her neck it was so charged. He finally took a step back, but then dipped his head so that she had no choice but to meet his eyes. They were full of so much fire and heat that she almost lost her breath. It shouldn't have been so hot at that moment, but yeah, it totally was.

"Get your coat on, I'm going to go bring my car closer. If you're not at the door in thirty seconds for me to help you out to the car, I *will* carry you, do you understand me?"

"Wow, Tate," she snapped, the heat he had in his face building up her spine until it spewed out of her mouth. "You're actually going to trust me to put my own coat on? Thanks for being so generous."

It was obvious that he slicked his tongue over his teeth to keep from responding the way he wanted to. Rolling his lips inward, he pulled in a deep breath through his nose.

"Now you have twenty seconds," he said before he spun and walked to Casey's door. About one second after the door shut behind him, she heard him yell, "Damn it!" clearly not realizing that she could hear him. Not willing to risk actually having to be carried by him, she grabbed her coat, only putting a tiny amount of weight on her right leg. The pain was still there, but not as sharp as before. She yelled a goodbye to Casey when Tate whipped open the door, a look of chagrin over his face when he took her in waiting for him. Rachel held up a hand, wanting to stem the inevitable *I'm so sorry, Rachel* that was probably choking him.

"Apparently I become a raging bitch in those situations. Let's just call that exchange even, okay?"

One of his hands gripped hers, and he gave her a small smile, his other hand clasping her elbow while he helped her across the snow covered driveway to where his car sat idling. After he closed the door behind her, she breathed out in relief. That so wasn't his fault, and she hoped he knew it. Truth was, she was just as freaked as he probably still was, despite what the nurse had said to him. Lashing out at Tate's understandable *you woman me man* display couldn't even really be blamed on the little nugget. Nope, that was all her.

They were quiet on the drive to her doctor's office; not even any music filled the car. The way that white snow covered everything was still beautiful, still welcome at this point of winter. No blackish-gray slush weighed down the curbs yet, and the way that the fluffy snowfall from that morning clung to the branches of trees made their leafless state a little bit more bearable. Tate swung the car into an expectant mother spot, and looked over at her once he'd pulled the key from the ignition.

"I know that inside that exam room, it seems to be acceptable that I hold your hand while she listens for the heartbeat." He smiled when he said it, but his eyes still held a worried tinge from earlier. "Even though I know May is probably right, could you please humor me for the next thirty minutes? I don't particularly like how it made me feel when I didn't know what was wrong or if you were okay. I'm probably going to need to touch you a bit more than normal, just to put myself at ease, okay? Please?"

It made her nose burn and her eyes dry out in a very unwelcome way. But she nodded, not looking away. He lifted a hand up and brushed a thumb across her cheek, just for a second, before tucking her hair behind her ear.

"Thank you," he said simply, before leaving the car. While he was walking around to her side, she gasped in and out a few times, feeling like she'd just accepted a damn marriage proposal or something, the way her heart was stuttering. He opened her door and held out a hand. She stared at it for a second and then looked up at him waiting for her.

Rachel placed her hand in his, and didn't even try to pull away when he wove his fingers through hers, keeping them firmly together the entire way into the office. He didn't let go while she checked in, or while they sat on the chairs, picking ones that didn't have an armrest in between them. They briefly separated when she stepped on the scale for May, not missing the way the nurse's eyes met hers knowingly when Tate smoothed a hand up and down her back as they walked through the door into the empty exam room. She felt so warm, so soothed, that she had almost forgotten to be worried. Though, by the way that the pain only came when she moved her leg, she was fairly sure everything was fine.

Her doctor came in, giving a small, easily missed look of surprise at the way Tate had dragged a chair over so that it was against the exam table where Rachel sat. One of his hands covered hers, his thumb rubbing back and forth against her knuckles, and it made her breasts feel heavy and tingly with each swipe of his finger. Doctor Madison asked her a few questions, pressing against Rachel's belly in a few different places and nodding at her answers. And when she gave an easy smile, Rachel felt tension flow quickly from both her and Tate.

"I'm pretty sure you pulled your groin muscle when you tried to sit up too quickly. Not really a good story for an injury, I know. Just try to take it easy for a few days, sit as much as possible, and I'll give you a muscle relaxant that's safe for baby in case the pain gets to be too much."

She looked over and smiled at Tate, who gave her a small wink and squeezed her hand. "Well, I have to work at a bridal expo this weekend, it might be hard for me to sit."

"I'll help you," Tate said decisively.

Doctor Madison grinned and nodded at Rachel. "Don't turn

down an extra set of hands. But, even if you have a chair or a stool in your booth, sit as often as you can and you'll be fine."

Rachel narrowed her eyes at Tate when he had a very annoying look of triumph on his face.

Pulling the magic little heartbeat finder out of her white lab coat, Doctor Madison looked at Rachel with a question in her eyes. "While you're here?"

Rachel nodded quickly. Since it was the coolest, most awe-inspiring sound she'd ever heard in her fricken life, that was a no-brainer. Laying back on the hard cushion of the table, she pushed her pants down while Tate stood from his seat to move closer to her head. She looked up at him as the doctor squirted the gel onto her stomach, smiling a bit at the way he took in every detail with unconcealed fascination.

When Rachel tightened her grip on his hand, he looked down at her with a contented curve of his lips. When the fast whooshing sound filled the room, they both smiled reflexively. While the doctor cleaned off her belly, Tate leaned down and pressed a kiss to her forehead, lingering a moment longer than Rachel expected him to. He took a breath while his lips stayed against her skin, and she felt that intake of air all the way down into her toes. When he pulled back, he took his hand away as well, and she had to stop herself from following its retreat.

It was the tenderness in every gesture that burrowed its way under her skin. They'd had passion, more than once, but the sweet and gentle touches that he gave her were so foreign between them. And what scared her even more was that it didn't feel even remotely uncomfortable. There was a huge part of her that wanted to arch and purr like a cat under each stroke of his hand. Burrow her head into some warm crook of his body and stay there.

"So," she started, trying her hardest to shake off those feelings when the doctor left the room and there were a few feet of space separating them. "You're staying at the house now, right?"

"Yeah, as of two days ago. Still a lot of empty rooms, but Casey is chomping at the bit to remedy that for me." He watched her while she smiled in response. "You sure you want to wait so long to move in?"

She rubbed her hands against her thighs. "Truthfully?"

"Of course," he answered, furrowing his brows.

"I uhh, I'm not sure ..." she started, faltering at the look on his face. It was the thought of living with him for months without the safety buffer of the baby that scared her shitless. But she couldn't say that right now. They'd had this tiny little pocket of time this afternoon in the car, on the walk inside and in the exam room, that was perfect and uncomplicated. She wasn't ready to burst it yet, it was too fragile and, selfishly, she wanted to let it linger. "I'm not sure I'll be able to hold out at my parents for another four months. My mom kinda drives me up a wall."

He pinched her chin, tapping his thumb there before dropping his hand. "Whenever you're ready, then so am I. Now, let's go set up a bridal expo booth."

She groaned, but followed him out of the room, and back into the quick burst of reality.

15

"RACHEL, if you don't go sit down-"

"You're going to what? Glare me to death? Tate, this is *my* booth for *my* business, you can't seriously expect that I'm going to just sit here like an invalid while you set everything up."

He grinned, and turned his back to where she was sitting, quite unhappily, on her little black stool, that little rounded belly pushing out. Instead of reaching out to run his hand over the small curve like he wanted to, Tate moved chairs around the table, squaring the plates and shining silver utensils to match the picture that Casey had sent him on his phone.

"You heard the doctor," he said, trying to straighten the middle of the short square vases stretched across the table. "Plus, I'll be out of your hair as soon as this is all set up, then you can dictate this little area to your heart's content."

She gave a discontented *hmmph*, and he smiled knowing Rachel couldn't see it. It had been an interesting day with her, thinking he'd just stop over at Casey's to say hello when he saw Rachel's black muscle car in the driveway. And here he was, hours later, seeing her on the angry patient end of the spectrum. He'd seen a few different sides of her today, and once they knew the baby was fine, he'd loved it. He'd loved holding her hand, rubbing her back, touching her face, kissing her forehead. All of it.

It was sort of like someone sheathed a hot dagger through his breastbone, knowing that those types of moments were fleeting, only allowable in a situation like that, but he'd decided to shove that knife in to the hilt, take the opportunity when it was presented to him.

"Hey, when you're done with that, could you grab me that blue bag? I want to have the folders with all my package information in close reach, so I don't have to go digging for it in case I actually need it."

Instead of waiting to finish the table, he handed her the bag right away.

"You sure you don't want me to stay? Or at least call one of your interns to come and help you?"

She shook her head, not meeting his gaze. "I already sent them a text, and Peyton is coming for a couple hours this evening so I can grab some food and let her know what to do tomorrow."

"Okay," he said, still feeling hesitant to leave her. "Does everything look the way you wanted it to?"

After pushing cautiously off the stool, Rachel walked around the table, and smiled at another vendor who was across the aisle from her, making similar last minute touches. She'd finally caved, even though he could tell she didn't want to be wearing maternity clothes. But she'd popped last week, and didn't have much of a choice.

And thank the Lord, she'd told him that pregnancy muumuus were strictly forbidden, so everything she wore lately hugged her like a second skin. Every inch of her curved now, more than just the flare of hips to a small waist and back up to her pretty damn near perfect cleavage. And the gentle rounding of her stomach was currently covered in a yellow lace top with a white shirt underneath it, and a gray pencil skirt that he had to actively keep his eyes off the way it curved around her backside.

Maybe most men wouldn't pay attention to what a woman wore, but having Casey as a sister, and then being with Natalie - who was as clothing-conscious as Casey - he couldn't really help it. When she dragged a finger over the back of one of the black chairs and bit her lip while looking over the table, he set his hands on his hips and looked away, blowing out the air in his lungs very, very slowly.

It would be a special kind of torture, the best kind probably, to see her every day once she moved in. As much as he'd wanted her to, truly believing it was the most logical situation for all three of them, he didn't think she'd actually say yes to his idea. Especially after his monumentally dumb-ass move to kiss her. Well, he'd only felt like a dumb-ass for the first two seconds until he realized she was more than kissing him back. It had felt like she wanted to devour him whole, then lick her lips and come back for seconds.

But, despite the wanting of her - which he was beginning to think would never go away - he wouldn't push her. It was a precarious balance they'd have to reach, to embark on this new journey together, and even if he had to take five cold showers a day while she lived with him, he'd do as she asked and keep the line firmly between them. Firmly platonic. Platonic. Yeah. That sounded ... horrifying.

"Hellooooo, where'd you go?"

It was on the tip of his tongue to say hell, he was going to hell for the way he was thinking of her. Instead he just shook his head and ran a hand down his face. "Sorry, zoned out for a second. So, it looks okay?"

She nodded, her eyebrows scrunched like she knew he was a complete liar. "Yeah, you definitely have a fallback career if this lawyer thing doesn't work out."

He pulled his keys from his coat after slipping it on, then fixed

Rachel with a serious look. "Call me if you need anything. I mean it."

Snapping one hand up to her forehead, she saluted him. "Sir, yes sir."

Tate snorted. "I'll take that, sarcasm and all. What time do you need me back here to pick you up?"

"Eight thirty should be good. Peyton will be here with me from six to eight, and then I'll just have to tidy up a bit so it's ready for them tomorrow."

"You got it."

"How come I don't get a salute?" she muttered.

"Keep dreaming, Hennessy. I'll be here at eight fifteen to help clean up," he said over his shoulder as he left her space. When he saw her smile, he walked out of the bustling convention area with a bounce in his step.

RACHEL LET out a heavy sigh as she sank back down onto her beloved stool. The first couple hours, she'd hated it. But after six hours at the damned expo, she never wanted to go anywhere without the four legged piece of heaven. Reaching down to find her water bottle, she groaned when she felt the empty cylinder. Everything, right down to her fingernails, was throbbing and aching. Apparently a human the size of an orange could completely annihilate any sort of stamina she used to have. She slipped her ballet flats off her feet, and rubbed the heel off one foot against her calf with a groan. And here everyone told her that energy bounced back in the second trimester.

Lying bitches. All of them.

"Are you sure you don't need anything else before I go?" Peyton had already secured the tie on her hot pink wool pea coat, which Rachel eyed with the kind of envy that only a pregnant woman can feel for cute clothes. The bubbly little blond had one foot out the door already, that much was obvious. But it was just heading into prime social hour on a Friday night, so Rachel shook her head, waving a hand in dismissal.

"You can head on out, you've been a great help tonight. I'll come the last couple hours tomorrow so I can pack everything up, but call me if you or MacKenzie need anything before then, okay?"

Peyton nodded so frantically that it looked like her curly blond hair was having a seizure. "We will. Thanks Rachel."

A few people were still milling around the convention hall, some actively seeking information, others just wandering around the see what free stuff they could score. Rachel smiled at one young woman who looked over her display, eyes flicking away quickly when she noticed Rachel looking back at her.

So far she had three potential brides who had taken information while asking her some fairly in-depth questions about what she could help with, which was more than she'd anticipated for the first day. Tilting her wrist so she could see what time it was, she figured that she should start cleaning up a bit before Tate showed up. Arching her other foot, she slipped her shoes back on and sat up a bit straighter, thinking that a slouch on a stool might not make the best impression.

The woman from a few minutes earlier turned the corner she had just came from, her gaze meeting Rachel's directly this time. She turned her head and called to someone out of sight while Rachel rose from her stool.

"I love this table set up," she said, bright blue eyes flicking over the black, cream and white place settings across the sleek black dining room table Rachel had borrowed from her Aunt Maura. "Are you a florist?"

Rachel shook her head with an apologetic smile, considering this was about the eighth time someone had asked her that today. "Wedding Coordinator, but I have some great florist connections. When are you getting married?"

"Oh," she said with a quick flick of her hand. "It's not me, it's my cousin. She thought going to an event like this to plan a wedding was 'horribly gauche'," she used her fingers to make quote marks in the air. "But I told her there can be some really good ideas here, especially since she can't figure out what she wants to do for decor and doesn't use Pinterest. C'mon, who doesn't *Pinterest*?"

Two things snapped through Rachel's head. One, this girl's cousin was probably snooty, erring on the side of bitchy. But, she might very well be a rich one, and her budget would probably have room for a wedding coordinator, so Rachel kept that happy smile pasted right on her tired-ass face.

"You're very right. If she's having some problems coming up with a direction for her wedding, I'd be happy to speak with her, it's one of the things that a coordinator can do." Rachel held out a hand. "I'm Rachel, by the way. I'm the owner."

Never failed. Saying those words zapped her with a boost of energy, grounded in pride in what she was doing.

The girl took Rachel's hand. "Caitlin. Let me grab Natalie a second, I think she'd love this set up. It screams rich, which is kind of her thing."

Rachel tilted her head, noticing that Caitlin had a narrow face with long thin nose and wide eyes that looked vaguely familiar. And just as it snapped into place with the name she said, Caitlin reappeared with her cousin in tow. Definitely rich and definitely a bitch.

She was wearing wide-leg, high-waisted camel color pants with an ivory silk blouse tucked into them. No necklace, no earrings. Just a wide gold cuff on one really tiny wrist, and a camel colored leather clutch in the other hand. Rachel felt the color drain right the hell out of her face as recognition mirrored through Natalie's big brown eyes.

She lifted one perfectly manicured eyebrow while her gaze flicked across Rachel's pregnant stomach.

"Nat, isn't this a gorgeous table setting?" Caitlin asked with a wink at Rachel, completely oblivious to the silent *what the hell are you doing here* stare-down going on next to her. "Rachel's a wedding coordinator, you should totally have her help you out."

Natalie found her voice before Rachel did, clearing her throat delicately. "I'm quite capable of planning my own wedding, Caitlin."

Caitlin rolled her eyes. "Obviously. Everyone is *capable* of it. But if your dad is giving you carte blanch, why wouldn't you have someone help you? Look, I'm gonna go use the restroom. You do what you want." She aimed a small smile at Rachel, crinkling her nose in apology. "Nice to meet you, Rachel."

There was so much, so freaking much running through Rachel's head in those short seconds of silence after Caitlin walked away. First was *holy friggin shit, Tate is going to be here any minute*. Second was *I want to knock her on her tiny ass*. And third, well third was just a repeat of the ass thing. Everything else fled when Natalie gave her a condescending little smile, narrowing her eyes and tilting her head at the same time.

"I see congratulations are in order," she said, her cultured voice holding a perfectly even, quiet tone, the way it always did. Rachel inclined her head, praying every prayer she'd ever said to keep her patience. They were in public. She was representing her business, so she would keep her mouth sewn shut if she had to.

"To you as well," Rachel said, voice practically choking on the words. Not even remotely surprising was the large shining rock she saw perched on Natalie's left ring finger. "When is the big day?"

Lifting her finger to look at the ring, she smiled slightly before answering. "September twelfth of next year. I'm surprised you actually care to ask."

I don't. I hate your bitchy ass and want to wipe that smug smile right off your face for what you said about my friend.

"It's my business to care about when people get married,"

Rachel chose to say instead, shrugging her shoulders. "That was pretty fast, Natalie. Love at first sight?"

"Not that it's any of your business, but Blake was an old family friend I recently reconnected with. We're perfect for each other."

"Well, that's wonderful for you." In an unconscious thought, Rachel rubbed a hand across her belly, the tiny bubbles of movement that she'd started feeling the week before dragging along the inside of her stomach. Maybe little orange baby could feel her stress. Rachel took a few discreetly deep breaths to try and lower her rapidly rising blood pressure.

Natalie watched the movement, eyes narrowing again. "I'm a little surprised to see you expecting, Rachel, you never really struck me as the maternal type. I remember how much you enjoy ... socializing."

Rachel bit down on the inside of her cheek until she tasted the coppery tang of blood. And she probably would have been able to keep the carefully blank look on her face until she saw Tate stride up to them, forehead creased in confusion when he noticed Natalie.

Oh. Shit.

This was a pretty big unknown, how Tate would react to seeing Natalie again. It wasn't like Rachel was worried he'd see his ex in all her ivory-shirted glory and fall prostrate in front of her, but still, unexpected run-ins could wreak havoc. Rachel had been fortunate that she hadn't seen Marc since the day she packed all her shit, but then again, seeing your boyfriend handcuffed to the bed by someone who looked an awful lot like Natalie made a girl pretty reticent to see said boyfriend's face ever again.

This was worse though. To see your ex-fiancé and your, umm, baby mama facing off. Rachel was no slouch, she'd always been happy with her looks, but standing next to the perfectly svelte I-just-walked-off-the-set-of-a-Vogue-shoot Natalie would make just about anybody want to throw on a pair of Spanx.

They were sooooo different, she and Natalie. It made just a little bit of her wonder how Tate could have been attracted to someone like Natalie, *and* someone like Rachel. But, considering the unborn baby rumbling around inside of her was planted there by a seriously determined Steadman sperm who'd found its way around the two measly days she'd forgotten her birth control, Rachel decided to give herself a point in the column of 'Tate wants me more than he wanted you'.

"What are you doing here, Natalie?" Tate said as soon as he was closer. Natalie jerked around, eyes the size of basketballs. Not even the healthiest dose of NARS Orgasm blush could combat the way she lost every speck of color in her face.

"Tate?" Ugh. Her voice even trembled a little on his name. Rachel had to fight the eye roll that was just dying to come out.

Sweeping past a still gaping Natalie, Tate faced Rachel and linked hands with her, looking straight into her eyes. "Are you okay?"

"Settle down, I'm fine," she said, voice hushed so Natalie might not be able to hear. "We're just having a little girl talk about my maternal instincts." Tate grimaced, but still kept his back to Natalie.

"Wait," Natalie said, and Tate turned slightly to look over his shoulder at her. "Are you ...? Tate, you're not *with* her, are you?"

And as bad it was, a teeny tiny little thrill shot right through Rachel. Ohhh, this could be fun. She may not be able to beat Natalie's ass for what she said about Casey, but this? This she could do, without even a shred of remorse. Pulling on Tate's arm, where their hands were still linked together, he didn't have much choice to stand by her side, fully facing Natalie now. The heat of his skin seeped into her, and she couldn't resist dragging her thumb up and down along the side of his hand. His fingers tightened in response, and he dragged her closer, pressing Rachel firmly along his side, so she was touching him from the tops of her shoulders all the way down the length of her arm.

"By *with me*," Rachel started, slowly rubbing her free hand across her belly, not at all missing the way that Natalie's eyes zeroed in on the movement before shifting her gaze back over to Tate, "do you mean that I'm pregnant with his child and am living with him? Well then yes, Natalie, he is *definitely* with me."

And when twin spots of angry color popped into Natalie's cheeks, Rachel lips curled into a satisfied smile.

Ha. Bring it, bitch.

16

"THIS IS A JOKE, RIGHT?" Natalie sputtered. In all the years that he'd been with her, he could safely say that he'd never seen Natalie sputter, and he was thrilled to be able to look at her objectively and know that it wasn't a good look on her.

Nothing. He felt nothing standing only a few feet away from her after all these months. Well, that wasn't entirely true. He felt every inch of himself that was pressed against Rachel, in some little rebellious show of solidarity against the woman that he'd had every intention of marrying at one point.

But, man, the veil was good and off now, because the disdain that coated every word out of Natalie's mouth was so thick and heavy that he wanted to kick his own ass for not hearing it, or not paying attention to it, for so long.

"No joke, Natalie," he said, briefly looking down at Rachel and smiling. "Rachel and I are expecting our first child in July, and I closed on a house in Ada for our family last week."

None of it was a lie. And when he felt a tiny quick inhale from Rachel at the words 'our first child', which heavily implied more to come, he couldn't stop the wide grin spreading across his face. Natalie narrowed her eyes and searched across his face for any sign of deceit. But the truth was, he was damn proud to have Rachel standing next to him just then. She was making something of her life during an incredibly difficult and unexpected situation, something that Natalie wouldn't have the slightest clue how to do.

"I don't believe it," Natalie stated, her pinched features not giving way.

Tate shrugged. "It doesn't matter whether you believe it. It's the truth." And with no agenda behind it, other than just the desire to do it, Tate extracted his hand from Rachel's so that he could smooth it up her back and grip the back of her neck. With his thumb, he drew lazy circles on the smooth skin he found there, knowing that if he went high enough on her neck, he'd be able to feel the silky strands of her hair. Rachel turned her face to look at him, and what shone out of her eyes made his heart thump in a pretty unmanly way.

Lord help them both, she was turned on by what he was doing. What *they* were doing. Natalie cleared her throat, an uncomfortable scrape of sound, obviously not blind to whatever was brewing between Tate and Rachel.

"Well," she said on a sniff, and then lifted up a hand that was decorated with a diamond much bigger than the one-point-seven-five carat rock he'd given her a couple years ago. "Some people are fine with lowering their standards. Personally, I'm not one of them. I wish you both all the best, of course."

She turned to leave, but Rachel called out before she could walk away.

"Natalie?" she called out, eyes hard and mouth flat. Natalie raised an eyebrow in answer. "It's true that I've never particularly liked you, and I'd wager a whole lot that you always felt the same about me. But the second you opened your mouth about Casey, it became personal. So, the next time you see me, I suggest you run your scrawny ass in the opposite direction, okay?"

Not surprisingly, Natalie didn't say a word in response, simply turned and took fast steps away from them. Tate's hand was still on Rachel's neck, even though Natalie was well out of view. And with the words she'd snapped still hanging in the air, he exerted just enough pressure so that she turned to face him, and leaned down so that their foreheads almost touched.

"The only reason I'm not kissing you for that little performance is because you've asked me not to do that anymore." Her eyes flared and he clenched his teeth to keep from closing the distance between his mouth and hers. For just a few long seconds, they shared breath, neither of them moving. She pulled her head back a few inches, so he backed up the same amount, and released her from his hold. They both exhaled at the same time.

"I don't know," she said, shaking her head. "You really thought I was convincing?"

"You mean when you threatened her?" he asked dryly.

"Yeah."

"I think it's safe to say that she'll steer clear of you in the future. Why?"

Rachel shrugged and grabbed her coat from behind her table full of supplies. Tate pulled it from her hands, and held it open. She smiled and then slipped her arms through the sleeves.

"It's just," she hesitated while pulling her hair from the collar of her coat. "The thing I don't like about being pregnant is that I feel it seriously threatens my status as a bad ass. I mean, how can I do a credible job of a verbal bitch slap when I have to turn and waddle away, you know? Sure, I *say* that Natalie better run when she sees me, but let's be honest, I couldn't catch her right now if I wanted to."

Tate laughed, and took the heavy purse from her hands.

Rachel turned and fisted her hands on her hips. "You think I'm joking?"

"Oh no, I know you're completely serious, trust me. I think you'll bounce back pretty soon after labor, don't worry."

"I fricken hope so," she said on a sigh, the weariness that had stayed hidden during their conversation with Natalie starting to show in her body language and across her face. "Let's get out of here, my feet feel like they're going to fall off."

On the walk through the convention center and into the frigid parking garage underneath the building, they were both quiet. Rachel because she was tired, most likely, and Tate because he couldn't quite shake the way she'd looked back up at him. What she kept saying was that the lines needed to stay firm, and obviously he understood why she said it. He really, truly did.

But there was so much in both of them that was bubbling just beneath the surface, and eventually it had to boil over. When he'd agreed to step back, he'd meant it, one hundred percent. And honesty compelled him to admit that if she ever realized how easy it would be for her to move those last couple inches, he'd meet her there with no hesitation.

He let the car warm up for a few minutes and he watched while Rachel settled into the passenger seat that she had reclined back almost as far as it would go.

"Anything else I can get you? Pillow? Blanket?"

"Shut it," she said on a yawn. "It's your child that's doing this to me, the least you could do is cut the sarcasm."

He smiled when she immediately closed her eyes. The air coming out the vents finally turned warm, and when he looked back over at Rachel, her breathing was deep and even. Easing the car out of the parking garage, he laughed under his breath, not wanting to do anything to disturb her.

It wasn't terribly late, but the selfish part of Tate was growling at him to not bring her back to her parents' house. Instead of driving to US-131 heading south, he made a left onto I-96 heading east, towards his house. Let her get pissed at him when she woke, he'd deal with that later. Instead he settled in his seat, soaking in the yellow-orange glow of street lamps as he drove under them, and let that growl turn into a satisfied roar.

RACHEL WAS HAVING a completely kick-ass dream. The smell of Tate was everywhere, crisp and clean and right in front of her nose. She burrowed into the scent and reveled in the way that his arms tightened around where they were banded underneath her knees and behind her back. Almost like he was carrying her. Yup. Best dream ever. Because pregnant Rachel was not a light Rachel.

She let her arms drift up around his neck, the short hairs at the base of his skull soft and prickly underneath her fingers. And then dream Tate cursed, which was odd, because he wasn't a guy who typically said naughty words like that. Which meant dream Tate was possibly hotter than real Tate. So she dug her fingernails into his skull and dragged them lightly through his hair. Then dream Tate groaned out the f word, which was definitely out of character.

She didn't think he'd be able to get any hotter after their little performance in front of Natalie earlier. Sweet mother of all things holy, when he'd grabbed her neck like that, she about stripped him down right there in the middle of the convention hall. And this dream must be her shiny prize for maintaining some sense of public decency.

But what she wanted to know, in this extremely pleasant haze, was when dream Rachel was gonna get laid, because dream Rachel and real Rachel were about ready to come out of their collective skin, they were so horny. Pregnancy hormones? No freaking joke.

And when she felt herself being laid down on a nice firm mattress covered in freshly laundered cotton that, oh hell yeah, smelled like Tate, she could have sworn she heard the hallelujah chorus playing in surround sound. Tate's arms slid out from underneath her, and he smoothed the hair back from her face, which made her smile.

And then ... nothing. Wait. What? Dream Tate was supposed

to rapidly undress her and then spend hours tasting every inch of her with his extremely talented tongue. Something ... hang on ... something wasn't right.

Her eyes popped open, and she caught the silhouette of broad shoulders in the light coming through an open door. But, not her bedroom door. Apparently not a dream. And that, well it made her want to cry, because that had the makings of being completely epic.

She must have fallen asleep in his car. But enough of what she'd been feeling lingered in her head, just enough to make her feel impulsive and yup ... still horny. But more than that, she just wanted him. All of him, with no excuses of alcohol. She wanted to feel his skin under her hands and remember every second of it.

"Wait," she said before she could think better of it, her voice a little husky from sleep and good ol' sexual frustration. He turned back towards her, and she realized that she was in one of the downstairs bedrooms at his new house. Nothing on the walls yet, and a few boxes were stacked in the corner next to the dresser. When the mattress sank in from the way he perched on the edge, it caused her to roll towards him a little bit.

Rachel wrapped one hand around his arm where it was perched on the bed, his skin warm and solid to the touch. The hairs on his arm felt wiry against her palm and she slowly moved her hand up a few inches, dragging it back down again. Without looking up, she could practically feel the way he was staring at her.

"Why did you bring me here?" she asked, still staring at her hand against the tan skin of his forearm. He didn't answer, so she finally looked up at him. In the dark of the room, his features were indistinct, his eyes a burning shade of black.

"Because I wanted you here," he said simply. "Is that okay?"

Instead of answering, she nodded, feeling her hair catch on the pillow underneath her head. She pushed to sit up, and he shifted to let her. She could have taken her hand off his arm, and she could have gotten off the bed and insisted he take her back to her parents' house. There were actually a million different things, smarter things, that she could have done just then. But instead of any of those, her hand followed up his arm, across his shoulder to cup his jaw.

She leaned forward until there were only a couple of inches separating them. His eyes bored into hers, neither of them willing to shut their eyelids like common courtesy suggested they do. Gazes locked, she tilted her chin so that his top lip fit perfectly in between hers, and then lightly touched her tongue there. She pulled back and smiled, hopefully in a way that he knew exactly what was making her happy. Him. He was making her happy.

And ho boy, she wanted to make him happy in return. His other hand slid up her waist, his thumb resting just underneath the curve of one breast. And then he smiled back.

They met somewhere in the middle, lips meshing and pulling, tongues sliding, hands pushing against each other's skin and through each other's hair in a frenetic way. Like if either of them stopped to think for even a second, they'd lose the moment. And no way was Rachel going to click her brain back on in a moment that would actually let her see Tate naked, when she was sober. Even the idea of stopping made her skin tingle in rebellion, like her body would keep going with or without her consent.

Up on her knees now, she shifted backwards to let Tate come onto the bed. She hastily undid the buttons on his shirt, and then gave a whimpering little sigh at the sleek muscle she uncovered underneath it. After briefly removing her mouth from his, she went right back to kissing him, one hand drifted down his chest to the toned stomach that vibrated under her touch.

Everything disappeared from her mind completely, except the way his hands felt coasting along her body, the way his skin felt underneath hers. Surrendering to what he made her feel, just by touching her, made everything inside of her feel heady and delirious and potent. That was it - Tate made her feel powerful.

She shoved at his shoulder so that he lay down on the bed, and swung her leg so that she straddled him, she pulled her shirt over her head and tossed it across the room. The look in his eyes was nothing short of reverence, and his large hands followed the places that he stared at. Over the front curve of her stomach, briefly touching where her belly button pushed out, down her thighs, tightening his grip on her hips, then down over her shoulder to coast across the sheer black lace that covered her breasts.

"You are the most beautiful thing I've ever seen," he said quietly, eyes steady on hers. She leaned down and they kissed again, in a way that was so lush and luxurious that she started moving her hips above him in a slow, seductive rhythm. He groaned into her mouth and bit down on her lip. They made quick work of everything else covering them, pushing and pulling at shirts and bras and pants until they were skin to skin.

Tate sat up to press a kiss on the throbbing space above her heart and then looked up at her with so much feeling radiating from his eyes that she almost had to look away. Instead she raised her hips up and had to draw in a sharp breath when she lowered herself onto him, taking him into her in one sudden movement.

The way that he pushed and she moved and they came together was the most pure moment of passion Rachel had ever felt. And when they were both covered with a light sheen of sweat, she threw her head back, shouting his name. He followed moments later with his fingers digging into her hips until she thought she'd bruise, and she knew that she was completely and totally ruined for anyone else.

Damn it.

17

IN HIS THIRTY-FOUR years of life, Tate had experienced very few 'morning afters'. If he was being exact, he'd had two. Both of them with the same woman. But instead of stabbing pressure behind his eyeballs, a throbbing skull and a disappointingly empty bed, this morning-after was vastly better. Instead of cool, rumpled sheets next to him, Rachel was curled up on her side, face half buried into one of his pillows. The rat's nest that used to be her hair covered the other half of her face and every third breath, she let out a small sound too quiet to be considered a snore.

The sheet only covered her to her hips, the slight roundness of her belly finally uncovered for him to stare his fill. Instead of pressing one hand against it like he wanted, not daring to wake her, he just looked.

Everywhere.

She had light freckles that spread underneath her collar bone and they stretched around her shoulders, barely detectable unless you were looking for them. There was only one of a darker shade, and it landed on her upper arm. The way his blood rushed and raced through his veins just by looking, he knew this wasn't just because she was carrying his child. It couldn't be. He'd never felt a fraction of this for Natalie, this deluge of every minute detail about her.

And the way that she'd been looking at him when she had leaned forward to touch her lips to his, she had practically lit the room. A smile spread across his face. Tate rolled to his back, but kept his head turned so he could watch her. There was a warm contentment uncurling through him, the kind that a man *wanted* to experience, the kind that came from watching a beautiful woman sleep and knowing that he'd never get sick of doing it.

He rubbed a hand down his face, wanting to laugh at the thoughts tripping through his head. They were the kind of thoughts that you could only dare to speak out loud to some other poor sap who'd experienced the same thing, the same feeling of winning the damn lottery just because she'd chosen him. Even without the mind-blowing sex, and it really truly had been, he just felt like he could breathe deeper, breathe easier.

And then he did laugh, softly because he couldn't keep it in. Dylan would probably kick his ass if he'd heard even a smidgen of what Tate was thinking. If he laid there any longer, he may end up composing a sonnet, so he rolled out of the bed, careful not to disturb her, and made his way upstairs. He hadn't put much in the upstairs fridge, but the coffee maker was up there, and he figured that even if he couldn't make her a decent breakfast, he could at least bring her a cup of the Ethiopian Sidamo that he loved.

While the coffee maker dripped and filled the kitchen with the smell of the bold roast, he stood by the slider that opened to the large deck, everything covered with a thin layer of white and ice. This year there'd be no Christmas tree or decorations given that he'd just moved in, but seeing the large expanse of yard behind the house, completely untouched by any footprints, he couldn't stop the visions of next winter. There would be toys on the floor, maybe a snowman taking up space in the backyard, a sled ready to take down the hill down the street. He felt another slow grin, thinking that he might be getting ahead of himself since the baby would only be five or six months old at that point. But with a sleeping Rachel downstairs, curled up in *his* bed, he could see Christmases for the next few years in this house with no trouble at all.

A few short beeps came from the coffee maker, and he poured the steaming liquid into two mugs. Not sure how Rachel took her coffee, he stirred some sugar into one just in case she didn't want it black and turned to head back downstairs. And then he had to work not to drop the heavy ceramic mugs when he saw Rachel come up the last step and turn into the room.

She wasn't looking up at him, but at her fingers where they were trying to close up a few buttons on the gray dress shirt he'd worn yesterday. The last place he'd seen it was draped over the corner of his dresser when he'd left his bedroom. Her legs were bare where the end of the shirt hung around her thighs, and her hair was only slightly tamed from earlier.

She looked like sex and sin and every single thing he'd ever fantasized about in one slightly rumpled package. By the time she noticed him, standing there and gawking like an idiot, there were still two buttons open at the top of the shirt. He wanted to kiss her so damn bad, but he stayed rooted in place. One of her eyebrows lifted, and he lifted one of the mugs in answer.

"You're actually going to let me drink that?" she asked, her voice still a little scratchy.

"Why wouldn't I? Pregnant women can still have about two hundred milligrams of caffeine a day with no known side effects."

"It weirds me out that you know stuff like that." She accepted the cup, curling her hands around it to capture the heat. "How long have you been up?"

"Just as long as it took that to brew. I was going to bring it down to you, I wasn't sure if you had someplace you needed to be this morning."

She shook her head, taking a slow sip of her coffee. "I sent my mom a text last night letting her know I wouldn't be home, which makes me feel like I'm eighteen again, by the way. I'd just like to be back home by eleven to shower and head back to the expo by one. Even though I told the girls I wouldn't be there until later, my groin feels a lot better, so I'll be fine to go this afternoon."

"You sure? The doctor said not to push yourself."

"Quite sure," she said, watching him over the rim of her mug, her eyes giving absolutely nothing away. Tate was about three seconds away from morphing into a complete girl. *What are you thinking? What did last night mean?* It was par for the course, really, considering his frame of mind since the second he woke up.

"You can shower here, you know. Give those double shower heads in your bathroom a spin."

Her hand paused where it was lifting the mug back to her mouth. She narrowed her eyes just a bit, enough for him to know that she was treading as carefully as he was right now. It was like they were both trying to balance on the same log, but moving in opposite directions, just trying not to fall off. And he hated it, hated that they were both doing it.

The last time they'd been like this was at the airport, after Rachel told him she was pregnant. That had been like navigating a minefield. This, well, it wasn't much better. And it made him feel edgy to get them back into a better, more comfortable place. Unfortunately, he wasn't quite positive what that place might be.

"And use what exactly? Your dude body wash? No thanks. I'd prefer not to smell like you for the rest of the day, thank you very much."

"The smell didn't seem to bother you last night when you basically inhaled the skin off my neck and told me you wanted to devour me." The words fell out before he could snatch them back in, and the way her eyes widened told him she was pretty shocked as hell right along with him. Apparently that edginess shuffling under his skin landed them smack dab into the banter that always seemed to follow them around.

She scoffed. "I didn't say that."

"Oh, sure you did," he continued, figuring that if he was going to start down this road, to push a few of his favorite buttons, he might as well see it to the end. It certainly wasn't a game he was accustomed to playing, so he channeled his little brother as best he could. Now this, this Dylan would be proud of. Moving forward one step, he dragged his eyes all the way down her body and then back up, relishing the spots of color that had appeared on her cheeks. "I'm pretty sure you said it right before you ripped my shirt off. Glad to see you didn't tear any buttons off in your haste."

She slicked her tongue against her teeth and it took everything in him to keep a grin off his face. The glare that she sent him pretty much shot straight to his groin. Oh yeah, this was kinda fun. In fact, maybe this could ramp them up to another round somewhere in this kitchen. With the sharp turn, she plopped the mug down, and the sharp crack of ceramic against the counter sounded like a gunshot in the kitchen.

"As much as I enjoy this little recap, I really should get back home." Her face was closed off, and he felt a small stirring of panic. They'd just been having fun, right? Only Rachel's face didn't look like she was having fun. At all.

"Rachel," he started, and she held a hand up to stop him.

"No, this was my fault. Obviously I need to learn to keep a lid on my pregnancy hormones. Next time I'll handle matters myself."

Now it was his turn to set down his mug, only he did it slowly and carefully. Her fault. Handle matters herself. Pregnancy hormones. Those three sentences broke down into separate words and then into individual letters that didn't make any sense as they swept through his head. First he was confused. Then, as he stared at her, and the blank look that she was trying to keep pasted on her face, he just got pissed.

"That's how you're going to play this," he said, keeping his tone carefully even. "I helped you, what? Scratch an itch?"

She pursed her lips, working her jaw back and forth. Her mouth opened, and then she closed it again. And that was new, Rachel thinking twice about what she was going to say.

"I don't believe you," he said firmly in her silence, his eyes not wavering from her for even a second.

"This is exactly why I was afraid to move in," she said, quite obviously avoiding his statement. "This can't keep happening, Tate."

He laughed. He couldn't help it. This woman had balls made of bricks to be able to look him in the eye and say that after last night.

"This isn't funny," she snapped.

"I couldn't agree more. I had absolutely no intention to sleep with you last night, had no problem respecting the boundaries you put in place. You called me back. You kissed me. And I do not believe you that you just couldn't control some pregnant woman hormonal overload. It meant *more* than that, it meant more than that to me, and you know it." Tate punctuated it by pointing a finger at her, and he practically shook with everything rushing through him.

He was angry, sure, but that battled fiercely with disappointment. It was a toss-up which one would come out on top. There was more to this, to last night, and to this morning, he *knew* it. And all he wanted to do was push and push until she admitted what it was. But the way she paled a bit as he spoke, he knew he'd rein in the anger.

"You're right," she said, eyes lowering to the floor briefly before coming back up to meet his. "That was all on me."

He rubbed a hand across the back of his neck, shaking his head. Self-preservation radiated off of her, covering her like full body armor. Pushing buttons was definitely not the right approach, not with as quickly as she'd shut down. Rachel obviously had control of whatever switch in her head allowed her to do that. And with that fact clear, Tate decided that a tactical retreat, with hands raised in concession, was the only smart thing left to do.

Because if he pushed too hard, he'd concede the biggest victory he'd achieved with her: her decision to move in with him. And if she changed her mind about that, he probably wouldn't be able to look himself in the mirror for quite a while. "You didn't exactly have to push me very hard. This is on both of us. I shouldn't ... I just saw this morning go a little differently in my head. And that's not your fault."

"Maybe not, but I'm sorry all the same. I'm the one who wanted the rules, and I broke them at the first opportunity. I won't do it again, I promise." Not exactly what he wanted to hear. It chafed to give her even the smallest smile. But he did, and the relief was clear in her eyes. One of her hands tugged on the end of the shirt she was wearing, like her lack of pants was suddenly very obvious given the direction of their conversation. She flashed a tiny grin, and then gestured towards the stairs. "I'm gonna go get dressed. Thanks for the coffee."

After she'd gone back downstairs, he sank into one of the stools tucked against the kitchen island and let out a heavy breath. Trying to navigate a pseudo-relationship with the woman that he'd accidentally impregnated and was still insanely attracted to was more exhausting that anything he'd ever experienced in his entire life. And all of this without adding a child into the mix. A quick glance at the clock told him that as soon as he dropped Rachel off at home, he'd be within an acceptable time frame to drink. If the last twenty-four hours didn't earn him some alcohol, then he didn't know what would. He tapped out a text to Dylan.

Tate: Are you working today?

Dylan: When am I not working?

Tate: Good point, I'll see you in a bit. Save a seat at the bar for me.

Dylan: Women troubles?

Tate: Brother, you have no idea.

18

ACROSS SEVEN MASSIVE TELEVISION SCREENS, various college football games raised cheers and curses among the packed sports bar. From where he sat at the main bar area, Tate had the best view of the entire space. Almost every wall was exposed brick, all the chairs black, and in the rare space where there wasn't a television screen mounted, there were large framed prints showcasing vintage sports paraphernalia. The one closest to Tate was a black and white poster from the 1968 World Series, when the Detroit Tigers played the St. Louis Cardinals, the heavy mahogany frame dark against the red and brown toned bricks.

It was a cool place, the Bombay Grille & Sports bar. It made him feel just a touch guilty, that Dylan had managed it for the last two years and Tate had only been in there once. Another thing that he could add to the list of fights that weren't worth having with Natalie. Even though it was located in a trendy part of Grand Rapids, she couldn't fathom going someplace that had a single television mounted anywhere for public viewing.

Tate tossed back the last swallow of his first drink, a vodka tonic that Dylan had yelled for a flirty bartender to mix up for him. A hand clapped him on the shoulder right as he set his drink down, and Tate turned his head to see Dylan slide into the empty stool next to him, one of the few open seats left.

"It's amazing, no matter how much Michigan sucks this year, I still fill almost every seat when there's a game on," Dylan said, motioning to the bartender to get Tate another drink. The brunette practically bounded over to where they sat, smiling at Dylan in a way that made dimples dig into either side of her mouth.

"Anything else, boss?" she asked, eyes barely touching on Tate now that Dylan was around. Yup. Another one bites the dust.

"We're good, Chrissy, thanks." She let out a very inconspicuous sigh when she turned to a new customer, and Tate let out a chuckle.

"Another one in love with you?"

Dylan shrugged a shoulder, flashing a crooked grin that got him out of a whole lot of trouble growing up. "She'll get over it. They all do after about month, and they realize I'm kind of an asshole to work for."

Tate chuckled and took a sip of the freshly made drink, the dry bite of the gin and tonic welcome after the train wreck of a morning with Rachel. Out of the corner of his eye, he watched as Dylan kept his eyes constantly moving around the bar, making sure the staff were doing what they were trained for. It felt a little strange, being there, to talk to Dylan about what was going on. It wasn't just that his little brother worked in an establishment that served alcohol, since Tate wasn't someone who ever drank all that much, it was strange because he and Dylan had never really had that kind of relationship.

Casey and Dylan, the two youngest of the Steadman kids, had always been the closest. And the twins, well, they were twins. Tate had always fallen somewhere in the realm of a comfortable sibling relationship; getting along with all of them, but not necessarily having one of them for 'himself'. It'd never bothered him though, always burying himself in his school work, and then burying himself, quite literally, into his relationship with Natalie.

"What's up, big brother?" Dylan asked, not taking his eyes off of where a skinny waitress was delivering an impressively large tray of food without spilling it. Some groans over a thrown interception filled the bar, so Tate waited until the disgruntled football watchers quieted down before answering.

Twisting the low-ball glass around in a circle, Tate thought about what he even wanted to ask.

"That bad, huh?" Dylan laughed at Tate's obvious hesitancy. "I'm not surprised you're twisted up in so many damn knots. Rachel has that kind of effect on people."

He tried, he tried really hard to not get defensive at that statement, so casually made. "What effect?"

"I just mean she's the kind of woman who brings out those, uhh, strong feelings. Rachel is an admittedly proud ball buster. You and I have both seen her knee someone in the 'nads for brushing up against her in the wrong way. I'm thinking that men either want to run from her, or screw her. And not much in the middle."

And that he had no choice but to turn in his seat and fix Dylan with the coldest damn glare he'd ever aimed in his brother's direction. "And which one do *you* feel towards her?"

Only it had no effect whatsoever, except to make Dylan lean back in his chair and let out a full, loud, and annoying laugh. When he finally stopped laughing, at least a dozen people around them had turned to see what was going on.

Dylan wiped a hand under his eyes, and then let it drop over his heart. "Shit, Tate. That's the funniest thing I've ever heard come out of your mouth."

"I fail to see how."

"Dude," and he punctuated that with a slap on Tate's shoulder. "I fall right smack dab in the harmless middle. She's Casey's really funny, very mouthy, *I want to keep her sharp bits far, far away from my man parts* friend. That's it." He tilted his head, and thought for a second. "Well, and she's carrying my brother's child and making me an uncle for the sixth time. But, that's it."

"I'm losing my mind, Dylan. She is making me insane from trying to figure out where the hell we stand. If there is one thing that I've ever needed to get right in my entire life, it's this. And I don't ... I don't know what to do." Tate tossed back the rest of his drink, relishing the sharp burn against the back of his throat. It felt good to admit that, because he'd only had the fragment of the thought, not even wanting to think those words together in his own brain. There was a small portion that felt liberated. A very, very small portion. Every other part of him just felt absolutely scared shitless.

"And you're asking *me*?" Seeing Dylan look miffed was new. Hell, all of this was new.

"Apparently."

Raising his eyebrows, Dylan finally looked straight at Tate. "Of any one of the five of us, I'm the last one to be in a serious relationship. Forgive me if I'm a little skeptical."

"C'mon, you expect me to ask Casey what to do? She'd scalp me if she thought I'd screwed with Rachel in the slightest."

Dylan smiled. "Or worse, she'd send Jake after you. And his Ranger ass would make you disappear without a trace."

"Thanks," Tate said dryly. "You're being incredibly helpful."

"Need another one?" Dylan asked, gesturing to Tate's empty glass.

Tate shook his head and then waited while Dylan pulled a waiter aside to point something out.

Turning his bar stool so that he faced Tate, Dylan's face was set in a serious expression. "When Mom told me about Rachel and the baby ... honestly Tate, I was so damn relieved."

"What?" Tate asked when he finally picked up his jaw which had fallen somewhere around the floor. "Why?"

And instead of serious, Dylan just looked a little uneasy,

scraping a hand across his mouth. "Casey and I are the ones who didn't go to college, just falling into these jobs that we loved, and happened to be good at. But it was okay for her because she's the baby, the only girl, and Mom and Dad pretty much think she shits diamonds. It's different with me."

"They're proud of all of us, you know that. They say it enough."

Dylan shrugged and then took a long drink of the ice water in front of him. The thought that his incredibly self-assured, admittedly cocky little brother could feel even the least bit like he didn't measure up made Tate feel itchy, uncomfortable. "Yeah, but I see it in Dad's face every once in a while, like he keeps waiting for me to 'live up to my potential'."

"Wait, so what does that have to do with me and Rachel?"

"Dude," Dylan said on a short laugh. "Me doing something stupid wouldn't surprise anyone. But you coming home and telling our parents that not only did you knock someone up, it was Casey's best friend? That's the kind of epic screw up that people would bet their entire life savings that Tate Steadman would never do. Not gonna lie, made me feel like I had a little breathing room, at least for the next nine months."

Hot anger came first, making the back of his neck feel like it was on fire. Tate clenched one hand into a fist, counting down from ten until he felt like he could feel his pulse slowing. Thinking of Rachel, of their baby, as an epic screw up made him want to punch a lot of somethings. Probably not Dylan though, because Tate was fairly sure that his brother would be a much dirtier fighter than he was. But once the anger receded just a bit, enough to process rational thought, he just felt a little sad.

"You doing yoga breathing over there to calm down?"

Tate laughed, shaking his head. "You're such an ass sometimes."

A cheer roared through the restaurant and, by silent agreement, they decided to watch football for a couple minutes. When a commercial break came on, Tate looked at Dylan, then back down at the shining bar in front of him. "You know, you have yet to give me any semblance of useful advice."

"I'm thinking."

Tate rolled his eyes. "Think faster. I do have things to do today."

"Look, as much as Rachel knows how to run her mouth, she's tough to read, right?"

"Right." Tough to read. Guarded. Ensconced by the Great Wall of China. All of the above.

"But she's no idiot. We all know you were asking her to marry you for the wrong reasons when you first found out."

"You know what, Dylan? I'm pretty damn sick of apologizing for that. I've admitted it was stupid to pretty much every member of our family by now. Want me to call Aunt Evie, too? I don't know if she realizes that my brain wasn't working on all cylinders in that moment. Don't bring it up again," Tate snapped out.

Dylan pointed a finger at him, looking weirdly satisfied by his outburst. "See, this? This is a side of you that I like. You've been so buttoned up for the last six years, probably because Natalie took a lot of pleasure in shoving the same stick up your ass that was surgically implanted in hers. But now, you've got this 'Tate's kind of a badass' thing going on. And you need to keep following where this path is leading you. You are more yourself than I've seen in a long time, because your ass has landed in a situation that you never would have chosen before. And you need to give Rachel the credit to recognize when you're being genuine. When you're asking her to marry you because you want to *marry her*, not because you think it's what you should do."

Tate sank back, letting the hard curved back of the barstool support him. "It sounds stupidly simple when you say it like that."

"Yeah well, I'm good like that...making everything look stupidly simple." Dylan said it evenly, but Tate could hear the slight edge to his words.

His lungs expelled a heavy breath, like they were working overtime to keep the push and pull of oxygen moving through his body. "Don't be such a girl, Dylan. You know what I meant."

Through his peripheral vision, Tate saw Dylan's mouth lift in a grin. "Yeah, I do. Look, you're both smart people, which means you'll produce a genius child who will undoubtedly bring unending joy and happiness to you. And I'd bet my job that if you don't push her, if you just be what she needs you to be, then she'll figure it out eventually. And so will you."

The sharp crash of dishes hitting the concrete floor made Dylan groan. "Sounds like I need to go fire someone."

Tate laughed, but grabbed Dylan's shoulder before he cleared his stool. "Thank you, really. For the drinks, and the advice. I appreciate it, brother."

Looking slightly uncomfortable with the praise, Dylan gave a short nod and cleared his throat. "Anytime."

Not needing to hang around any longer, Tate started to thank Chrissy, but when he saw her staring at Dylan with a wistful look, he just smiled and walked out into the freezing air. Everything smelled so clean in the winter, even though a sharp inhale would just about freeze the nose shut. Tate smiled, thinking about what Rachel had told him once that her favorite part of winter was the fact that she had a justifiable reason not to shave her legs. When he reached his car where he'd parked it a few blocks down from the Bombay, it had a light coating of snow covering it. He quickly started it up and let it idle while he brushed off the front and back windshield.

Rubbing his hands together once he sat down inside, Tate let the words of advice that Dylan gave overlap with memories of the last twenty four hours.

She's guarded ... tough to read.

Rachel asking him to stay. Leaning forward and kissing him.

Let her see that you're genuine.

Rachel pushing him onto his back and straddling his lap.

Keep following where this path is leading.

Him feeling across every inch of her skin, tell her how beautiful she was. And her eyes, how they lit from within when he said it.

Be what she needs you to be.

Handing her a cup of coffee while she wore that damn shirt.

She'll figure it out eventually.

It was enough to drive a man crazy, trying to filter through all of that. And maybe Dylan was right, for so long Tate had done what he thought he should do, that even though his feelings for Rachel were true enough, real enough, he was still pushing where he should rest, where he should trust in the certainty of what was growing between them. No pun intended, with the baby, but in the way that she pushed and pulled right along with him. It would be enough for him, for right now, to know that Rachel was giving him these little glimpses as to what she wanted. And because it was what he wanted too, Tate could back up a few steps.

Maybe this was the new Tate, the right Tate. Right in the uncertainty of where he'd found himself. The relieved breath that came out of him felt good. Really, unexpectedly good.

19

WITH THE EXCEPTIONS of finding her ex-boyfriend handcuffed to a bed by another woman and then getting herself knocked up by someone who was emphatically not a boyfriend, Rachel didn't usually find herself truly surprised in life. But unfortunately, she'd just added another thing to that list.

Tate Steadman was tricky. Oh yeah, he was a tricky one, this baby daddy of hers. And of course, he was a lawyer, so why was she surprised? She shouldn't have been. But the whole picture was narrowing in, all the little pixels sharpening until she could see *like* every little blade of grass on her dad's HD TV.

Tate was stepping back. Respecting her very narrowly held up standards as she'd enforced them a month ago after her little *slip into bed naked* moment. And he was doing everything so right and so perfectly that she could only come to one conclusion: he was trying to trick her into falling in love with him.

What an *asshole*.

And one of the things that forced her to come to this conclusion was that she found herself standing in the middle of a Pottery Barn with Tate and Casey, the latter of whom was doing her best to spend all her brother's money, and the former being all considerate of every single thing Rachel might want.

"Tate, don't be ridiculous. You cannot use the same couch that you bought in college." Casey sounded positively scandalized, like her brother had just suggested they line the walls of the house with dead puppies or something. "You're almost forty. You can afford new furniture."

"Your insanely awful math aside, considering that I'm thirty four, that couch is perfectly fine. It's comfortable. It's irresponsible to spend money on a new couch when I don't need one."

Casey rolled her eyes, and Rachel had to stifle a laugh at the corresponding glare that Tate sent his sister's way. "Yeah, well, sweatpants are comfortable too. Doesn't mean that we wear them everywhere we go."

The sigh that came from Tate sounded a whole lot like the ones Jake issued whenever Casey-logic was in full force. And that was to say that Casey-logic didn't usually make much sense to anyone outside of Casey. Tate quirked a grin at Rachel, seeing her watch the exchange with narrowed eyes.

What was he playing at, with that adorable little self-deprecating grin? Sure, he'd been steady and supportive the entire time, when he wasn't making inappropriate proposals or assuming she'd wind up in his bed every time they were alone. It was a strange teeter totter that Rachel felt like she was trapped on. The steadier he was, the more he tried to balance the two of them, the more she felt like she was going to fall onto her ass. He soothed, and her head spun faster and faster. He accommodated, and she felt like someone tilted her axis.

It made her want to scream at the top of her lungs until her vocal chords burned straight through. Certainly not the most logical response, she could admit it, but the unsteadiness that he made her feel was enough to send her into a padded cell. Because even though she needed that distance between them like she needed oxygen, she wanted real. And this polite harmony they'd found themselves in was intensely disconcerting to her. Because what it did was make her want to kick at it until it all shattered around her.

Dangerous - that's what it was. Dangerous because every bit of it reminded her of her mom. Dangerous because of how easily it fit inside of her, the craziness she felt for him, no matter how much she wanted to rip that part of herself out. But dangerous or not, she was having a craving. A craving for the Tate who not only pushed her buttons but completely obliterated them. The mussed-up Tate that didn't let her get away with anything.

Gah. Bad, bad thoughts for her. Because it was making her paranoid, that he was doing all this niceness and hand-holding to get at her from a completely different angle. So when he asked her opinion on almost every single thing in the damn store, she felt like chucking a lamp across the overly crowded showroom. And a nice lamp too. One of those really sturdy wood ones that Casey kept cooing over like it was Tiffany diamonds or something.

"Good Lord, Casey," she grumbled. "It's a freaking lamp. You can probably get the same one at Target for like twenty bucks."

"Au contraire, my prego friend. This is a legit craftsman style lamp, it fits with the style of the house. And with the columns framing the stairs into the basement, and the mantle on the fireplace, this will go perfectly." And Casey punctuated it with a girly little point of her finger at the lighting fixture in question, like it would magically jump in her purse.

"Do you like it, Rachel?" Tate asked, not making eye contact, but flipping a price tag on a throw blanket that Casey had snuck into the cart. His eyebrows raised imperceptibly at the digits he found on the other side, but he didn't take it out. Which was good, because Rachel had actually felt the plush cream fabric and died a little inside at how nice it felt. It would be like snuggling under friggin' clouds and rainbows and angels wings.

Rachel heaved a sigh, not at all trying to be quiet about it.

"Yes. It's the greatest lamp I've ever had the privilege of seeing. And my life won't be complete at your house if that's not the lamp sitting on the end table."

Casey squealed and clapped, then wrote down the item number. Tate rolled his eyes, but his face hinted at a smile.

"But", Rachel said, voice firm and eyes as narrowed as she could get and still see out of them. "You need to wrap this up, Spendy Girl. My doctor appointment is in an hour, and I've been standing for so long that it feels like someone is trying to shove a bowling ball down my spine."

"Why didn't you say something?" Tate said and practically shoved her into a ridiculously comfortable armchair.

"Hey," she said, and swatted his hand away from where he was trying to put her feet up on a coffee table that probably cost more than Tate's mortgage payment every month. "Look, you're the one who feels my opinion is necessary in this little endeavor. I'm just trying to get it over with."

Tate rubbed a hand over his chest and gave a mock groan. "Ouch. That ... that stings a little, Rachel."

"Yeah, well, as fun as is spending all your money, Tate, maybe I'll be a bit more excited when I get to pick out the stuff that I'm going to buy. Because I will be." She pointed a finger at him. "Buying stuff, that is."

He lifted his hands in surrender. Internally she rolled her eyes, because it was so bloody obvious that he wasn't taking her seriously.

Casey smiled and then tucked a picture frame into the cart next to the blanket of happiness. "You're about the only woman I know who wouldn't find even *this* the tiniest bit thrilling."

"He's obviously trying to be placating, but I'm serious; I'll have plenty of time to contribute to the furnishing of this house. I've already given you my budget for my bedroom that you've promised to make fabulous. Plus we still have the nursery to discuss, and I've got ideas."

Casey gave a little squeal of delight over that, then patted Tate on the arm and practically bounded to the cash register to hand over the overflowing cart and monstrous list of items that needed to be delivered.

She'd pored over catalogs and websites the last few nights, when the movements in her belly kept her from sleeping. It was so easy, laying there, rubbing a hand over the gentle rolls and pushes that came from inside, and picturing that teeny little human sleeping in the cribs that she was looking at. She'd always been pretty good with saving money, feeling better when she had a safety net. But since leaving Marc, and the rent-free arrangement with her parents, she had more of a nest egg now than she'd had in her whole life.

It felt good, knowing that despite the unplanned way she was becoming a parent, that providing the things her child needed wouldn't be an unbearable burden for her. Because even though she would be living with Tate, there was no freaking way she was going to let him pay for everything. The roof he was providing for them was a pretty damn nice one, and so the other big things were responsibilities that she couldn't wait to shoulder.

Maybe that sounded weird. Because even though she and Tate hadn't sat down to talk about who was paying for what, she knew he'd have no issue affording whatever the baby needed. But she didn't *want* him to do everything. It would be a sticking point for her, to be sure. The ability to contribute to this family they'd created.

And right through the wide opening into the next area of the store, she could just see the corner of the set she had her eye on. The one on display was exactly the one she'd found online. Gray, with framed ends and ribbon molding. The lines were all straight, making it classic. Timeless. The display bedding they had it paired with was pink and white, and there would be none of that in her baby's room. Not that she minded. A little gender neutral decor was fine with her if it meant saving that surprise for whenever Nugget came into the world. And like Nugget knew she was thinking of him (she said him, because hey, let's be honest, it was probably a him), he gave a steady somersault, making her grin widely.

"What are you smiling about?" Tate asked, sitting across from her in another display chair.

She motioned for one of his hands, and surprise made his jaw pop open. Then he quickly moved next to her. Rachel took his large, warm hand into hers and laid it right over where she'd felt the gymnastics and pressed down. They sat there waiting in perfectly still silence while the store continued to bustle around them. She shifted his hand once, hoping that he could feel the slight movements that she could still feel.

When she curled his fingers under hers so that he pressed in more, the baby gave an answering kick. It was subdued, but Tate's face gave her the answer as to whether he felt it. He blinked rapidly, and his smile was slow and full of wonder. His gaze was fixed on her stomach where their hands were still pressed together. His dark eyes looked up to her, and they looked a little shiny. She smiled back at him, feeling warm and amazing and not at all crazy for the way his brown eyes made her feel.

"That..." he said, voice hushed and more than a little rough. Then he stopped and shook his head. "That's the most miraculous thing I've ever experienced. Thank you."

"You're welcome," she replied, equally quiet, not wanting to be the one to break the bubble around them. Then Hurricane Casey swept back into their little pocket of space and plunked on the arm of the chair that Rachel was in. Her eyes widened when she saw Tate's hand still firmly lodged underneath Rachel's.

"Did you ... did he just move?" But before Rachel could answer, Casey yanked Tate's hand away and put her own on Rachel's belly, pressing in a couple spots with a wide smile on her face. "Hi, little pumpkin," she crooned. "It's your Auntie Casey. Won't you move for me? Show me that I'm your favorite already?

I'm way nicer than Uncle Dylan, so if you move for him first, I'll be really, really upset."

When there was no answering movement, Casey pouted and pulled her hand back, making Rachel laugh. "You say that as if I'd let Dylan feel me up."

Tate damn near growled, and Rachel and Casey gave a simultaneous eye roll.

"Get a grip, Steadman. It's a figure of speech," Rachel said in as dry of a tone as she could manage, when the growliness was actually fairly hot. Actually really hot. And ooh, as much as she wanted to blame the hotness on hormones, she'd be a lying hussy if she did. Nope. That was a universally accepted turn-on.

He sighed and looked over at Casey. "So, dare I ask for a receipt for this little outing?"

"Only if you don't value the good mood that you're currently in," Casey said as she stood, swinging her monstrous purse over her shoulder. "I'll mail it to you, so that I'm far, far away when you get it."

Tate raised an eyebrow when Rachel laughed under her breath. "Your sense of self-preservation is inspiring, sister, truly."

"Just one of my many positive traits. I keep a list if you ever need reminding."

20

As soon as Rachel pulled into the parking lot of her doctor's office, she saw the car immediately and let out a mournful, completely overly dramatic groan that was wrenched from the depths of her tortured soul. The car was fairly impractical for the winter, considering it was a rear wheel drive convertible, but her mom had always said that if she ever ended up in a ditch, the candy apple red color would ensure that she never stayed stuck for long.

But of course, it was possible that other crazy Michiganders drove convertibles during the winter. It was the vanity plate that read 'NTRLRED' that definitively gave it away as her mom's car, immediately bringing to mind the abject mortification of when she and Kate had to endure watching their parents giggle over some inside joke that was hidden within those seven letters about her mom's natural hair color.

Gag.

When Rachel carefully pulled her car into the only open 'expectant mother' spot, there was a blur of color outside of her driver's door before she could even pull the key out of the ignition. Her door was yanked open and her mom's beaming face appeared along with the cold December air.

"Surprise! I hope it's okay that I'm here," her mom said breathlessly, like she'd sprinted across the icy parking lot, taking a hold of Rachel's arm and helping her out of the car.

No, no it's not freaking okay that you're at my first ultrasound without being invited. Get in your impractical car and drive your ass right on back to work. That's what she thought, at least.

"Umm," was what she said instead. Glad that she could focus on walking across the slick surface of the ground, Rachel tried to figure out a nicer way to say, *yeah, what the hell are you doing here?*

"Madelyn, you made it," Tate called from behind them. Aaaaaaand apparently Tate was not all that surprised. What the what?

"Hang on," Rachel interjected when her mom started to reply, she turned her head to Tate as they reached the glass doors leading into the office building. "You knew she was coming?"

He gave her a sheepish grin, one that practically dared her to not forgive him, and *ooooh* did that piss her off.

"It was a peace offering."

"Uh huh. What peace did you need to make again?"

Her mom harrumphed a laugh, only it sounded like a ball of tar was stuck in her throat. "Other than the fact that he's whisking you and my first grandchild away to a gorgeous house? And that he knocked you up in the first place? Because maybe that's what he needs to make peace over with your parents who worry incessantly and don't know much about what's going on."

Rachel gaped. Because really. What else was she supposed to do with all of that? And she could admit that she hadn't been all sharey with her parents, because she didn't really want to hear all the parental reactions to what was going on. If you couldn't be twenty-eight years old and not keep a few things from your parents, then when the hell could you? And deep down, way, waaaaaay deep down she retracted behind that little concrete wall she'd erected to defend herself from becoming her mother. In the process, she was well aware that the wall did more than keep Rachel from becoming her mom. It kept *her* from her mom.

Oh, crappity crap crap. She was such a bitch. And not a pregnant, conveniently-blame-it-on-hormones bitch. Like straight up, I-have-an-emotional-problem-to-work-through bitch.

The warm air of the lobby was stifling the shit out of her in the midst of all these personal revelations and she had to work to take a deep breath. Tate was still incredibly, conspicuously silent after her mom's little rampage, which probably meant he'd heard the same thing when they'd talked earlier.

"Well," Rachel started, voice a little more hesitant than she liked. "I'm fine with you being here." At the triumphant expression that bloomed on her mom's face, Rachel pointed a finger. "But Tate's off the hook. It's not like he forced me into anything, okay? We made all these decisions together. So no more guilt trips, got it?"

The look that Tate sent her pretty much went straight into her damn panties, it was so grateful and relieved and good Lord, what was he *doing to her*?

After they both received a rib-cracking hug from her mom, they rode up the elevator in comfortable silence. Rachel checked in with the woman at the desk, went to pee in her little cup, and by the time she was about to sit back down between her baby daddy and her emotionally unstable mother, a girl in scrubs and an unfortunate little ponytail on top of her head appeared at the glass door, waving her clipboard and calling Rachel's name.

"Hi!" she said brightly, her bleach blonde stub at the back of her head bouncing along with every movement of her head. "I'm Megan, and I'm your ultrasound tech today! How super exciting is this?!"

"Umm, more than I can handle really," Rachel said, trying to pull her eyes away from Megan's unnatural hair movements. She gestured behind her. "Is it okay if they both come along?"

Megan's violet eyes widened. Yeah, violet. Obviously colored contacts and high ponytails were her two most favorite things ever, along with sickening energy levels. "Of *course*. We can totes fit two adults in the room with you. Is this your mom and husband? That's so presh. C'mon back, guys. It's a baby party!"

Rachel rubbed a hand at her temple when her mom asked what presh meant, and if it was acceptable for an over fifty woman to use it.

"No, Mom. Not acceptable. Ever," she said firmly, and tried to ignore the way Tate was fighting a smile in her peripheral vision. Thank the sweet little baby Jesus that Megan decided to keep her mouth shut after that, directing them into a darkened room, and told Rachel to lay back on the reclined chair. Both her mom and Tate took up spots on her left side so they could view the small screen that was positioned to her right. Megan rolled a stool next to Rachel on the table, and held up a white bottle.

"This is the gel that your doctor uses to listen to the heartbeat, but I usually warm it up so it's not so icky. Could you pull your shirt up for me?"

"Sure. But only because the gel won't feel icky," Rachel said. Someone tapped her shoulder in warning, but she didn't look back to see who it was. Probably Tate. He was way more into following societal cues than her mom was. Once her pants were shoved within inches of her vag, and her shirt pushed up, Megan became remarkably serious. The ultrasound wand was similar to the heartbeat thingie, getting pressed down into her skin until Rachel felt like it would pop through. The screen showed a confusing blend of white staticky stuff and black blobs. After pressing down in one spot for a longer moment, Megan let out a really undignified squeal.

"There the little bugger is! It was hiding from me. See the little leg and arm waving at you?"

And she totally, completely did. Two skinny little legs, a slightly larger than normal head, and an arm, right there in front of her.

"Oh God," came her mom's wavering voice from behind her, and Rachel recognized the sound of her quiet tears. Tate hadn't grabbed her hand like normal, but pushed his hand under the nape of her neck and squeezed tightly while all three of them looked. Just looked. Even Megan kept her trap blissfully shut.

A little hand moved, and one of the legs followed suit, and Rachel felt a little nuclear bomb of happiness go off in her chest. Megan started taking measurements with the wand and the keyboard that was attached to the screen. She was talking, something about how things looked, and it all sounded good, but there was no way Rachel could tear any part of her attention away from the little movements on the screen. What was even freakier was how some of the larger ones corresponded with movements she could feel in her stomach. One of Tate's hands smoothed the hair off her forehead, and she managed to tear her eyes off the screen to look back at him. He gave her a small smile, and winked. She smiled back and turned her gaze back to the screen.

"Pretty amazeballs, huh?" Megan asked in a hushed tone. "I never get sick of seeing it."

Tate cleared his throat, his hand back at the base of Rachel's skull, a reassuring weight. "It kinda makes it hard to imagine not believing in God when you see something like this. It's nothing short of a miracle."

Her mother coughed on a sob and a hot brick pressed at the back of Rachel's eyeballs. She blinked rapidly to try to make it go the hell away. Speaking was not even remotely possible, not with all these freaking emotions pushing at her from every direction. The three of them were talking, but Rachel just swallowed down the lump in her throat, and it was one big ass lump. Her mom sniffled and asked for a tissue, and it made Rachel clench her teeth down so tightly she thought they might crack. Rachel did not want those tears to be contagious, but the burning behind her eyes kept getting hotter and hotter as Megan kept checking off all the things that looked healthy and normal about the baby.

"And do we want to know the gender today?" Megan asked with a wide, toothy smile.

"No, thank you," Tate answered quickly, giving Rachel another squeeze. "We've decided to keep it a surprise."

"Oh," Megan breathed. "That's totes fun. Nobody does that anymore. I dig it. But, you've got one healthy little baby here, and everything looks perfect, congratulations."

She was so sincere when she said it, Rachel kinda felt like apologizing for being so judgey. But really, using 'totes' twice in twenty minutes? Overkill. Instead of that though, Rachel smiled at her and thanked her for everything. Megan beamed, and proceeded to hand her about million printouts, including one where she'd typed in 'Hi!' into a conversation bubble popping up from little Nugget's head. Megan left the room, telling them to take a few minutes if they needed, and Rachel used one more paper towel to wipe the rest of the gel off her skin. As soon as she stood to straighten her clothes, her mom wrapped a strong arm around her shoulders.

"Thank you, Rach. I can't believe I just got to see my little grandbaby! I'm thinking I should be something other than 'Grandma', you know, like a cool nickname or something."

"How about granny?" Rachel asked with a small smile. Her mom smacked Rachel's arm, and pursed her lips.

"What does your mother go by, Tate?"

He held open the door and then followed them into the brightly lit hallway. "She's just plain ol' grandma."

"Well," her mom said, and sniffed, her eyes still a little red around the edges. "I think I need something distinctive. Like GG or Nana or Glammy or something."

Rachel stopped, and her mom almost ran into her back. "Glammy?"

"I saw it on Real Housewifes of Atlanta. Is it too much?"

Rachel let out a sigh, and walked back out into the crowded waiting room.

21

WHILE NO ONE would accuse Rachel of being overly sentimental, there was one way in which she could proudly and unashamedly proclaim herself as just that.

Christmas. She freaking loved Christmas.

And since no one else in her family wanted the Glee Christmas Soundtrack (either volumes one OR two) blasting away at ear-numbing levels, she gladly slapped on her Bose headphones and immersed herself into her April 11 bride's binder, trying to nail down exactly which centerpiece options would fit into Danielle's healthy budget. With line items in front of her, and Lea Michele singing her hot little tush off, Rachel felt a happy sense of relaxation bleed through her.

So far, she was exceeding her own business plan at every point. Last week, she had to turn away a bride because her plate was perfectly, make her bank account do friggin cartwheels, full. It was successfully keeping her mind off her previous paranoid thought of Tate somehow trying to trick her into a relationship with him.

Pfft.

As if. Well, she'd had to firmly insist that she didn't need to be a part of his family Christmas get-togethers because that was blurring the lines just a bit for her. Even through their text exchange, she'd felt his disappointment like a slap across the face, and it made her feel all grinch-like.

Tate: I know you mentioned that Christmas morning is your big family tradition. Are you sure you couldn't spare a couple hours on Christmas Eve?

Rachel: I appreciate the invitation, but is that really the best idea? I don't want your parents getting the wrong idea about us.

She could practically hear the song echoing through her head.
You're a mean one, Mister Grinch.

Tate: They're aware of how we're doing this, I promise. I just thought it might be nice for you to be part of our family Christmas. Because you know that you're family now, right?

You really are a heel.
She rubbed a hand against the soft flannel of her dancing snowman pajama pants that barely stayed up, considering how low she was wearing them to accommodate her growing belly. The harder she pushed her palm against the fabric, the less she felt the pressure building in her chest.
You're as cuddly as a cactus.

Rachel: I know. I still think it's better that I stay home.

And then there was silence.
You're as charming as an eel, Mister Grinch.

Tate: Okay. Whatever you feel is best

Rachel shook her head, fast and hard, thinking about it now. A few days later still feeling like he'd stabbed her right in the flippin' heart. And even knowing that maybe she could have bent on this one thing, without any major repercussions, considering how much she loved that family, she just ... didn't. And there was no way she was going to examine the part of her that was screaming to not be so damn stubborn. Not now, at least.

Opening up a new page on her internet browser to compare price options for wedding favors, Rachel barely noticed the knock on her bedroom door.

"What?" she bellowed when the knocking got louder and louder and louder and didn't go away.

Kate poked her head in, making a dramatic sweep of the room before entering. "You gonna cut me if I come all the way in?"

"Nope," Rachel said, popping the 'p'. She pulled the headphones off her head. "The mess alone would make me vomit, not to mention the fact that it's Christmas Eve and that's just not very nice."

Kate plopped on the edge of Rachel's bed, and Rachel snatched away Danielle's binder as soon as Kate started flipping through it. Her sister rolled her eyes and turned the laptop so she could see the screen.

"Is there a purpose for this visit?"

"What are you working on?" Kate continued undeterred.

Rachel sighed, arching her back. "One of my April brides wants to hand out French macaroons as a wedding favor, and I'm doing some price comparisons on whether it's something I should do locally, or if there's a specialty bakery that could ship and still stay within budget."

"Well, that sounds boring," Kate said as she pushed from the bed. Rachel watched her from the corner of her eye, not missing how her little sister would peer at the baby stuff accumulating in the corner of her room, but not touch any of it. After a few webpages worth of silent snooping, Rachel finally snapped her laptop shut and leaned over to plug it back in to its spot on her nightstand. Kate stopped where she was in front of Rachel's closet, spinning in place and leaning against the white painted door. She wore the same pajamas that Rachel did, an annual gift from their parents that they were supposed to wear the following Christmas Eve and then throughout the morning of Christmas Day. Of course, Kate's hung nicely on her thin, not at all curved hips, and the bright blue long sleeved shirt was loose on her frame.

"Seriously, Kate, what's up?"

Kate shrugged one shoulder, clearly chewing on the inside of her cheek. "You're due in, what? Four months?"

Okay. This conversation needed to be marked in the calendar, as it was the first time Kate had actively sought out information about Rachel's pregnancy.

Rachel nodded. "Close. Early June, so a bit longer than that."

"Hmm. Cool."

"Yeah, I guess." Curiouser and curiouser. "Kate?"

Kate heaved a sigh. "Okay fine, Mom said I need to take a greater interest in your life. Apparently she and dad think I'm 'avoiding the baby', so then I told her I couldn't avoid something that wasn't even born yet, and then she burst into tears and asked me why you and I hate each other."

"Oh, good Lord. Seriously?" Rachel swung her legs to the side of her mattress, flexing her feet to restore some of the feeling that she'd lost in them from sitting on her bed. And what surprised her so much was that when she looked back up, Kate was twisting her fingers, and her face actually looked fairly ... tortured. Rachel schooled her face to keep from gawking. Her sister could be described as a lot of things, but emotionally tortured? Nuh-uh.

"It's not that I don't care," Kate said on a rush. She moved from the closet door and sat back down on the bed next to Rachel, causing them to sink towards each other a bit. The dark purple from her comforter looked practically garish in the gap that showed between their matching bright blue pajama pants. There was an even bigger space that spread in the silence.

But Rachel kept her lips firmly closed while Kate continued fidgeting. It was one way that they were similar, that oh-so-difficult job of putting normally pushed down thoughts and feelings into words. "Because, I'm like, excited? That you're having a baby and everything. I think it'll be cool to say that I'm an aunt. But ... I don't know ... I'm only twenty. I don't even know what major I should stick with, and you're over here popping out a kid and making all these big decisions that make our parents cry-"

"Hey, that's so not my fault."

"Doesn't make it less true." Yeesh. Fair enough. Rachel raised her eyebrows in concession, gesturing for Kate to continue. "I guess I just don't even know what to say that might help, ya know? Mom's cray cray about all this, that's nothing new, but at least that's something I'm used to. You about to become a mom? That's like a whole level of weirdness that I don't even know what I'm supposed to do with. So I guess it's just easier to not ask about anything. I don't hate your baby or anything. Or you."

The smile that spread on Rachel's face was unconscious, it barely even registered until Kate whacked her on the shoulder.

"Ow, what the hell was that for?"

"I'm glad you find my emotional ramblings so freaking funny, asshole."

"Oh, chill out. I'm smiling because you and I? We're pretty much the same in that way."

"Yeah?" Kate asked, turning sideways a bit, just enough that their knees touched. "Because the other day, I knew I was being stubborn, like really, over the top stubborn about something and even though I knew it, I still wouldn't give in. And I've kinda found myself doing that with you lately. I know I should ask, see if you need, like, emotional support or anything, but I just don't.

And even me feeling pissed at myself about it isn't enough to make me stop. Do you ever do that? I might not feel like such a bitch if you do."

Gah. What Rachel wanted to do was deny the hell out of *that* statement. Instead, she ran her thumb over the screen of her phone, still seeing her conversation with Tate all laid out. And right along with it was the nagging guilt that she hadn't been able to shake even for a second since she told him no. Even knowing that he had the best of intentions for inviting her. But she found herself nodding, not able to admit it out loud.

Instead of replying, Kate nodded in return. The sound of Rachel's music still came through the headphones that were lying on her bed, and the tinny, far-removed sound of *Oh Holy Night* filled the room. Without asking, Rachel knew that nothing was going on tonight. No big family dinner, no presents to be opened. Christmas Eve was typically Chinese takeout and *A Christmas Story* on TV. And here she sat, in pajamas, in her room, working. Something in her cracked, just a little.

"I'm a really, terribly, awful person." Except ... wait ... she just said that out loud. And the shock that registered on Kate's face is what told her that the thought hadn't stayed safely in her head like she'd planned on, it had come right on out, subconsciously and completely unfiltered.

"Well, I'm that way too, it doesn't make us terrible."

Rachel shook her head, standing off the bed and pacing the short distance of her room. There wasn't much space to walk around anymore. Any baby stuff that her mom purchased was slowly taking over the corner next to her dresser. Sure, she could've moved it to Tate's by now to make things easier, but she hadn't. Because she was a raging bitch who was avoiding him other than when she had a doctor appointment. She pushed a shaking hand into her hair and dug her nails into her scalp, needing that quick bite of pain to center her thoughts. And still,

Kate sat quietly on Rachel's bed, watching with a brow crinkled in clear confusion, and maybe a little concern.

"I, uh," Rachel started and then pivoted to face the wall, not even wanting to meet her sister's eyes. "The Steadmans always do their family Christmas on Christmas Eve, and Tate invited me, because he said I was part of the family now."

"Okaaaaaay."

"I said no," Rachel said on a rush. "And I had no reason to, other than I felt like I shouldn't, you know?"

Kate tilted her head. "You afraid you're going to defile him under the Christmas tree or something?"

"Kate."

"What?" Her sister shrugged unapologetically, then gestured somewhere towards Rachel's bump. "It's a justifiable concern." When Rachel just stared, Kate rolled her eyes. "Okay, fine. We're in serious mode. Listen, if the only reason you're not going is because you're doing the stubborn thing, then yeah, you're being stupid. Is that what you want me to say?"

Of course that was what she wanted Kate to say. Because that 'stubborn thing' was its own living, breathing, powerful entity that she'd battled against her entire life. And to hear someone else describe that knowledge, the willful decision to let the stubbornness win? It wasn't pretty. In fact, it went down like a bitter, chalky pill. Rachel let out a hard breath and turned to her closet, not even really seeing anything in front of her.

"Well?" she asked to Kate over her shoulder. "Are you going to help me find something to wear or not? I sure as hell can't go in these pajamas."

22

TATE STRETCHED his mouth in a smile, hoping it did a credible job of looking authentic. As much as he felt like retreating to his quiet, unoccupied house and brooding, he knew that being at his parents' house was a better idea. It was easier to get distracted here, with his five nephews whooping and hollering and making a general mess of every room that they stepped into.

"Rachel couldn't come?" his sister in law Jen asked, after giving him a tight hug. He tried to keep the sigh in, he really did, but obviously he failed given the pity that filled her bright green eyes. So he didn't even answer, just wished her a merry Christmas and moved into the kitchen after she squeezed his arm. His brothers and dad were helping the boys put together a race car track in the basement, and Casey was holed up in her old bedroom on one of her preciously few phone calls with Jake while he was deployed to Afghanistan.

"How's she feeling?" Jen said from behind him, clearly not taking his lack of answer as his intended code for 'let's not talk about Rachel right now'. "Has her morning sickness passed?"

Tate reached into the fridge and pulled out a beer. "Yeah, I think so. I mean, she threw up in my office once, but other than that she hasn't really mentioned it."

"Well, she must not have the nausea from hell like I did. Because even though you're not around her much, trust me, she'd tell you if she had it."

And didn't that casually stated sentence feel like a red hot poker got shoved into his eye. Would she? Tate wasn't so sure that Rachel would tell him if she was struggling with something like that.

Leaning back against the closed fridge, Tate watched Jen help his mom with something over by the sink.

"I don't know if she would."

Jen huffed out a laugh, sharing a smile with Tate's mom. "We've all met Rachel. One of my favorite traits of hers is that mouth that she's got on her. If the child that you implanted into her was causing nausea twenty-four-seven, then yes ... you would know. I'm pretty sure I called your brother every four letter word I could think of when I was pregnant with Mason."

"Yeah, I remember." He cringed when she whacked him across the shoulder.

"Listen, you men think it's so bad to deal with the hormonal pregnant lady, but if it were up to the men to carry the children? The human species would've died out long ago."

"The miracle of childbirth, huh?"

Jen nodded, wiping her hands on the towel draped over the oven handle. "It is, don't get me wrong. But if you're not one of those glowing pregnant women? Those forty weeks are an eternity. And I'm not even just talking about being nauseated, or puking up everything that isn't a saltine. The swelling of every part of your body that could hold water, the feeling that your body isn't your own anymore, and the exhaustion ..." she shook her head again, her eyes fixed someplace that was outside of the kitchen. His mom made a commiserating sound. "Let's just say if I hadn't had Michael around? I think I would've ended up just sleeping on the bathroom floor because I didn't think I had the strength to walk my puffy ass upstairs to our bed. There's a lot of wonderful things about being pregnant, but it's also really, really hard sometimes. I can't imagine doing it alone."

With every word, Tate felt a rock land heavier and heavier into his stomach. He *didn't* see Rachel all that often. Certainly not as much as he wanted to, but short of showing up at her parents' house, he didn't think there was much he could do about that. One of the boys yelled from the basement and Jen rolled her eyes, but hurried off to make sure no one was bleeding.

If his mom noticed him stay in the room after Jen walked out, she didn't say, just kept her back turned while she continued making the filling for the twice-baked potatoes they always had with their Christmas Eve meal. The air in the kitchen was about fifteen degrees warmer than any other room of the house, considering the double ovens had probably been working all day long. Tate sat at one of the stools at the large center island, even though there wasn't really space for him to even lean his elbows on.

Every inch of the light colored granite was filled with bowls and dishes and glasses in preparation for their meal. One of the Steadman rules for Christmas - at least one meal had to be taken with everyone sitting at the same table; no tv, no phones, nothing except food and the family.

"Well, if you're going to sit there sulking, at least come and make yourself useful," his mom said without turning around.

Tate smiled, and stood to walk around the island to where she was. She gestured to the bowl she had just finished using and Tate took it to the sink and started washing it. "Am I sulking?"

"Just a little," she said, and nudged him with an elbow. After she'd finished filling the scooped out potato skins and placing the large sheet into the upper oven, his mom turned to watch him. He set the clean bowl onto the drying rack next to the sink and faced her, crossing his arms across his chest.

"Just say it, Mom, whatever you're thinking."

She smiled and reached up to pat his cheek. "I wish she'd have come, too, but she's not your girlfriend, and she's not your wife. If she's not ready to jump in with both feet, that's okay. It's time to pull your head out of your ass and enjoy Christmas with your family."

Tate laughed, but rubbed at his heart. "Really, Mom, please don't hold back because you're afraid to hurt my feelings."

Her returning smile was small, and not apologetic in the least. "Set the table, oh middle son of mine. When Casey's off the phone with Jake, she can help."

There was a soft knock on the front door just as Tate set the stack of dinner plates on the dining room table.

"Can you grab that?" his mom called from the kitchen.

"You need me to make the rest of the meal while I'm at it?" Tate yelled back while he walked through the dining room to the front door. "Maybe shovel the driveway? Wrap the rest of the presents?"

He was grinning at the response that was shouted back at him when he pulled the door open. And then he just stared.

Rachel stood there under the brightness of the porch light, holding a small red and green gift bag, looking nervous and beautiful and well ... beautiful was the only other thing he could think of just then.

"Merry Christmas," she said and stepped forward so that the light was behind her now, making her hair look like it was about to go up in flames. "I hope it's okay that I'm just showing up like this."

Something. He knew he should be saying *something*, but everything was stuck in his throat that had mysteriously closed up. Thankfully, he had enough presence of mind to step back and let her come through the door. By the time he'd shut the door behind her, Rachel had pulled off her coat and was hanging it in the hallway closet. He wanted to ask her if she was sick, or if her feet were swollen, or if she'd thought about sleeping on the bathroom floor because she was too tired. Instead, Tate rubbed a hand across his mouth and kept staring like an idiot. The bright green of her sweater made her hair look even more vibrant, and it was tight enough across every single perfectly proportioned curve that he had no chance in hell of not looking at her in ways that were probably inappropriate. And she was there. Beyond whatever she'd chosen to wear, or if she was sick, she was *there*. That was more than enough to make him feel a tad bit out of control.

"Okay, you need to say something because I'm kind of freaking out over here and your stoic silence isn't exactly helping matters."

While he had the advantage that no one else had realized she was there yet, he moved on instinct and stepped next to her, setting one hand on her slightly curved belly. Her eyes closed and she turned towards him, covering his hand with one of hers, still cold from being outside. Wrapping his other arm around her shoulders, he pulled her into him and set his chin onto the crown of all that bright hair.

"Merry Christmas," he said quietly, her hair tickling his mouth. She smelled like cinnamon. "Thank you for coming."

They stood there, just like that for a few long, wonderful moments. He felt her release a shuddering breath, and it made him smile a little. He liked to think that he wasn't the only one who felt thrown off.

Stepping back just enough that he had to stop touching her, she gave him a one-sided smile. "Yeah well, just remember how generous you're feeling when I make you go clean off and start my car for me when I'm ready to leave."

"Rachel!" His mom cried as she came around the corner, wiping her hands on a towel. She wrapped Rachel in a tight hug. Pulling back, she cupped one side of Rachel's face and smiled. "Merry Christmas, sweetheart. I'm so glad you could make it."

"Thank you for having me," Rachel replied, eyes flicking back to Tate.

"You're family; you never need an invitation. Now, you help Tate finish setting the table, and I'll let the others know that we can get started now that everyone is here."

When he followed the two women back into the kitchen, there was nothing forced about the way that he smiled this time. Nobody had seemed surprised to see Rachel, even though Dylan sent him an incredibly inconspicuous wink when he saw her setting out silverware next to the plates that Tate had just finished setting down. Casey had squealed at an inhumane level, and practically flew across the kitchen to wrap Rachel in a giant hug. And it seemed almost impossible to wipe that smile off of his face over the next few hours. The sky had darkened completely, and the lights from the ten-foot Christmas tree in his parents' family room seemed brighter. The candles around the dining room put off more light than they had before. And throughout the evening, as his whole family piled onto couches and the floor to watch his nephews distribute the gifts, Tate felt about as content as he ever had before.

Of course, it would have been nice if instead sitting just a few inches away from him, Rachel would have been pressed up against his side, or maybe if he'd been allowed to rub her back and shoulders like he wanted. But still, she was *there*. And with every smile or laugh or teasing joke she threw at his nephews, Tate saw little glimpses of Rachel that he hadn't seen before. Her sweetness in helping Mason put together one of his new Lego sets. Her patience with Isaiah when he asked her a question about the baby, and her easy approval when he asked if he could feel when the baby was kicking. Her ability to snap Casey out of her post-Jake phone call pouting with a few easily spoken words.

The way his family loved her was so evident, and it felt good. Something else he'd been missing with Nat - he shook his head, stopping that thought. Instead of the comparisons, which were admittedly very easy to do, he just sat back on the couch and basked in the way it felt now. Rachel looked at the time on her phone, and Tate didn't miss how her brows creased slightly.

He nudged her lightly with his elbow. "Do you need to go?"

She looked around the room, and without following her gaze, Tate knew that nobody was really paying them any attention. "I probably should. It was starting to snow again when I got here, I don't want to wait too long and have to deal with bad roads."

"I can drive you, we'll get your car back to you sometime tomorrow."

"It's amazing," she said, looking thoughtful, "being pregnant hasn't hampered my ability to drive a car."

This time it was her turn to elbow him, and he laughed. "Alright, but I'm going to clean off your car. That's non-negotiable."

"And I have no intention of arguing with you about it. In fact, my keys are in the pocket of my coat, feel free to start it up while you're at it."

He stood, liking the way she was leaned up against the arm of the couch, feet tucked underneath a blanket. She had one hand underneath her belly, and every once in a while she would move it softly under the curve. He'd caught himself a few times from doing the same thing. He nodded at the bag by her feet.

"Don't forget your gifts."

She grinned, and leaned over to lift up the onesie that Jen and Michael's boys had given her. It was a light green color, almost impossibly small. And across the tiny chest area it read *You think I'm cool? You should meet my cousins.* "Yeah right. You think I came for you? I wanted the loot."

It didn't take him long to find her keys and clean off the couple inches of snow that had accumulated on the top of her car. The black paint was covered by snow, but he couldn't help but chuckle at the masculine lines of the vehicle. Soon he'd have to talk to her about it, see if she'd discovered yet that the low-slung muscle car wouldn't be the best choice for a car seat. Living in his house was one thing - he doubted she'd let him buy her a more appropriate SUV. Something with all-wheel drive and decent gas mileage. A few different options filtered through his head, thinking that maybe he could buy the car, casually mention that she could use it if she had to go somewhere with the baby. Leave her car for times that she was out by herself.

"Don't forget those side mirrors, Steadman," Rachel said from behind him, the crunch of the snow under her boots the only thing that had alerted him to her presence. The black collar of her coat was pulled up so that Rachel was covered to the chin, her cheeks showing a touch of pink from being inside the warm house. Tate opened the door to toss the scraper into her backseat, and then shut it again so that the car didn't fill with cold air. He rubbed his hands together and took the gift bags from her gloved hand so he could hand them to her after she'd settled into the driver's seat.

"So," he started, suddenly feeling nervous. He really, really hoped she didn't want to knee him the balls for asking. "Have you had any nausea?"

"Not for a few weeks, why?"

He scratched the back of his neck, feeling itchy at the suspicious look on her face. "I just ... if you're feeling sick or, you know, really tired, I want you to be able to tell me."

"So you can do what? Take it away for me with your gentle concern?" The small quirk of her lips betrayed her blatantly sarcastic statement, so he let out a small breath of relief.

"Are you sure you want to wait so long to move in with me?"

"What?" She looked fairly gob-smacked. And he certainly felt it. Ever since talking to Jen in the kitchen, he knew there wasn't much he could do for her the way things were now. And apparently this was what hovered at the back of his mind as a solution.

"Well," he said slowly, opening the car door again to set the bags down behind her seat, then closing it again. It was a stall tactic, plain and simple, and he really hoped she wasn't seeing right the hell through it. When he straightened again, and she was still staring at him like he'd just suggested they give each other matching tattoos, he decided to just lay it out there and pray it wasn't pushing her. "I want to be there for you, Rachel. Having you move into the house with me isn't just for the sake of the baby, it's for you, too. And right now, I feel like I can't do a whole lot for you, like help you when you're feeling sick or so tired that you want to sleep on the bathroom floor."

"*Why* would I sleep on the bathroom floor?"

He waved that off with an impatient hand gesture. "Sorry. Something Jen said earlier."

Understanding softened her eyes, just a little. "Was she spreading pregnancy horror stories before I got here?"

"Maybe."

"Believe me, if I had some magic sickness card to play where you'd wait on me hand and foot, I would so use it right now." He laughed and she smiled, a tacit agreement on the truth of that statement. "I'm okay, Tate. First trimester kinda kicked my ass, but I've felt a lot better the last few weeks. I promise, if I start puking again, you'll be the first person I call."

He moved aside so she could walk to the car. There was no part of him that wanted her to leave, and even though his ears were about to drop off from the cold, he would have stood out there all night just talking to her. "Even if you're feeling better, you could still move in earlier."

"I know," she said simply. The way the snow fell, in large, quiet flakes, made him feel like they'd just been stuck into a settling snow globe. "I ... I'll think about it."

Not a no. Not a kick in the balls. He could barely hold back the triumphant shout building up in his chest.

She turned to go, but stopped before opening the door, looking back at him. There was a different look in her eye than he'd ever seen. It wasn't heat, or anger, or confusion, and it wasn't determination. Those were variations that he could pinpoint easily in those hazel irises. This was peace, contentment. And he figured that it must be how he'd looked all evening with her sitting next to him. Rachel stepped from the door until she was right in front of him, and reached up to wipe some snow off of his dark blue sweater.

"Thank you for inviting me," she said, still cleaning the fluffy white flakes from his shoulders. He didn't dare move, because he wasn't exactly sure what this version of Rachel was doing.

"You're welcome. I'm really happy you came."

Searching his eyes for a few seconds, she pushed up on her tiptoes and placed her lips against his. They were soft and smooth, and she kept them pressed there on his for a long moment before he couldn't stop himself from reaching his arms around her, pressing back.

She pulled back, kept her eyes closed. "That was just a thank you, Tate. For knowing I needed this before I did."

He leaned his forehead down until it touched hers, resting one of his hands on her shoulder, then squeezed when he stepped back. The small smile she gave him barely moved her lips, but he felt it everywhere. It was strong and real, and it told him that she was happy.

And that was enough for him for tonight.

23

OH HOLY MOTHER of all things holy, her bladder was going to explode if she moved so much as an inch. Rachel groaned and squeezed her eyes shut even tighter. The bright sun streaming into her room practically singed through her eyelids. Taking stock of all her bits and pieces, Rachel decided that waking up when thirty weeks pregnant was vastly overrated.

Keeping those lids firmly clamped shut, she blindly threw her hand around on her end table until she felt the smooth screen of her phone. It felt disorienting, but her head was so fuzzy from sleep, from deciphering dream from reality from yum ... fantasy, that she needed some backup to bring herself into the present.

"Siri, I don't feel like opening my eyes. What time is it?"

"I'm sure you don't," Siri crooned in her soothingly annoying voice. "It's April first, and it's seven forty eight a.m."

Umm, huh? That wasn't right.

"Are you sure, Siri? I'm fairly certain it's December."

"No comment."

Rachel whipped into a sitting position, heart racing. What the effing eff? She rubbed the heel of her hand into her eye socket, clearing the last of her sleep from her mind. Then looked down at her massive stomach.

Thirty weeks.

It didn't seem possible, as she sat there, knowing that it was roughly fifty degrees outside already. Spring was pretty fantastic in Michigan, but that wasn't her issue. It was that last night, she'd dreamed ... again ... of that stupid kiss she'd given Tate on Christmas Eve.

Almost as if she concentrated hard enough, she could feel that bitter cold again, those wet, fluffy snowflakes that she'd swept off Tate's sweater. Sometimes, probably due to the flood of heaving, monstrously powerful hormones that raced through her every second of every day.

Every second of the last three months. And that's what seemed impossible.

But finally, everything crystallized into a sharp picture of reality.

Siri, that snooty bitch, was right. Again.

Rachel had stayed so flippin' busy there were some days she thought she might actually lose her mind, which must explain the time warp she was feeling like a nasty hangover at the moment. And shit, had she been busy.

Aside from the craziness of the holidays, she'd steadily maintained a roster of eight-ish brides. And with the help of Payton and Mackenzie, she'd pulled off three style shoots for her website, and pulled off some the most kick-ass amazing weddings she'd ever seen. Even a month later, she couldn't think about Dani's French inspired wedding with its shades of pink and ivory and gold and the perfect pink macaroon favors without getting a little choked up. The kick-ass-ness of that one had been off the *hook*.

Once winter had melted away, there was the insanity of registering and baby showers. Three of those, to be exact. And Casey had wormed her way into managing every single one, making them the most ridiculously well decorated baby showers that Rachel had ever seen. The party favors that the women went home with were actually enough for Rachel to contemplate hiring Casey. Seriously. Little tins of Rachel's favorite tea with a Casey-made tag that said *A baby is brewing.* Mini-pedicure sets in a mason jar. Gourmet popcorn tied up in a brown paper bag with another Casey-made tag that said *Rachel's about to pop!*

Seriously, that girl was born to be an event planner. If only Casey was able to part herself from her beloved wallpaper, Rachel just might have to offer her a job.

Once those were done, the days just kept going faster and faster and faster. And the biggest benefit to that was that it had been effortless to stay at a safe distance from Tate. Especially after that Christmas Eve at his parents' house, she couldn't untwist the thought inside her head that the 'safe distance' was for her safety, as much as for Tate. Because once she moved in ... there wouldn't be much that was safe. Or distant.

They texted a few days a week, saw each other at all of her appointments, and she'd started moving bits and pieces of her life over to his house, since they'd reached an acceptable compromise. Instead of waiting until those last few weeks before her due date, Rachel agreed to move in after her third trimester was underway. The smile he'd given her when she'd told him at a doctor's appointment had almost caused her to spontaneously orgasm. Seriously, hormones. And it was nice, being able to give herself time to settle in, and not have to do one giant move.

Casey had given her strict instructions that under no circumstance, even if her life depended on it, was Rachel to open the door into her bedroom or bathroom. And that really was no hardship. She'd literally been dumping bags and boxes in the hallway, taking Casey up on her offer to take care of everything. They'd had one conversation about the nursery, which Casey had also begged to decorate, and Rachel would be a filthy, dirty liar if she said she hadn't been hugely relieved that Casey had gushed over the furniture Rachel was going to buy. Something about modern simplicity or blah blah blah.

Whatever she wanted to call it was fine. And Rachel would have bought it even if Casey hadn't loved it, but with time rapidly slipping away between now and that pesky little due date, the furniture purchase was something that needed to be done soon and she didn't want to have to pretend to look for something different. Rachel hadn't even thought to ask Tate what he thought about the furniture, but because he'd been so invested in making sure she liked it, it felt fairly safe to assume that he'd just wave off his approval and show up when it was time for him to assemble it.

Assembling their child's furniture. Which was in the room across from hers. In the house that she'd be sharing with Tate. Those realities still managed to cause her heart to pound a little harder. Buying a few pieces of furniture probably wouldn't seem like that big of a deal to most people. Exciting sure, but not something so symbolic, as it was to her.

The first *real* way she was contributing since this whole thing started, besides housing the little nugget for forty loooooooooong weeks. This was her way of proving to Nugget that even though she didn't have to, she *wanted* to do something, to make all the hours she was working worth it, to put her stamp on whatever the new picture of their day-to-day life was going to be. It was all so foreign, to think like this, to think about what that new normal would be, once she walked through Tate's front door.

Truthfully, there wasn't even a single bit of this that was familiar, even though she'd lived with Marc. That was so different. First was the obvious, they'd been in a serious relationship for almost two years when he asked her to move in. And second, she hadn't been pregnant with his child. And third, well, that was becoming more and more obvious as she continued on with whatever this was with Tate.

Marc *never* did to her mental state what Tate could do with one teeny tiny look. It was one of the most disconcerting things she'd ever experienced. There wasn't any part of her that was fooled about her relationship with Marc. Rachel knew full well that there might be a comfort in that relationship that some people couldn't overlook, but it had soothed her. It made her feel like she wasn't destined to end up right where her parents were.

But now? She found herself standing on the front porch of Tate's, wait ... of her house, about to turn the key into the lock. Tate had given it to her a couple months ago, telling her that she could use it whenever she wanted. They really were in a good place, something that had been instigated by their Christmas truce. The kiss ... that might have been ill-advised, but he'd just been standing there, so handsome and so *good*, she just couldn't help herself. And it had shifted things, that small press of her lips against his. Like it had become something more powerful because of its simplicity. They seemed to understand each other now. He still wasn't pushing, that wasn't new, but the difference was that she didn't feel crazed because of it.

With a soft click to the right, Rachel pushed open the heavy front door, pulling the shiny silver key out of the lock and tossing her keys into her purse. The house was still, which wasn't a surprise because she'd asked Tate to let her officially move in by herself. She wanted to take it all in, walk through all the rooms, without worrying if she was reacting 'right' to everything she saw.

"Welcome home," she said, needing to hear something in all this space, and maybe needing to hear those specific words out loud. The lamps really did look amazing on the thick wood end tables that framed the deep brown L-shaped couch. Everything in the family room looked soft and warm and comfortable, masculine in the lines and colors, but with plush pillows and blankets and soft rugs to soften the edges. There'd been a large painting added on the wall next to the fireplace, a sepia toned photograph of a solitary tree in a snow-covered field in a heavy mahogany frame. Rachel dragged her hand along the back of the couch, pulling in a deep breath and catching just a hint of Tate along with it.

In the stillness of the room, the trill of her cell phone seemed particularly jarring. Pulling it from the inside pocket of her purse and rolled her eyes. Casey.

"No, Casey, I haven't looked at my room yet," she said by way of an answer.

"Well, you better get on it. I can't just hide in the warehouse for the next two hours waiting for you to call me and tell me how freaking awesome it looks." Then she hung up. Rachel smiled and tossed her purse onto the kitchen counter. There was a small piece of white paper tucked in between two bright red apples in the basket in the middle of the island. She leaned forward and plucked it out, shaking her head slightly as she read.

Quit wasting time looking in the kitchen. GO LOOK AT YOUR ROOM.
(Casey forced me to write this.)
-Tate
P.S. Welcome home. (She did not force me to write that.)

After taking a couple steps away, Rachel quickly pivoted and reached back to grab the note, not spending too much time questioning why she wanted to keep it. When she reached her door, she left her hand on the knob for second before she turned it and pushed the door open.

"Hooooooly crap," she breathed when she finally regained her breath. She was standing in what was unequivocally the most beautifully *her* room she'd ever seen. Ever.

The walls were covered with an almost decadent looking silver and cream wallpaper; the bed was covered with crisp white covers, which stood out against the tall, dark gray headboard that came up behind it. Past the foot of the bed, Casey had created a small sitting area with two white tufted chairs and a small light aqua table between them. In fact, everything was white and gray, except for that little table, a couple pillows on the bed and a tiny bud vase on one of her mirrored side tables, which all had that same shade of light bluish green. Everywhere she looked, she fell just a little bit more in love. The small covered bench in her closet that had a gray and white chevron fabric on it, the white lacquered frame on her dresser that held one of her sonogram pictures. It was all so clean, and crisp, and bright, and as damn near perfect as she'd ever seen.

The bathroom was more of the same; whites and grays and tiny pops of aqua. Rachel went to sink down on the gray bench that was at the foot of her bed when she saw the white bassinet on the far side of her bed. It was almost impossibly tiny, where her baby would sleep in just a couple months; the gray and white bedding that lined the slats was perfectly soft to her touch and, when she pushed, the whole thing rocked softly back and forth. The bridge of her nose started burning like a mother effer when she saw the tiny white envelope that was propped up on a plush white teddy bear. Her name was written on the envelope in Liz's flowing script.

Her finger trembled a little when she pulled the thick white card out of the envelope.

Rachel-
Casey and I could think of nothing better than to give your precious baby a safe place to sleep for those first, most important, weeks of life. We already love him or her so incredibly much, and it still feels like a tiny portion of how much we love you. Now stop trying not to cry and call Casey to tell her how amazing your room looks. (She made me write that.)
XOXO- Liz and Casey

Rachel gripped the card so hard she was surprised that it didn't rip in half from just the force of her emotions. Her friends never stopped surprising her, even after fifteen years, with how much love they showed her. She let out a slow breath, *feeling the overwhelming everything from the last hour ebb away just a bit.* Enough that she was able to leave her room in search of her phone. First she sent a text to Tate letting him know it was safe for him to come home. Without waiting for his reply, she called the library that Liz managed first.

"Thank you, thank you, thank you," Rachel said as soon as Liz's voice came up on the other line.

"You're so welcome," Liz replied, the smile evident in her voice. "Do you like it?"

"You know I do. I know I should probably be pissed at your extravagance," Rachel paused when Liz laughed. Then she smiled, pushing one hand against a foot or an elbow that was pushing back. "But, I'm pretty sure this kid is worth it."

"Most definitely. So did Casey weep in relief that you love your room?"

Rachel pulled a water bottle from the fridge. "I didn't call her yet."

"What? Why not?"

"Beeeeeeeecause I'm stubborn and everyone kept leaving me notes telling me to call Casey. Naturally, I did the opposite."

"For some reason, I'm not surprised in the slightest," Liz said. "But you should put the poor girl out of her misery, she's probably on the verge of a breakdown."

Rachel laughed, and they said their goodbyes. Unable to resist, she took another sweep of the room, loving absolutely every little detail she found. And when she went to pull up her call screen, the phone trilled in her hand. Casey.

"Oh, hey Case," Rachel said, very nonchalant.

"You are killing me!" Casey wailed. "If you hate it, and don't dare call me to tell me, I'll just ... I don't even know what I'll-"

"Oh geez Louise," Rachel interrupted. "I love it, and you know I couldn't do anything but love it considering your mad skills."

Casey exhaled heavily. "Really?"

"Shut up. You know it kicks ass. I seriously love every single inch of that room, but that bassinet is really amazing. Thank you, for all of it."

"No prob. K, I gotta go. I've been paged three times by my manager while I was waiting for you to call. Glad you love it. Muah!"

She tossed her phone on an end table, and fell back into the couch, still grinning. The trees in the backyard were starting to bud with leaves and the pops of bright blue sky flicked through the branches. Watching the easy movement of the trees, Rachel didn't hear the warning sounds of the garage door opening. It wasn't until the door through the kitchen clicked open that she knew Tate was there. Small, tight goosebumps pulled across her arms and the back of her neck when she heard him set his keys on the granite, the sound incredibly loud in the quiet house.

The cushion behind her head sunk in a bit when he placed his hands on it, and she tilted her head back to look at him. His smile was so wide, practically blinding her with the expanse of ridiculously straight, white teeth.

"Hi."

"How long have you been here?" Tate asked.

"About an hour. And yes, I called Casey to rave about my room."

His smile grew, which hadn't seemed possible a minute ago. "She killed it, didn't she?"

Rachel nodded, then rolled her head on her shoulders, feeling a slight ache from looking up at him. One of his hands slipped down to her shoulder, and he gently rubbed along the sore muscle. Oh hell yeah, a built in masseuse. It was a fleeting, buoyant thought, not tethered in reality. Because as soon as she felt all warm and relaxed, she started feeling warmer. And less relaxed. Because she kinda wanted to grab his hand and shove it down the front of her shirt.

Moving faster than she thought possible at thirty weeks pregnant, she pushed off the couch and turned to face him. His eyes read amusement, so she breathed out her relief. Awesome. Must not look like a raving psychopath during the first five minutes of sharing a roof with him.

"Umm, I'm going to go ... look at my room some more." She patently ignored the pleased little grin that pulled at his lips. Ass. He knew exactly what she'd been thinking. Well, maybe not *exactly*, because he'd most likely be chasing her down the hallway. So, just to be sure, she pushed the lock on her doorknob after she'd entered the Tate-free zone. And while those first few minutes weren't much, Rachel sagged against her closed door.

Day one. Sanity still intact. Thank the Lord.

24

IT FELT AMAZING TO HIM, how easily he and Rachel slid into a routine over the next couple weeks. They didn't always eat together, but at least four nights a week they did. She didn't relax much, which was something he hadn't known about her. It seemed to him that she was constantly working, always answering phone calls and texts to emotional brides, solving issues that he couldn't have imagined even if forced. Her laptop was an extension of her hand, and the way she'd tried to maneuver typing around her round belly had made him laugh. It earned him one hell of a glare, but it had been worth it. Sometimes she holed up in her office for a couple hours in the evening, and sometimes she spread everything out around her on the couch, with some HGTV show playing in the background, taking up bits of her attention. It was so different from his fairly structured days. He had a schedule that Maggie kept religiously organized. Very little surprised him while he was in the office, but now, he came home to something unexpected every single day.

And there was a rather large part of him that felt like he'd come out of his own skin with how happy that made him. During her first week at the house, he'd walked into the house to find

Rachel, Casey and Liz cuddled together on the couch, watching some Cameron Diaz movie, all three of them shaking with laughter. The sound had followed him downstairs, where he'd sat on the couch, just listening to them be so happy. It had quieted down a couple hours later, and Tate made his way up the stairs, hoping to pick over some of the food that had been left on the counter. The television screen was dark, but all the kitchen lights had still been left on. With a full plate, Tate walked around the edge of the couch and then stopped short when he looked down.

Rachel was sound asleep.

She had barely moved from where she sat earlier in the night, her head lay to the side, leaning against the back of the couch, and her legs stretched forward onto the coffee table, covered by the blanket that she'd unofficially claimed as her own. He set his plate down on one of the side tables, and crouched in front of her.

Her breathing stayed even when he said her name, and he brushed a hand down her arm, trying to rouse her.

Next, he laid his hand on her belly, feeling one spectacular roll underneath him. And still she slept. He said her name again, rubbing his hand back and forth slightly.

Nothing.

She didn't look terribly comfortable, and maybe it was selfish, but he didn't try to wake her again. Carefully, he put one arm underneath her knees, and the other behind her back, and lifted. She stiffened for just a second, then slumped against his chest while he walked her down the hallway. The warm puff of air from her exhalations hit him at the base of his throat, and he had to grit his teeth at that tiny intimacy. Her bedroom had been dark, so the only light that pushed into the room came from the hallway. He gently laid her down onto her bed, and she immediately settled herself on her pillow while he covered her with a blanket from one of her chairs.

He let out a heavy breath, staring at her curled up on her side.

With one finger, he reached out and pushed a strand of hair off her face, feeling a bit like a creeper when he felt down the line of her jaw. Like this, she looked so sweet, and it made him smile.

"Thank you," she whispered, right after he turned to leave her room. "That was a really long walk from the couch, and I just didn't feel like doing it."

"Liar," he whispered back when he faced her again. Her eyes were still closed but she was smiling. "Goodnight, Rachel."

"Goodnight," she said on a mumble and then went right back to sleep.

For obvious reasons, that had been his favorite night so far.

Another night, he actually left the office early and had every intention of making dinner for them, when he was greeted by the smell of lasagna and garlic bread upon walking into the house. Rachel was wearing an apron, tenting out from her pregnant belly, and it should have made her look ridiculous, but it didn't. And he probably should have been dismayed at the absolute disaster that she'd left the kitchen, but he wasn't. They'd cleaned up together, and only had one minor incident with dish bubbles ending up on the tip of her nose. She'd pretended not to be amused, but those eyes of hers, they practically glowed whenever she was happy.

And then there was the previous night, when he'd walked in to find every single inch of the kitchen counter had been covered in tiny white paper bags filled with little chocolates. Rachel had been in the middle of tying thin green ribbons around each one.

"Need any help?" he asked, and before the words had cleared his lips, she'd chucked a roll of ribbon at his chest.

"Yes. We have two hundred and thirty bags to tie, now get your ass to work."

And truthfully, it wasn't the fact that he didn't know what he'd find every day that surprised him. It was how much he loved it. It was another one of those little things that Rachel seemed to bring out in him. Or maybe that he was allowing to come out in himself.

"Don't worry about a thing, okay? I'll make sure that the deejay sticks with your exact set list." Rachel lifted one of her legs, flexing her foot forward and wiggling her toes a few times, then dropping it back to the floor. Her mouth was flat, like she was mad, but her tone stayed perfectly pleasant. "No, he won't play any Miley Cyrus. Trust me, my ear drums pretty much demand it too. Yup. You just enjoy your week, I'll take care of everything else."

From where he sat on the opposite end of the couch, he grinned at the obvious relief Rachel expressed when hanging up the phone.

"Tough one?"

Rachel lifted her eyebrows briefly in concession. "I don't know if tough is the right word, she just stresses about things she doesn't need to. I think she needs to get laid."

Tate choked on the sip of water he'd just swallowed.

"What?" Rachel asked. "She does."

Again she pushed her foot up and stretched her toes.

"Do your feet hurt?"

She snorted. "Always. No, I'm trying to decide if I should repaint my toenails before this wedding on Saturday. But it's just a shit ton of effort right now, to reach those bad boys."

"I'll do it." The words just came out. And the shocked look on Rachel's face probably matched his.

"You want to paint my toenails for me?"

It wasn't that he'd actively avoided touching her the last couple weeks, but he figured that if there was any body part he could touch without feeling like he would lose control, it was her slightly puffy feet. So he nodded.

"If you need them painted, I'm your guy."

"Uh-huh." She slid a look over at him. After a few second of scrolling through her phone, she looked at him again. "Are you serious?"

There wasn't much he could do for her at this point, and he just wanted to fix everything. To take care of everything for her. So yeah. He was serious. Down to the marrow of his bones serious that if painting her toenails was the most helpful thing he could do for her, he'd do it every day. Lose his man card in the process, absolutely, but he'd still do it.

Instead of answering like that though, he just lifted a shoulder, keeping his focus on the screen of his laptop in front of him. "Sure. Shouldn't be too hard."

She continued to study him, and the skin on the side of his face almost prickled from it. When she slowly stood and walked down the hallway, he let out a heavy breath, not at all sure why he suddenly felt like he'd just set himself up for a huge test. And failure was not an option here. Because failure meant Rachel would run so far and so fast that he'd never catch her. Not in the way he wanted to.

While she was a surprisingly easy person to live with, considering the pregnant mood swings, she still carried herself with a touch of wariness around him. He could see it in her eyes, sometimes more than others. But whenever they touched, it was brighter, sharper, like a vivid armor she kept around herself. After it would flash around her, she'd retreat to her room or her office. And he let her, knowing that this was exactly what Dylan had been talking about. Tate wasn't going to push her, not yet. He'd just keep doing what he could for her, taking these opportunities when they presented themselves.

A small bottle of light pink nail polish appeared next to him, and he glanced up at Rachel, taking it from her outstretched hand. The color was soft and feminine, which surprised him, but he liked it. He flipped the small bottle over and looked at the name. Hearts and Tarts. Definitely fit her.

Rachel had settled herself back on the couch, and tossed a towel at him.

"What's that for?" he asked as he pulled a footrest from the deep reading chair next to the slider, placing it so that he would face Rachel.

"Well, unless you don't care about possibly getting pink nail polish on the carpet or your clothes, feel free to not use it."

Tate laughed. "Oh ye of little faith. Now I have to go towel-free just to prove you wrong."

They were both quiet when he looked at her, reaching down to lift her right foot, placing it on his knee that he'd lowered so she wasn't uncomfortable. She had small feet, even though they were a little swollen-looking, and he went about the task of moving the small brush back and forth, back and forth until he reached her big toe. Rachel hadn't spoken a word, and he felt her gaze on the top of his head like a laser beam. He wrapped one hand around the top of her foot so he could shift it at a better angle to paint her big toe, and he let his fingers drift across the soft skin, quite purposefully, just to see if she'd say anything, or maybe threaten to kick him in the head.

She didn't. She was completely and eerily still. Tate set the finished foot back onto the floor, and picked up her left foot. This time he moved slower, making sure he held her foot in place this time, not because he needed to. Because he damn well wanted to. Tate wasn't a foot guy, but at the moment, he had to pretend he was anchored in place, so that he wouldn't lean forward and kiss each toe. It was a slightly disturbing impulse, and he almost let out a hysterical laugh.

Man card, officially gone.

When Rachel slowly pulled her foot back, Tate realized that he was finished, but he kept his grip on her.

He shook his head, then stood to help her up, offering her both hands. It took more of an effort for her these days, to get up from the low-slung couch. He could see a difference in the two short weeks she'd been living there. Normally she waved him off, but this time she barely hesitated before putting her hands into his. Her fingers were cool compared to his, but strong as they wrapped around his hand. He stepped back, pulling her up easily.

She still hadn't said a word since he'd sat down in front of her, but instead of making him nervous, it made him feel like he'd breached a great, hulking wall to get to her.

Her head was tipped down, looking at her feet, and when she looked back up at him, he was expecting a smile, but she didn't give him one. Her look was searching, and he realized that she was still holding onto him.

Don't kiss her, don't kiss her, don't kiss her. He chanted it through his head, screaming it at the impulse that charged through him to do just that. Her chin tilted up, just a scant inch, and his heart thundered until he was sure she could hear it.

Don't kiss her. Don't. Kiss her. Kiss her. Kiss her.

When her lips parted, he felt the chant change in his head. But the second he dipped his head, she yanked herself back and almost fell into the couch again. Tate reached out and grabbed her elbow to steady her, but she all but ripped her arm out of his grasp.

"Rachel," he started, feeling like an absolute ass for doing exactly what he knew he shouldn't.

"It's fine, I just ... I have to go ... go do something."

While she hustled down the hallway to her room, or *sanctuary* as he was starting to think of it, he sank down onto the footstool. He dropped his head into his hands, scrubbing them harshly down his face.

The selfish way he'd handled every second of that made him feel like he was swallowing a pine cone. He had to figure out a way that he could help, could be there for her, could fix things, without making her run.

While he listened to the sounds of her opening and closing drawers in her room, determination filled him.

He knew exactly what he could do.

25

"SON OF A MOTHERF-" TATE bit off the end of that particular sentence, grinding his teeth together and breathing slowly. He could do this. He had to do this. He was a lawyer, for crying out loud. He should be able to put together three pieces of furniture by himself. But the instructions might as well have been written up in Chinese for all the sense they made. Yeah, he'd pitched those suckers across the room after he'd mangled the changing table together.

But this crib, he was seriously considering shoving his foot through the wall just to release the thrumming of anger he felt for this inanimate object. Gripping one of the main posts, he counted to twenty, and then looked back down at the pile.

Rachel better appreciate this. Because after waiting the two hours after she'd gone into her room for the night, Tate had sneaked back upstairs and started the shockingly hard task of unpacking boxes and assembling a crib and dresser without making too much noise, in the middle of the night when he should be sleeping, considering what his next few days of work were like. But he couldn't risk it, her walking into that room, and seeing boxes laying everywhere.

Nope, it had to be done tonight. They'd danced around each other for the last ten days since he almost kissed her, being almost painfully polite to each other. Definitely no more toenail painting. But maybe this gesture could break them past it. No, it *had to*, for his own sanity.

When he'd called Pottery Barn to order the crib and dresser he'd seen in the store, there had been a little whisper of a voice that made him pause, that he should have at least asked Casey what she thought, but since he already had the woman on the line, and she'd been so accommodating in helping him set up a very specific delivery time when he'd explained what he was doing. So he'd barreled ahead, and now he was cursing himself with words that hadn't passed his lips in *years*.

It would be worth it in the end, that much he knew. The furniture was stark white, which he figured was a good choice for going with whatever decor Rachel and Casey decided on. Or in all honesty, what Casey decided on. And the front and sides were the typical slats, but the back of the crib arched up in a beautiful sleigh design. In addition, he'd bought the matching six-drawer dresser. They were both so solid looking, a little old fashioned in design. Expensive as hell too, but beautiful nonetheless. Just thinking about the finished product renewed him into a more calm state of mind. He turned his wrist so he could see his watch.

1:36 am. He'd probably want to slit his own throat at the office in a few short hours.

"Alright, let's try this again" he said, and crouched down onto the floor, smoothing out the crumpled instructions.

About two hours later, he stumbled out of the room and face-planted onto the couch, sinking into sleep with a slight smile on his face that he'd successfully conquered the furniture beast for his fair lady.

"What the hell are you doing out here?" Rachel said from somewhere above him, jarring him awake. Tate rubbed at his face, and squinted up at where she stood next to the couch, gripping her coffee mug in both hands. She was still wearing her pajamas, which he'd learned were probably just meant to be an instrument of torture for him, the few times he'd seen her in them. Small black cotton shorts stopped just beneath the curve of her bottom, and the thin-strapped black tank top she wore was tight. Tight *everywhere*. And even though she slept with a bright pink sports bra underneath it, the swells of her breasts didn't want to be contained into anything these days. The brightness of the bra she wore, her wild, sleep-mussed hair, and her greenish-brown eyes were the only pops of color among her pale skin and the black clothes.

He wanted to eat her alive.

Wait. She'd asked him a question.

"Uhh, I slept out here."

Her face quite clearly read *No shit, Sherlock*."I saw you go downstairs though, right before I went to bed."

"Yeah, I had to come back up here to do ... something." He sat up and scratched the top of his head. "Look, let me grab some coffee and then I have something to show you."

"Same something you came back upstairs for?"

He hummed in agreement, still trying to wake up fully after the abbreviated night of sleep. Suddenly he was nervous. Really, really nervous to show her the room.

"Actually, I can have my coffee later. I'll show you now." And he took off down the hallway, not even really hearing if she immediately followed. He pushed open the door that he'd closed last night, and stood just outside of it, waiting for her. His traitorous heart was beating frantically, like it was facing a guillotine instead of a pregnant woman about to look at some furniture.

Rachel came to a stop outside the nursery door and just stopped. Just stared. Tate searched her face and it was the surprise that he saw only appeared briefly, in the widening of her eyes, and the dropping of her jaw. Then confusion, in the drawing in of her brows. She briefly shook her head, just a tiny little movement. And then her face paled, almost impossibly, considering her skin was such a light shade of ivory to begin with, but it paled anyway.

"What is this?" she asked, her voice low and hushed. It sounded dangerous, the way she said that.

Officially not the reaction he wanted, which involved a bright, wide smile and undying gratitude that was shown in the form of a long, lingering hug and some gushing excitement.

"Well," he fought to keep his tone light, "I bought and assembled nursery furniture for you. One less thing for you to worry about."

"And you didn't think you should ask me before you did this?" She practically growled that last word, and his heartbeat slowed and slowed until he wasn't sure it was going to keep going. She wasn't just surprised.

She finally looked over at him, just a short, loaded glance. Oh no, Rachel was pissed.

Tate nodded slowly, striving for calm among the explosions of disappointment and anger that pushed against him. This felt so familiar, and he knew why, because this was *always* her reaction. And this always seemed to be his. "Yeah, I probably should have asked if you liked this style."

They were both still standing just outside the door, and Tate motioned for her to go in. Only, instead of moving, Rachel planted her feet and propped clenched fists on her hips. Like she was preparing for battle.

"It's not just about that."

"Okay," he conceded. "I didn't want to bring it up, because I figured you wouldn't want to, but yes, I felt like I kept pushing where you didn't want me, forcing you to back away. I thought this would be a nice gesture, to fix it."

"To fix it."

"Yes, I almost kissed you, and it freaked you out." He felt a little frantic now, at the blank look on her face. "I wanted to fix it."

She shook her head a few times, and then her eyelids fell shut, like she couldn't bear to keep them open. She pushed a hand through her tangled hair and then opened her eyes to stare at him. "It must be hard for you, Tate."

"What must be?"

"To be the savior of the world, swooping in whenever some helpless peon needs you."

"Excuse me?" he asked incredulously. Yup, that short fuse of anger was good and lit, simmering and bubbling and boiling under his skin, just waiting for her to rip the lid off.

"Unbelievable. You really don't see it, do you?"

He spread his hands. "I'm just trying to do something *nice* for you, so you'll have to tell me what this is about. Because what I see right now is that I did something that needed to be done. Something that was my responsibility to begin with, and all I did was take care of it."

The color that had fled her face was back, a bright flush of color in her cheeks. It was the color of suppressed anger. Any chance he had to be calm snapped like a twig at her stubborn silence, especially after she started speaking.

"And that was somehow your cross to bear, huh? Had to do the 'right thing', had to fix the problem, and you *had* to do it without communicating with me first?"

"Even though that's a monumentally insulting statement, I'm going to choose to ignore it for the time being." He dug his fingers into his throbbing temple. "You're pissed because I didn't ask you first? Or because you didn't get to pick it out? Because I'm really trying to figure out the problem here."

She tilted her chin up, so defiant in her stubbornness. It *used* to be a trait he liked. Right then though? Nope. He sure as hell didn't. All he could do right then was just try to keep his balance, considering they'd spun so quickly into a direction he was never anticipating.

"This is not about me being able to pick out furniture,

although you are absolutely right that that's not what I would have chosen. This is about you constantly making unilateral decisions about things that involve both of us." She stepped closer to him, her chest heaving and her eyes on fire. "Did it ever occur to you that I might want to be financially involved in making such a major purchase for our baby? In fact, I remember *telling* you that I wanted to help, and you brushed me off. Do you remember any of this? That maybe, just maybe, I have a shit ton of money saved up right now because my business is doing really well, because I have lived rent free for the past year, and because, in case you've forgotten, this is *my child too*."

"In case I've forgotten," he repeated slowly. He felt so blindsided it was almost ridiculous. Because even though he was good and swept up in the tide of anger pulling them both along, she was right, he'd never once thought that she might want to buy something like that. And that pricked his pride *just enough* for him to not admit that she was right. "Is that supposed to be a joke? We live together. I bought this house so we could do this together, and you ask if I've forgotten this is your child too?"

"Tate, you are not the sole provider in this relationship. Being able to do this was *important* to me. I'm not your wife, I'm not even your girlfriend. I moved in here because it made sense. But that doesn't mean you get to steamroll all over me whenever the hell you feel like it."

He laughed, harsh and cold. She looked a little shocked at the sound. "So because I try to do something nice, I'm steamrolling? Well, I'll certainly remember that for future reference."

From the movement of her jaw, it looked like she was practically gnawing on her tongue to keep from saying something, and that sparked a tiny thread of thought in his head. He laughed again, this time softer, more disbelieving. "You know, I never thought you and Natalie had anything in common, but I see it now."

"Excuse me?" Her eyebrows shot up, along with her volume.

"Oh yeah. I had to keep my skills as a mind reader fairly sharp during my time with Natalie. Good thing too, considering I now have to be one with you."

"What are you *talking* about?"

"You didn't tell me either."

"I didn't tell you what?" she snapped out, not backing down an inch.

"You didn't tell me that you *wanted* to buy the furniture. You didn't tell me that you had something picked out. How the hell do you get to be mad at me for doing exactly what you had planned all along?"

She sucked in a breath, and he could hear it shake as it filled her lungs. "Don't do that. Don't you dare do that to me."

He threw up his hands. "Do *what*?"

"Don't you *dare* be all rational when I'm in the middle of a really good pregnancy rage, okay? It's not fair, because I cannot just make myself be calm."

She was practically shaking, and even though the words could've been humorous, she was incredibly serious.

"That's right." He nodded his head. "Because we do everything on your terms, don't we? Because *nobody* is allowed to push Rachel, to call you out on all the bullshit that you throw around. You want equality in how we do things? But only when I'm the one who has to clear decisions with you, isn't that right?"

"No, I ..."

"No? Because that's what it sounds like to me. You? You are a hypocrite, Rachel. And that's someone I never thought you'd be."

Her jaw set, but she still tipped her chin up just enough to raise his hackles. She still refused to back down.

"Do you need me to say you're right, that I should have said something about the crib? Will that make you feel better right now? Fine. Tate, you were right. I was wrong."

"Wow, hypocritical and patronizing ... that's an impressive combination."

The look in her eyes changed when he said that, and an angry quiet fell between them. There was a vague sensation that this is what happened when both sides of a gunfight needed to reload their weapons, the next wound inflicted by whoever could draw first.

She shifted on her feet, and he had a fleeting desire to ask if she needed to sit down, but he knocked that thought right on its ass. She was a big girl, if she wanted to sit, she could figure it out on her own.

He speared his hand into his hair and tightened his grip to the point that his scalp burned. That sharp tug of pain was just enough to pull back the reins on his anger. But damn it, there was still a roaring part of him that wanted to be one to walk away, *finally* be the one to walk away from her. Because he never was. But he pushed against that, knowing that this was too important for him to even consider it.

"You're right," she said quietly. "I should have told you. And because I didn't, and because you didn't-" she waved a hand between them. "We have this now ... these ugly words."

It hurt, to hear her say that, and know how true it was. Such a stupidly simple miscommunication. And worse than that, Tate was so disappointed in himself. It was so hollow, hearing her say that he was right with such sincerity.

"Rachel-"

"No, don't. We were both wrong." She was already backing away, her eyes studiously avoiding his. "And it's beautiful furniture, thank you. Casey will have no problem making that work. So, you have nothing to apologize for. Nothing. This kind of *insanity* is what I don't want, what I can't have. Not for me, and not for our baby. So we'll agree not to rehash this, and not bypass each other with big decisions anymore."

Tate tilted his head, watching her retreat down the hallway, back to her room. There was something more behind that, behind the way she spit out the word insanity. Because while they both overreacted, he certainly wouldn't go so far as calling it that.

He started after her, and she turned around to face him where she stood just inside her bedroom door.

"No, Tate."

"No?" He drew up, feeling those two words like a hot knife, sliding right in between his ribs.

She looked exhausted when she shook her head, then determined as she walked in and started shutting her door. "I *can't*, okay? I can't do this with you."

Something big had just slammed down between them, and buried underneath it was any hope he'd kept alive for them to build their romantic relationship. When it came to him and Rachel, there was an overwhelming sense of being on a merry-go-round. Every time he turned around, he'd get quick glimpses of something amazing and beautiful and precious, the kind of thing he wanted for forever, the way he was quickly seeing forever with *her*. But it was gone as fast as he could turn his head to look at it again, swallowed up by flashing lights and sounds around him. But this time, Tate had the feeling that he wouldn't get another look on his next trip.

It nagged at him, what she'd said, for the rest of the day. And despite the fact that he'd barely had time to inhale a quick sandwich at his desk, it stayed right there, those last couple things she'd said with so much feeling. Maybe it was just the fact that they'd actually fought that was making him unable to let them go, or that she hadn't let him apologize. Like that was far less important to her than just getting the conversation over with. Deep down though, he knew it was more.

Well past normal office hours, somewhere around seven thirty, Tate eased open the garage door and tried to make his entrance as quiet as possible. He'd seen Madelyn Hennessy's car in the driveway when he'd pulled in, and while it wasn't the first time she'd been over, it was the first time that Rachel hadn't given him a heads up. He'd told her every time that she didn't need to let him know when she had people come over, but he had the distinct sense that this time it wasn't because she was actually listening to him. She was probably still very ready to ignore him.

He'd hoped to sneak downstairs, but from the mudroom off the kitchen, he could hear the murmur of their voices in the family room. Before he walked into the room, he stopped, not to eavesdrop precisely. Just to make sure he wasn't walking in where he wasn't welcome. And if he managed to gain insight into that otherworldly creature he happened to live with, well, that would be an added bonus.

"I just didn't know this would be so hard, honey." There were sniffles and the wavering tone of voice that only accompanied a crying woman. Not Rachel though, Tate was fairly certain that Rachel would have surgically removed her tear ducts if possible. "I feel like you don't need me anymore now that you've moved out. And when I told your dad how I felt, he said I was certifiable. Me! I'm the sanest person I know."

"Uh-huh."

He'd been about to walk back out the door, sit on the porch until she left, but something held him there.

"You don't think I'm sane? Are you siding with your father? You're always on his side."

"Mom." Rachel's voice sounded muffled, like she was covering her face with something.

"No, tell me. I can take it."

Rachel sighed. "I don't think you're insane, Mom. But, I do think you thrive on drama. And that's, I don't know ... exhausting after a while. And I can't have that twenty-four-seven. Not at this point in my life."

"I exhaust you?"

There was a stretch of silence when Rachel didn't immediately answer and Tate didn't even dare breathe in case they heard him.

"Well, to be fair, getting up to pee exhausts me right now, but yeah, you do. And I just ... I need a peaceful place right now. Does that make sense? For me and the baby? I kinda feel like I need a nap if I spend too much time with you and Dad. I don't see how you two don't get tired of all that back and forth after thirty some years."

Tate raised his eyebrows at that one, feeling the picture getting clearer in his head, the pixels around the edge starting to tighten up into something recognizable.

"Huh. He does love it when we bicker. Trust me, *loves it.*"

"Eww. Seriously, just ... stop talking." Madelyn laughed, and Tate smiled at the sound, the remnants of her tears making the sound watery. "Look, I'm glad you miss me and all, but I've been here for almost a month, Mom. And I still see you, and I will still need you when the baby is born, okay?"

"Okay." More sniffling. "Can I come over every day after work?"

"Uh no."

Sniffle. Sniffle. Then a heavy exhale. "Well, you just take some time to think about it. I brought you some more clothes. I went into that other big baby supply store, it's like the uptight, snotty version of Babies R' Us and I felt judged. I don't think I'll *ever* go there again, but they have some seriously cute shit."

"Bitches. Let's boycott." They laughed and then Tate recognized the groan that Rachel always let out when she stood from the couch. He straightened from where he had been leaning up against the wall, listening while Madelyn gathered her things and hugged Rachel goodbye. After the door had clicked shut, Tate rounded the corner into the kitchen. From where he'd stopped next to the center island, he watched silently as Rachel stood staring at the door.

"That's why, isn't it?" he asked, feeling a little guilty when she started, pushing a hand onto her chest when she saw him standing there.

She let out a short puff of air, then narrowed her eyes at him. "That's why *what*?"

"Why you work to stay so contained. Because she's not. Is that it?"

"You have no right to judge my mother."

Lifting his hands, he shook his head. "I'm not. I happen to think your parents are great, but I would imagine that it might have been overwhelming growing up. And would probably have a major impact on how you've learned to react to things."

Given the size of her belly, she couldn't cross her arms like she wanted to, and Tate worked to not laugh when she finally gave up and laid them on top. "And what's the point to this psychoanalysis?"

Tapping one finger on the granite, he watched her struggle to keep the emotions from her face. But the bits that he saw looked an awful lot like fear.

"Just trying to figure you out, and this actually makes sense. I'm surprised that no one's called you on this before."

Rachel huffed. "And how would you know that?"

"Because you look terrified right now." Even though he wanted to walk to her, he stayed right where he was, wanting to keep this honest little space alive between them. But she laughed, and he felt it crack a little at the edges.

"So what if it is the reason that I am this way? Some people don't like to hit every tick mark on the crazy scale during the course of one day."

"Come on, Rachel. You know there's a happy medium between crazy and completely shutting down every time something takes a turn you're not expecting."

She shrugged, but looked at the floor. "Maybe so. But you can't blame me for wanting our child to grow up with the kind of emotional stability that I sure as hell never experienced."

Tate pinched the bridge of his nose, wanting to scream at her, just to get her to show him that she could see how important this was. "You're just ... you risk missing out on a lot, if this is the way you choose to do things. And that makes me sad for you. For us."

"Why?"

He dropped his hand and stared at her. "You don't know why that would make me sad?"

Again, she shrugged.

"Rachel," he shook his head, unwilling to tear his eyes away from her, "since the night I followed you to that bar, I have been trying to figure out what to say or do to get you to give me a chance. I've given you space, I've pushed when I probably shouldn't have, but if this," he held up a hand and then rubbed the back of his neck with it, "if this is what I'm competing against? Then I was doomed from the start. And it's not about the baby, this is about you and me. For too many years, I did what I thought I was *supposed* to, did the safe thing. But I'm not going to settle for that anymore, because the only time in my life that I have felt like I am being set on fire from the inside out is when I'm with you. And that is what I want, forever. But if what you want most out of life is safe and predictable and emotionally complacent ... then you're right, you should keep running from whatever it is that will not go away between us."

Rachel nodded slowly, watching him. If he hadn't seen her jaw tense during his little 'heart vomiting out of his chest' moment, he'd have thought her completely unmoved by what he said. But her eyes looked so serious, and something in them actually made him have a hard time holding her stare, but he did hold it. There was a pounding, an incessant beat through his head, through his bones and through his veins that told him that if he looked away, if he didn't let her see every ounce of earnestness inside him, then she might never open up to him.

"You might be right. About all of it," she finally said. "But the thing is, this is one more thing about me that's not your problem to fix."

26

PINTEREST WAS where Rachel spent the majority of her time, when it came to work. Truly, a greater invention for an event planner had never been created. But instead of looking up ideas for the rustic/country themed wedding she was working on, she found herself skimming through quotes on positivity, thinking that maybe something could touch the depths of her singed soul after the verbal smack-down that Tate had given her.

-Leave a little sparkle wherever you go.

Uh huh. She felt all sorts of sparkly lately.

-Some days you just have to create your own sunshine.

That person could kiss her ass.

-She believed she could, so she did.

Insert eye roll.

Dragging her thumb down the screen, another quote caught her eye.

Comparison is the thief of joy- Theodore Roosevelt.

She clicked on it, staring at the bold white lettering on the chalkboard background. Something about that resonated, sending little ripples of recognition as she read it over and over and over.

Isn't that what she'd been doing? Comparing everything. Comparing Tate to Marc. Comparing herself to her mother. And it definitely felt like she'd been robbed of joy as of late. It wasn't like she was unhappy, per se, but ever since Tate had stared across that room at her, about knocking the breath from her with the words he'd spoken, she'd felt ... off.

For the last two weeks, she could pretty much count on two hands the amount of words they'd exchanged. But that one sentence, it echoed, every single time she looked in the mirror, looked down at her gently moving stomach, at whatever was on the screen in front of her.

Because the only time in my life that I have felt like I am being set on fire from the inside out is when I'm with you.

"Shit," she said on an exhale. No matter what she did, those words, oh those words just wouldn't go away. She could easily say that the last twenty days had included more introspection than she'd had in her previous twenty eight years. Combined. It said something - that motherhood was only a handful of days away - and it was *not* the thing consuming her thoughts.

What she'd wanted to do when he'd said that was a terrifying combination of rip his shirt off and just hug the shit out of him. Just let him hold her. Tell him that she was one tiny shove from falling in love with him. And that tiny shove had been the glaring clarity in which he saw her. She'd suspected that Liz and Casey knew exactly why she was the way she was, but they just loved her enough not to shove her face in it. Clearly, Tate didn't have that issue.

Oh no. He'd stripped her all the way down, saying to her what she'd never actually wanted to say to herself. And he'd still looked her in the eyes, so intensely that she'd *felt* it, and told her that he burned for her. A sharp jab made her stomach push to one side, and Rachel smiled, pushing a hand against the limb in question. An elbow maybe? It disappeared back to a more comfortable position after she pressed against it, and she could breathe more easily again.

"Nugget, what am I supposed to do about your dad?" she whispered, like if she spoke any louder, she'd actually get an answer. "I'm pretty sure I don't deserve him, especially not with how I've acted, but ..." she breathed in and out a few times, letting her heartbeat steady a bit. "But ... I want to fix this. And I don't know how."

There. Not so hard to admit.

Her phone rang, and Rachel smiled when she saw Peyton's name on the screen.

Not that she wanted to play favorites with her interns. But Peyton was totally her favorite.

"Hey, Peyton. What's up?"

"Umm, we have a problem."

"On a scale of one to ten ..."

"Eh, probably a seven."

Rachel pushed herself into a sitting position, rubbing her forehead. "Hit me."

"I was working on the labels for the programs for Saturday's wedding. And I sent Michaela a picture, because I thought they turned out great. And, well, she said the color and the font are wrong. And the paper. And I'm kinda freaking out."

Pfft. That wasn't even a four.

"Okay, let me call Michaela. This isn't the first time she's randomly decided to change her mind without telling anyone. Let's meet in two hours at the Panera on Canal. They have the upstairs room we could use. I'll see if I can get her to come with me. Only bring one finished program, we'll have a better chance of convincing her they'll still work if she's not overwhelmed by seeing three hundred of them."

"Thank you," Peyton said, sounding relieved.

It was a good distraction for the next few hours, allowing her a little vacation out of her own head. She and Peyton successfully soothed Michaela, who decided that she was a genius for picking those options in the first place.

"So," Peyton said as they walked out to their cars. "When's your due date again?"

"Twenty-two days. Not that I'm counting. I swear, this kid moves even a centimeter and I have to seriously concentrate on not peeing myself."

Peyton laughed, but held the facial expression of a young woman who didn't really want to hear about the joys of being incredibly pregnant. "So, what do we do if you go into labor early?"

"Oh, from your lips to God's ears, my sweet girl. If I were that lucky, Casey said she's willing to help you with Michaela. She knows where my binder is, and on the odd chance that I'm actually in labor during the wedding, and can't call to tell you, she has both you and Mackenzie's phone numbers."

Opening Rachel's car door for her, Peyton gave a confident nod. "We'll be fine if it comes to that. You can be kinda scary sometimes, but you taught us well."

Rachel laughed and then dropped into the driver's seat with a groan. "Thanks."

As she drove home, everything that had successfully been pushed to the back of her head came back in a rush. Since she'd woken that morning, Rachel had the oddest sense of an hourglass having been tipped over, and each little grain of sand that passed through into the rapidly filling bottom chamber gave her a sense of unease. This thing with her and Tate, she needed to fix it. Who knew when she'd have the baby, it could be hours, and it could be days past her due date. But nonetheless, this twosome was about to become a threesome, and not in the filthy porno kind of way.

He'd said that it wasn't about the baby, it was about the two of them. And it wasn't like she didn't understand what he meant, but she also didn't want her child to feel the same yo-yo of a mother that she had. On the other hand though, she hadn't had this little Nugget her whole life, so it wasn't just about that. Rachel and Tate. Is that really what it boiled down to? That she was too afraid of looking in the mirror and seeing Madelyn Hennessy to even give him a tiny chance?

But how well could she really prove it to him once her days were consumed with diapers and sleep cycles and nursing? And even now, she was still trying to figure out what she wanted to prove, exactly. That he was completely and one million percent right about her? That she was a complete bitch for how she'd jerked him back and forth with her inability to let him in? That she felt the exact same fire boiling over inside of her?

Even if it was just *one* of those things, she could only get started with the process by taking one step at a time. The first, and hardest, step would be to seek him out. When she got back to the empty house, knowing he wouldn't be home for a couple more hours, she thought over and over about just how difficult this would be for her. It flashed her back to the conversation with Kate on Christmas Eve, about how they both knew when they were being stubborn, and couldn't physically make themselves stop.

That's how it had been, just exactly like that for the last fourteen days. There was some immovable barrier that she could feel whenever she imagined going to him, even when she wasn't sure what she might say to him. It lashed around her ankles to hold her place, like vines that sunk through the foundation of the house to keep her where she was. It covered her mouth like a vise, tightening and closing every time she thought about letting him in.

No, it screamed at her, *don't let him get to you. It's not safe. Don't give him the power to break you.* Because that was something else she knew, knew it like God Himself had descended from the heavens to whisper it in her ear, that if Tate ever betrayed her the way Marc had, it would ruin her. Ruin her for eternity and beyond any hope of repair. Even the safe, tepid boundaries of her last relationship had felt like jagged shards when she realized how long Marc had been unfaithful.

And even though Tate didn't have it in his genetic makeup to cheat, there were other ways he could crush her. Just these fleeting glimpses she'd allowed, of what life could be like for them, showed her just how definitively he could destroy her if he ever decided she wasn't it for him.

But the other part of her, the part that had been growing and stretching over the last few days, unequivocally knew that he would never hurt her. That he was the kind of man that if he maintained possession of her heart, he would protect it with every breath he took. Like in a hot, growly alpha kind of way without being a total douche.

Rachel shifted uncomfortably where she sat on the couch, pressing a hand on her continually aching back.

"Kid, you're killing me. Any chance you could go easy on me tonight? I may be doing something drastic."

The answering foot that pushed against her ribs made her lose her breath, but she still smiled. Baby steps. That's what she needed. Something to break the ice, and just one thing that would make him see that she was trying. She grabbed her phone, pushed off the couch, and got to work with the time she had left until he got home.

HE'D BEEN home for about thirty minutes. From where she stood around the corner, she'd heard the garage door open and close, his car door slamming, then the back door click shut, and his quiet steps go immediately through the kitchen and down the steps into the basement. It was the new routine.

They hadn't really shared a meal, just him grazing in the kitchen when she'd be watching tv at night, and with maybe a polite inquiry as to her day and how she was feeling, he'd retreat back to his own living space. Not tonight though, she'd change up their new hellish routine. Hellish because every single pound of guilt landed squarely on her stubborn-ass shoulders.

It was heavy. And annoying. And needed to go.

Padding down the hallway on bare feet, Rachel tugged the neckline of her white scoop tank down, just a smidge. Because they'd officially entered summer-like weather, she pretty much lived in dresses, but this was one she hadn't busted out yet. Busting out being the operative term. And she wasn't stupid. If one was attempting to make an emotionally vulnerable gesture to a man that you might possibly be in love with, it never hurt to show some cleavage.

Evened the odds a little bit. She'd started with a flowy white dress, but that just screamed *bridal*, so she switched to her basic, long black tank dress, and that looked just a little too pregnant hoochie considering how tight it was on her now, so she ended up with the white scoop tank and her light aqua skirt that skimmed the floor. Very easy, breezy, please-don't-ignore-what-I'm-about-to-do.

After making sure there was no sign of Tate coming upstairs, she quietly sneaked into her office, where she'd put all her supplies right before he'd walked in the door. Once she'd set everything out the way she wanted it, she felt a quick, hot burst of nerves. Shit. This could so backfire.

It could be too late.

He could laugh.

He could walk away.

He could ...

"Stop it," she whispered to herself, fanning her suddenly hot face. No. No more of this scaredy-cat shit. She needed to be the person that could actually grow some lady balls, take the kind of first step to the relationship that not only Tate, but that she deserved too. Blowing out a hard breath, willing her nervousness to go the hell away, she walked over to the top of the stairs. For just a moment, she listened carefully and heard the faint sounds of typing, the rustle of papers being moved.

"Tate," she called out. "Could you come up here?"

It was quiet for a few seconds, and it seriously felt like three years before he answered.

"Yeah, I'll be there in a minute."

Oh sure. Of course he was making her wait for an entire *minute*. Like she wasn't going to hyperventilate in that monstrous amount of time.

Just baby steps, you're not proposing to him, she repeated to herself in between pulling in huge breaths. She was well on her way to staring a hole into the top of the dining room table when the sound of him walking up the steps dominated the entire room. And like the complete chicken shit coward she was, she didn't look at him right away. From the complete lack of sound, she knew he was standing at the top of the stairs, staring at her.

"Rachel ..." he said, the confusion heavy in his tone.

When she turned to him, she swallowed hard, because he looked so freaking good after *days* of not really letting herself look at him. His face was scruffier than she'd ever seen it, and as hot as that was, and holy heavens, it was hot, he kinda looked like crap. He'd changed after work, wearing a worn gray t-shirt from his law school alma mater, and worn jeans.

"What is this?"

Oh yeah, she hadn't spoken yet.

"Chinese food." With a vague hand gesture towards the table, she smiled at him, and his face relaxed a little bit. Then she shrugged. "A peace offering. And an apology."

With slow, sure steps, he moved towards her, and she moved to the chair she normally sat in when he reached the table. One side of his mouth curved in a smile.

"That looks suspiciously like my favorite food from my favorite restaurant."

"Crab Rangoon, fried rice, and Empress Chicken with no water chestnuts. And I made sure to ask for extra almond cookies."

He pursed his lips briefly.

"I asked Casey," she said, answering his unspoken question. Why the freaking hell wasn't he sitting down? She was about to jump out of her skin when he pulled out the chair across from her and started dishing out food to the two plates she had sitting out. Other than the sounds of shuffling cartons, the clink of her fork against the plate, him breaking his chopsticks apart, it was completely silent.

Music. She was *such* an idiot. Why didn't she think of music?

Barely tasting the food that she'd put in her mouth, Rachel watched the slow movements of his jaw as he tasted his.

"So," he said, after he finished chewing. And then he didn't say anything else, just settled back in his chair and stared at her. If there was a prize for most stubborn, Tate would most certainly be giving her a run for her money. And she couldn't blame him one teeny, tiny bit. Yeah, she'd underestimated this man. No way was he going to let her off easily.

She nodded and then reached over to the empty chair next to her, pulling a small white bag from the yellow cushioned seat. Tate watched, not moving, as she set it in between them on the table.

Lifting her chin towards the bag in a 'go ahead' gesture, she worked to keep her face even. And that was really freaking hard at the moment, because she so wanted him to understand what she was trying to do. After another bite of his food, Tate reached forward and snagged the bag with one hand, then his forehead wrinkled in confusion. His eyes flicked up to hers and then he set down his chopsticks, used two fingers to pull out one of the pieces of paper in the bag. She watched his lips move slightly while he read, then one side of his mouth twitched like he was fighting a smile.

"Am I supposed to ask or answer this question?"

"That's totally up to you. I just," she took a sip of her water, recognizing the stall tactic for exactly what it was, "I thought it would be nice to learn things about each other, not about the baby, or with Casey being the middle man between us, just Rachel and Tate. And I promise to answer, no matter what the question is."

The breath that Tate released came out of his nose, and he just kept staring at her, eyes moving slowly over her face. Her fingers pinched together where she'd set them on her lap so that she wouldn't fidget or move away from his scrutiny.

"We don't have to though," she rushed on when he still didn't say anything. "I rented a movie too, we could watch that-"

"Would you rather," he interrupted, speaking slowly, keeping his gaze steady on hers, "have no one show up for your wedding? Or your funeral?"

A relieved smile spread her lips, and she rolled them in between her teeth while she considered.

"My funeral. Because I wouldn't know the difference."

"I suppose I'd have to agree with that," he said, setting the bag back down on table. "Your turn."

"Would you rather travel back in time to meet your ancestors? Or travel to the future to meet your great-grandchildren?"

He tapped his chopsticks against his mouth while he thought. "Do I get to come back to my own time?"

"I would assume so."

"Hmm. Would I be meeting my great-grandparents? Or further back?"

"Tate."

"Hey, I don't know how you intended this game to be played."

"Only a lawyer would make this game difficult with exploratory questions."

Tate grinned. "Go back and meet my ancestors. There's always the possibility that I could live to be over a hundred years old, and see my great-grandchildren be born anyway, but meeting my ancestors? Yeah, that's what I'd want. Seeing how their choices in a much more difficult time of life influenced where our family ended up and the type of people they were? That'd be incredible."

They ate until they were stuffed, and traded questions easily over the next hour. Tate was always thoughtful in how he answered, deliberating before giving his opinion. And to her surprise, he laughed easily and often, especially when she was torn about whether she'd rather live in a world with absolutely no problems, or live in a world where she was in charge of everything.

Hey, so sue her. Being in charge was fairly awesome. And even though she wouldn't have really answered that way, it was totally worth it to see the creases around his mouth deepen with his rich, booming laugh.

She'd missed him, and even sitting across the table from him, she ached thinking about the time they'd lost. And really, it wasn't like she wanted to sit and rehash what had happened, so this was a fairly perfect way for them to start getting back to normal. Whatever the hell that would be for them.

By the time they were cleaning up the table, the sky was almost completely dark, just traces of a pinkish-purple sunset left over the tops of the trees in the backyard. Rachel stretched her legs out in front of her after settling into the couch, watching those colors fade into the bluish tinge of dusk. Tate sank next to her, holding out one last piece of paper out for her to take.

She shook her head and then yawned. "No, it's your turn to ask."

"Are you gonna fall asleep on me again? Make me carry you to bed?"

Rachel scoffed. "*Make* you?"

He laughed again, and the sound made her feel so ... unsettled. Because it was soothing. And arousing.

And it made her look away from him, take a few deep breaths.

"Would you rather take a dream vacation for two weeks, by yourself? Or spend five days at home with the person you love?"

The question dropped between them like an anvil, and it absolutely decimated any hold that she had on her feelings. Staring across at him, there was absolutely no doubt in her mind which of those two she would choose if Tate was the one she'd be staying home with. When she didn't answer right away, he looked back at her. Every part of her skin felt tingly and tight with the way his dark eyes held hers.

"You terrify me, Tate," she whispered.

His eyes fell closed, but he shifted closer to her, angling so he was facing her. Oh holy shit, she wanted to snatch the words back, shove them back into mouth, and give them less power. One of his hands reached out, disentangling her wound-up fingers, and he used his thumb to trace the knuckles.

"Don't you," he stopped and dipped his head down so he knew for sure she was looking at him, "don't you think that's how it's supposed to be?"

"I don't know, Tate." She practically sobbed out a breath, and pulled her free hand up to clench it in a fist over her hammering heart. Like she could force it to slow down, lessen the insanely powerful grip he seemed to have on it. "But I don't *want it* to feel this way, can't you understand that?"

"What are you so afraid of?"

Her eyes and her throat burned, a pushing, insistent rush of emotions clogging them up to the point that she wasn't sure she'd be able to hear or see him for much longer. She pulled the hand over her heart, and cupped the side of his face, smoothing her thumb back and forth over the spot where she knew those smile lines curved in. The way he leaned his head into her touch made her want to claw her heart out of her chest, because it felt so good that it *hurt*.

"Everything," she answered.

"I don't buy it." He shook his head, and her hand dropped off his face with the determined movement. He picked it up, gripping both of her hands in his. "You are the most fearless person I know."

She wasn't fearless, not with him. But she *was* weak and just a little selfish. Pulling her hands from his, she smoothed them up the soft cotton of his shirt, reveling in the warm, solid muscle she felt underneath. Cupping both hands behind his neck, she pulled him into her.

"If I could be fearless for anyone," she whispered against his lips, "I promise, it would be you."

Then she kissed him.

He immediately wrapped his strong arms around her, angling his head to deepen the kiss. His movements weren't hesitant or unsure. But neither were hers.

This felt desperate, urgent. Like he would be capable of changing her mind by the way he curled his tongue into her mouth. By the way he nipped and pulled at her lips with his own. She started to pull back, but he speared a hand into her hair and held her to him.

Swept up. It was the only thing she felt tapping at her thoughts outside the heat of his skin, the firmness of his lips, the hot slide of his tongue against hers. She was totally and completely swept up. His hand moved from the back of her head, to slide down and cup the back of her neck, using his thumb to tilt her chin at the absolutely perfect angle.

The whimper she heard must have been hers, but it felt like it came from somewhere outside this maelstrom of need and heat and intensity. It felt *vital*, like she wouldn't be able to breathe without him pushing air into her lungs.

And she wrenched herself back. "We can't."

Stupid, stupid, stupid, stupid, emotionally handicapped pregnant person. Yup. That was her.

He was breathing as heavily as she was, and the passion

hadn't abated from his face despite the distance that hung between them now. "Only because you won't *let us.*"

She touched his face again. "I'm not running, I promise. Not like before. But Tate, we can't afford to do this wrong, to screw this up. We don't have the luxury of attempting a relationship the way that everyone else does. I know tonight was us, just us," she took his hand and laid it over her stomach, "but we still have someone else to think about. Someone that needs us not to be crazy and impetuous. I don't want to be that kind of mother."

The breath he let out carried the weight that only a man with a serious case of blue balls can have. "I know."

"Okay," she said, and pushed herself to stand up, absently rubbing her belly. With one hand hanging off the back of his neck, Tate stood too, tucking a piece of her hair behind her ear.

"Do you still want me to carry you to bed?"

She laughed under her breath, loving the mischievous light in his eyes. With a meaningful look somewhere near the vicinity of his zipper, she shook her head.

He groaned. "Not helping."

"We both just need a good night sleep, okay?"

With his thumb and his forefinger, he pinched her chin lightly, tilting it up. "I have a feeling you'll sleep better than me."

27

SHE WAS GOING to completely and utterly *die* from pleasure.

Tilting her hips up and arching her back, she and Tate were touching everywhere. One of his hands held both of her wrists, stretching her arms above her head, anchoring them in place with his implacable grip. And as much as she wanted to dig her nails into his back, the helplessness that came from his physical dominance was gah, so freaking sexy.

He moved slowly, thoroughly, never rushing his smooth movements even though she bit down on his earlobe. An insistent pulse started somewhere around her core, and she tilted her pelvis to meet the starting spark.

"Rachel."

"Mmmmmm," she moaned in response. When he said her name like that ... yeah ... just yeah.

"Rachel ... wake up."

Wake ... what? Who the ever loving hell would interrupt the most delicious of deliciously orgasmic dreams?

"I know you can hear me."

"Mmmpppphh. Go 'way."

Maybe if she just kept her eyes shut, she could go back. She'd been so, sooooooo close.

A warm hand coasted down her arm, pulling her further away from the lovely haze that still lingered behind her eyes. And as much as she wanted to roll onto her stomach and bury her head under a pile of pillows, that just really wasn't possible in her current physical state. Instead, she blindly reached down and pulled the pillow that she used to prop up her stomach and slapped it over her eyes and practically burst into tears.

No sexy times.

Still massively pregnant.

She was going to completely and utterly die from embarrassment.

Tate chuckled. Well, if any sound could drag her firmly back into consciousness, it would be that low sound.

"It's so rude to wake a pregnant woman who was blissfully unaware of how much she'll need to pee as soon as she stands up."

"I know, which is why I made that thick cut maple bacon you like."

"Okay." She sat up, letting the pillow fall to the side in her haste. "You're forgiven."

Watching Tate walk out of her bedroom, she somehow managed to keep a ridiculously dreamy sigh from escaping. That man. Oh, that man looked so friggin good in black dress pants and a white oxford. The broad sweep of his shoulders tapered down to slim hips and long-ass legs, and yeah, she could watch him walking away aaaaaall day long.

With the lingering feelings from her dream, Rachel had a vivid idea of following him into the kitchen, pulling the shirt from its cleanly tucked state and ripping it open, buttons flying ...

Damn it. Bad Rachel.

Stretching her legs out, Rachel carefully slid over and swung her feet down to the fuzzy gray rug that ran along the length of her queen size bed. Nugget must have liked that, because Rachel could pretty clearly feel two little feet plant somewhere around her hip bones and push outward.

"Kid. Seriously, cut me some slack here. I just got woken up, mid-happy times, and I think I just peed myself a little."

After taking care of her bladder issues, Rachel wrapped herself in her short cotton robe and walked down to the kitchen, following the smell of bacon like a delicious, pork lined yellow brick road. Tate was standing at the kitchen sink, his back to her, putting the skillet into the dish drying rack. Wiping his hands on a towel, he turned and gestured towards the island. There was a heaping plate of bacon and a plate of three waffles. Not that she wanted to look a gift horse in the mouth, but this was awfully strange. She lifted an eyebrow as she sat.

"You trying to butter me up for something?" She crunched down a strip of bacon and moaned at the crispy salty goodness. "Beeeeeecause it's working."

Tate smiled. "Maybe a little. You eat, I'll be right back."

Curiouser and curiouser.

But hey, she had bacon and Eggos - there would be minimal complaints from her. Just as she popped the last bite of waffle in her mouth and pushed the square black plate away from in front of her, Tate made his way back upstairs. The white dress shirt was covered with a black suit jacket, and he was straightening the knot on a vibrant blue tie.

Don't think about how you'd like to use that tie ... do not think about how it would look if you tied it around his eyes so he couldn't see what you were doing ... don't think about ...

"Rachel, are you listening to me?"

"Huh?" Yeesh, that sounded all breathy and turned on.

"I said I wanted to talk to you about last night."

Aaaaaand that punched her fantasies right in the throat.

"What about?"

He moved to the other side of the island and propped his

hands in front of him. "I get what you were trying to do, and I really appreciate you making the effort."

"But ..."

"But," he tilted his chin down and stared across at her, "I need to get inside that head of yours, just a little. Last night felt like the first time you've really been honest with me, about us. But I still have no idea what scares you so much."

With a tiny shrug of one shoulder, Rachel dragged a finger along the beveled edge of the granite. "Maybe I think you're too good-looking for me."

He slowly raised an eyebrow.

She huffed out a breath. "Fine. It's ... it's partially my mom, like you said."

"Well, I want to know more. Rachel, you were one hundred percent right last night, about us not being able to do this the way everyone else does it. And I think the only way we can do it, in this crucible that we've been thrown into, is to be honest. I'm not going to judge you, but I have to know what I'm dealing with."

"So you can fix me?" She said it without heat, but she saw his jaw set anyway.

"No. You don't need fixing. But I do think you need someone to push you. And I *want* to know, Rachel, I'm not asking out of politeness or pity, I want to *do this* with you." He pushed off the island, spread his arms out, moving towards her. The expression on his face was so sincere, so pleading, and it made her hurt inside. "But you have to give me *something*. Not any little question games to pacify me, as enjoyable as last night was, I need and *want* more than that with you."

Discomfort clawed its way up her throat at the thought of putting this into words. Her eyes fell shut and she shook her head, feeling like the connection between her brain and her mouth was just ... severed.

The sharp sound of his hand smacking on the counter snapped her eyes open. His eyes were blazing, like he had something boiling up in him that would be able to reach in through her and yank out an honest answer. And part of her wished he could, that it would be in his control, not falling all onto her. That he could take his warm, capable hands and dig down into her soul and untangle it.

"Still? I still get nothing?"

"You don't understand," she burst out. "My whole life I have had a front row seat to the complete dysfunction of my parents' relationship. Or, maybe dysfunction isn't the right word. I don't even know what you'd call it. Angst, drama, whatever. My mom is constantly pushing and poking at him, crying and then kissing, questioning this and that and everything, and then they lock themselves in their bedroom for hours. And yeah sure, I get they love each other. But at what cost? Their sanity? Because that is not love to me. That is not how I want to live my life, in some constant state of ... agitation."

"And I agitate you?"

"What?"

He took another step, his eyes calmer than before, just by a bit. "Do I agitate you? Is that why you constantly push me back?"

"No," she protested immediately. And he didn't. He ... he pushed under skin like a burr, making her look at everything differently, just by being there. He prickled against her skin, like electricity that raised every hair on her body, like every nerve ending in her body had been sparked to life. He incited more feelings in her than anyone ever had before. He refused to let her retreat into her comfort zone, and he absolutely triggered something inside of her. Oh holy mother Mary, because she was in love with him. He did all of that because she was totally and completely in love with him. She met his gaze, feeling frantic. Desperate. "I don't know how to do this, Tate."

"Rachel, you always have a choice in how to react to something. If you don't want to repeat your parents' relationship, then don't. It's not that hard."

Hot tears pushed at her eyes, at her throat. "And that's so easy for you to say, isn't it? That it's not hard to suddenly change how I've reacted to things my entire life. It's not easy, Tate. Not for me. And you should respect that I'm trying. Can't you see that?"

"Yes, yes I can see that you're trying, but imagine how it feels for me, just for a second." He shook his head, and took the last step between them, grabbing both of her hands in his. "Every single time we take one tiny step forward, you sprint backwards and I don't know how to stop you, because you don't *want me* to."

Suddenly she felt cold. Ice cold, down to her toes. And, yup, she had to pee again. "Maybe this was a bad idea."

"Yeah," he ran a hand through his hair, ruining any semblance of a style. "Maybe I should have waited until after work."

Rachel shook her head, every emotion billowing up her throat in red tinged clouds, and she could not push it back down. "No. Me living here. Look at the last month, Tate. Half of my time here we've been fighting. I am *trying*, Tate, and as hard as I try to not end up with all the craziness? We're doing exactly that."

Tate straightened slowly, stepping back slightly, mouth agape. "So, because I want to know what's going on in your head, the thing that's keeping us from really trying to be together, you think it's a mistake to live here?"

Panic dried her throat, made her eyes blink rapidly. She didn't really mean it. What the hell was wrong with her? It was like her tongue had been effing hijacked. "Tate..."

And then he turned and walked away, sweeping up his briefcase that was sitting on the floor. Rachel rolled her lips into her mouth, using the motion in order to keep her from crying out, from wailing that he was so, so right and that she was a coward. Tate stopped and turned to face her. The hallway light wasn't turned on, so he was mostly in shadow. Fitting really, as he was apparently the harbinger of death for her emotional distance, ripping down every single brick she'd built with his bare hands.

"You are absolutely right. If you can't see exactly what we have in front of us, what we have the opportunity to be, then you are right. If you can't be honest enough with yourself to see that, to see that I am right in front of you, then it *was* a mistake. And as much as I have fallen in love with you, because I cannot *help* but fall in love with you, Rachel, I will not be someone who keeps pushing where I am constantly rejected. So I promise, I will not bring this up again. That's on you."

The door slammed shut behind him, and in the vacuum of sound that followed it, all she heard was the uneven breaths that sawed in and out of her lungs. He loved her.

He loved *her*.

She really, really loved him back.

And then the tears fell. Two hot, quick drops onto her face. A hiccuping sound fell from her open mouth, and she crumpled onto the counter. Huge, wracking sobs shook her body, and when she turned her head to the side, rolling her forehead on the cool granite, tears slicked down her cheek and into her ear.

The release that she felt was almost staggering, and she managed to suck in a huge, cleansing breath. Swiping at her damp cheeks, she managed to steady herself mentally. Now all that remained was to figure out how to stop being a giant shit head.

She turned, standing from the stool. And a rush of warm liquid slid down the inside of her leg.

Not pee.

That was so not pee.

"Great," she wailed, feeling the tears push past her eyes again. "I'm leaking from every damn hole I've got!"

"WHAT THE HELL took you so long?" Rachel cried when Liz oh so casually strolled into the front door.

Liz turned her wrist to look at the slim silver watch she always wore.

"It took me seven minutes, Red." She was so annoyingly calm when she said it, setting her purse down on the entryway table, like they didn't have a *hospital* to get to. "Didn't you say you aren't even having contractions yet?"

Rachel scoffed. "I've had one. And hello, amniotic fluid went spewing down my leg, okay? Would you want to chill at home?"

A tiny smile quirked Liz's mouth, and she gestured to the duffel bag that Rachel clutched in one hand, maybe possibly to keep it from the out of control shaking that seemed to be plaguing her limbs. Early labor right after fighting with Tate, apparently not the most calming thing in the world.

"Do you have everything you need in there? We could take a couple minutes before we leave."

"Listen, Blondie, I want to get to the damn hospital, okay? So all the lovely little nurses can hover around me and hook me up to needles full of happy drugs. My overnight bag is perfect, don't you worry your skinny little ass over it."

Liz clucked her tongue. "Name calling is so unnecessary, considering I'm the only ride that showed up. Where is Tate, anyway?"

"His cell went right to voicemail, and when I call his office, Maggie said he dropped his phone in a cup of coffee and went right to the cell phone store to get a new one set up. She promised to send him on his way to the hospital as soon as he got back." Rachel decided not to mention the fact that Maggie was very quick to bring up that Tate seemed 'off' when he arrived. And since she was most decidedly at fault for that, Rachel decided not to mention that either. A sharp, crawling pain starting at the base of her stomach pinched at her, turning the skin hard as rock. Rachel clenched her teeth. "Yeah, let's just go, okay?"

"Contraction?"

Rachel nodded, blowing out a breath when it eased about twenty seconds later. Liz reached forward to take her bag, and rubbed a hand down her back. "Come on, I left my car running so it wouldn't be too hot in there for you."

"I take it back. I love you and your skinny ass."

As much as Rachel wanted someone to wheel a gurney out to Liz's car, the two of them walked into the ER entrance, where a very nice security guard grabbed a wheelchair to bring her to the registration desk. A few more contractions pulled at her during that tedious process, handing over insurance cards and filling out what felt like a bajillion pieces of paper. Couldn't she just sign one that said 'yeah, I'm popping out a kid, and I'll let you do whatever will make that happen'? Probably would have saved a shit ton of time.

Liz was on cell phone duty, making sure Rachel didn't miss a call from Tate while they were waiting for a labor nurse to come and wheel her back to triage. So far, nothin'. A big, fat, silent nothin'. What if he didn't go right back to the office? What if he was still uber pissed at her?

It wasn't like he didn't have reason to be.

All she'd had to do, just one little thing, was open her mouth and say that he showed the greatest capacity for driving her insane with how much she loved him, and it scared the bejeesus out of her.

Liz held up Rachel's phone. "Another one from your mom. She wants to know when she should come."

"Just tell her to calm her crazy ass down, she doesn't need to rush over here."

"Ummm, no. I probably won't tell her that."

Rachel groaned when another contraction hit her, and it happened to be at the same time that a young nurse in bright blue scrubs came through the doors.

She crouched in front of Rachel. "Having a contraction right now?"

Liz answered from behind her. "It started about ten seconds ago."

"Okay. Let's get her back to triage to check her out."

The shining floors and soft cream walls all bled together while Rachel breathed through the tightness in her middle. Liz and the nurse helped her strip out of her pajamas and into a generic robe, then settled her into the bed to get her hooked up with her IV needle.

And holy effing shit. Rachel may have called the person administering *that* a Nazi from the flaming pits of Hades. But whatever. Apparently the IV was sort of necessary, but wasn't it possible to make it not hurt like hell?

"I just got a text from Casey," Liz said from the hard plastic chair up against the wall. "Do you want her to come until Tate can get here?"

"No, I think her optimistic cheerleader bullshit would make me want to punch her right now. She'd probably be all 'you can do it! Just envision the baby! Work with the pain!' No. I love her, but no."

Liz chuckled and tapped out a reply on her phone.

"Wait. You didn't tell her I said that, did you?"

Liz opened her mouth to answer, when her nurse, Samantha pushed back the curtain to her little cove of pain and walked in with a smile.

"Alright, we're going to wheel you up to your room, where you'll stay until you have the baby. Could still be hours yet, but we want to get you nice and comfortable until then."

Panic worked its way through her veins. Tate really wasn't here yet.

"Will, umm, well, if someone shows up for me, will they tell them what room I'm in?" Liz gave her a sympathetic smile, and Rachel saw a suspicious brightness to her blue eyes. Rachel jabbed a finger in her direction. "Do not start crying, Blondie. Seriously. I've already lost my fair share of liquid this morning."

Samantha laughed. "Yes, they'll direct anyone who comes for you to the labor and delivery room. Whether they're allowed in the room is totally up to you."

Rachel chewed on that as they wheeled back through the same generically clean hallways. She'd sent a text to her mom and Kate, letting them know she was at the hospital, but the thought of her mom hovering around nurses and doctors while awaiting the birth of her grandchild filled Rachel with a whole different kind of panic than thinking about Tate not being there yet. She knew her mom wanted to be in the room.

Hell, she probably wanted to cut the cord, but she just couldn't go there ... not yet. Maybe when she'd progressed a little bit, and Tate actually got his hot ass into the room, she'd be able to think about what role she wanted her mom to play in this day.

Samantha helped settle her into the large delivery room. It was big, much bigger than she'd expected. On the opposite wall from the bed was a flat screen TV, a long bench sat underneath tall windows, and a reclining chair sat in the corner behind her IV pole. And in the other corner was a little plastic bassinet under a warming light.

Her breaths came faster with the burn of a contraction. Holy shitting shit, she was going to meet her child today. Tears pushed hot and hard against her eyes, from excitement and pain and well ... sheer terror that Tate still wasn't there yet. Her phone sat conspicuously silent next to the bench where Liz had pulled out her Kindle.

"Seriously? You're reading?" she asked, gaping over at Liz. "I'm about to pop out a kid right now."

Liz raised an eyebrow at Samantha, who just calmly went about her business of shoving her hand up Rachel's hoohah. Umm, ow, she thought as she squirmed higher in the bed.

"You're just about four centimeters dilated, Rachel," she said as she snapped off some bright blue plastic gloves that weirdly matched her scrubs. "Will you be having an epidural today? This is the time we start thinking about calling an anesthesiologist for you if that's something you want."

"Uh, yeah. Send him on up. Right now. Ohhhh holy mother of all things holy, this is a good one." Rachel breathed out slowly as the pain climbed and climbed and shit ... kept climbing. The monitors hooked around her stomach shifted a bit when she tried to get comfortable. Samantha watched the paper spitting out of the computer next to the hospital bed, and smiled at Rachel.

"Sure thing. I'll go page him. Press your call button if you need anything, okay?"

Rachel nodded, and let her head fall sideways on the pillow underneath her. There wasn't a single cloud in the bright blue sky, but the beauty of the day did nothing to make her feel better. What if she had reacted differently this morning?

If Tate had been in that kitchen even five minutes longer, he'd have been with her when her water broke. Maybe he would have kissed her, eased her into the passenger seat of his car, held her hand tightly the entire drive to the hospital, and then rubbed her back through each contraction. Instead, here she was. By herself, for all intents and purposes.

Not that it wasn't nice that Liz was here, but it still wasn't who she wanted in that room with her.

She just wanted Tate. Pretty much forever. He could steady her, calm her down. Keep her focused. And he wasn't *here*.

"Red? Are you okay?" Liz walked around the side of the bed and clasped one of Rachel's hands.

"No," she whispered. "I think I really screwed up."

Another contraction hit her, and she squeezed down on Liz's hand, not really giving a shit if she broke her friend's fingers into a million little pieces.

"He'll be here," Liz whispered back. The pressure around her middle started easing and Liz reached up to smooth the hair back off of Rachel's slightly sweaty brow. "Do you want a distraction? Or should we analyze his absence to death?"

Rachel laughed slightly, adoring her friend a whole helluva lot just then. "Distraction, please."

"Well, I'm thinking that I need a makeover. I'm getting kind of sick of my style."

"Oh, thank you tiny baby Moses. It's about freaking time, Blondie. You do your stupid model-esque body no favors by dressing in the blandest clothes possible."

Liz smiled. "I don't even dare tell Casey, she'll have all my money spent thirty minutes later."

"So, what style are you thinking? Naughty librarian? It would be appropriate. Maybe liven up your time in between the stacks at work. You know, garter belts and what not. Those pencil skirts that seem respectable but really aren't."

"I don't know if that's me. What about that kinda bohemian style? I like all the layers and stuff."

"Boho chic?"

"Sure."

Rachel reached out and smacked Liz's shoulder. "Hell no. Boho chic is just something made up so that the Olsen twins style has a nice name to it. 'Bag lady' doesn't have the same ring to it. So, no. Not happening. If you start coming around me with a headband wrapped around your forehead, I will beat the snot out of you."

Liz laughed. "Okay, no headbands. Did that help?"

"Oh sure, we killed a whole three minutes." Another contraction ebbed and flowed, stemming their conversation while Rachel breathed through it. When it faded completely, she shook her head, the desperation filling her again with the absence of pain. "Where is he, Liz?"

Her friend's face held all the misery that Rachel felt sinking in her gut.

"Rachel," Tate called out as he ran into the room, sinking down by her bed, grabbing one of her hands. "I'm so sorry, I got here as fast as I could. I'm so sorry I'm late."

And for the second time that day, Rachel burst into tears. Vaguely she registered the warm skin of Tate's thumbs wiping away her tears, the soft words that he murmured into her forehead as he held her the best he could with all the wires and tubes hooked into her.

"I'm so sorry, Tate," she said, voice wet with tears. "I was such a bitch this morning. And well ... for basically the last nine months. I'm so, so sorry."

He opened his mouth to say something, and a slight man wearing gray scrubs and white coat came in the room.

"So, someone here is ready for some pain control?"

"Yes, that's me, oh I love you," Rachel said in reply, just as another contraction gripped her. Tate held her hand while she moaned through it.

The doctor laughed, introduced himself to Tate and Rachel and went about pulling out his magical supplies, including one frighteningly large needle. Liz came over with her purse slung over her shoulder and kissed Rachel on the forehead.

"Love you, Red. I'll wait for your text that the little bundle has arrived."

"Thank you, Liz." Rachel squeezed her hand. "I love you, too."

"Alright sir," the happy drug doctor said once Liz had cleared the room. "If you'd like to sit on the stool in front of your wife, I'll do my business back here."

Tate watched her, still gripping her hand while she attempted to sit on the side of the bed where Samantha was directing her. His eyes were dark, fathomless. His hair was a complete wreck, and his tie had been yanked from its firm knot around his neck.

He looked achingly handsome. Perfect, at least to her.

"Why do I need to sit on the stool?" he asked, totally and quite obviously, not correcting him on the husband/wife assumption.

"She's my priority," Samantha said, gesturing at Rachel. "And if you keel over when he puts that needle in her back, I'll have no choice but to leave you on the floor until she's all set. So, you'll be making my job easier if you sit down, okay?"

And so he sat. Rachel curved her back and hugged the pillow the way Samantha told her to. Tate didn't faint, but his eyes did widen slightly when Dr. Happy (or whatever his name was) hooked Rachel up with his magic drugs. Not long after the pinch and pressure in her spine, a calm, soothing warmth spread through the lower half of her body.

Samantha checked her one more time before she left, five centimeters this time, and the room was strangely quiet when the door clicked shut.

"The uh, the phone store was really busy. And then Maggie wasn't at her desk when I got back to the office. That's what took me so long. I'm really sorry."

"It's okay." She shrugged, looking around the room, anywhere but at Tate, really. The hospital was newer, and the soft blues, grays, and greens in the room reflected that. When Tate sat on the long bench against the wall, he let his head fall back onto the window behind him.

"What happened?"

Staring down at her hands knit together in her lap, she told him about her morning. Out of the corner of her eye, she saw him clench his fists when she mentioned how her water broke only a few minutes after he left.

"I'm such an asshole."

"No," Rachel said, and tried to shift higher on the bed, but with the lower half of her body in a pleasant state of numbness, it was pretty damn impossible. "You had no clue, Tate. And it's not like you dropped your phone in your coffee on purpose."

"I'll admit, I was pretty tied in knots after I left the house." He stared at the wall opposite him, at a large framed picture of the Big Red lighthouse in Holland, perched at the edge of Lake Michigan. Maybe he was trying to dissect the painted waves hitting the side of the pier, because it was easier than focusing on how spectacularly they'd screwed up this day. The last month, really. "Look, I shouldn't have pushed so hard this morning. I see that now. And considering where we find ourselves at the moment, I suggest a truce."

"Until you cut the cord? Then we throw down again?"

He laughed, and it made her heart squeeze. Pushing off the bench, he stretched his arms up towards the ceiling, and then walked over to her. Snagging the same stool that he sat on for the epidural, he sank onto it when it was pushed up against the bed.

"At least for the hospital stay. I meant what I said earlier, I won't push you again. You know how I feel, and that won't change." The squeezing in her heart turned into a tight-fisted grip, pushing all the blood into the rest of her body. Moving slowly, Tate picked up the hand laying closest to him, lifted it, and pressed a kiss into her palm. "I'm excited to meet our baby."

She smiled, eyes swimming until he got all blurry and blobby looking. "Me too."

And that was right about when shit got real. That terrifyingly exciting knowledge that she was about to become a mother. That within, God willing, the next couple hours, she would finally see that little Nugget who kicked and punched and rolled inside of her. Emotions swelled and spilled over, uncontrollable and unrelenting.

Her phone chimed.

"Tate, could you see who's texting me?"

Squinting at the screen, he smothered a smile. "Your mom wants to know if she can bring you ice chips."

Chime.

"And umm, if you need a cool washcloth for your forehead."

Chime.

"Or someone to rub your back through the contractions."

"Oh for shit's sake, tell her I have a giant needle in my back to take care of that for me."

He did as she asked, this time letting the smile loose.

When the phone chimed again, he just laughed and didn't elaborate on what it said. Probably for the best. She had what she needed right now. She had Tate.

Over the next couple hours, Tate got her what she wanted; a couple grape popsicles, and yes, a cool washcloth for her head, because it kinda felt awesome. During three more checks from Samantha, she was two more centimeters dilated, and something-something effaced. Whatever. She just wanted someone to tell her when to push and get this show on the road.

But at least until then, she had her happy drugs flowing through her dilating vag, and Tate right by her side.

29

SHE WAS GOING to murder the anesthesiologist.

Slowly, with relish.

And where the ever loving hell was her mom when she needed her?

Yeah.

She needed her mom. Someone besides this bonehead who impregnated her who did not understand what the excruciating, blinding pain of contractions felt like.

"Ohhhhhhhhhhhh," she moaned when another rolling contraction gripped her. Writhing in place, she tried to focus her breathing while Tate laid a cool cloth on her fiery-feeling fore-head. The agony eventually eased, and she finally had her voice back. "You get his ass back up here, this shit isn't supposed to run out!"

"I'm so sorry, sweetheart," Tate murmured. "Is there anything else I can do?"

"Yes," she snapped, whipping the washcloth off and chucking it at his handsome face. The stupid handsome face that got her into this mess. "Quit touching me!"

Oooh, and the a-hole chuckled.

"And if you call me sweetheart one more time, I will rip off your testicles."

Before Tate could respond to that little gem, Rachel's mom came swooping into the room.

"Ohhhhh baby, I got your text. I'm here! I'm here. Okay. Whose ass do I need to kick?"

From the other side of her bed, her mom wasn't crying, yet. Thank you, sweet merciful Lord in Heaven for that. Oh no, she wasn't crying. She was pissed.

Her blazing hair looked like absolute shit, probably from running her hands through it. Oh yeah, mama bear was in full affect. "Tate, can you sue a hospital for a faulty epidural? Because this is unacceptable. Can I go talk to the nurse? I just ... I need to do something."

Yeah, the blind fury of her mom actually soothed her a little bit. Weird.

Completely ignoring Rachel's very serious dictate to keep his hands off of her, he rubbed a hand down her thigh at the hem of her hospital gown. There were lingering tingles from the epidural, but she could feel every place he touched her. "Come on, we already talked to Samantha. This can happen every once in a while, and it's not always a terrible thing. Now Rachel will easily feel when she needs to push."

Both women scoffed. Rachel almost smiled at how identical the sounds were.

Another burst of fire and pressure and pain cracked through her body. Her mom grabbed her hand, and Rachel grabbed right back. Tate's jaw clenched and she saw the puff of his cheeks when he exhaled harshly. If she hadn't been wracked with pain, she could probably appreciate the intensity of his dark brown eyes when he watched her. Like he just wanted to suck away every bit of that pain and take it on to his own body.

Ha. Amateur. He'd die on the spot.

Just as the pain was easing, Samantha walked back into the

room, followed by the doctor who'd been in earlier to introduce herself. She was short and slight, couldn't have weighed more than a hundred pounds, and tiny pieces of black hair poked out underneath her surgical cap, which was covered in pink and purple polka dots.

"Besides the contractions, how are you feeling?"

"Peachy."

Samantha just smiled, already quite used to Rachel's terse answers. Both women had donned surgical gloves and peered down into the Promised Land. Someone, she didn't really know who, shoved right on up there then.

"You're looking so close, Rachel," Samantha said, sounding pleased. "You're at a good nine and almost completely effaced. If you feel any desire to push, just try to hiss out your breath until one of us can get in here, okay? Hit that button if you even think that you need to."

And then like the words pushed a button somewhere deep inside of her body, she *did* need to push, and she was completely useless to try to resist it. As soon as she ground out the words, everyone in the room was in motion. Another nurse swept in, Tate stood at one side and her mom on the other.

The contractions fell and rolled on top of each other, and she barely registered the numbers that someone counted as she pushed. One on top of the other, short moments to breathe in between. Bouncy calls of encouragement from one unfortunately chipper nurse, which got a quelling glare from Rachel. Sniffles from her mom, who held one of her legs back while she pushed. A brief touch of Tate's lips on her forehead when she sank down into the bed after one bitch of a push.

It revived her. A yell from the doctor that the head was out, lots of dark hair.

And in a final burst of searing pain, like a circle of bright flames shot through her heart, her head and every pore on her body, Rachel pushed one more time. Then a sweet, mewling cry filled the room.

Relief. It was so instantaneous that Rachel wept.

"It's a boy!" Samantha called out, and plopped the wriggling, wet, kind of purple-ish, completely perfect baby right on her chest.

Never had she felt so much of everything. So much love filled her, so much perfect, instant love. His puffy little eyes looked right up at her, his perfectly formed little lips forming an 'O'.

"Hi," she whispered tremulously. "I'm your mom."

Tate sank down to a crouch next to her, his head touching hers. "Rachel, he's so perfect."

She nodded, and barely managed to tear her eyes away from her son to look at Tate. His eyes were bright and shiny, flooded with emotion, and without stopping to think or care, she lifted her chin and softly kissed him. Their lips just rested on each other's for a moment, neither of them trying to make it into more. Because it was perfect.

The next few minutes flew. Cleaning and washing the baby, swaddling him into an impossibly tight little bundle and handing him off to Tate. The doctor finished up taking care of Rachel, the nurses cleaning her up and getting her ready to take him back into her arms, which positively ached to hold him again.

And through all of it, her mom was sitting on the chair in the corner, just ... stunned.

"Mom?"

Her eyes snapped up. Two tears spilled over onto her pale cheeks. "Holy shit. You just had a baby."

"I did," she said on a laugh, and then smiled gratefully at Tate when he laid that perfect little baby back in her arms. It was ridiculous actually, how much easier she breathed being able to just touch him. "Do you want to hold him ... Grandma?"

And then her face crumpled. Her mom sank her head into her hands, her shoulders shaking with the force of her tears.

Rachel just shook her head, Momma Bear was gone. Crazy Mom, back. She drew a finger down his tiny little button nose, his skin so soft, almost translucent.

While the sobs continued in the background, Tate leaned down and told Rachel he was going to go down to the waiting room and tell his parents and Casey, who'd been waiting the last hour. She nodded, and then about burst with gooey, sparkly happiness when he leaned down and pressed a tiny kiss on their son's scrunched, wrinkly forehead.

"See you in a minute, buddy," he whispered. He looked at Rachel, cupping her face. "You were incredible, I hope you know that."

"Well, duh."

He laughed, and then left the room. By the time the door swung shut behind him, Rachel's mom had pulled herself up from the chair, and other than her red eyes, she looked fairly emotionally stable.

"Oh honey, he's so amazing." The hand that she reached out to brush over the tiny hospital cap on his domed head was shaking just a bit. "What's his name?"

"Oh. Umm, we didn't pick one out yet." He let out a tiny grunt, pushing his lips into a pout, and Rachel grinned. Were all babies so freaking cute immediately after being born? Because she'd missed that so far, if it was the case. "Since we didn't find out the gender, we figured we might as well meet him before deciding."

Her mom nodded, a chunk of hair falling from behind her ear to fall over her shoulder. She pushed it back and motioned for the baby. Rachel carefully shifted her arms and let her mom's hands take him from her. Her heart gave a pinch, just a teeny one when he was clear of her fingers, but she breathed through it.

The smile on her mom's face made the pinch more than worth it, because it was wide and completely full of awe.

"Hello, sweet boy. I'm your grandma. And you're the most

handsome thing I've ever seen in my life, but don't tell your grandpa I said that. He'd pout."

The pinch turned into a thump, and then a pounding, resonant beat in her head as Rachel watched her mom fall in love with her son. Her nose burned, and she swallowed hard.

"I'm so sorry, Mom."

A surprised look covered her mom's face when she glanced up. "For what?"

The boulder in Rachel's throat did not go down easily when she tried to speak around it. It vaguely registered that immediately after giving birth, still flooded with hormones, was probably not the best time for a talk that was twenty-eight years in the making. But she pushed past that, exhaling heavily. "I've judged you, Mom. Like, a lot. And as long as I can remember, I've pretty much tried to be ... well, to not be you. And I'm sorry."

"Oh, honey. Did you think I didn't notice?"

"You knew?"

"I know you," she said simply. Her mom smiled, and there was nothing condescending about it, it was soft and maybe a little sad. "And what you feel for this little man, after knowing him for ten minutes? Stretch it across almost thirty years. It never goes away. Not ever."

Rachel nodded, soaking that in. It was sobering, and more than a little terrifying. How could you love someone so much that you barely knew? How could you function every day, knowing that so much of their life was out of your control? Even now, less than thirty minutes into being a mother, she knew that if someone so much looked at her son wrong, she'd rip their throat out. With her teeth.

"Rachel, I show my love for people differently, and I've always been aware of that. And long ago, I decided not to give two shits about whether people judged me for it."

"Mom," she said, and kinda hated herself for the way her voice cracked on the word. "I've probably judged more than anyone else."

"Oh, that's highly doubtful. I've met my fair share of assholes."

"But there's nothing wrong with the way you are." And as she said the words, she knew how unequivocally *true* they were.

"I know that, trust me. I'm more than confident in my own skin, honey. And that's because I know it's not necessary to compare myself to the people around me, whether they're my family or friends or just some random person passing me on the street." Carefully, she stood and walked over to the bed, settling the baby back into Rachel's arms. "Your father, you and your sister, and now this little guy? The love I feel for you feels like a fire that will consume me sometimes, body and soul. And that can be terrifying. But I would never change it. And you, my first born, just needed the right person to show you that you have the exact same heart burning inside of you that's inside of me."

"Tate," she whispered, swiping at an errant tear on her cheek. Seriously, with the crying. What the hell?

Her mom nodded. "Tate. And that precious boy you're holding. They lit something in you that will never go away. I'll admit, I didn't know if it was Tate at first, but there's no way anyone could miss it, not looking at the two of you. There are a lot of people in this world who are content to wear numbness like a badge. But not you, honey. Never you." Wrapping one arm around Rachel's shoulders, her mom leaned in and hugged her tightly, placing a kiss on the crown of her head. "I love you, Rach. And now you know exactly how much."

"I love you too, Mom."

The door swung open, and Tate smiled broadly at them. "Ready for some visitors?"

Samantha walked in right behind him, clapping him on the back. "Hold that thought. We're gonna get him to try to nurse and then move you guys to your post-partum room. Which is where you'll be until you're discharge. Tell them to cool their jets for about twenty-ish minutes, okay?"

Rachel's mom left to go sit with her dad in the waiting room, after snapping a few hundred pictures on her iPhone. Little man latched on like a champ, and Rachel about screamed at the stabbing pain.

"Good Lord," she hissed, as her toes curled up at the foot of the bed.

"Does it hurt?" Tate asked. She just stared, when she wasn't wincing like an idiot. He chuckled, shaking his head. "I swear, I missed him like crazy when I was out there talking to everyone."

She smiled at him, even though it still felt like someone was stabbing her boob. "Who's here?"

"My parents, Casey, Liz, and your dad. Casey asked if she could post to Facebook yet."

Rachel groaned. "Please tell me you said no."

"Well, I was informed that it's a faux pas to post without a name anyway." Tate leaned forward, unwrapping the tiny fingers that were clenched in a tight fist. When he lightly touched the palm, the fingers immediately wrapped around his pointer finger. They smiled at each other. "What are we going to name this little man?"

"Asher," she whispered, pressing a finger against the tight skin of her breast, and the suction of his mouth popped. Settling him onto the other side, and barely even registering that she was totally baring her major boobage to Tate and the two nurses that were gathering her stuff to move rooms.

"Asher," Tate repeated. Then he smiled at her, searching her eyes. "I like it. What does it mean?"

"It means blessed."

Tate clenched his teeth, looking more than a little emotional, and then nodded. He blinked a few times and cleared his throat. "What about a middle name?"

"How about Elliot?"

One side of Tate's lips rose in a smile, and he breathed out a soft laugh. "My dad's name?"

"And your middle name," she pointed out.

"Right." He laughed, sounding embarrassed. "Really? You're sure?"

Taking a deep breath, she looked away from Tate's fathomless expression, and stared down at their son. It felt like she might actually explode, she was so ... happy. So she nodded, and looked back up at Tate, wanting to kiss him, *really* kiss him. And the way his eyes flicked down to her parted lips, he totally noticed. It'd be so easy to just lean forward. Instead she smiled. "Asher Elliot Steadman. It's perfect."

"Well, I like it," Samantha stated, pushing a wheelchair towards the bed. "Let's get you movin', mama. I just spent my whole shift with you, so I'd like to see you settled before I head home. Plus, you've got some very pushy women in the waiting room."

Rachel laughed. "Oh, you have no idea."

30

THE AVERAGE NEWBORN went through ten diapers a day.

Ten.

So, as Tate hooked the stretchy tabs around Asher's little hips, he figured that this was roughly diaper number two hundred and one. Because, if he and Rachel had learned anything in the last sixteen days, it was their son was above average in every way.

The scrawny little legs kicked away while Tate attempted to button those damn little snaps at the bottom of his onesie.

"C'mon, little man. Gimme a break. I know you're hungry, but your mom will kick my ass if I bring you back to her unclothed." The answering coo made Tate smile, something he'd done a whole lot lately. He was tired, beyond exhausted actually, but that wasn't anything that a couple extra cups of coffee every day didn't fix. And really, it was nothing on the level of exhaustion that Rachel was feeling.

Their new running joke was that since one of the meanings of Asher was 'happy', he must be happiest when he got full access to Rachel's rack. Hey, rack was her new term, not his. Asher wanted to be attached to them, almost all the time. Not that Tate could blame him, because they were fairly spectacular. Tate cleared his throat, feeling slightly uncomfortable that he was lusting at Rachel's chest when thinking about how often Asher needed to nurse.

But really, they were phenomenal right now. Firm, and high, and ...

"Pull yourself together, man," he muttered, and lifted Asher from the changing table up onto his shoulder. While he had been over eight pounds at birth, he'd just recently regained the full pound that he'd lost in the hospital. So, Asher's teeny little butt fit right into the palm of Tate's hand when he held him. Placing a kiss on his son's head, Tate walked across the darkened hallway into Rachel's room. In the five minutes it had taken Tate to change the dirty diaper, she'd sank back into the bed and fell right back asleep.

One strap of her nursing tank was undone, and she clutched a burp rag in both hands. The soft light from the small lamp on her nightstand covered Rachel in a golden glow, lessening the dark circles that he knew were underneath her eyes. She'd just nursed two hours ago, around midnight, and when Asher had stirred again, Tate had tried everything to get him back to sleep without needing to wake her.

When pacing the room, with Asher swaddled tightly, and rocking him side to side didn't work, Tate had softly called Rachel's name.

"Wha?" she'd said as she bolted upright in the bed. "What time is it?"

"2:15. Sorry, I tried to get him back to sleep and couldn't. I think ... I think he's hungry again."

She'd motioned for the baby with her hands, eyes still firmly shut.

"Oh wait," Tate said and lifted the baby up higher. "Yeah. He needs a diaper change. I'll be right back."

"Mmmhmmm." And then she'd flopped back down.

Standing over her softly snoring form, Tate so badly wanted

to just go make a little bottle of the breast milk they had set aside in the freezer so that he could just let her sleep. But, Rachel felt very strongly about doing it herself, at least for the first month. And if there was one thing he'd learned in the last nine months, was that if Rachel had her mind set about something, nothing short of a nuclear bomb would deter her from the course she'd chosen. And even then, she might fight through it.

Tate sank down onto the empty side of the bed, his side of the bed.

Yeah. *His* side of the bed.

Since coming home from the hospital, he just ... started sleeping up there. The first couple nights, he'd started on the couch, not wanting to be so far away from both of them if Rachel needed his help. The third night, Rachel had just grabbed his hand, led him down the hallway, and pretty much shoved him on the side of the mattress that had been empty until then.

And in all the nights that had followed, neither one of them had seen fit to change the new routine. Since Tate couldn't feed Asher, he was in charge of diaper changes and getting Rachel anything she needed during the night. Sometimes it was water, sometimes it was a snack, sometimes it was just sitting and talking to her to keep her awake while she nursed the baby.

Tate gently nudged Rachel's arm while keeping a squirming Asher balanced on his shoulder. She groaned, but pulled herself up into a sitting position. Leaning over, she grabbed her nursing pillow from the floor and wrapped it around her stomach. Once that was settled, she pushed out a heavy breath and popped her eyes open, almost comically wide. Blinking a few times, she looked over at Tate, her eyes briefly skipping down his bare chest.

Was it purposely cruel for him to not put a shirt on? Quite possibly. But, he figured that if he had to share this bed with the majesty that was Rachel's cleavage, then she'd just have to deal with the fact that he preferred to sleep in only athletic shorts.

Settling Asher in her waiting arms, Tate didn't move his gaze away while she bared herself to get the baby latched on. Rachel made a brief noise when Asher started suckling, but it wasn't the litany of curse words that she'd let loose that first week of nursing.

Like he did during most nighttime feedings, Tate sat propped up against the massive upholstered headboard and just watched the perfection of his son and the rumpled, exhausted beauty of Rachel. Asher's dark hair stood out in stark contrast to Rachel's pale ivory skin, and Tate couldn't help but reach out and run his hand across the downy soft hair that stuck up in odd angles across his head.

"So, you're sure you don't want me to take one of these night time feedings with a bottle? I hate waking you up."

"Another week of this and I may take you up on that." Tearing her gaze away from Asher, Rachel smiled softly at Tate. "You really would do that, wouldn't you?"

"Sure. At least I know that if I fall asleep at my desk, Maggie will wake me up before a client catches me."

She laughed. "You haven't really fallen asleep at work, have you?"

"No. But, that first day back at work, I was close." He rubbed the back of his neck. "I barely slept the night before."

Rachel's forehead wrinkled as she was thinking. "I don't remember him being up more than usual that night."

"He wasn't. I uhh, I watched him sleep for a long time that night."

"Why?"

"Just thinking about being at the office the next day, after being with you two for those first few days after we got home. It was like I missed him and I hadn't even left yet. Does that sound stupid?"

He saw her swallow hard, then look down at Asher for a while. When her eyes came up again, they were suspiciously bright. "No, it doesn't."

"Rachel Hennessy, are you *crying*?"

"No," she sniffled. "Okay, maybe. I still have hormone overload."

Tate chuckled. "You don't even have to start working again for a few weeks. What are you going to be like then?"

"Oh Lord, I'm going to be a wreck. And even though your sister is pretty much taking over my company so I can actually have a maternity leave, Tate, I don't even care right now. What's *up* with that?"

While she lifted Asher up to burp him, Tate watched the way her face practically vibrated with thoughts. They'd only briefly discussed what she was going to do work-wise, but because her company had been so new at that time, the reality of how busy she would be might have made her change her mind. It was almost impossible to believe that there had ever been a time where he thought she was hard to read.

And he wasn't idiotic enough to think that just because he knew that he was in love with her, that he suddenly had some magic decoder ring into Rachel's thoughts. He was just ... learning. And every single thing he'd learned, he loved. She was grumpy when she first woke up. She hummed when she changed diapers. It took her an insanely long time to do her hair, even just to go to the grocery store. She couldn't stand clutter, which would prove interesting as Asher grew up and accumulated more toys.

While she'd never turned down any of the many visits from their family and friends in the last two weeks, she needed her alone time to rejuvenate her.

"I think," she said, pulling him from his ever-rotating list of things he loved about her. "I think I might want to reduce what my max number of brides will be. There was one point this spring that I was juggling ten of them, and I just can't imagine doing that again. I think somewhere in the six to seven range sounds doable. Even with Casey helping me out, which I think she'll be doing more, that's a lot of work. Plus, I don't want to be gone every weekend, that's when you'll be home from work, and I just ... I don't, umm, I'd miss that, I think."

And one of the other things he loved? She was absolutely, one hundred percent losing her battle of fighting against *them*. The *them* that Tate knew would be incredible, as soon as she knew that she was ready for it. He resisted the urge to fist pump, and just nodded. "Makes sense to me."

Asher was settled on the other side now, even though he was practically sound asleep, only making random pulls at Rachel's breast. She absently rubbed his back, and closed her eyes for a few long moments. When she opened them again, she looked over at Tate while he stretched his arms above his head and groaned at the small pop in his shoulder. Neither of them said anything when she pulled Asher off, they just watched him sleep. And yeah, he was fairly comatose. One arm was flung above his head, and the other held tight across his stomach. Now that the post-birth puffiness had dissipated from his face, it was clear that he had Tate's long, straight nose, and the shape of Rachel's lips.

Like she was reading Tate's mind, Rachel curved one pinky finger and traced it around the bow of Asher's mouth.

"It's so hard not to just keep touching him, you know?"

Yeah. Tate did know. And it wasn't just the baby he had a hard time keeping his hands off of. As much as he promised Rachel he wouldn't push her, he kind of wanted to grab her by the shoulders and shake her. Didn't she see it? How amazing and perfect this was?

In no way did Tate operate under the illusion that it would always be this harmonious, but the past two weeks had been about as mentally and physically draining as he'd ever experienced. And despite that, together he and Rachel had been a *team*. Almost like it was choreographed, each of them knowing exactly where to move, the kind of perfect dance that he always desired. Sometimes, he actually had to bite down on his tongue to not tell her that he loved her, that she was impossibly beautiful to him, that she was an even better mother than he'd imagined, and that if he ever had to go to bed again without her next to him, he might forgo any shred of his pride and just beg to stay by her.

"Yeah," he ground out, hoping his voice didn't sound full of all the emotion inside of him. But the way she looked at him, he knew that she heard something. "Here, let me swaddle him. You should get back to sleep."

Without meeting her eyes, but feeling them on him, he took the baby, wrapped him tightly in the little contraption that Maggie had gotten for them. The first few times he'd attempted it, he'd had absolutely no clue where arms and legs and the head went, but now, it only took about four seconds for Asher to be rendered completely immobile. Placing a few soft kisses on Asher's sweet smelling forehead, Tate took a few seconds just to relish the feel of him, the perfect weight in his arms. And if it wasn't manly to tear up just by holding his son, then Tate sure as hell didn't want to be a man. Clearing his throat, Tate set him down in the bassinet next to Rachel's side of the bed.

"Alright, buddy. You let your mom sleep for a few hours, okay?" he whispered and then turned back to the bed. But instead of being curled into her pillow, Rachel was still watching him, her eyes rimmed with red like she was trying not to cry. Again. The whole giving birth thing had unleashed twenty-eight years' worth of repressed emotion for her, because the crying thing? At least once a day. He loved it. But this time, she was rubbing at her chest, pressing into it. "What's wrong?"

"I..." she started, her voice heavy with unshed tears. Pinching her eyes shut, she flattened her hand and kept it right over her heart. When he sat next to her on the bed, her eyelids lifted, like it was an effort for her to do it. "I love you, Tate."

"Rachel..." He reached for her, overcome with warmth and love and *relief*. But she grabbed his hand before it could touch her face, motioning for him to listen.

"The past two weeks, I've been trying to figure out exactly

when I started falling in love with you. And until just now, I couldn't figure it out."

"When?"

"The first night, when I got fired, and you came after me." She pulled his hand up from where she'd been holding it in her lap, bringing it up over the same place above her heart that her own hand had been moments before. The skin was warm, the thick beats of her heart heavy under his palm, and there was a small part of him that wanted to curl his fingers in under her skin and wrap his hand around the pulsing rhythm, just to be that much closer to her. "I felt like someone different that night, because of you. Because of how you immediately believed in me, how you let me be *me*, with no judgments. And I could apologize in a million different ways for how I've run from you since then, but I think it's better to just love you instead. Because I do," she whispered, one tear falling over her lashes. "I love you so much, Tate."

He moved his hand from her chest, up her neck and into the hair at the base of her skull. And until she reached up to swipe at his cheek, he didn't even realize that he'd shed a tear too. Pulling her towards him, he tilted his head and then softly brushed his mouth against hers, once, twice and then deepened the kiss until she opened fully for him.

Their arms wrapped around each other, and he pulled her against him, wishing he could anchor her there permanently. Her tongue twined in his, soft and warm and sinuous in how it moved against his own. It made the hair on the back of his neck stand on end with the sheer pleasure of being able to touch her again. He pulled back, and smoothed a hand down her hair, then kissed the tip of her nose.

"I'll be right back," he said and stood off the bed.

"Where are you going?" she asked, incredulous. He just winked and left the room, practically sprinting down to his bedroom downstairs. Former bedroom. Not anymore, he thought with a wide grin. Yanking open the top drawer of his dresser, he stuck a hand under the neatly folded stacks of t-shirts until he felt the smooth velvet box. By the time he made it back upstairs, he actually felt short of breath.

Not nerves. Just ... anticipation.

Rachel was standing at the foot of the bed, tapping her foot and looking mildly pissed off, hand perched on her hip.

"Steadman, for future reference, that is so not an appropriate time to--"

And then she stopped when he kept walking until he was a foot away from her, which is when he sank down to the floor. Onto one knee.

He hadn't practiced. He hadn't given one second of thought as to what he'd say when he was here. With her staring wide-eyed at him, one hand covering her mouth, in the dimly lit room of their bedroom, their son fast asleep, he knew how perfect that was. The unexpected timing, him not having the perfect words was just ... completely right.

"Marry me."

Then he flipped open the small black box, and the hand fell away from her mouth when she saw the ring.

"Oh, Tate," she breathed. "Is that ... wait, what *is* that?"

He laughed, and shook his head. Turning the box, so he could pull the ring out to place it on her finger. Her hand was shaking slightly when he slid the thin platinum band over her knuckle.

"The middle stone? That's a raw diamond." He rubbed his thumb across the irregular edges of the stone, which was close in shape to an oval and completely surrounded by tiny pave diamonds. "Rachel, one of the things I love most about you is your rough edges, that sharp tongue and wit that keeps me on my toes. You, my love, are the most raw and real thing in my life, and I would never change a single thing about you. So," he pressed a kiss to the patch of skin just above the ring, "I decided that you needed a ring to reflect that. Now, are you going to answer me?"

The brilliant smile she gave him when she yanked him to his feet almost took his breath away. "Yes."

He swept her up off her feet, swinging her around with a laugh, feeling so buoyant that he thought he might not be touching the floor either. He kissed her, sweetly and tenderly, knowing that there would be time for passion later.

"I love you, Rachel."

She grinned, then drew her eyebrows down over her eyes. "Wait. When did you get that ring?"

"Oh, that old thing?"

"Tate..."

Letting out a deep breath, he buried his head into her throat to just pull in her scent. "I bought it the day you went into labor."

She pulled her face back. "What?"

"That's partially why I was so late. I knew that morning, I knew you'd find your way to me, even if I had to wait awhile."

"Wow, you really do love me, huh?"

He laughed. "Yeah."

"And you need me."

"Always."

"And you want me."

With a groan, he laid her back on the bed, wrapping his arms around her back to draw her into him. "That too."

The little minx started to press sucking kisses along his throat, then up his jaw.

"Rachel..."

"Hmm?"

"How strict are you going to be on that six week no sex thing that the doctor said?"

She leaned up, kissing his lower lip softly. "At least three more weeks, hotshot."

Tate rolled so that he held himself over her. "Are you sure?"

Unfortunately, even the tug he gave her earlobe with his teeth did nothing to sway her. "Not happening."

He pressed a hard kiss to her mouth and rolled off of her, heaving a sigh that made her laugh.

"Three weeks?"

"Three weeks."

"Fine. But after that, you're mine."

EPILOGUE

TWO WEEKS AND SIX DAYS LATER

"HOW DO I GET THIS OFF?" Tate groaned from somewhere behind her.

"Just rip it, I don't care." And she didn't. As much as she loved her wedding dress - which she did - at the moment, she could have cared less if he'd whipped out a machete to cut it off of her.

Holy shit. Her *wedding* dress. Even though the Grecian style gown, with delicate gold overlay straps wrapping around her neck, under her bust, and then around her back was freaking fabulous, she wanted it gone so she could finally, *finally* be with Tate.

It was a perfectly random thing to do, sure, just decide to get married a little more than two weeks after they'd gotten engaged, in his parents' backyard, with only family and close friends present. But, they saw no reason to wait. And since Tate had been very clear that once those three weeks were up, she would be his, she figured what the hell, let's make this shit legal.

Tate and Rachel, no attendants, saying their vows in front of the Steadman's pastor. Asher asleep in Mrs. Steadman's arms, wearing a little onesie with a clip-on black tie. White chairs in the emerald green grass of the expansive yard. White lanterns hanging from the boughs of the oak tree above them. Strands of white lights making a canopy over the large deck where they all ate a simple dinner afterward. Bunches of yellow and pink roses in short square vases on each white table.

Simple. Simple and completely perfect.

Finally, mercifully, the dress loosened, and he whipped her around to face him. His mouth descended to hers, and he practically devoured her. Moaning at the taste of him, the feel of him surrounding her, filling her, Rachel devoured him right back. He pushed the straps of her gown down off of her shoulders, and let out a shaky breath at the way she basically spilled out of her white bustier.

Yeah. That look in his eye? It was hers. Forever.

Dragging her pinky finger along the edge of the scalloped lace, she stared up at him, biting down on her lip.

Wrapping a hand around her waist, and then pushing it down so that he cupped one butt cheek, Tate gave a lovely little growly sound that made her smile.

"If you keep looking at me like that, I don't know how gentlemanly I can be."

She quirked an eyebrow. "Is that a promise?"

And just like that, her dress pretty much disappeared, and Tate threw it somewhere in the corner of their hotel suite. They got one night. And even though they'd joked that with Asher at her parents' house, they should really use the time to sleep, ha, yeah right. They could sleep when Rachel no longer had use of her legs, and Tate was passed out in a sexually blissed-out coma.

Using both of her hands, Rachel yanked open the collar of Tate's white shirt, dragging one finger down the hot skin that covered the muscles tightening his stomach. He picked her up, holding her weight under her thighs, and he walked them to the bed with their mouths fused. When they fell backwards, Tate pulled his weight off of her, just staring.

"You're my wife," he said roughly.

Rachel nodded. "And you're my husband."

Pressing his forehead against hers, he whispered against her lips. "I promise to love you without reservation, comfort you in times of distress." She breathed out a quiet laugh as he repeated their wedding vows, then kissed him softly. But he pulled back again, staring into her eyes. "Encourage you to achieve all of your goals, laugh with you and cry with you, grow with you in mind and in spirit, always be open and honest with you, and cherish you for as long as we both shall live."

Rachel wrapped her arms around his neck, wishing she could just embed him under her skin, loving him so much that it felt like it was exploding out through her fingertips.

"How did I make it so long without you?"

He smiled when he looked down at her, dragging a thumb across her lips. "You'll never know what that feels like, ever again."

It was still a little odd to her, that tears could push out of her eyes when she was so blissed-out happy. But with a soft drag of his thumb, Tate cleared her cheek, leaning down to kiss the damp skin. No more fears, no more fighting it, because this man had her back. Had her heart. And he always would.

ACKNOWLEDGMENTS

Chelsea Wright with Chelsea Lauren Events for showing me the event planner ropes. Rachel thanks you too, because she wouldn't have had any interns without you telling me about yours. If she was real, she'd be forever grateful.

Timothy Newhouse, P.C. for making sure I didn't make Tate sound like an idiot posing as a lawyer, which I would have undoubtedly done left to my own devices.

Amanda Welniak, for being my labor and delivery nurse pro. Even though I gave birth to two babies, I didn't remember half of this stuff. Nate, you did good marrying that one.

Najla Qamber, you made a cover for this book that makes me sigh a little every time I look at it. Not only did you give Rachel the perfect shade of red hair, you are so incredibly easy to work with and your talent is stunning.

Caitlin Terpstra, THANK YOU for making an offhand comment on Instagram, because you were a perfect beta reader. Twist my arm, you'll probably be getting book 3 soon.

InkSlinger PR (especially Nazarea Andrews!) for coordinating my release day and saving my sanity in the process.

Quite late in the process of my first book, I learned that the women I connected with online could become real and true friends; Brenda Rothert, Stephanie Reid (who I henceforth shall call Queen Beta Reader, because you just point out all those little or big things I somehow missed), Jade Eby, Katrina Kirkpatrick and Whitney Barbetti.

Jade, formatter, proofreader and general sounding board. Thanks for making my books so stinkin' pretty on the inside. I am so happy I finally got to hug the crap out of you this spring.

Katrina, it's odd to have someone who's not inside my head 'get' my characters, but you do. I seriously feel like Rachel is as much yours as she is mine. I still want our kids to get married so we have a justifiable reason to hang out forever and ever.

Whitney, you kinda came out of nowhere while I was writing this one, and I'm so insanely grateful for you. Thank you for being funny and kind and intuitive and supportive and freakishly talented. And for reading Outlander at my, ahem, *gentle* nudging. Above all things, we are now forever bonded in our love of Jamie Fraser.

Even though I'll probably never meet her, I want to thank Diana Gabaldon too. I can't believe I went until 2014 without reading a single word that you'd written. You're gracious with your readers, intelligent and lush in your writing, and if I can impact a single person with my writing in the way that you've impacted millions, then I'll be a very happy woman.

My family- parents, sister, and my various in-laws who were so ridiculously and wonderfully supportive of my first book. Not gonna lie, hearing that you guys actually *liked* my book? Felt quite amazing.

My husband and two young sons, whom I adore. You put up with a lot this time around, what with me writing this book in a quarter of the time that it took to write the first one. To be married to someone who has been 100% supportive of me chasing my dreams is amazing, and I couldn't be more thankful.

And lastly, to my Lord and Savior. Countless time in the last year, I've whispered "I trust you, Jesus" while attempting this journey. And You always, always, always prove to be worthy of that trust. Thank You.

ABOUT THE AUTHOR

Karla Sorensen has been an avid reader her entire life, preferring stories with a happily-ever-after over just about any other kind. And considering she has an entire line item in her budget for books, she realized it might just be cheaper to write her own stories. She still keeps her toes in the world of health care marketing, where she made her living pre-babies. Now she stays home, writing and mommy-ing full time (this translates to almost every day being a 'pajama day' at the Sorensen household...don't judge). She lives in West Michigan with her husband, two exceptionally adorable sons, and big, shaggy rescue dog.

Find Karla online:
karlasorensen.com
ksorensenbooks@gmail.com

Tristan

Amazon

Standalone title

Hooked: A dark romantic comedy co-written with Whitney Barbetti

Amazon Universal Link

Stay up to date on Karla's upcoming releases!

Subscribe to her newsletter

Made in the USA
Las Vegas, NV
22 September 2024

95645964R00184